THE REINDEER HUNTERS

THE
REINDEER
HUNTERS

Joan Wolf

A DUTTON BOOK

DUTTON
Published by the Penguin Group
Penguin Books USA Inc., 375 Hudson Street,
New York, New York 10014, U.S.A.
Penguin Books Ltd, 27 Wrights Lane, London W8 5TZ, England
Penguin Books Australia Ltd, Ringwood, Victoria, Australia
Penguin Books Canada Ltd, 10 Alcorn Avenue,
Toronto, Ontario, Canada M4V 3B2
Penguin Books (N.Z.) Ltd, 182–190 Wairau Road,
Auckland 10, New Zealand

Penguin Books Ltd, Registered Offices:
Harmondsworth, Middlesex, England

First published by Dutton, an imprint of Dutton Signet,
a division of Penguin Books USA Inc.
Distributed in Canada by McClelland & Stewart Inc.

First Printing, November, 1994
10 9 8 7 6 5 4 3 2 1

REGISTERED TRADEMARK—MARCA REGISTRADA
LIBRARY OF CONGRESS CATALOGING-IN-PUBLICATION DATA
Wolf, Joan.
The reindeer hunters / by Joan Wolf.
p.   cm.
ISBN 0-525-93848-6
1. Man, Prehistoric—Europe, Southern—Fiction.   I. Title.
PS3573.O486R4   1994
813'.54—dc20   94-14437
                                                          CIP

Printed in the United States of America
Set in Electra
Designed by Eve L. Kirch

For Joe, who loves swift horses

Introduction

Twenty-five thousand years ago, our planet lay in the frozen grip of the last Ice Age, the Pleistocene. Glaciers covered northern Europe, reaching as far south as England and northern France. These glaciers locked up so much of the world's water that the level of the sea was substantially lower than it is today, and the English Channel was dry land.

One would not think such an inhospitable world conducive to the growth of human culture, but it was during this very period of the late Pleistocene that one of the most creative and successful of prehistoric peoples appeared in southern France and the Pyrenees. This is the Cro-Magnon people, known to modern anthropology as the Magdalenians.

The Magdalenian period was perhaps the golden age of Stone Age man. This period saw not only improvements in tools and hunting weapons, but also the creation of the magnificent paintings found in the caves of Lascaux, Niaux and Altamira. This culture is chronicled in my two previous prehistoric novels, *Daughter of the Red Deer* and *The Horsemasters*.

The Magdalenians were hunters and gatherers, and the freezing climate they lived in was host to a multitude of cold-weather animals. Mammoth and wooly rhinoceros were to be found in the valleys of Ice Age France. Most important of all, there were reindeer—great herds of reindeer—roaming the tundra and sparse woodlands of the time. Hunting and gathering can offer humans an extremely viable way of life if the game is as plentiful as it was during the late Pleistocene.

Ironically, it was actually the warming of the climate that created a major crisis for this successful prehistoric hunting society. About 12,000 years ago, the glaciers began to withdraw, pulling back so that the margin of the ice eventually lay in central Sweden and south-central Finland. This warm inter-glacial period is called the Alleröd, and during this time temperatures were probably close to what they are today. One would think that mankind would have found this warmer world a far more congenial place than the frigid Pleistocene had been.

But the cold-weather game did not like the warmer weather. The great winter migrations of the herds into areas such as southern France and Britain halted, as the reindeer, following the cold weather and the glaciers, retreated ever farther to the north, taking with them the main food and clothing supply of the people who hunted them.

This is the time in which I have set my story. As in my previous prehistory books, the language the characters are supposedly speaking is "translated" into modern English. The setting is the French side of the Pyrenees Mountains.

Cast of Characters

Liev:	Nardo's second sister. Born to the Wolf Clan.
Tyr:	Liev's husband. Born to the Red Deer Clan.
Tora:	Mara's sister. Born to the Wolf Clan.
Harlan:	Tora's husband. Born to the Bear Clan.
Mano:	Tora's son. Council member for the Wolf Clan.
Haras:	Tora's son. Born to the Wolf Clan.
Nessa:	Tora's daughter. Born to the Wolf Clan.
Adun:	Nessa's husband. Born to the Red Deer Clan.
Lora:	Tora's daughter. Born to the Wolf Clan.
Dane:	Lora's husband. Born to the Red Deer Clan.
Varic:	Nevin's son. Council member for the Eagle Clan.
Freddo:	Council member for the Red Deer Clan.
Nat:	Council member for the Bear Clan.
Hamer:	Council member for the Leopard Clan.
Matti:	Council member for the Fox Clan.
Lina:	Matriarch of the Red Deer
Fara:	Lina's daughter. Born to the Red Deer.
Pettra:	Lina's daughter. Born to the Red Deer.
Rilik:	Chief of the Atata Kindred
Crim:	man of the Atata Kindred

THE REDU

Kerk:	the chief
Paxon:	the chief's son
Madden:	secondary chief
Wain:	secondary chief
Aven:	Paxon's friend
Cuch:	secondary chief

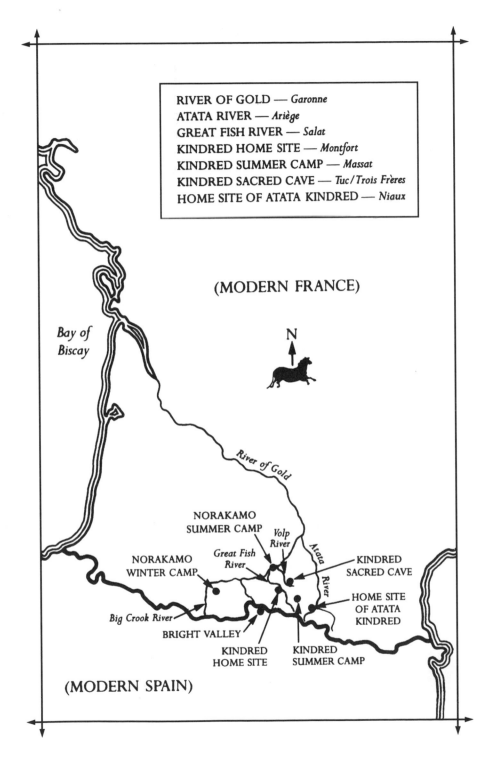

RIVER OF GOLD — *Garonne*
ATATA RIVER — *Ariège*
GREAT FISH RIVER — *Salat*
KINDRED HOME SITE — *Montfort*
KINDRED SUMMER CAMP — *Massat*
KINDRED SACRED CAVE — *Tuc/Trois Frères*
HOME SITE OF ATATA KINDRED — *Niaux*

(MODERN FRANCE)

Bay of
Biscay

N

River of Gold

NORAKAMO
SUMMER CAMP

*Volp
River*

NORAKAMO
WINTER CAMP

*Great Fish
River*

*Atata
River*

KINDRED
SACRED CAVE

HOME SITE
OF ATATA
KINDRED

Big Crook River

BRIGHT VALLEY

KINDRED
HOME SITE

KINDRED
SUMMER CAMP

(MODERN SPAIN)

PART ONE

The Norakamo

Chapter One

Nardo snaked through the high grass, his belly so close to the ground that he would be invisible to any eyes that might be watching from the Norakamo camp. He felt a light tap on his left shoulder, and immediately he passed the signal along to Dane on his other side. In a moment's time the whole raiding party had come to a stop.

Nardo lay perfectly still, the fresh, sweet scent of wet grass and flowers in his nostrils as he watched the first gray light of morning brighten the eastern sky. His reindeer skin clothes were wet with dew and the ground under him was cold, yet he was aware of no discomfort.

At last the red rim of the sun peeked over the horizon. The twelve men in the grass lifted their spirits to the rising god and, in the quiet of their own hearts, recited the dawn prayer. Then, with Nevin in the lead, the entire raiding party began to snake forward once more.

The horse herd also had awakened to greet the morning. As the pearly light of dawn slowly brightened into day, the horses' coats turned from a uniform shadowy gray into varying hues of brown and chestnut. Foals reached up their heads, eager to nurse, while their mothers stretched their thick, short necks downward to graze on the rich valley grass. Nardo and the men of the Kindred were downwind of the herd, so the horses fed peacefully, undisturbed by the scent of strangers.

The raiders assessed the herd with expert eyes. Their aim was simple: each man was to catch a mare and ride her back to the Big Ford, where the rest of the raiding party waited with their remounts. Then the men of the Kindred would be on their way back to their safe summer grazing camp in the high mountains, with the Norakamo mares and foals to add to their herd.

Nardo had just decided to try for a short-backed chestnut with a dark foal nursing at her side when the peaceful morning air was shattered by a shrill, piercing whinny. The chestnut mare Nardo was watching lifted her head, and her nostrils flared in alarm.

Ever impatient, Varic had moved too quickly!

Nardo scowled and leaped forward, grabbing the short, stiff mane as the frightened chestnut mare backed away from him. He vaulted onto her back, not taking the time to use the halter he carried slung over his shoulder. The mare squealed as she felt his weight, then she reared. Her foal, abruptly dislodged from his breakfast, fell to his knees. Nardo dug his knees into the mare's sides and flung his weight forward to bring her down. As her front feet touched the ground, he cast a quick glance around to see how the rest of the raiding party was faring. That was when he saw the band of men galloping toward them out of the hazy morning light.

Dawn was a favorite time for both the Kindred and the Norakamo to stage a raid, since it was usually possible to catch the enemy unaware. Not today, however. Today the Norakamo were horsed and ready. Nardo cursed and raked the horse herd with his eyes, searching for his uncle, the raiding party's leader. They had to get out of here quickly!

The chestnut mare snorted, alarmed by the sound of galloping horses and by the stranger on her back. Her foal, catching his mother's fright, squealed and butted his head against her side. She swung around on her hindquarters, circling nervously. Nardo finally caught sight of his uncle. Nevin had not caught a mare, but was on foot on the outside of the herd, shouting to his men. With horror Nardo saw the horsemen bearing down on the solitary unhorsed figure.

"*Nevin!*" It was impossible for Nardo to control the frightened mare without a halter, so he slid from her back and began to run.

Nevin was the most famous horse raider of his time. For three handfuls of years he had been stealing horses from the Norakamo, and it seemed this morning as if the Norakamo had determined to put an end to his career. Ignoring the rest of the raiding party, ignoring even the possible loss of their precious horses, they were clearly intent upon capturing Nevin.

The herd's lead mare gave another shrill, piercing whinny and began to gallop away down the valley. The rest of the panicked mares followed immediately. There were shouts from the mounted Kindred raiders, who were being swept along helplessly by the stampeding herd. Only the fact that Nardo was on the outside of the herd saved him from being trampled to death. As it was, one mare knocked into his shoulder, sending him crashing facedown into the wet, aromatic grass.

By the time Nardo leaped to his feet, the Norakamo had his uncle surrounded. Nardo's fingers tightened on his javelin as he assessed the situation. Nevin was turning warily in the midst of the circle of his enemies, his short spear raised, but he was trapped. Nardo ached to go to his uncle's assistance, but he was realistic enough to see that his single javelin would make no difference to the outcome of this encounter.

The Norakamo were going to capture Nevin, and they would demand a great number of horses for his return. If Nardo was captured also, his father would lose half the herd.

Then, as Nardo stood there watching, one of the Norakamo horsemen surged forward into the circle, his javelin raised. One of the other men in the circle bellowed, "Loki, don't!" but the javelin had already buried itself in Nevin's chest. Nevin bent forward at the waist, then slowly collapsed into the knee-high grass.

A rush of color, red as Nevin's blood, suddenly swam before Nardo's eyes. A great roar of fury and anguish erupted from his throat. He leaped forward, swift, graceful and deadly as a cave lion in the morning light, straight for the man who had killed his uncle. He had the satisfaction of feeling his spear bury itself in living flesh before the horses closed in around him.

Alane was bringing the morning's water from the river when her father and the men returned to camp leading three horses with bodies slung across their backs. She rushed forward so quickly that water splashed out of the basket on her head and wet her hair. Her father roared out his wife's name: "Adah! Come quickly! One of these men is injured."

"Aiiiya!" Alane's mother ducked out of her tent and came running. The rest of the women in the camp called to their children, and all stood in breathless silence at the thresholds of their tents, watching as the scene unfolded before them. The tents all formed a large circle, so everyone had a good view of the men as they untied one of the bodies and carefully lowered it to the ground.

In the silence, a flock of geese rose like smoke from the river, their wings hammering the air as they climbed into the sky.

"This is the one who is hurt," Alane heard her father saying. "The other two are dead." The shadow of the flying geese passed over the men and horses, and Tedric added grimly, "One of the dead men is Nevin."

Alane's heart began to hammer. Then she raised her hands to the basket on her head and carefully lowered it to the ground. Her hands were shaking and more water spilled onto the beaten-down grass of the campsite.

"I thought you were only going to capture him," Adah said, her voice sharp with fear.

Tedric gestured to the body that was slung across the third horse. "An evil spirit must have possessed Loki. He ran Nevin through with his spear. The injured man killed Loki in revenge."

A high-pitched scream came from one of the tents as Loki's mother learned of her son's fate. She rushed forward, and the men lifted Loki's body from the horse and laid it gently upon the ground. His mother fell to her knees and began to keen loudly. A few other women joined her.

Alane could feel her heart beating in her throat. She looked at her father's grim face and wondered if he had made any attempt at all to save Loki's life.

"We do not want this one to die, then," Adah said, gesturing to the man who lay stretched unconscious upon the ground. She raised her voice to be heard over the sounds of grief that were pouring from the throat of the bereaved mother and said to the men, "Bring him into the medicine tent and I will tend to him."

One of the keening women looked up and demanded, "Where is the shaman?"

"I am here." The voice was mellow and deep, the voice of a singer. The slim man approaching the center of the campsite was wearing the great horsehair cape that signified he had been engaged in a religious ceremony. His face was thin, almost gaunt, with deep creases down each cheek.

"Hagen!" Loki's mother screamed to her brother, lifting her tear-blurred face. "Loki has been slain!"

The shaman halted and looked at Tedric. His lightless gray eyes bored into the chief's. "How did this happen?" he demanded.

Before he answered, Tedric deliberately gestured to his sons, who bent to lift the injured man under his shoulders and feet. Then two more men stepped forward to support him at the waist, as if his weight were too great for only two to carry. The sun shone brightly on the front of the unconscious man's shirt, which was soaked with blood.

As the procession moved off toward one of the tents, Tedric explained tersely to the shaman what had happened. Without a word Hagen went to examine the body of his dead nephew.

The rest of the men stood nervously by, regarding the dark-haired corpse that was tied by its hands and feet across the chestnut mare's back.

"I am thinking that the Kindred will not return home without Nevin's body," Tedric said to the shaman's back. "They will also wish to learn the fate of this other man."

"Until they come we do not want to keep the body here!" one man said.

"*Sa, sa,*" the others agreed fervently. The Norakamo were always uneasy in the presence of death. The ghosts of the newly dead were yet too close to the body for living men to feel safe.

Hagen rose to his feet. "Put it on the raft and take it to the far side of the river," he ordered. "The water will keep his spirit away from us."

The men nodded and moved with alacrity to do his bidding.

"Alane!" It was Adah, calling from the open doorflap of the

medicine tent. "Bring that water in here." As Alane bent to lift the water basket to her head, Adah spoke next to the shaman. "Will you come and look at the injured man, Hagen?"

The shaman stared once more at the body of his sister's son. Then, "I will come and look," he said.

The stranger stirred and sighed, and Alane hastened forward to see if he was finally waking. But after a moment he subsided back into sleep once more.

Both her mother and Hagen had said it was not the spear wound in his shoulder but the great bruise on his temple that was keeping his spirit from returning to the land of the living.

"He came roaring into our midst like an enraged bull," Alane's father had said. "He killed Loki and wounded Oden and Larz before I finally felled him with my spear handle."

Alane thought of this conversation now as she gazed down into the face of the unconscious man. The skin on his temple had been broken by Tedric's blow, and under the jagged tear a huge lump had risen. Her mother had told her to keep putting cool, wet buckskin cloths over the lump, and now Alane dipped a fresh piece of buckskin into the water basket, which was lined and made waterproof by salmon skins. She removed the now-warm cloth from his forehead and replaced it. He did not stir. Alane resumed her post by the injured man's side.

All the Norakamo understood the code of the blood feud, and so they knew that it was in the best interest of the tribe that this man live. Loki's action in killing Nevin had changed the rules by which the tribes played their raiding game, and the Norakamos' one hope of avoiding a devastating vendetta lay with this man. Loki had killed Nevin; Loki had been killed by this man. If he lived and could be returned to his tribe in health, then perhaps the Kindred would be satisfied that vengeance had been done.

He was a young man, Alane thought, her eyes on the stranger's face, although the dark stubble of beard indicated that he was not a boy. Alane's gaze moved next to his naked chest and shoulders. *Dhu,* but he was strong! Surely a man built like that could not be killed by a blow on the head. She reached over and spread her cool fingers on his sound shoulder. His skin was much darker than hers, and it was too hot. She frowned.

He should drink. It was not good to be so hot and not drink.

Alane filled an antelope horn with water and dropped to her knees at his side. Slipping one arm under his head, she raised him, propping his head upon her shoulder. His head was very heavy; his eyelashes were amazingly long and thick against the hard line of his cheeks. Alane lifted the horn to his lips.

"Drink," she commanded. Centuries before, the Norakamo had spoken their own language, but after many years of living in the lands of the Kindred, they had gradually adopted the other tribe's language. They used their original tongue now only in certain prayers.

There was no response and Alane trickled a little water upon his closed lips. It dribbled down his chin, but after a moment his lips moved. "Good," she said softly. "Come now. Drink." She held the cup once more to his lips, pressing its rim upon his bottom lip to encourage him to open. She smiled when she saw him swallow.

A shadow fell upon her. She looked up and saw Hagen standing between her and the light from the open doorflap. Hung around his neck was the feathered stole he wore when he healed.

"You should not be holding that man against you," the shaman said in a cold voice.

Alane could feel her face flush and was angry with herself for such a reaction. She was doing nothing wrong! "My mother said that he must drink," she said.

"Your mother should not leave you alone with a Kindred murderer," the shaman said, his voice even colder.

"He is still wandering in the land of the spirits," Alane replied. "He is no danger to me, Hagen." Carefully she lowered the Kindred man's head until he was lying flat. She looked up once again at Hagen, her face a mask of calm.

Alane was well aware of the long-running power struggle between her father and the shaman. Both were strong, dominant men and each felt that the other was always trying to encroach on his circle of authority. Hagen had recently tried, and failed, to win Alane to wife for one of his nephews, and Tedric's refusal still rankled.

The sound of the chief's voice floated into the tent, and then came the sound of steps approaching. Two young men came rushing over the threshold to drop to their heels beside the man lying on the reindeer skin bedplace.

"Nardo!" the bigger of the two men said urgently, "Nardo, it's Dane! Varic is here, too. Can you hear me?"

"He is in the land of the spirits," Hagen said in the same cold voice he had used earlier to Alane.

"He is so pale," the man called Varic said. His dark brown hair fell forward around his cheeks as he leaned over the unconscious body of his fellow tribesman.

"Dhu," said Dane. "If he should die!" There was anguish in his voice.

"He will not die," the shaman said. "His heartbeat is strong. He is gathering power from the spirits to heal his body. When he is powerful enough, he will awaken."

The man called Varic raised his head, and Alane saw that his brown eyes were set very widely apart, giving him a peculiarly childlike look. When he spoke, however, his voice was hard and full of menace. "For your sake, shaman, and the sake of your tribe, I hope you speak true."

Alane shivered.

Her involuntary gesture attracted Varic's attention, and he looked at her for the first time. "You are caring for my cousin?" he asked.

As he spoke, Adah came in the door. Alane's eyes darted to her mother, and Adah responded by answering the stranger for her. "This is the chief's daughter. She has been keeping watch on your kinsman while I attended to other matters."

Varic's widely spaced eyes did not move from Alane's face. "He will like waking up and seeing you," he said, and Alane's eyes fell before the frank admiration in that look.

Adah said, "If you try to move him, man of the Kindred, you will do him harm. It will be best to leave him in our custody until he is healed."

The man who had identified himself as Dane lifted his head and gave Adah a piercing look. Alane's mother responded in a reassuring tone: "We know well it is to our advantage that he recover. You may trust us."

Varic's voice was deeply bitter. "Your treachery killed my father. How can you expect us to trust you?"

Alane regarded him with deep surprise. If Nevin was this Varic's father, she thought, then why had vengeance been done by someone else?

There was a movement by the door, and Tedric came into the tent. Evidently he had heard Varic's last words, for he crossed his arms and said impassively, "My orders were to capture Nevin, not to kill him. Loki acted on his own, and he has paid for it. This man"—Tedric pointed at the recumbent figure—"killed Loki. A life has been given for a life. It is finished."

Involuntarily Alane glanced at Hagen. His face was set like stone. He did not speak.

Slowly Varic rose to his feet. "It is not finished," he said to the Norakamo chief, "until my father's sister's son has been returned in health to his mother's house." He paused, then added with cold deliberation, "And to the house of his father, Rorig the chief."

There was a reverberating silence. It was Adah who finally asked, "This man is the son of your chief?"

"Sa. His name is Nardo and he is the son of our chief."

Tedric said grimly, "I hear you."

Varic looked down once more at his cousin's unconscious face. "I am thinking that you are right when you say it would be ill to move him. Therefore I will leave him with you and take my father's body home." He stood up again, and this time he looked at Alane. "Take good care of him," he commanded.

Alane bowed her head. Dane touched the unconscious man on the cheek with a gentle finger, then rose to follow his fellow tribesman out of the tent.

In grim silence the men of the Kindred loaded Nevin's body onto one of their horses and took the path downriver toward the Great Ford. After the corpse was well out of sight, Hagen, dressed in his great horsehair cape, went around the entire encampment, sprinkling water for purification. Then, chanting the proper incantations, he threw four javelins: one toward the Altas in the south; one toward the plains in the north; one toward the east, where the sun rose; and one toward the west, where the sun set. The javelins, he told the tribe, would drive back Nevin's ghost should it seek to return.

"Now," said Tedric to his wife as he came back into the tent, "this man must get well!"

Adah took over the sick watch, leaving Alane to see to dinner for her father and her brothers. There was deer meat from yesterday's hunt, and Alane seasoned it with wild onions and thyme and cooked it in a stone-lined fire pit. With it she served a salad of sorrel and hawthorne berries.

The men ate hungrily, and Alane moved quietly around the hearth, offering more meat and filling their cups with mint tea. It was not until the men were finished that she took some food for herself. It was always the way of the Norakamo women to eat only after the men had been satisfied.

"Father," she asked after she had finished chewing her first piece of meat, "why did not Nevin's son avenge his death?"

Tedric drained his tea and held out his cup for a refill. "He was probably caught in the herd's stampede." He waited until Alane had filled his cup before he added, "But even if that had not happened, the primary duty of revenge would still have fallen to this Nardo."

"I don't understand," said Stifun, Alane's second brother.

"The Tribe of the Kindred does not count kinship as do we of the Norakamo," Tedric explained. "They make their first prayers to Earth Mother, and to them it is the mother's line that is the important kinship connection. A man of the Kindred belongs to the kin group of his mother, not of his father."

Alane's eldest brother, Rune, ran his fingers through the pale bangs that hung almost to his eyebrows. "We know that, Father, but I still do not understand. . . ."

"Nevin was this man's mother's brother. To the Kindred that is the closest of all male ties," Tedric said.

"Even closer than son to father?" Fenris, the youngest boy, asked incredulously.

"Even closer than son to father" came the reply.

There was silence as Tedric's three sons tried to comprehend such a strange thing. Then Alane said, "He is the son of the chief. Do the Kindred pass the chieftainship from father to son as we do?"

"Sa," said Tedric grimly. "They do."

Alane was clearing away the antelope horns in which she had served the stew when Irek and Piet, the elders for each Half of the tribe, appeared in the open doorflap. Tedric gestured them in. Shortly after they were followed by Hagen, who was accompanied by his nephew Vili. Tedric scowled when he saw Vili, who had no right to attend a chief's council. He did not challenge the shaman's decision, however, but sat in disapproving silence while Alane poured tea for all the men. Then she retired to a corner of the tent with Stifun and Fenris and picked up the basket she was weaving.

Finally Tedric opened the discussion. "So," he said heavily, "it seems we are dealing with the life of the chief's son."

"Are you certain he will recover, Shaman?" Irek asked.

Hagen took a small sip of his tea. "I think so," he said.

"You told the men of the Kindred that he would definitely recover!" Tedric bellowed.

Hagen shrugged, unperturbed by the chief's anger. "He should. But sometimes unforeseen things happen. You all know that."

He is such an eel, Alane thought with exasperation. Her head was bent over her basket, but her ears were attuned to the voices of the men.

Tedric looked from Irek to Piet to Hagen to Rune. Deliberately he did not acknowledge the existence of Vili. The summer sun had not yet set, and the men's faces were easily visible in the light from the open doorflap. Tedric's eyes came back to Hagen. "This man must live," he said, slowly and deliberately. "We do not want a blood feud with the Kindred. They are a much larger tribe than we are."

"We are as good as they at horse raiding!" Vili said furiously. He had not missed Tedric's deliberate insult. Like his uncle, Vili had a narrow, hollow face, but his lips were oddly full. He had been the husband whom the shaman had proposed for Alane, and she had been vastly relieved when her father refused him. There was something about Vili that repulsed her.

Tedric raked his fingers through his thick beard. "Horse raiding is a game," he said shortly. "A blood feud is serious."

Vili jutted out his chin. "I am not afraid of the Kindred."

What a fool Vili is, Alane thought scornfully. Her fingers flew automatically over the basket, their skill so deeply ingrained that they could work without the attention of her brain.

"If the Kindred call for a blood feud, we will not back away," Rune said to Vili. His blue eyes moved to the shaman's face. "But we would be fools if we did not do what we could to avoid a war of vengeance."

Hagen said, "My nephew Loki lies dead and my sister weeps." His face was impassive.

"Loki killed first," Irek said. "I was there and I saw."

"Loki was a Norakamo!" Vili was almost shouting. "His murderer, who lies at our mercy, is a man of the Kindred!"

A fool and a coward, Alane thought, *to want to take advantage of a helpless man.* She looked up from her basket and her eyes met those of her brother Stifun. He made a disgusted face, and Alane nodded in silent agreement.

"What are your thoughts on this subject, Hagen?" Piet said forthrightly. "Do you think we should slay the son of the Kindred chief?"

Alane smiled. Everyone knew how the shaman hated plain speaking. He preferred to work by innuendo and suggestion. She understood perfectly that he had brought Vili with him to do his dirty work, to say the things Hagen would not want to say himself.

However, no discomfort showed on the shaman's face as he returned Piet's look. "I am a healer, not a murderer," he said. "I have said that this young man will recover, and he will. But I thought it would be well for you to understand the mind of Loki's kin. Loki rid the tribe of its greatest enemy; it is hard to see his death go unavenged."

Vili growled in agreement.

Tedric said, "I understand your grief, but Loki chose to act outside my orders. Under the circumstances he has no right to vengeance."

"I agree," said Irek, leader of the Black Half of the tribe.

"And I," said Piet, leader of the Red Half.

Hagen rose to his feet and Vili hastily followed. "The tribe has spoken," Hagen said. He put his hand on his nephew's arm.

Alane watched the two men depart, and then her eyes went to her father's face. Tedric looked grim.

"Mother is sitting with the Kindred man," Rune said into the silence.

"Tell her to remain there," Irek said. "Just to be sure."

Chapter Two

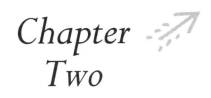

Someone was pounding him over the head. The pain was excruciating, and Nardo groaned and opened his eyes. He had to make it stop.

Sunlight was pouring through the open doorflap and, narrowing his eyes against the brightness, Nardo realized with surprise that he was alone. No one was hitting him. Carefully, moving his eyes and not his head, he looked around.

He was in a tent. Not a Kindred tent, though. This tent was circular, tapering upward to a tall, narrow smoke hole.

Where am I?

Gritting his teeth against the agony in his head, he tried to sit up, and it was then that he felt the pain in his shoulder. He looked down and saw the deerskin bandage wrapped around his bare torso. He was covered to the waist by a reindeer skin rug and, sliding his hand under the rug, he verified that he was naked. Cautiously he lay back down again.

What has happened to me?

He was ragingly thirsty and he ran his tongue over his dry, cracked lips. It was warm in the tent, and the air held the bittersweet scent of healing herbs.

He tried to gather his thoughts, but the last thing he could remember was setting forth with Nevin. After that there was nothing.

A woman's voice spoke from the open doorflap. "You're

awake. Good." He struggled to sit up again, and she came to kneel at his side, putting out a hand to press him back.

"I'm hurt," he said. His voice came out in a croak.

"Sa, you are hurt. But you are getting better. It is important that you be quiet." She spoke his language, but her accent was unfamiliar.

"What happened?" he demanded. "How did I get hurt? Where am I? Who are you?"

"Softly, softly," she said. "I will answer all your questions, but first you must drink some water."

Ignoring the thunder of pain in his head, he managed to push himself up on his elbow, and she held the antelope horn to his lips. He drank thirstily.

"That is good," the woman said.

He had flopped exhaustedly back to the bed skins after drinking, but now he said, "I want to get up."

"In a little while you can get up."

His mouth set stubbornly. "Now."

"Don't you want your questions answered?"

He looked up into the face of the woman. She was no longer young; her fair hair was streaked with gray, and there were lines at the corners of her blue eyes and her mouth. Fair hair and blue eyes . . .

"Are you Norakamo?" he asked harshly.

"Sa."

He stared up at the high cone of the Norakamo tent. "Tell me," he said.

There was a long pause. "You don't remember anything?"

He said fretfully, "I remember leaving camp with Nevin. After that there is nothing."

"You came to raid our horses."

This did not surprise Nardo. The Norakamo and Kindred had been raiding each other's horses for generations. The raiding helped increase the raider's horse herd, but the main reason for the forays was that next to hunting, horse raiding was one of the main ways the young men of both tribes could prove their manhood.

The distant sound of children's laughter floated through the open doorflap of the tent. There was the noise of running feet and the laughter became louder. The woman added, "My husband, the chief, was waiting for you."

There was a pause as Nardo assimilated this information. Then he demanded, "How did he know that we would be coming?"

"We wounded two of your men on our last raid. My husband was certain that Nevin would retaliate quickly."

A muscle quivered in the corner of Nardo's mouth as he realized how accurately the Norakamo chief had read his uncle. The woman was going on, "My husband gathered our men together. 'We must capture Nevin,' he told them. 'Rorig will pay many horses to get back such a man.'"

Nardo said nothing.

"That was the plan," the woman continued. "And they were almost successful. They were ready for Nevin, they cut him out from the rest of his tribesmen, they had him surrounded. Then . . ." Her voice wavered. She paused. "You do not remember what happened next?"

"*Na*," he said harshly. He had a bad feeling about what was coming next.

The woman said simply, "One of our men disobeyed his chief's orders and killed Nevin with his spear."

Nardo lay as still as a stone, staring up at the smoke hole.

"You saw this," Adah continued after a moment, "and you came running to avenge your uncle's death. You were like an enraged bull, my husband said. You killed Loki, the man who had killed your uncle, and you wounded two more of our men before my husband hit you on the head with his spear handle and brought you down."

There was a long silence.

"Then Nevin is dead?" Nardo asked at last.

"*Sa*. Nevin is dead, and Loki, his slayer, is dead also."

More silence. Outside, the children's voices rose shrilly in argument.

"Where are the rest of the men who came with us on the raid?"

"They took your uncle's body home to his kin."

"They left me here with you?"

"It was not safe to move you, and they knew we would take good care of you," Adah said.

He did not answer, but closed his eyes. *Nevin is dead*, he thought. *Nevin is dead.* Why could he not remember?

"Sleep a little now," he heard the woman's voice say. "When next you wake you may eat."

I shall never sleep with my head pounding like this, Nardo thought, just before he slid back into unconsciousness.

When next Nardo woke his head was still aching, but the terrible pounding was gone. He opened his eyes and saw a different woman sitting beside his bedplace. Her head was bent over the moccasin she was stitching, and a shining sheaf of the palest hair Nardo had ever seen had fallen forward to screen her face.

"I'm thirsty," he said, and the woman looked up.

"You're awake. Good. I have water here for you." Her voice was low-pitched but very clear. The hand that she laid upon his brow was wonderfully cool. She dipped some water into the antelope horn and knelt beside him. "Can you sit up a little or shall I help you?"

Nardo found himself gazing up into the most beautiful face he had ever seen. "Help me," he said.

She slid an arm under his head and lifted it, then she held the horn to his lips. She did it so easily, so naturally, that he knew she had done it before. He let the full weight of his head fall back on her breast, and he drank all the water in the horn.

"More?" she asked.

"Na."

He let her lower him back to the skins. "How long have I been lying here?"

She held up two fingers. "So many days."

"That must have been some blow your chief gave me," he remarked and watched with fascination as faint color stained her cheeks.

"My father wished to stop you from killing more of our men," she said. She averted her eyes, obviously uncomfortable with the way he was looking at her.

"Your father? Then you are the chief's daughter?"

"Sa."

Her skin was as pure and delicate as a young child's. He asked, "What is your name?"

She gave him a quick, startled look. "That is not a question a man of my tribe would ask a woman."

He had heard that the Norakamo were very strict with their girls. He said with easy reasonableness, "You have been taking care of me for two days. Surely it is not inappropriate that I should know your name."

She reflected for a moment, clearly uneasy. At last she said, "My name is Alane."

"Alane," he repeated, tasting the word on his tongue. "Alane, I want to get up."

She forgot her embarrassment in alarm. "You cannot get up!"

"I cannot get up until you leave," he agreed. "I do not have any clothes on."

She was shaking her head. "You cannot," she repeated. "You will fall and open the wound in your shoulder."

"Perhaps." Cautiously he levered himself to a sitting position. His shoulder hurt and his head ached, but he knew he would be able to get up.

"I thought you couldn't even raise your head for water!" she said.

He grinned at her. "Be a good girl and leave so I can get up."

Alane felt a flash of annoyance that this Kindred man thought he could dismiss her so easily. "I will get my father," she said stiffly.

"Good."

She rose to her feet and walked proudly toward the door flap. Nardo watched her appreciatively until he could see her no more. Then he began the laborious task of getting to his feet.

When Tedric entered the injured man's tent, he was surprised to find Nardo had actually managed to get to his feet without help. The first thing the scowling, black-haired young giant said was: "My father will not give you a single horse for my return. You owe him my life, Chief of the Norakamo."

Tedric was not at all surprised by Nardo's words. Both of their tribes shared a fanatical devotion to horses, and Tedric would actually have been surprised if Nardo's first thoughts had been for something else. On this subject they thought alike. The name Norakamo actually meant Horsemasters, and it was said by the shamans of Tedric's people that long ago it was the Norakamo who had brought the art of riding horses to the people of the Kindred.

"I had no thought to demand a payment for you," Tedric replied. "One of my men took your uncle's life, and you took the slayer's life in revenge. It is finished. When you are well enough to ride, you will be returned to your father."

"Are you certain it is finished?" Nardo asked. His voice was harsh, his brown eyes hostile. "What of the slayer's family? Won't they demand my life as blood revenge for his?"

"There will be no revenge," Tedric replied. "I am the chief of this tribe; my father and grandfather were chiefs before me. I have said that it is finished, and my people have heard me."

Nardo's gaze bored into the eyes of the Norakamo chief. Then the younger man nodded. "Sa. I see that you are a chief." He swayed a little and his scowl returned.

"You should not be standing," Tedric said and moved forward to help.

Nardo held up a hand to stay him. "I was dizzy for a moment. I am all right now." He took a step forward to prove his point, and staggered.

Tedric slid his arm around Nardo's back and braced him with his shoulder. Among his people Tedric was tall, but the younger man was almost half a head over him. "Dhu," said Tedric feelingly. "You are no lightweight, son of Rorig. Let us get you back to your bedplace before you fall."

Nardo swore, but clearly he was not going to be able to remain upright for much longer. His head was pounding again. With Tedric's help he lowered himself onto the reindeer skins of the bedplace and shut his eyes.

"I will get my wife," he heard Tedric saying. The darkness reached out for Nardo and, grateful for a place to hide from the renewed pounding in his head, he slid back into it.

Alane was returning from the river, riding one of her father's horses and leading two others she had taken for water, when she saw the first horseman come around the bend in the river. By the Norakamo camp the River of Gold was broad, and the sweet meadow grass grew right up to its edges on both banks. The bright summer sun danced on the clear water, demonstrating vividly to any who might wonder just how the river had gotten its name.

A whole line of horsemen had come into Alane's view by now, each of them leading two extra horses. *Kindred,* she thought as she watched them advance through the high grass. All around them butterflies and small birds rose out of the wild-flowers, and on the river a mother goose honked to her young as if in warning. Alane thought: *They have come for the chief's son.* She pressed her calves against the sides of her horse, urged him into a canter, and hurried toward the safety of camp.

Others had seen the horsemen by now. As Alane rode into camp she could see Norakamo women herding their children into tents. In a few moments the camp circle, which shortly before had been noisy with the daily activities of busy women and children, was silent and empty. A huge bearded vulture glided over the deserted campground, casting its shadow on the beaten-down grass. Alane shivered and made a quick circle with her fingers to ward off evil.

Then Tedric emerged from his tent, walked to the center of the empty circle, crossed his arms on his chest and stood there waiting. He had not gone with the hunting or the herding parties since they had brought the injured chief's son into their camp. He had been waiting, Alane knew, for just this moment. Her eyes went back to the line of riders, and she saw that they had halted at a little distance downriver. As she watched, one man gave his two extra mounts to another to hold and began to ride forward alone.

Tedric looked at his daughter. "Tie those horses up, Alane, and get into the tent."

Alane looked at the approaching horseman and then back at her father. She wanted to hear what would be said. If she moved quickly enough, she reckoned she could manage it. She squeezed her legs, pushed with her seat, and the mare she was riding exploded into a full gallop. The two mares whose ropes she held squealed and galloped alongside. Tedric scowled.

Alane tied the three mares to the hitching post behind her father's tent, ran to the front of it and ducked inside just as the single horseman entered their camp circle. Her mother and her youngest brother, Fenris, were also inside the tent, standing next to the doorflap, obviously prepared to listen. Alane joined them.

"Greetings," she heard her father's voice say. "I am Tedric the chief, son of Hal, son of Urik, born to the Black Half of the Tribe of the Norakamo."

The stranger responded in turn, also identifying himself by family and by kinship. "I am Rorig the chief, son of Berta, grandson of Mira, born to the Eagle Clan of the Tribe of the Kindred."

Silence fell as the two men regarded each other. Then Tedric said, "You have come for your son."

"Sa," replied the other. "I have come for my son. Has he awakened?"

"He has awakened," Tedric replied. "I will take you to him." His voice grew louder as he turned to face his tent. "Fenris!" he called. "Come and hold the chief's horse." Alanc's brother gave her a quick grin before he darted out the doorflap to answer his father's call.

Alane had not been allowed back into the injured man's tent since he had awakened, but she had seen him for the past few mornings washing in the river with her brother Rune. Her mother said he was well on the path to recovery. She gave Adah a quick look, then peeked out the tent doorflap and saw that the group of Kindred horsemen were still keeping their distance. To the watching eyes at the doorflaps in every Norakamo tent, time seemed to pass very slowly. Finally, however, the Kindred chief emerged from the medicine tent, and after him came his son. They were followed by Tedric, the shaman and Rune.

Alane's eyes were attracted by a flurry of motion among the Kindred horsemen. Obviously they had recognized Nardo. Rorig raised a hand to signal, and one of the riders began to gallop toward him, leading a beautiful long-maned gray mare. It did not take Alane long to recognize the rider as Dane, the man who had been so distressed to find Nardo unconscious. Dane pulled up, leaped off his own horse and held out his cupped hands to assist his friend to mount.

Nardo shook him off, jumped onto the gray mare's back and

picked up his reins. His father said something to him and he grinned, his teeth very white in his dark face. Then the three men cantered back toward the waiting group of tribesmen.

Tedric and Rune watched them go. Then the two Norakamo men turned and walked toward the tent where their womenfolk awaited them.

Rorig had agreed to share a meal with the Norakamo later in the day, but for now the band of Kindred men rode a short way back downriver and pitched their own camp. Once the horses were hobbled and grazing peacefully, a group of the men went all the way back to the Great Ford in hopes of getting a deer as it tried to cross the river. They wanted to have some meat to bring as a guest offering to the feast. Rorig and Nardo were among those who remained behind, Nardo because he was still too weak for hunting and Rorig because he wanted to talk to his son. While the rest of the men busied themselves with camp chores, father and son leaned against their rolled-up sleeping skins, watching the horses.

The peaceful scene before them was unshadowed by a single cloud. The sky above was cobalt blue, and the horses grazed peacefully among the fluttering butterflies and the vivid flowers. There was a shadow in Nardo's eyes, however, and a pain that was not physical sounded in his voice as he asked, "How is my mother?"

"Very distressed," Rorig replied. "Nevin was her only brother."

Nardo scowled. "They surprised us, Father. They were on horseback and waiting for us. Tedric says his plan was to capture Nevin, that he did not plan on a killing."

Rorig nodded. He was a good-looking man, with dark, leathery skin molded over strong facial bones. His black, gray-streaked hair was worn loose to the shoulders, and about his forehead was bound a buckskin headband decorated with three perfect golden shells. His eyes were hooded as he watched the grazing horses. He said, "Do you think he is speaking true?"

"Sa," said Nardo almost reluctantly. "They were very anxious for me to recover. Mother could not have given me better care than did Tedric's wife. I think they do not want a blood feud with us, and they must have known they would be courting one with the slaying of Nevin."

With his eyes averted from his son's face, Rorig said, "I am sorry, Nardo. You will miss Nevin sorely, I know."

Nardo's mouth set grimly. He nodded without speaking.

A little silence fell. Then Rorig said, "I do not want a feud with the Norakamo either."

Nardo lifted his brows in surprise at his father's forceful tone.

On the far side of the river a small group of red deer, three does and three fawns, came down to the water for a drink. Nardo's gray mare raised her head from grazing to watch them, then lowered her nose once again into the lush grass. Rorig said, "While you were in the high mountains at grazing camp, I went to the Summer Gathering at Big Rivers Joining."

Nardo gave his father a thoughtful look. "You do not usually make such a journey."

"That is so," Rorig agreed. "But I have been hearing tales from the traders that made me uneasy, so I thought I would go and see for myself."

Nardo was silent, waiting.

"Things are changing in the world outside our mountains," Rorig said at last. "Trees are growing on the grasslands where once the aurochs and the buffalo and the horse herds used to graze."

"Sa?" Nardo said softly.

"The people who dwell in the river valleys to our north are going hungry, Nardo."

Nardo shrugged. "The Horse Eaters have offended the Mother, and she has punished them. Why should this make you uneasy, Father?"

Rorig did not reply.

Across the river one of the fawns had finished drinking. He stood close to his mother's side and peered under her belly, watching the horses on the other side of the river. Nardo smiled faintly at the sight.

"The weather is changing," Rorig said at last. He raised his face to the sky. "You can feel the sun, how warm it is. In the days of my boyhood it was never as warm as this."

"Warm weather is a blessing," Nardo said. "In the warmth of

spring the salmon come back to our rivers. It is warm when the reindeer bear their fawns and the mares their foals. In the warm weather the snow melts from the high pastures, and Mother Earth blesses us with thick green grass for our herds."

"This is how it is for us in the mountains," Rorig agreed. "Our reindeer still climb into the high pastures each summer and descend to the lower hills when the snow begins to fall. It is still cold enough in the mountains for the reindeer. But they are no longer coming to the river valleys, Nardo." Rorig turned somber eyes toward his son. "I have heard that many tribes have already left their ancestral hunting grounds to follow the reindeer north." Brown eyes looked into brown eyes. "I am thinking that someday one of these tribes that are losing their game will hear how good it still is for us. I am thinking they may even try to push their way into our mountains." A beat of silence. "If ever we should face an invasion, Nardo, I would rather count the Norakamo as friends than enemies."

Rorig could see understanding dawn in his son's eyes. There was a long silence. Then Nardo said, "Do you really think such an invasion possible?"

"It is not impossible."

"We do not want Horse Eaters in our mountains!"

Both men stared with possessive eyes at the lovely animals grazing so serenely on the banks of the golden river.

"It is in my heart that it would be wise of us to cry a peace with the Norakamo," Rorig said. "No blood feuds." Pause. "No more horse raiding."

"No more horse raiding!" Nardo repeated in astonishment. "But, Father, what will we do for fun if we can no longer go horse raiding?" Rorig did not reply, and after a long while Nardo sighed. "It takes two to cry a peace. Do you think the Norakamo will agree?"

"I think they will agree to almost anything if it will avoid a blood feud with us," Rorig said.

"Sa," said Nardo somberly. "I think you are right."

The Norakamo were roasting huge haunches of deer over an open fire in the center of their camp circle when the men of the Kindred arrived. The Kindred horses were taken by a group of young boys, and the visitors were invited to join the circle of males.

Nardo could remember no other occasion when these two tribes had met on friendly terms with each other, and the mood of the gathering was tense. The death of Nevin loomed large in the minds of all. It loomed large in Nardo's mind also, but he remembered his father's words and turned to Rune, who was seated beside him, and asked him something about his horses. Rune ran his fingers through his long bangs, glanced around the circle himself, replied and then made a complimentary remark about Nardo's gray. Nardo gave a genial grin and leaned over to relay the comment to Dane, thus drawing him into the conversation.

Across from Nardo the shaman sat in brooding silence. Nardo had scarcely seen Hagen since he had awakened, the residue of his nursing care being left to Adah. But Nardo had sensed the hostility of the Norakamo shaman. Now, as Nardo watched, the young man next to Hagen leaned over and said something in his ear. The two of them glanced at Tedric, and Hagen said something in reply. Both men had their backs rudely turned to the Kindred men on their other sides.

But the chiefs, Rorig and Tedric, were speaking together with obvious good humor, and Nardo could feel the tension in the group relax slightly.

The meat was passed around, and conversation, at first extremely stilted, became easier as the men traded hunting stories and talked in endless detail about horses. The mood of the gathering, while not exactly cordial, at least was not actively hostile. The shaman and his satellite sat in silence, but no one seemed to pay them much attention.

The sun was hanging low in the western sky when Tedric asked Rorig and his son for a private conversation. The Kindred chief accepted gravely and gestured to Nardo. Rune got up also and the two younger men followed their fathers into the privacy of Tedric's tent.

Adah was there to welcome them, and Nardo immediately looked around the large tent for Alane. He felt a pang of disappointment when he did not find her. He had caught only tantalizing glimpses of the chief's daughter during the days of his convalescence, and he had been hoping to see more of her today. He thought with exasperation that these Norakamo were overly strict with their girls.

The four men sat around the stone hearthplace, and Adah took the tea cauldron off the small fire. Nardo had learned that the Norakamo made their tea with mint instead of sage, and he had also learned something of their tea-serving customs. Now, as Adah ceremoniously filled a single large clay cup with the hot liquid, he murmured in his father's ear, "Take only a few sips and then give it back to her."

Rorig's face remained expressionless, but when Adah presented him with the cup he did as Nardo had told him. Adah received the cup back, returned to the pot, refilled it and then brought it to Nardo. He sniffed the minty fragrance appreciatively, took two sips and handed it back. Adah repeated this ritual, offering the cup to her husband and last to her son. Then she retired to the recesses of the tent. Tedric cleared his throat, a signal to the others that the real business of the meeting was about to begin.

Nardo sat in silence and listened as Tedric assured his father that the Norakamo did not want a blood feud. Tedric said this at length and several times over, and after a little while Nardo ceased to pay attention. Instead he looked at Rune, who sat across the small hearthplace from him.

There could scarcely be men more physically different than the two who gazed at each other over the stone hearthplace. The Norakamo's sun-colored hair was cut in long bangs across his forehead and then tied back by a band made of the skin of deer antlers taken in the velvet. His face was narrow, with a thin, straight nose and wide-spaced light blue eyes. He had a slim, pliant body that looked as if it would never withstand the rigors of a hunting life, but Nardo, whose cousin Varic was built the same way, knew well how deceptive such slenderness could be.

Now Rorig began to talk, and Nardo transferred his attention to his father's words. Rorig was speaking of the warming weather and the disappearance of game from the river valleys to the north. From the look upon Tedric's rugged features, Nardo suspected that what Rorig was saying was not news to the Norakamo chief.

"We do not go to the Gathering at Big Rivers Joining, we go to one farther west, but I have heard the same things," Tedric said. "There is much unrest among the Horse Eaters." With some ceremony he rested his hands upon his knees and said, "It is in my heart that during these troubled times there should be friendship and not enmity between our tribes."

"I have felt this also," Rorig replied.

Tedric looked pleased. "The Norakamo and the Kindred are children of the Horse God. In the past we have let this divide us; now is the time for it to bring us together."

"Your words are good," said Rorig. "But how is this friendship to be accomplished? Our people have been at odds for many lives. It is not easy to change the feelings of the heart."

Tedric was stroking his short blond beard. "It is true that the young men of my tribe will be reluctant to give up their horse raiding. If we are to succeed it will be necessary to make this friendship between our people with something more binding then mere words."

"I agree, but how are we to do that?" asked Rorig.

A small silence fell. The air in the tent was scented with mint from the tea and with the fragrance of the other herbs which were hanging from the tent poles to dry. The chief's tent was very large, but to Nardo's eyes, accustomed to the clutter of his mother's house, it looked almost unfurnished. Sleeping skins were piled along one wall, and the cooking gear was arranged upon a large stone by the hearthplace. There were two handfuls of large baskets also lining the walls; Nardo thought that the rest of the family's belongings must be stored in them.

Finally Tedric spoke. "We must make a bond of kinship," he said. His blue eyes were steady on Rorig's face. "That is the only way. And in order to do this, I will give my daughter to your son in marriage."

There was stunned silence as both Rorig and Nardo stared at the Norakamo chief. Finally Rorig found his voice. "How can this be? My son is to be the next chief of our tribe. He cannot come to live among the Norakamo."

Tedric's gaze did not waver. "Among my people it is not customary for men to live with the families of their wives. We would not expect your son to live with us. It is the Norakamo custom for a woman to join the family of her husband."

A steady drumbeat began outside the tent. Then came the rich, hypnotic voice of the Norakamo shaman.

"I do not think you understand." Nardo could see that his father was striving to speak mildly. "Among the Kindred, a child belongs to his mother's clan. Since your daughter's children would be of her clan, not of ours, they would have no place among us. The kinship you speak of would not be accomplished."

Tedric did not seem at all perturbed by this objection. "The Norakamo do not have clans as do the Kindred," he said. "Our tribe counts kinship by halves. However, the children of a Norakamo marriage always belong to the half of their father. My daughter has always known that her children would be of their father's lineage. In this one instance, for the good of both our peoples, would it not be possible for her children to be of the clan of your son's?"

Rorig looked amazed. "I do not think you realize what you are asking of your daughter," he said. "First you propose sending her to live her life separated from all the women of her blood. Next you say that even her children will not belong to her. How can she, or any woman, live in such a way?"

Tedric shrugged. "That is the way it is for a girl. She does not grow old in the tent in which she was born. Her fate is to be given to a man, not to grow old sitting by her mother's side."

Nardo felt a stab of pity for the lovely girl he had seen so briefly. Outside, the voice of the shaman rose and fell, and the beat of the drum began to hurry.

"If I do agree to such a marriage," Rorig said slowly, "what will you want from me?"

Tedric smiled and waved a casual hand. "Nothing that is not usual. You must pay me bridewealth for her, that is all."

The shaman was singing about the creation of Raven, a tale that was familiar to all the Kindred. In some things, then, we are alike, Nardo thought.

Rorig said, "Bridewealth. You are saying you will expect a gift from me in return for your daughter?"

Tedric's thick blond brows lifted. "Do you not give bridewealth in your tribe?"

Rorig shook his head.

Tedric's blue eyes widened. "You give your daughters away for nothing?"

Rorig's dark face was impassive. "We do not give our daughters away," he said. "Unlike yours, our women do grow old in the tents in which they were born. It is our men who change households when they marry."

Nardo glanced across the fire and saw Rune's incredulous look. Evidently the marital ways of the Kindred were as astonishing to him as those of the Norakamo were to Nardo.

"What would you expect me to pay in bridewealth?" Rorig asked.

Tedric smiled again. "Five handfuls of horses."

"What?" Nardo almost leaped to his feet. "You must be mad."

Tedric nodded. "That is so. It should be much more, but I am a generous man and I understand that our ways are strange to you. Therefore I will only ask for five handfuls."

Nardo began to speak again, but Rorig gave his son a look. Nardo closed his mouth.

"What you have offered is indeed generous," Rorig said to the other chief. "Must the five handfuls of horses be paid all at once?"

Tedric stroked his beard and looked thoughtful. Finally he said, a little reluctantly, "It is paid three times, at each step of the marriage ceremony."

Nardo thought furiously: The son of a hyena was thinking of asking for it all at once.

With infinite courtesy Rorig asked, "Will you explain?"

Tedric continued to stroke his beard, clearly trying to organize his thoughts. "First, I must begin by telling you that while it is true that a married woman goes to live with her husband's people, she does not do this right away. At the beginning of the marriage the husband must come to live among his wife's family." His eyes moved to Nardo. "This is so he can establish bonds with his wife's father and brothers," he explained.

That is impossible, Nardo thought. I cannot live among the men who killed my uncle. He looked back at Tedric, his face impassive.

Rorig said, "For how long does the husband stay with his wife's family?"

"Until the birth of the first child."

Rorig nodded.

Tedric smiled happily; he felt he was doing a good job of explaining. "The bridewealth is given three times, then," he said. He held up a finger: "One, when the marriage is agreed to." He unfolded a second finger: "Two, on the bonding day when the husband first lives with his wife." Now came the third finger: "And three, when the first child is born. That is when the woman is truly a wife and she leaves her father's family and joins the family of her husband."

A thoughtful silence fell and Tedric turned to signal to his wife. Adah came forward, and once again the ceremony of the tea was repeated. When Adah had retired to her corner and the men were once more alone around the fire, Rorig said, "Let me be certain I am clear about this. If my son should marry your daughter, you would expect him to come and live among you until their first child was born?"

"Sa."

"I would give you one part of the bridewealth when I accepted your offer, the second part when they began to live together, and the third part when the first child was born."

"Sa."

"At that time your daughter would come to live among us and her children would belong to the Clan of the Wolf, which is my son's clan."

"Sa."

"I understand." Rorig moved his legs, a signal that he was about to rise. "I will think about your generous offer, Chief of the Norakamo, and I will give you my answer tomorrow."

Everyone got up. It was not until Nardo was ready to pass through the doorflap that he asked Tedric, "We are speaking of your daughter, Alane?"

The chief crossed his arms on his broad chest. "We are speaking of my daughter, Alane."

The men Rorig had left behind at camp had built a temporary corral along the river out of the rawhide ropes they always carried and some wooden posts they had cut down in the stand of woods to their east. After the returning party had put their horses in with the others, they unrolled their sleeping skins along the perimeter of the corral and lay down to sleep.

Nardo's shoulder was aching after the long day, and he lay flat on his back and stared up at the growing sliver of Horse Foal Moon in the night sky. The crickets were chirping loudly in the high grass, and frogs were croaking in the river. An owl hooted, and grunts came from horses in the corral as they lay down to rest. The smell of fresh manure drifted to Nardo's nostrils, a familiar and comforting odor. The men had built two large fires to warn away predators, one at each end of the horse corral. They would take turns tending it during the night.

Rorig spoke in a low voice from his sleeping skin beside Nardo's. "It is in my heart that such a marriage might be a good thing for both our tribes."

Nardo's eyes were on the moon. "They want me to live among them, Father. I cannot live with people who have slain my uncle."

Rorig moved restlessly, and then was still. He understood Nardo's objection very well. Among the Kindred the important male relative to a boy was not his father but his mother's brother. Rorig was of the Eagle Clan, and Nardo was of the Clan of the Wolf, the clan of his mother. He did not share a lineage with his father at all. The blood that counted, Mother's Blood, he had shared with Nevin, his uncle. Nevin had been the one to teach him the skills of hunting and riding, to instruct him in all his religious duties. Nevin had been the one to sponsor him when he was initiated, first as an adolescent and then as a man. Rorig had also done these things, but for his sisters' sons, not for Nardo.

Rorig said now in a soft voice, "Tedric was right when he said that a bond of kinship is the only way to make peace between our tribes." Nardo did not reply; his dark eyes still gazed at the moon. Rorig went on, "It would be a good thing for you to live for a little while among the Norakamo, Nardo. As Tedric said, you would learn to know the men of your wife's blood. Your cousins would visit you, and they too would learn to be friends with these people. It is the way to build a bond between our tribes."

A horse squealed somewhere on the other side of the corral rope, and there was the sound of scrambling hooves. The two men listened, but the herd remained quiet.

Nardo said quietly, "And what will my mother and my sisters say to such a marriage?"

"You must remember, Nardo, that Tedric was not the slayer of your uncle. You killed the man who killed Nevin. Blood has been exacted for blood." Rorig's voice came a little louder, as if he had turned his head in Nardo's direction. "You have grown friendly with Tedric's son, I think."

"Sa. Rune is a good man."

"It will not be so impossible to live among these people. And it is only until the birth of your first child. Less than a year."

"And my mother? She will understand this?"

"Your mother and sisters think the rainbow arches over your head," Rorig replied. "I am thinking they will be in favor of any marriage that will keep you within their household."

From nearby came the sound of grass tearing as several of the horses decided to graze. From across the river a jackal howled. Another answered, and then the howling turned into excited yipping as the two greeted each other.

Nardo regarded the night sky and reflected upon his father's words. If he married this Norakamo girl it would mean he would not have to move away from his mother's house. He would escape the divided loyalty all the men of his tribe lived with: husbands in one house and sons and brothers in another.

This would be pleasant. And Alane was very beautiful. But the thought of parting with five handfuls of horses made him angry.

"I do not think Tedric is being generous," he said. "I think he is asking for more horses than he would get for his daughter from among his own people."

"You are probably right" came the serene reply.

"Dhu, Father! We cannot afford to give away so many horses!"

"We can afford it. It will be hard to part with them. It will be hard to choose which ones we must let go. But we can afford it, Nardo." The moon was in the western sky. Soon it would disappear and the night would belong only to the stars. One of the men tending the fire began to pile more wood on. The flames leaped higher. The yipping from across the river had ceased.

"You are serious about this, Father," Nardo said.

"We do not want the Horse Eaters coming into our mountains, my son."

Rorig rarely addressed Nardo as "my son." Nardo looked through the darkness at his father's faintly visible face. Then he replied quietly, "It is in my heart that you speak true, Father. It is as Tedric said, the time has come for the children of the Horse God to come together."

"You have seen this girl? She is not distasteful to you?"

"She is not distasteful to me."

Bat wings beat through the air. The horses in the corral moved restlessly. Rorig let out a long, slow breath.

"You cannot make a promise to Rorig until you have spoken to my mother," Nardo said. "If she objects to my marrying into the tribe that killed her brother, then I cannot make the marriage."

"I would not ask you to go against your mother's wishes, Nardo," Rorig said.

Nardo closed his eyes and tried to ignore the ache in his shoulder.

"I will accept Tedric's offer with the understanding that first you must have your mother's approval."

Nardo was silent.

"Do you agree to this, Nardo?"

"Sa," Nardo said slowly. "I agree."

Chapter Three

The clan council meeting the following morning did not go as smoothly as Rorig had hoped. When he told the men gathered around the campfire of Tedric's marriage offer, Varic protested furiously.

"These people murdered my father!" he cried. "How can you think of making a bond of kinship with them?"

Rorig once more explained his reasoning.

"Nardo killed the man who killed Nevin," Mano, the representative for the Wolf Clan, said to Varic. "Vengeance has been done, Varic."

The rest of the council members murmured their agreement about the issue of vengeance. What they objected to was the five handfuls of horses.

It was a long meeting, with a great deal of animated discussion. The chief of the Kindred was not as absolute a ruler as was the chief of the Norakamo. Unless Rorig got the approval of the clan council, he would not be able to accept Tedric's offer.

At last, over the angry objections of Varic, the council decided to accept Tedric's offer of his daughter. Their peace offering to Varic was the stipulation that Mara, Nardo's mother and Nevin's sister, must agree to the marriage as well.

Alane learned nothing of the proposed marriage until the following afternoon, after the men of the Kindred had crossed the

Great Ford to their own side of the river. Tedric then gathered his family within his tent and told them what had been discussed between the two chiefs.

"They have to consult with the boy's mother before they can offer bridewealth," Tedric said to Adah. "But I could see by Rorig's eyes that he is as eager for this bond between our tribes as I am."

"Has he agreed to the five handfuls of horses?" Rune asked.

"Sa."

Rune laughed. "You did well, Father."

Tedric grinned. "Sa. The Kindred know nothing of bridewealth. I told them five handfuls was less than the usual amount for a chief's daughter."

"What of Larz?" Stifun's voice intruded into the conversation. "Larz wants to marry Alane. You know that, Father. He has spoken to you."

"His father has given me no horses," Tedric said. "There is no bargain if horses have not been given."

"You asked for too many horses," Stifun said, defending his friend. "Larz and his father have been trying to collect them, but you asked for too many."

Tedric shook his head in wonder. "A spirit must have been speaking through me. It is true what you say, my son. I asked Larz for too many horses. And because of that Alane is free to marry Rorig's son."

Alane had been silent, listening to her family with stunned incredulity. Now she found speech. "If I marry this stranger, then I will have to go and live among his people. You cannot have thought of this, Father. You cannot mean to send me to live with the Kindred!"

Tedric lifted his hands in a gesture that signified resignation and turned to his wife. It was Adah who answered her daughter. "Alane, your father would not ask such a thing of you were it not of great importance to the tribe."

"Sa," said Alane bitterly. She threw the mitten she had been sewing to the ground. "It is worth five handfuls of horses to the tribe."

"It is not the horses," Tedric said angrily. "Do you think I would give my daughter to strangers were it only for the horses?"

Alane's stormy eyes challenged her father. "What is so important, then, that you must banish me to the tents of our enemies?"

"It is important that the Norakamo and the Kindred cease to be enemies," Tedric said. All the anger had left his voice; now it was quiet and very sober. "That is what is important." He looked around at the faces of his family. "Great changes are happening in the world outside these mountains," he said. "The great herds of reindeer that used to come south every winter to the river valleys are coming no longer. Our mountain reindeer have never traveled such great distances, have always been content to stay within our hills and move higher or lower according to the season, so we have not been affected. But the people of the valleys, who depend upon the reindeer for their food, their clothing, their tools, are growing desperate."

"Let them hunt some other animal, then," Alane said.

"The other game is also getting scarce, my daughter. Trees are growing where no trees ever grew before. The grazing animals also are going north. Whole tribes are going hungry."

Rune said to Alane, "Father fears the Horse Eaters will try to move into our mountains."

Tedric nodded. "Our horses have kept them away thus far; they fear us because we can ride. But we are not a large tribe, and if we have to defend our hunting grounds we will need help." Tedric shrugged. "You see?"

"Your father wants to make a bond of kinship with the Kindred," Adah said softly to Alane. "It is the best way to keep us safe."

"And what of the Kindred chief?" Alane demanded. "Why does he want a Norakamo woman for his son?"

"For the same reason," Tedric replied. "Rorig too is worried, and he does not want his foothills overrun by invaders. We are no threat to the Kindred. We know how to save and use our own pastures; we know where to find the reindeer, the red deer and the smaller game; we know how to fish the rivers. The horse raiding was a game between us, but now our deeper interests lie in being friends."

Alane's white face was set. "And you will use me to make that friendship."

"Sa, my daughter. I will use you. As Rorig will use his son."

Alane's nostrils quivered. "It is not Rorig's son who will have to dwell with strangers in a world far from his own kin."

Once again Tedric raised his hands in resignation. "That is the fate of a woman, my daughter."

Alane's gray eyes glittered. Without another word she stood up and stalked out of the tent. Those left within sat for a moment in tense silence. Then Rune said, "I will go after her."

Tedric nodded. "She must be made to understand the importance of this marriage, my son. It may well be that the future of the tribe depends upon it."

The sound of galloping hoofbeats resounded in everyone's ears.

Tedric's jaw set angrily.

Rune said, "I know where she is going." He stood up.

"The son of the Kindred chief may not appreciate a wife who steals his horses," Adah said.

"Alane is upset." Rune moved toward the door. "She does not usually take a horse without permission."

"Find her," Tedric said. "And make her understand."

Alane was where Rune had expected her to be, in a small cove of the river about three miles upstream of the Norakamo camp. She was sitting on the grassy shore, using her knife to skin a rabbit she had found in one of the tribe's traps. She did not seem surprised to see Rune, shooting him a quick look before returning once more to her work. The only visible sign of her feelings was the vicious way she was wielding her sharp flint knife.

Rune hobbled his mare and set her loose to graze with Alane's horse. Then he came to sit beside his sister.

"This Nardo is not such a bad fellow, Alane," he said. "I spent some time with him while he was in our camp, and he is a man I could easily learn to call brother."

"I am thinking it will be easier for you to call him brother than it will be for me to call him husband," Alane muttered as she efficiently removed the skin from the carcass.

Rune sighed. After a moment he said sadly, "It seems our family is not fated to make happy marriages."

Alane turned to regard her brother's pensive profile. Rune was twenty years of age, five years older than she and two years older than Stifun. He had been married, but his wife had died in childbirth the previous year.

Rune had been fond of his wife, a girl he had known since early childhood. Ordinarily Alane would have made a comforting gesture or comment, but she felt that Rune had betrayed her by taking her father's part in this matter of her marriage. So she said nothing, once more bending her head over her job so that her face was hidden behind the curtain of silvery hair that slid forward across her shoulders.

"Father insisted that they follow our marriage ceremonials," Rune offered next. "It will not be so bad, Alane. Nardo will live among us until your first child is born. You will have a chance to get to know him while you are still surrounded by your own family."

"I don't want to get to know him."

"Alane." She felt her brother's fingers on her arm. "Look at me."

Reluctantly she lifted her head. His blue eyes were very serious. "I meant it when I said this Nardo was a good fellow. I would have spoken against Father's plan if I did not think he would make you a good husband." She said nothing, but her angry gray eyes spoke for her. Rune made an exasperated gesture. "Dhu! He is a splendid-looking fellow, Alane. And he rides as well as I do! I am thinking you are upsetting yourself for no good reason."

"What if I say I will not marry him?" she said.

Rune looked faintly alarmed. "You cannot. Not if Father has promised. Not if the bridewealth has been agreed upon."

"Words must be spoken by the woman on the bonding day," Alane said. "What if I will not say them?"

Now Rune was really alarmed. He knew his sister better than anyone, and he knew she was capable of it. In most things Alane was a gentle and biddable girl, but once in a great while she would set her mind on something, and then she was adamant.

"This is not just a matter of you and Nardo," Rune said urgently. "This is a matter of our survival as a tribe. We are a smaller tribe than the Kindred, Alane. If the Horse Eaters of the plains unite and invade us, we will not be able to withstand them. We need the Kindred. In truth, we need them more than they need us."

In stony silence Alane began to disjoint the rabbit.

"I took your part over Vili," Rune said. "I knew you did not like him, and I asked Father to refuse the shaman's offer."

Alane's eyes glittered. "Father refused Vili because he did not want to give the shaman the advantage of having the chief's daughter in his family. His refusal had nothing to do with my wishes, Rune, and you know it!"

"Your wishes had something to do with *my* intervention," Rune said steadily.

Alane looked at her bloodstained hands.

"I think you can be happy with this Nardo," Rune said.

His sister's face said that she did not think the same way.

"He knew your name," Rune said. "When Rorig and Father were first discussing the marriage, Nardo asked Father specifically if we were talking about his daughter, Alane."

Her head lifted. "He did?"

"Sa." Rune looked quizzical. "How, I wonder, did he come to know your name?"

"He asked me. They are so boorish, these Kindred men, that they will ask a perfectly strange girl for her name."

"But you told him," Rune persisted.

She shrugged. "He was injured and I did not want to tell him how rude he was." She paused, thinking. Then she said bitterly, "That must have been my mistake. I told him my name and gave him this power over me."

"The marriage was Father's idea, not Nardo's," Rune said. "Try to be more open-hearted, Alane. It is not as if you really wanted to marry anyone else. You don't care that much for Larz. You know you don't."

"Larz is at least a Norakamo!" she cried with passion. "If I married him I would live among my own people, not be banished to a life among strangers."

Rune's eyes dropped from hers; he did not have a reply.

Alane was not the only Norakamo opposed to her marriage with Nardo. When Vili heard the news he stormed to the shaman's tent in a fury. Hagen was sprinkling his medicine bag with pollen when Vili pushed open the tent flap, and the shaman did not pause in his incantations to see who had come in. Vili stood just inside the door and waited, his eyes adjusting to the shadows on his uncle's long fingers as they went about their daily work of feeding the spirits that dwelled within his magic deerskin pouch.

Finally Hagen was finished. He picked up the medicine bag, put the long leather cord with which it was tied around his neck, and turned to Vili.

"So," he said. "What has happened?"

Vili came farther into the tent, which had an odor unlike any of the others in the Norakamo camp. The shaman's tent always smelled faintly of decay. "You won't believe this, Uncle," Vili said, "but Tedric has offered Alane in marriage to the son of the Kindred chief."

The shaman stiffened. "And has the Kindred chief accepted?"

"He has."

The tent was too dark for Vili to see his uncle's face clearly. Hagen said nothing.

"He refused me," Vili said, "yet he will give her to Loki's murderer!"

"He refused *me*," Hagen said softly.

"Sa. But you were asking for me."

"I was asking for my brother's son, and he refused me."

"It makes me want to puke," Vili said violently. "The most beautiful girl in all the tribe to be given into the hands of a murderer."

"There is power in Alane." The shaman walked slowly forward until he stood beside his nephew. "That is why I wanted her for you. I do not want her in the hands of our enemy."

"Speak to Tedric, then!"

Hagen smiled and his hand went to his medicine bag. "Tedric will not listen to me. I will have to take action on my own."

In the dimness of the tent Hagen's gaunt face looked almost like a skull. Vili shivered. "What action, Uncle?"

"The spirit of Loki cries out for vengeance against his murderer, and the tribe does not hear," Hagen said. "It will be up to you and me, Vili, to accomplish it."

The growing Horse Foal Moon had turned into the disappearing moon by the time Rorig and Nardo returned to the Norakamo camp, bringing with them word of Nardo's mother's agreement as well as two handfuls of mares for the first payment of Alane's bridewealth. Both tribes rode only mares, for it was not possible to keep stallions together in one herd.

Tedric led the Kindred contingent to a corral that had been built beneath the steep cliffs that rose along the river to the south of the Norakamo camp, and instructed the men to turn the mares into it. Then the Norakamo chief invited Rorig and Nardo to accompany him as he inspected the horses.

The men spent an intense hour going over each particular mare from nose to tail. The conversation was never boring. For example, the language of the two tribes had thirty or forty specialized words just to describe the color of a mare which to a member of a non-horse-owning tribe would be brown. They had words that succinctly summed up defects, such as retracted heels or sickled hocks. They had different words for a horse in each year of its life until it was fully grown. There were even specific words that applied to the conditions of herding horses at different times of day and in different seasons.

There was, however, one major way in which the two tribes differed in their horse keeping. Among the Kindred the horses belonged to the tribe, while with the Norakamo they were owned by individuals.

At first Nardo had found this difference difficult to understand. In his tribe each man had his own favorite riding horse whose use was reserved solely for him, but the rest of the horses, which served as remounts or were used for hauling, were owned and cared for by the whole tribe together. Rorig would have been unable to give these mares to the Norakamo if he had not had the approval of the clan council.

The Norakamo used horses for all the things that the Kindred did, but for them a horse meant even more. Among the Norakamo a man's wealth was measured by the number of horses he owned, and he used these horses principally to pay bridewealth. The status of an entire family depended upon how much bridewealth was paid for the wife.

Tedric rose from his inspection of the feet of the last mare, and smiled with great good humor. "You have brought me good stock," he said to Rorig. "I am pleased."

The Kindred chief inclined his head. "I have given you these children of my heart because I know you will take good care of them," he replied gravely.

"They will live among us in honor," Tedric said. Then he turned to Nardo. "Come. My daughter awaits you," and he leaped on his horse to return to camp. The others followed.

The meadow where the Norakamo always pitched their summer camp was wide and pleasant, and it was strategically located just upstream from the place where the Greatfish and the River of Gold met. Shortly downstream from that convergence was the Big Ford across the River of Gold. The steep cliffs just upstream of the camp made trapping deer easy, and the Great Ford just downstream was useful for the trapping of game traveling across the river. In addition to these hunting advantages, the River of Gold was filled with fish, and the soil along its banks produced a rich grass upon which horses thrived.

There were several large caves in the area which the tribe could use, but they lived mainly in their tents. Thirty of them were set up in two concentric circles on the grassy bank of the river. Small rope corrals had been erected behind many of the tents, and these were used for holding riding horses or horses the women looked after. The men continuously moved the main horse herd from pasture to pasture on the grassy plateau to the west of the camp. Nardo knew from his raiding days that once the summer was finished, the Norakamo would pack their tents and move to another camp farther to the west.

This was the main difference between the Norakamo and the Kindred way of life. The Norakamo were a nomadic people, moving in a regular cycle between a series of known camps and pastures. The Kindred also migrated according to the season and the pastures, but only a small portion of the tribe accompanied the herd. The rest remained behind in the home base.

The sky had clouded up while the men were at the corral,

and Nardo could feel rain in the air. A family of ducks was sailing down the river and a V-shaped wing of geese was flying over it in the opposite direction. Nardo could hear the rhythmic slap of their wings. Nardo thought it a good luck sign and paused for a moment, looking up, before he ducked into the chief's tent behind his father.

The air inside the tent was fragrant with mint. Nardo's eyes searched for Alane and found her seated beside her mother before the stone hearthplace. She had not looked toward the door when the men came in. There was a teapot hanging over the low fire, source of the minty fragrance, and the dirt floor of the tent had been carefully swept. Tedric said expansively, "Sit, my friends, and my daughter will serve us tea."

Part of the floor was covered with reindeer skin rugs, and Nardo took a place on one of the rugs between his father and Tedric. He watched as Alane poured the tea into the single large clay cup, willing her to glance at him.

She did not lift her eyes.

"Horses have been given," Tedric said to his daughter. "You may serve your husband."

She still did not look up as she walked across the floor and stood before Nardo, offering the cup. He took it from her narrow, long-fingered hands and sipped the hot minty liquid. He noticed that her eyebrows were not light like her hair but smoky in color. They gave her young face a look of beautiful gravity. He said in a soft voice, the voice he would use to soothe a frightened mare, "Thank you, Alane."

At the sound of her name her gray eyes flashed up; their look was unreadable. Then she took the cup back from him and returned to the pot to refill it before she offered it to his father.

Once the tea had been served, Adah came forward with a large chunk of meat, which she offered to her husband. He took a bite, cut it off close to his lips with a small flint knife, then passed the remaining chunk to Rorig, who copied his host's example before passing the meat to Nardo. As the men ate, Alane sat with bent head, her eyes on her folded hands.

He is such a boor, she thought. *He talks to me as if I were a child, but he looks at me . . .* She shivered as she thought of the way Nardo looked at her.

What if I threw the tea in his face? she thought next. But she knew she would not. However much she resented the fact that her parents were willing to sacrifice her happiness for the good of the tribe, she could not deny that the good of the tribe was at stake. If they demanded this of her, she would comply. But her heart quailed at the thought of being alone with this too-large, too-bold stranger.

Nardo looked at the girl in the corner and thought impatiently, *Are we never going to have a chance to be alone?*

Time passed and it seemed they were not. Alane remained at her mother's side while the men ate and traded hunting stories. Nardo pretended to listen and watched Alane out of the corner of his eye.

It was the custom for the unmarried women of the Norakamo to wear their hair loose, and Nardo could feel his fingers itching to slide into the shimmering mass that streamed down Alane's back to her waist. It would be so soft, as soft as rainwater. . . .

"How long is it between the first giving of horses and the bonding day?" he asked Tedric abruptly.

The men's voices stopped, and three faces looked at Nardo in surprise. Then Tedric grinned. "We will have the bonding day at the full of the next moon."

"My son is eager to take his bride," Rorig said, his voice dry.

Nardo smiled imperturbably. "I did not mean to interrupt your story, Father," he said, and settled down to listen to one of Rorig's favorite tales. In half a moon he would have all that pale loveliness beside him in his sleeping skins. He could be patient for half a moon.

Chapter Four

A Norakamo marriage was not just a single exchange of vows but a long ceremonial process which began with the preparations for the wedding. As with all Norakamo girls, Alane had been working on her bridal tent ever since her moon blood had begun to flow. It had taken many long hours of preparing skins and sewing them together, but the tent was ready, and her father and brothers cut saplings in the forest and put it up. Adah also helped her dig out a fire pit under the tent's smoke opening. Each of the women of the camp presented her with a bride gift. She received cooking pots of soapstone, of animal skulls and of clay. She received baskets and bone needles and spoons made of antelope horn. From her mother she received a winter sleeping bag to share with her husband. Such a bag was made by sewing four reindeer skins together with the fur facing inside. When used with a reindeer hide beneath it for insulation, it would keep sleepers warm in even the bitterest weather.

Alane went through all of these preparations with a bitter heart. Since she had been a small child playing with the deerskin dolls her father had made for her, she had dreamed of her marriage time. And now all the joy she had expected to feel was transmuted into anger and fear. Instead of some fair-haired Norakamo boy to share her bridal tent and her life, she would be forced into exile with a stranger. Yet all the women acted as though she ought to be a happy bride looking forward to welcoming her husband. Never had Alane felt so alone.

Never would she forgive her father and mother for what they were doing to her. Never would she forgive them for using the welfare of the tribe as a spear to hold to her heart. She would go through with this marriage because she had to. She would leave her home and live in a strange land among a strange people because she had to. She would live her life an exile, alone, and she hoped her mother and father would be miserable every time they thought of her.

As for her future husband . . . she tried to think of him as little as possible, but at night sometimes she dreamed about him and woke up trembling. He was so big . . . too big. She had taken care of him when he was ill, and she knew the strength of that big body. He frightened her. She was not used to men as big as that.

They saw little of each other in the weeks that preceded their marriage, but whenever they did meet, he would give her a boyish grin. The smile did not fool Alane. She knew that it had taken four men of her tribe to subdue him after the death of Nevin.

Well might he grin, she thought bitterly. He had to live among strangers only until the birth of his first child. Then he would be going home. Perhaps he was being forced to wed her in the same way that she was being forced to wed him, but the consequences of their marriage would fall most heavily upon her. It was always that way, she thought, for a woman.

Her only hope lay in the thought that she might prove barren. If that should happen, then Nardo would divorce her. A barren woman was an object of pity to the Norakamo, but Alane thought it preferable to be pitied among her own people than honored by strangers.

Two days before the marriage day, Rorig returned, bringing with him Nardo's mother and a host of other kin. Rorig and the men drove the horses for the next payment of Alane's bridewealth to the corral, and Tedric and his sons went with them to inspect the new arrivals. Adah took Mara and Nardo's two sisters into her tent to meet Alane and to have tea.

The Kindred women were cold. Rorig had had to work hard to get Mara to agree to the marriage, and she had no intention of being one jot more pleasant to these women of the tribe who had murdered her brother than was absolutely necessary. The Norakamo women were wary. Over the teacups they sized up one another.

He looks like her, Alane thought as she sipped her tea and regarded her future mother-by-marriage from beneath lowered lashes. Mara was very tall for a woman, with long black hair worn in a single thick braid down her back. There were streaks of gray in that braid, and lines beside her large brown eyes. Her high-boned nose and cheekbones were sharper than Nardo's and gave her a look of arrogance.

Mara looked like a formidable woman. Among the Kindred she would be a matriarch, the leader of a family. Her daughters deferred to her. No doubt she would expect her daughter-by-marriage to do the same.

A spark of temper stirred in Alane. *She is in for a surprise,* she thought, and lifted her chin. From Mara her gaze went to Nardo's sisters. They were both a good deal older than he, and the elder, the one called Riva, had a sad expression. Riva looked up and caught Alane's eye. She said, gesturing toward the wall, "Those baskets are very lovely. Such skill in basket weaving will be welcomed by the women of the Kindred."

"My daughter is a very fine weaver," Adah said with pride. "Her baskets are much admired among our people."

"What material do you use?" Mara asked Alane, looking if possible even more arrogant than before.

"A plant that grows along the River of Gold," Alane replied. She raised her eyebrows, indicating faint surprise. "Do not the women of the Kindred weave baskets?"

Mara's brown eyes narrowed. Steadily Alane returned her gaze. It was Mara who looked away first, dismissing Alane from her attention as she turned to Adah and said, "You must tell us about your marriage ritual." She made it sound as if it was certain to be barbarous. "We do not want to make a mistake and perhaps offend you."

"Certainly," Adah said, ignoring her tone. "But first you must let my daughter serve you more tea."

Gritting her teeth, Alane complied.

———

The scene in the corral during the horse inspection was
equally tense. To Nardo's kinsmen the idea of bridewealth was
utterly foreign. They bitterly resented handing over their precious horses to enrich the herds of Tedric, and they also thought
Tedric was showing bad taste by "selling" his daughter in such
a fashion. Nardo felt they were fortunate to get through the
inspection without insults being exchanged.

The women were still sitting over tea when the men returned. When Nardo walked into the tent, Mara's arrogant face
warmed to beauty. Nardo said, "The tea is made with mint,
Mama. Isn't it good?"

There was an uncomfortable pause. Then, "It is good," Mara
said.

Nardo looked from his mother to his wife-to-be. Alane's face
wore its most unreadable look. Obviously the women had not
been getting along.

Adah was scarcely able to disguise her relief at the men's
appearance. She said to Mara, "We have set up a guest tent for
your family. If you will come with me, I will take you and your
daughters to see it."

Mara rose with dignity and brushed her long buckskin skirt
to smooth it. "You may come also, Nardo," she said.

"Sa," he agreed. His eyes searched his mother's face, and she
came to him and touched his forearm. He slipped an arm around
her shoulders and gave her a gentle hug. "Come," he said softly,
"we'll talk."

As they went out, Rorig looked at Tedric. "My wife is missing
her brother," he said. "This is . . . difficult for her."

"I understand," Tedric replied.

Alane threw the dregs of the tea onto the fire and walked
out.

As soon as Adah left mother and son alone in the tent, Mara
said, "It is not too late to repudiate this marriage, Nardo, if you
do not like it."

Nardo cocked an eyebrow. "Was it as bad as that, Mother? I
have always found Alane and her mother to be very courteous."

"She is pert," Mara said.

Nardo deliberately misunderstood. "Adah?"

"Alane. Your . . . intended wife."

"She has never been pert to me." Nardo sounded regretful.

"I am serious, Nardo! Rorig bullied me into agreeing to this marriage, and now that I am here I think I made a mistake. These people are foreigners. How can we take a girl who has no blood ties with us into our tribe?"

Nardo let out his breath. "Let us sit down," he suggested, pointing at the hearth rugs Adah had provided. After Mara had complied and they were sitting face to face and eye to eye, Nardo said gravely, "I cannot back out of this marriage now, Mother. If I did such a thing, it would gravely insult the Norakamo. Instead of making them our friends, we would have them serious enemies. This we cannot afford to do."

Mara bit her lip. "I am sorry I ever agreed to this," she repeated.

Nardo waited.

She said, with seeming irrelevance, "This Alane is very beautiful. You did not tell me how beautiful she was."

"She is beautiful," he agreed, "but that is not why I am marrying her."

"Is it not?" Mara said. Her voice was dry.

He grinned.

After a long moment Mara sighed. "You are right. We cannot back out of this marriage now. I suppose I will just have to make the best of it."

"Alane is a very biddable girl," Nardo said. "You will get along with her just fine, Mother."

Mara cocked an eyebrow in the exact same gesture that Nardo had made earlier. "I think you may be in for a few surprises, my son," she said. "She did not strike me as a particularly biddable girl."

Nardo looked surprised. "She didn't?"

Mara got to her feet. "Na," she said rather grimly. "She did not."

It rained the morning of Alane's bonding day, and she sat inside her family's tent like one of the dolls her father used to make for her and let Adah dress her. She did not speak, but listened instead to the sound the rain made beating against the buckskin tent. Her wedding shirt was decorated on each shoulder with a pattern of horse's milk teeth, and the hem of her skirt was adorned in a similar fashion. Adah had made the garments, not Alane.

"Nardo's mother and sisters seem pleasant," Adah said tentatively as she took out her ivory comb. The women had spent yesterday together; all of them had been chillingly polite.

"Pleasant?" Alane said bleakly. "I would not call them pleasant."

"His mother is a little . . . haughty perhaps. But his sisters are certainly pleasant."

Alane did not reply. The thought of spending the rest of her life among those women chilled her to the bone. Her mother began to comb out her hair so that it spilled around her shoulders and down her back. Alane thought: *Tomorrow I will put my hair into a braid.* She thought of what that meant about her change in status, and repressed a shiver. *Tomorrow,* she thought, *I will be a wife.*

Adah finished with the ivory comb and stepped back to look at Alane. "You are very beautiful, my daughter," she said with pride. "You and your new husband will make a handsome pair."

Alane did not trust herself to answer.

"The first few times you lie with a man, it will hurt," Adah said. "You will grow to like it, but don't expect to find pleasure right away. It is enough simply to do as your husband tells you."

Panic knotted Alane's stomach. She nodded.

Adah placed a necklace of small white shells in Alane's hands, then she herself picked up a reindeer skin rug. "Come," she said gently. "It is time."

The rain had ended while Adah was getting Alane ready, and they stepped out of the tent into brilliant sunshine. The meadow grass glittered and gleamed with millions of individual drops of water. The green of the grass and the varying reds and yellows and blues of the wildflowers were blindingly vivid.

"Look," said one of the women waiting outside in a hushed voice; she pointed upward.

Alane raised her eyes and saw a rainbow, its perfect arch spanning the river like a bridge. As she watched, another rainbow formed right above it, its arch as perfect as the first.

"An omen," Adah said softly. "It is an omen for you, Alane. You and Nardo are the rainbows that will join our two tribes together."

"Sa. Sa. Sa" came the reverent whispers of the women.

Alane stared at the colors in the sky. Could it be so? she wondered. Could it possibly be so?

The women of the camp had been waiting to escort Alane to the bridal tent, where her bridegroom awaited her. Two of the women carried stone lamps, and the rest brought baskets filled with berries and nuts and grains. These were to help the young bride begin her housekeeping. They began their procession through the camp, passing over the wet grass and under the cobalt sky with its startling rainbows.

The shaman, who did not have a part in the Norakamo marriage ritual, was standing outside his tent watching the women cross the camp. Alane felt his strange, lightless eyes upon her and repressed a shiver. She had known for a long time that Hagen was interested in her, and she had been puzzled. Norakamo shamans did not marry but devoted all their power to their relationship with the spirit world. When Hagen had wanted to marry her to Vili, then Alane had thought she understood his interest. He saw her as a pawn in his power struggle with her father.

But Tedric had refused, and still the shaman watched her. Alane did not like it, but did not know what she could do to stop him. Unbidden, the thought flashed through her mind that perhaps Nardo would do that for her.

The women had reached the bridal tent by now, and the men of the tribe who could not fit inside were waiting in front of it. They parted to let the bridal procession reach the door, and Adah called out loudly, "She is here!" The women waited outside the tent, exchanging smiles, until Tedric came out.

He asked his wife the ritual question: "You have brought my daughter?"

"I have brought your daughter," she replied.

Then Tedric went to Alane, lifted her in his arms and carried her into the tent so that she would not have to step over the threshold.

The tent was dark after the brightness of the day, and when

her father set her on her feet again, Alane blinked with sun-blindness. As her vision slowly cleared, she saw that the tent was filled with Nardo's and her kin. Adah came to stand by her side. "The necklace," her mother breathed into her ear.

Alane looked at the shells she was holding in her hands. *I will not show fear in front of all these people,* she said fiercely to herself. *I will not show fear in front of him.* Holding herself very straight, she walked to where her future husband was sitting and, standing behind him, she slipped the shells around his neck.

His skin was warm and smooth under her fingers. It looked very dark against the translucent white of the shells. They were strung together with sinew from a reindeer's hind legs, and to fasten the necklace Alane had to tie the sinew at the back of Nardo's neck. He wore his hair much shorter than the men of the Norakamo, but still it was in the way of the sinew. Alane was beginning to wonder wildly how she was ever going to get the necklace tied, when he bent his head forward so that the glossy straight black hair parted and she was able to tie the knot. Thankful, Alane stepped back. Then Adah was coming forward with the reindeer skin rug, which she spread beside Nardo. Alane sat beside her bridegroom.

Irek, the elder for the Black Half of the tribe to which Alane belonged, came forward to face the couple, with Tedric at his side. The tent was quiet as the elder turned to Tedric.

"This man has given horses for your daughter?" he asked.

"Horses have been given," Tedric replied.

Irek turned to Alane. "Your bridewealth has been paid, my daughter," he said. "Will you take this man to be your mate?"

Silence. Behind her father Alane could see Rune take a step forward. Then she said in a low voice, "Sa, I will take this man."

Rune stepped back.

Irek turned to Nardo. "You have given horses for this woman. Her father gives her to you in marriage." Pleased murmurs came from all the company as Adah stepped forward with the bridal crown to place upon Alane's flowing hair. Then the women began to bring in the food.

The tent grew very hot from all the bodies packed into it. The afternoon slipped away and Nardo began to wonder irritably if anyone was ever going to leave. He tried to talk to Alane, but she gave him no encouragement. Her profile, which was the only view of her he got, was aloof and withdrawn.

Mara had left early, saying she was not feeling well. No one was surprised by this. Mara had looked pained during the entire ceremony. One of Nardo's sisters went with her and one of them remained.

Finally the first of the Norakamo guests began to drift away toward their own tents. As soon as it became clear that it was acceptable to leave, Nardo gave Dane a hard look. That young man grinned, but it was not long before he and the rest of the men of the Kindred had disappeared from the bridal tent. Adah came to kiss her daughter, then she and Tedric left. This was evidently a signal; in less time than it took a horse to gallop across a pasture, the bridal couple was alone.

"Dhu," Nardo said as the last of the guests disappeared out the doorflap, "I am stiff from sitting for so long." He got to his feet and stretched, raising his arms above his head to unkink his spine. He was so tall that his hands almost touched the roof of the tent. He looked at his wife, who had not moved. "I thought they were never going to leave," he said humorously.

No reply.

Perhaps she needed a little time alone. He had been sweating for the past few hours, and he felt sticky. He said, "I'm hot. I'm going to go wash in the river."

She nodded without looking at him.

She was not very encouraging, Nardo thought ruefully as he strode down to the riverbank. Perhaps the Norakamo encouraged this kind of modesty in a bride. He took off his shirt and splashed cold water on his sweaty torso. Then he removed the decorated headband his mother had made him and dunked his whole head.

He immediately felt better. He shook his wet hair out of his eyes and thought of the cool loveliness of Alane waiting for him in the tent. His heartbeat increased. He would warm her up. He had no doubts about his ability to do that.

She was sweeping the floor of the tent with a broom made of beech branches when he pushed open the doorflap. She was still dressed in her wedding clothes. He glanced around to see if she had spread out the sleeping skins. She had not. He felt a flicker of annoyance and did not bend low enough to get in the doorflap. He hit his head and cursed. Alane jumped and swung around to face him. For a moment he looked into her unguarded eyes and saw there the dark, lost look of a frightened child. Then she had her aloof expression back in place.

"You startled me," she said.

Nardo stood silently at the door. He had not put his shirt back on and his hair still dripped upon his shoulders. Alane carefully placed her broom behind a basket and turned to face him. She was holding her slender body very straight and her face looked calm, but even from the door Nardo could see the pulse fluttering in her throat. Her eyes flicked once over his bare brown torso, and then she dropped her lashes.

Nardo did not mistake that quick glance for admiration. The girl was afraid of him.

"May I get you something to eat?" she asked.

He shook his wet head. "I was eating all afternoon."

She folded her hands at her waist and looked at them. "Oh."

Slowly he walked into the tent and approached her. "Alane."

Bravely she lifted her head. He felt as if he were looming over her. "I would like some tea," he lied and moved toward the reindeer rug so he could sit down and reduce his size.

She could not hide her look of relief. "I will fix it for you."

He watched the slim figure of his wife as she blew the embers into a flame and added enough wood to make a small fire. Then she placed the soapstone teakettle on the stones in the fire pit. "It will not take long," she said.

He sat and waited and thought about that look he had seen in her eyes. When the tea was ready, he accepted a cup from her and watched while she poured one for herself.

"I don't have to give the cup back to you?" he asked.

She shook her head, and her hair rippled around her shoulders. His fingers itched to touch it. She said, "Within the family the tea is just drunk."

He nodded gravely, sipped, and gestured for her to join him. She sat as far away from him as she could without being obviously discourteous. He felt that if he made the slightest unexpected move, she would spook like a frightened filly.

He was furious at the way he had been kept from her these

past weeks. He could have banished this fear if he had been given the chance. He said now, "I am sorry we were not allowed to know each other this last half moon. Is it always thus among your tribe, that a woman must marry a man who is a stranger to her?"

She answered a little breathlessly, "It is our custom to separate bride and groom after the first giving of the bridewealth. But ours is not a big tribe and usually the partners have known each other since childhood."

He took another sip of his tea. "But you do not know me."

The bitterness was audible in her voice as she replied, "That thought did not disturb my father or my mother."

Nardo was forced to admit that it had not disturbed him either. During the past two weeks he had never once wondered what Alane's feelings might be about their marriage. He had followed the strange Norakamo customs without argument, willing to believe that this was how life was for a Norakamo girl. The only thing that had been on his mind was how much he wanted to lie with her. He was as bad as Tedric, he thought now. Worse, because he should know better.

He stared into his half-empty teacup. "Are you a maiden?" he asked.

There was a world of indignation in her reply. "Of course I am a maiden!"

I knew it, Nardo thought gloomily. He took another sip of his tea. His hair was almost dry and had begun to slide forward over his temples. He extracted his headband from the waist of his trousers and tied it around his forehead. Alane held her tea and watched him out of the corner of her eye.

He sighed. She was beautiful, and he wanted her, but if he took her tonight it would be as bad as rape, a crime that was almost unheard of in his tribe. Nardo had lain with enough girls to have learned the way of pleasing a woman, but he was not arrogant enough to think that his skill would prevail over Alane's obvious terror. He said resignedly, "I am thinking I would not like my sister to have her wedding night with a man she did not know. We do not have to lie together tonight, Alane. It will be easy enough for us to wait until you are more comfortable with me."

She turned her head and looked at him. Her eyes were as clear as lakewater between her long, dark lashes. She said, "Tomorrow I will be expected to braid my hair to show I am no longer a maiden."

He gave her his most disarming grin. "Then braid it." Thoughtfully she reached up to touch her hair. He added, just to make sure she understood, "We are only delaying the loss of your maidenhood, after all."

Her eyes were luminous. "I would like to wait a little . . . if you do not mind."

Not mind. Dhu. "Of course I don't mind," he said.

Alane smiled and said, "You are kind."

It was the first time she had ever smiled at him. "My name is Nardo," he said.

"Nardo," she repeated tentatively.

It will be worth it in the end, he told himself resolutely, and took another sip of his tea.

Chapter Five

Outside the tent the eastern sky had changed from black to gray. Alane awoke feeling slightly cramped. It was a moment before she realized why she was lying at the far edge of her sleeping skins. With a flash of annoyance she realized that Nardo was taking up the rest of them.

The faint glow from last night's fire showed her that he was still asleep, lying on his stomach with one arm thrown over his head, his hand loose and relaxed next to his fanned-out hair. It was a disarmingly childlike posture, belied by the massive and muscular bare shoulders that protruded above the buckskin cover. Exercising great caution, Alane began to get to her feet.

He was instantly awake, rolling over and sitting up with all the quickness of a seasoned hunter. He looked at her out of completely alert brown eyes. She swallowed and said, "I am going down to the river to draw the morning water."

He watched her for a moment in silence, and then he nodded.

Alane stood up. She had changed out of her wedding clothes last night when Nardo had left the tent to go and check on his horse. As was usual for her in the summer, she had slept in a sleeveless buckskin shirt that reached midway down her thigh. Very conscious of the fact that he was watching her, Alane put on a skirt and moccasins, raked her fingers through her loose hair, and left the tent as quickly as she could.

The river was alive with waterfowl watching for the fish that came to the surface every morning to feed. On the opposite bank a great blue heron croaked *Krank, krank, kranhk!,* stood silent a moment, then repeated its hoarse call. The loons on either side of the river called *kwuk-kwuk* to one another, while the call of the grebes was a slightly different *kum kum kum.*

Alane bent over the river, watched the small fish gliding beneath the shallow water, then plunged her hands into the peaceful coolness and threw handfuls of clear water onto her face. Then she stood erect before the advancing dawn, her face to the sun. In the silence of her heart she offered her prayers for the new day.

Once her water basket was filled, she lifted it to rest on the crown of her head. Walking with the level gait of one long used to carrying such a burden, Alane returned to her tent.

Her husband was standing at a little distance from the tent doorflap, also facing in the direction of the sun. Alane realized he too must have been saying his morning prayer. He had pulled on his wedding shirt, but it was untied at the throat and his feet were bare. He saw her coming and bent to hold the flap open for her. Alane lifted the water basket from her head and carried it into the tent. She went immediately to the clay pot that stood against one of the reindeer skin walls and poured the water into it. Then she put the water basket next to the pot and went to the hearth to start the fire. The tent was small and Nardo seemed to take up far too large a portion of the space. "I will have your breakfast for you very shortly," she said stiffly.

Nardo watched as she took the still glowing end of a piece of wood from last night's fire and blew it into flames. She added kindling and then rose to go and get a few pieces of heavier firewood from the stack by the doorflap. He said, "I am going to take Bluebird down to the river for a drink. I won't be long."

She looked at him in surprise, her attention caught by the mention of a horse. "Bluebird? Is that your horse's name?"

"Sa."

Alane pictured the beautiful gray mare that Nardo rode. "How did she ever get the name of Bluebird?"

"My mother named her. In my tribe it is the custom for the women to name all the horses." He had not yet put on his headband and his hair was hanging in his eyes. "I agree that it is an unlikely name, but when she was a new foal she was blue-gray in color and my mother said she flitted around just like a little bluebird. So that is how she got her name."

"Your mother named her," Alane said flatly.

Nardo heard the note in her voice and gave her a sideways look. He made no further comment, however, but put on his moccasins and went outside.

By the time he returned, Alane had a breakfast of tea and plums and hawthorne berries ready for him. He ate hungrily in silence, then held out his empty cup for more tea. "I am to go hunting with your father today," he said.

She poured more mint tea into his cup. He did not seem quite as intimidating when he was sitting down and wearing a shirt. "I hope you have good luck," she said with formal politeness.

He looked at her for a moment, then drained his cup, put it down and glanced around the tent. "Someone was supposed to bring my things over here yesterday. I do not want to wear this shirt for hunting."

"It is a very fine shirt," Alane said in the same polite tone as before.

"My mother made it for me. It is for ceremonial occasions only. She will kill me if I get blood on it." His tone was humorous, but Alane did not respond. He felt a flicker of annoyance. He had behaved very well last night, he thought. The least the girl could do was to be pleasant to him!

"Your things are in here," Alane said, and she rose and went to one of the large baskets that she had woven to furnish the tent. She lifted the lid.

Nardo came up behind her, dwarfing her as he peered over her shoulder at the neatly folded pile of clothing inside. Alane stepped out of his way and watched as he searched among the clothes, extracted a shirt, a plain headband and a pouch. Then he stripped his wedding shirt over his head and dropped it carelessly back into the basket on top of all the clothing he had just disarranged. He pulled on the old hunting shirt he had chosen.

Alane stared in dismay at the crumpled heap that was his

wedding shirt. He returned to the hearthplace, bringing with him the deerskin pouch that had been in the basket. He ran his fingers through his hair to smooth it, and then he tied the headband around his forehead. Next he extracted from the pouch a small item wrapped in deerskin. He saw her looking at it curiously, and he held up a small, razor-sharp flint implement. "My beard scraper," he said. "Do you think I could have some water, Alane?"

"Sa." She went to the water pot and scooped water up into an antelope horn. She then put the horn into a basket holder that kept it from tipping over, and gave it to him.

She poured more water into another basket and began to rinse the teacups. Out of the side of her eyes she watched as he shaved. The men of her tribe kept their beards trimmed short, but they did not scrape them off the way Nardo was doing.

"Do all the men of the Kindred scrape their beards so?"

"Sa. In the summer it is cooler, and in the winter it is better not to have facial hair that can ice up."

Alane thought about that. "Is it very cold in the high part of the mountains?"

"In the winter it is." He wrapped the razor in the deerskin and put it back into the pouch. "I had better find Bluebird some grass. The area behind the tent is almost all grazed down."

"There is still some good grazing along the river upstream."

He took the pouch over to his clothes basket and carelessly dropped it in. "If anyone comes looking for me, tell them where I am."

"Sa," Alane said.

He walked to the doorflap, paused, and almost automatically looked behind him at the floor. He met her inquiring gaze and said ruefully, "I cannot get used to not having a dog at my heels."

Alane stiffened. "You keep dogs in your tribe?"

"We certainly do."

"In your tents? Living with you?"

"Sa." He smiled. "They are tame. You will like them."

After he had gone, Alane moved slowly to his clothes basket. With her lips set in disapproval, she folded all the shirts he had disarranged, put the pouch back on top, went and fetched the decorated headband that was lying next to the sleeping skins, put that in also, and closed the lid.

Dogs, she thought bleakly. I did not know about the dogs.

The Kindred guests were to stay with the Norakamo for another week, and the morning after Alane's wedding Tedric had planned a big hunt. This was not merely a recreational treat for the visitors; the wedding feast had sorely diminished the tribe's meat supply.

About two hundred people dwelled within the Norakamo camp, and in order to provide meat for that number the tribe's hunters needed to kill an average of four reindeer or six red deer every day. On the other hand, four buffalo or four aurochs would last the tribe for a week. This diet was often varied by the meat of ibex and boar. Quail and fish were also good summer foods that were readily available in the hunting area of the Norakamo summer camp. The grains and fruits and nuts gathered by the women were considered supplementary to the main diet of the Norakamo, which was meat.

The men who rode out on the hunt that morning included Nardo and Rorig and the two handfuls of other men who had accompanied the wedding party, as well as a large contingent of Norakamo. Both Nardo and Rorig made it a point of keeping Varic between them as they rode up the River of Gold. Nardo had hoped that Varic would refuse to attend the wedding, but when he had learned that the rest of the clan council was coming, he had insisted on coming as well. So far he had behaved acceptably, although his face wore a perpetual scowl.

Later in the morning, the hunting party caught a herd of reindeer as they were about to cross the River of Gold at the Big Ford. The men halted on the west bank of the river and stood silently, scarcely believing their luck. One or two of the Norakamo glanced worriedly at the Kindred horses, but once they saw that the gray mares would stand quietly, they returned their scrutiny to the reindeer on the opposite bank.

The leading group of reindeer hesitated at the water. The hunters did not move, knowing from experience that this hesitation was not caused by the sight of humans. Reindeer had very poor eyesight, and as long as the hunters remained immobile their prey would not be able to distinguish them. This was the reason it was essential that a good hunting horse be trained to stand still. Reindeer always hesitated before committing themselves to the water. As soon as the leaders went in, however, the rest of the herd would follow blindly.

Tedric was in charge, and he waited until the leading reindeer had reached the shallow water on the west bank before he gave the signal for his men to attack. Nardo's knee pressed against Varic's as they stood in silence. Then, at the single short cry, he lifted his spear and rode Bluebird into the river right up to her shoulders.

At this depth the reindeer were just beginning to regain their feet after swimming and the water was churning. Nardo veered away from Varic as he set his sights on a deer and brought his spear down, thrusting it between the shoulders of the scrambling animal. His long legs were wrapped around Bluebird's belly, enabling him to keep his seat. The reindeer lurched and fell, and Nardo wrenched out his spear. Blood sprayed onto both man and horse. Nardo looked up and into Rune's blue eyes. Rune grinned and made a gesture of approval, and Nardo grinned back.

The river was filled with men and horses and reindeer. Even though the reindeer had formidable antlers, they posed little danger to the men and horses. As the hunters well knew, reindeer never tried to defend themselves in water. They only wanted to get away. So the men pushed in among them fearlessly, stabbing again and again.

Reindeer fell, and the river ran red with blood. Yet save for the splashing and grunting of the struggling animals, the slaughter scene was eerily quiet. The men did not shout. Even when one man lost his seat and was dumped into the river, he remained silent while his horse was caught and returned to him. All the men had learned when they were boys that loud voices were not respectful to the animals whose gift of life meant survival to the tribe.

The push of the herd had separated Nardo from Rune, and Nardo paused for a moment to scan the scene before him when he felt a horse come up close behind him. Bluebird laid back her ears, and Nardo was reaching forward to give her a reassuring pat when he received a hard shove on the shoulder. Nardo was slightly off balance to begin with, and as Bluebird shied from the horse that had come up too close beside her, he was in danger of losing his seat. He managed to right himself and looked angrily over his shoulder at the man who had pushed him.

A pair of pale, hostile Norakamo eyes met his. The rest of the men were concentrating on the reindeer; no one had seen what had happened. The Norakamo man turned his horse away and mingled with the surging reindeer. His eyes dark with thought, Nardo turned Bluebird back toward the bank.

When the last reindeer had finished crossing the river, thirty dead animals lay in the shallow water of the ford. Tedric gave instructions in a soft voice, and the men began the work of hauling the carcasses out of the water.

Tedric sent for fresh horses and sledges, and the men loaded the dead reindeer onto wooden sledges and dragged them back to the camp. The women took charge of the hunting horses, washing them clean in the river and finding them grass. The men began the work of butchering.

While this work was going on, Nardo approached Rune. "Who is that?" he asked, nodding at a bloodstained, pale-eyed man who was skinning reindeer.

"That is Vili," Rune said.

"And does this Vili have any reason to wish me ill?"

Rune stared up into Nardo's impassive face. "Did something happen?"

"Just answer my question, Rune."

Rune said slowly, "Vili was the cousin and closest friend of Loki, the man you killed."

"The man who killed my uncle."

"Sa. The man who killed your uncle." Rune frowned. "What happened, Nardo?"

Nardo shrugged. "Nothing worth mentioning." His eyes were on the approaching figure of Varic.

Varic spoke to Nardo, ignoring Rune. "The Norakamo chief is giving away our meat," he said truculently.

Nardo turned his eyes to Tedric for a moment, watching what he was doing, and then he said to Rune, "Your hunters do not keep the meat from their kills?"

Rune's voice was low, but it was clear he was angry. "It is our belief that food belongs to the tribe, not to the individual hunter."

"Well, that is not our way," Varic replied too loudly. "Among the Kindred a man keeps what he kills."

"If the men of the Kindred wish to keep the meat of the animals they have slain, I am certain that can be arranged," Rune said coldly.

Nardo spoke. "We would not be such poor guests as to eat your food and not help you to replenish it." He stared at Varic and said steadily, "All of the meat is Tedric's, to do with what he will."

Varic gave an elaborate shrug. "It seems foolish to give all the meat to the chief, but if that is the Norakamo way . . ."

"Some men are not good hunters," Rune said. "Should their families suffer hunger because of this?"

"Of course not," Nardo replied.

Rune blew upward to unstick his hair from his sweaty forehead; he did not want to push his bangs away with his bloody hands. "You do not have any poor hunters in your tribe?" he asked with palpable disbelief.

Nardo put a hand on Varic's arm to keep him from replying. "You must understand, Rune," Nardo said, "that each household in my tribe has many men hunting for it. In my mother's household, for example, the hunters are my father, my aunt's husband, my sisters' husbands, my cousins' husbands, and me."

Rune was staring at him in amazement. "That is a lot of men for one household!"

"Sa. Someone is bound to have had luck in hunting."

"Do you all live together in one tent?"

Nardo grinned. "Na. That would be a little crowded. Each family sleeps in its own hut, but my mother's house is where the cooking is done and the food is stored."

"Your wife does not cook for you?"

"The women share the work. Some cook, some gather, some watch the children, some soften skins, some sew." Nardo shrugged. "My mother organizes the work. It is easier for all that way."

"Your wives do not mind taking orders from your mothers?" Rune asked incredulously.

"A Kindred wife does not live with her husband's mother but with her own mother," Nardo pointed out. "The women of the household have lived and worked together all their lives. It is not necessary for the mother to 'give orders.' "

Silence. Then Rune said, "But Alane will have to live with your mother."

"Sa. It will be different for her." Nardo's face was smooth, but he was not quite as successful at keeping the doubt out of his voice as he said, "My mother and Alane are both agreeable women. They will have no trouble cooperating with each other."

Rune looked skeptical, but prudently he held his tongue.

It was nearly the month in which the Norakamo bred their mares, and on the second day after the wedding, in an effort to further good relations between the tribes, Tedric invited the men of the Kindred to help the Norakamo search for a likely stallion. This was a complete change for the men, who spent the better part of the year driving all grown males away from their mares. Like the Kindred, the Norakamo allowed colts to remain with the herd through their yearling year, but once they turned two they were driven off. In doing this, the human caretakers were only emulating what a stallion would have done once his sons reached the same dangerous age. There could be only one stallion in a herd; if there were two, they would fight until only one was left. This was why both tribes kept only female horses.

It was breeding season, however, and the tribe needed a stallion. There were usually a few small herds to be found in the area of summer camp; some of the main herd's exiled sons were always successful in stealing a few mares to form their own harems.

Tedric had arranged for Rune and Larz to accompany Nardo and his touchy kinsman, Varic. At the last moment, however, Vili rode up to Rune and announced that Tedric had sent him also. Rune scowled and looked for his father, but the chief had already left camp. Rune did not believe Vili, but he did not want to accuse a fellow Norakamo of lying in front of Varic, so he nodded and motioned to Vili to fall in with the group.

The small party rode north along the River of Gold, and for the most part they rode in silence. It was an hour past midday when they spotted a small group of horses slowly approaching the river a little way upstream.

"It's Red Hawk!" Larz said. Like most of his tribe, Larz could recognize a horse much farther off than he could distinguish a human.

Rune recognized the mares. "So he was the one who made off with Frun and Mala and Lipi."

The five men drew rein and watched as the chestnut stallion stood guard while the three mares picked their way through the high grass to the river. Unlike the Kindred horses, which had long, silky manes, the Norakamo horses had thick short bristly manes. The stallion's exposed neck, powerful and arched, gleamed fiery red in the bright sun as he sampled the wind. Water was always a dangerous place for prey animals, and the stallion knew it. He would not take a drink himself until his mares had finished.

The riders were downwind of the stallion, so he did not catch their scent. A family of foxes, their fur as red as the stallion's, trotted through the grass a few feet from Bluebird's hooves. She quivered and Nardo patted her neck to distract her. The sky above was as blue as the drifts of Pyrenean hyacinth which grew in the cliff crevices on the far side of the river.

"Red Hawk would suit our purposes just fine," Larz said softly. Rune nodded.

They waited until the stallion had taken his drink and herded his mares away from the dangerous water, nipping their heels to make them move quickly. Then the men turned their own horses toward home.

"You will ruin the blood of the beautiful mares we gave you if you breed them with such a stallion," Varic announced rudely as they followed the game track along the river that led to the Big Ford.

Vili answered hotly, "There is nothing wrong with that stallion! He will give some strength of bone to the get of those thin-legged mares of yours!"

"Thin-legged!" Varic was incensed. "If you think so poorly of our mares, we will be glad to take them back."

"You can't take them back," said Rune grimly. "They were given for my sister's bridewealth."

"You certainly thought well enough of our horses when you came raiding them!" Vili threw at Varic.

"We use them as pack animals," Varic said. "We certainly wouldn't breed them."

Vili's fists clenched.

Nardo spoke calmly. "Varic, that is enough."

"Did you hear what he said about our horses?" Varic demanded.

"Sa. And I heard what you said about theirs first. You are a guest here, Varic. Remember to behave like one."

Varic hissed with fury, squeezed his mare into a gallop and headed back to camp alone. Nardo let him go, and the remainder of the ride was tense and silent except for an occasional remark exchanged between Nardo and Rune.

"Dhu!" Nardo complained to Alane as he came into their tent after he returned to camp. "What was your father thinking of to send Vili with a party that contained my cousin Varic?"

Alane looked up from the pot she was stirring. "Vili?" she said. "My father sent Vili with *you*?"

Nardo came farther into the tent. He frowned. "Why do you say 'you' in such a tone, Alane?"

Alane poked industriously at her pot. "You killed his cousin," she said over her shoulder.

"And that is all?"

She shrugged and refused to meet his eyes. "What else could there be?"

"I am asking you," he said in a dangerously quiet voice.

"And I have answered you," she snapped.

He let the matter drop, going to the water pot to ladle himself a drink.

"Did you find a stallion?" Alane asked, trying to change the subject.

"Sa. North of the Big Ford. A good-looking chestnut called Red Hawk. Your father said we will move the mares downriver tomorrow." He wiped the water from his mouth and put the antelope horn cup back on the flat table stone.

Alane smiled, her thoughts diverted from Nardo. "Perhaps I·

will go with you," she said. "I love to watch the reunion between the stallion and his old herd."

Nardo pictured the scene himself: the wild nickering and whinnying as old friends met; the rearing and nipping and interweaving of necks as the stallion was reunited with his mother. He looked at his wife in surprise. "Have you helped move the mares before, Alane?"

She put up her chin. "Sometimes I have ridden with Rune. Just to watch. Norakamo women can ride very well, you know."

Nardo felt a stab of exasperation. Everything he said to her seemed to be wrong.

From down by the river there came the sound of men shouting. Nardo cursed, jumped to his feet and headed for the doorflap. "It is probably that Varic," Alane said, following behind.

The fight had developed over a game that was very popular with the Norakamo men. It was called Sticks, and to play it the men hung from a tree branch a small rhomboidal plate of ivory with a hole in its center. This was kept steady by a stone affixed to the lower end. The men would stand around the plate in a circle, and when the signal was given, everyone tried to get his stick through the hole. The first one to do so was the winner.

Vili and a group of Norakamo men had been playing this game when they spotted Varic and two other Kindred men by the river washing their horses. Vili invited them to play.

It was not long before the playing became seriously aggressive. Sticks were brandished dangerously as men tried to spear the hole with their own stick while foiling the attempts of everyone else. The ivory plate danced as it was repeatedly struck this way and that. Suddenly there was a shout, a snarl, and two men were on the ground.

It was Vili and Varic, both rolling over and over in the dirt. They had given up their sticks and were trying to get their hands upon each other's throats.

The watching men all shouted. No one made a move to separate the furious pair, and after a moment they began to call encouragement to their own tribesman. Such was the situation when Nardo arrived.

If the match-up between the two men had been fair, Nardo thought he would have let them fight it out. Sometimes a good fight was just what was needed to clear the air. But Vili was much bigger and heavier than Varic, and even though his cousin was an agile and clever fighter, the amount of weight he was giving up was too much.

Nardo looked around for Tedric or Rune, but neither was in sight. Nardo cursed, stepped forward and roared, "Stop this now!"

Vili did not even glance around. He had Varic under him now and, with the loud encouragement of his fellow tribesmen, was preparing to slam his head against the ground. Nardo strode forward, put both hands on Vili's shoulders, and plucked him off of Varic.

Vili bellowed in protest and tried to pull away. Varic surged up and tried to take advantage of Nardo's assistance by attacking Vili. Nardo had to take one hand off Vili to hold off Varic. The two antagonists desperately tried to get at each other through Nardo, who was taking a battering in the middle but still holding on.

A new voice entered the fray. "What is happening here?"

"Rune!" Nardo panted. "I am trying to keep these two from killing each other."

"It looks to me like they are trying to kill you instead," Rune remarked with a laugh. Then he spoke sharply to two of the onlookers, who came reluctantly forward to take ahold of the infuriated Vili. Nardo then had both hands free to subdue Varic.

Rune glanced around the circle of men and told them to disperse. As the audience trailed off reluctantly, the antagonists gradually ceased struggling against those who were holding them. At a word from Rune, Vili's two subduers took him away also.

Rune said a little grimly to Nardo, "I am thinking it is time for your kinsmen to return home."

Nardo's nose was bleeding and he wiped it with his hand, thus smearing blood all over his face. "I will speak to my father," he promised. He looked at his bloody hand. "Dhu, I am glad you arrived when you did."

"Alane came and got me," Rune said. "I could not hear the fight from my tent."

"That son of a hyena was cousin to the man who killed my father!" Varic said to Nardo.

"It is true that Vili is cousin to Loki, but the blood spilled by Loki was avenged by Nardo," Rune said. He turned to Nardo, "There is to be no blood feud between your kin and Loki's kin. I thought that was understood."

"Then tell that to Vili," Varic flared. "He was the one who began the fight."

Nardo put his hand on his cousin's arm. "Come back to my tent with me, Varic."

Scowling, Varic complied.

Rorig agreed with Rune that it would be best for the Kindred party to leave the following day. Nardo spent the last evening with his mother, who was obviously unhappy at the thought of not seeing her son for perhaps another year.

He was Mara's youngest child, and her only son. The sole reason she had agreed to the Norakamo marriage was that it would mean Nardo could continue to live within his mother's household. At the time Rorig had proposed the match, this had seemed a desirable thing to Mara. Now she was not so sure.

The bond between husband and wife was not the strongest man-woman bond in a Kindred family. Husband and wife were of different clans. The strongest bonds were between those who shared the same blood: mother and son, sister and brother.

In agreeing to the Norakamo marriage, Mara had agreed to accept Alane into the Clan of the Wolf. This would make her of the same clan as Nardo. Mara was beginning to think this was not a good idea.

"I hope this marriage is not a mistake," she said to her son as they sat together around the small fire in the guest tent after supper had been eaten.

Nardo thought of his wife's chilly manner toward him, and hoped so too. But he said reassuringly to his mother, "How can it be a mistake? It has made a bond between our tribes, and that is what is important."

"So your father says," Mara replied astringently.

"Rorig is right. And once Alane has borne a child, I will be home again and things will go on as they always have." Ever since he could remember, he had known he was his mother's favorite. He smiled now and reached over to give her work-worn hand a small squeeze.

She smiled back with an obvious effort. "I will miss you, my son."

"Pretend that I am away on herding duty," he said. "It will make it easier, so."

She nodded.

"It will not be so long," he repeated.

It may not seem long to you, my son, Mara thought with faint bitterness. *But to me, who has just lost my brother, it will seem forever.*

But she could not burden him with her sorrow. And so she smiled, and agreed, and asked him about his hunting.

Chapter Six

The Kindred party had been gone for a week when the usual routine of the Norakamo camp was disrupted by the arrival of traders. The four newcomers were seeking to trade flint spear points and harpoon points from the flint knappers to the northwest, and shells and amber and shark teeth from the shore of the Great Sea. But in the eyes of the Norakamo, by far the most precious thing the traders brought was "the news."

Aside from its attendance at Gatherings, the only way a tribe could learn what was happening in the world outside its own hunting grounds was through these wandering traders. In exchange for a lavish meal and a gift of enough dried meat to sustain them until they could reach the next tribal camp, the traders would give of their goods and their information.

"So," Alane said as Nardo came into their tent after spending the evening around the fire with the newcomers, "what is the news?"

He crossed the meticulously swept dirt floor to where she sat sewing by the light of the stone lamp and sat down on the rug beside her. Alane rested the shirt she was making in her lap and looked up at him. He was sitting very close to her, and the yellow light of the lamp made his hair and brows and lashes look very black, his skin almost golden. Part of her was straining eagerly for his news, while the other part was nervously and acutely aware of his closeness.

"They bring news of much unrest in the world outside our mountains," he told her. "These traders came all the way from the land where the sun sets, and they tell a tale of tribes fighting with one another, of bloodshed, of the killing of men by other men."

Alane's eyes grew wider. "Dhu," she said. "That is terrible."

"Sa. It is the same story we have been hearing at the Gatherings. The unrest is because the reindeer herds are no longer coming south."

Alane's smoky brows were knit with worry. "I do not understand why such a thing is happening," she said. "There seems no reason for it."

Nardo shrugged and the movement of his big shoulders made him loom even closer. "There is always a reason for why things happen," he said. "The wind does not move, the leaf does not fall, the bird does not call without a reason." With the fingers of his left hand he smoothed his wrinkled buckskin trouser leg over his knee. His hand was big and powerful, like the rest of him, and Alane found herself staring at it as if mesmerized. Through the tent's skin walls she heard the sound of male voices bidding each other good night. Someone made a joke and several other men laughed. Nardo made an oddly graceful gesture with the hand she was watching and said, "It is in my heart that these people have offended the Mother, and because of this she has called her reindeer children back to the north."

"The loss of reindeer is death for a tribe," Alane heard herself saying in what she desperately hoped was a normal voice.

Nardo's voice was grim. "I am thinking that our greatest danger is that these traders will carry the news to other tribes that reindeer are still plentiful in our mountains."

Alane glanced up and found him watching her. His brown eyes were enormous. Quickly she looked back at the shirt in her lap. His scent filled her nostrils, a distinctly male odor of horses and buckskin and sweat. It was a scent Alane was quite familiar with, yet tonight, for some reason, it was having a strange effect on her. She was keenly aware of the fact that he was only a few feet away. Her heart began to accelerate, but not from fear. She wet her dry lips with her tongue and answered a little breathlessly, "That would be a terrible thing."

"That is why we married, Alane," he said. "So that our two tribes can unite to defend the mountains if we must."

She nodded. Then, when he did not speak, she managed to utter one word. "Sa."

"We have been married one week."

She swallowed. "Sa," she said again.

Then he asked the question she had been dreading. "How much longer will it be, Alane, until you have grown accustomed to me?"

Never! she thought a little hysterically. *I will never grow accustomed to you!* But she knew she could not say that. She even suspected that it was not true. She folded and refolded the shirt in her lap. "Another week," she said huskily. "Give me another week."

He reached out and put his hand over her frantic two, entirely engulfing their coldness with his warmth. "Look at me," he said softly.

Reluctantly she raised her eyes. He was smiling. Not the genial grin that she had seen him use so often with the men during this past week, but a slow, warm, intimate smile.

He was trying to disarm her. She knew that, resented it, and still she was disarmed.

"One more week," he said in that same soft tone. His eyes looked suddenly heavy in the flickering lamplight, and he yawned.

"You are tired," Alane said, glad of an excuse to pull her hands away and jump up. "I will prepare the bedplace."

When she turned around again after spreading the sleeping skins, Nardo was standing by the hearth, pulling off his shirt. He dropped it on the rug, yawned once more, then stretched his arms over his head. Alane watched with fascination as the great muscles in his shoulders and arms rippled under the smooth, coppery skin.

He was so powerfully male, and yet he was being so patient with her. A little unwillingly she acknowledged that fact. She felt that honor compelled her to return his graciousness, so she held herself very straight and made herself say, "Thank you for being so understanding."

They looked at each other over the lamp, and she saw his

face suddenly harden. She could feel her pulse beating in her throat. Then he blinked, shook his head, and said in a clipped voice, "You are welcome, Alane. But remember, it is only for one more week."

This time of year Alane was always busy making baskets for the men to trade at the Autumn Gathering. Two days after the traders had left she took one of the two mares her father had given her as a wedding gift and rode north along the River of Gold to cut more basket plant. The day was unusually sultry for the time of year, and after Alane had filled the baskets attached to either side of the horse's surcingle, she decided to cool off by wading in the river.

A pair of partridges rose from the grass in front of her as she approached the water, ascending over her head into the hazy sky. Alane kilted up her buckskin skirt and waded in until she was up to her knees. The cool water felt wonderful. A great golden eagle circled overhead, and she tilted her head back to watch.

She was peering down into the clear depths of the river, stirring the water with her foot, when she felt that she was being watched. She swung around in alarm to look toward the shore.

Nardo was standing there.

It seemed an eternity to Alane that they stood there gazing at each other. Finally he said, "I got back early from herd duty, and your mother told me where I could find you."

She looked behind him, as if expecting to see Adah, but there was no one. She stared back into the water, said, "It was hot, so I thought I would cool off in the river," and once more stirred the water with her foot.

"Alane." His voice had a distinctly plaintive ring. "I am so thirsty. Could you bring me a drink in your hands?"

She looked at him and frowned. "Why can't you get your own drink?"

He was standing on the grass at the very edge of the water, and now he gestured to his feet. "I don't want to get my shoes and trousers wet."

"All right," she said with palpable reluctance. She made a dipper out of her hands, scooped up some river water and, stepping gingerly over the rocks in the river, brought it to him. He bent his black head to her outstretched hands and drank. She could feel his mouth moving against her palms, and her stomach fluttered. When he had finished, he wiped the wetness from his mouth with the back of his hand, reached out to grasp her shoulders, bent his head once more, and kissed her.

A shock compounded of surprise and pleasure jolted through Alane. It was the totally unexpected pleasure that frightened her into raising her hands to push him away. For a moment she did not think he was going to release her, but then he did. She leaped back a few paces until she was safely in the river again, and hurled words at him: "You said you would give me one more week!"

"I was only trying to kiss you," he shot back. "Dhu, Alane. We are married!"

She lifted her chin. "I see now that you are not to be trusted."

Suddenly he lost his temper. Alane saw it happen and immediately began to back farther away. But Nardo followed, wading into the river, gripping her arms and pulling her toward him so he could kiss her again. Alane tried to raise her knee so she could get him in a place where it would hurt, but he evaded her, shifting his grip and muttering something under his breath. They began to struggle, Nardo trying to subdue her without hurting her. Which one lost their balance first was unclear, but the result was that both of them came crashing down into the cold water, Nardo first with Alane on top of him.

Nardo swam slowly back to consciousness to find himself lying on his back in cold water. As if from a great distance he heard an anxious voice calling his name. He tried to lift his head, winced with the pain and opened his eyes. He was lying with his head in Alane's lap. Her face was bent over his. It seemed to waver before his eyes. "Nardo," she said imploringly.

His name sounded wonderful on her lips. He tried to tell her that, but nothing came out. He closed his eyes to gather his forces. He felt her hand on his forehead, smoothing back his hair. He decided he might never open his eyes again.

She was speaking to him softly, and he suddenly realized that if he didn't open his eyes he wouldn't be able to see her face.

He lifted his lashes and she rewarded him with a tremulous smile. "Are you all right?" she asked.

It was lovely lying here with his head in her lap. Too bad the river was so full of rocks. He shifted uncomfortably. Alane slipped her arm under his shoulders and urged him upward. He could feel the softness of her breast against him. Nardo sighed and sat up, wincing as pain shot through his head. Evidently the back of his skull had made contact with one of the river's more formidable rocks.

Alane looked contrite. "It is all right," Nardo assured her gallantly. "I am fine." He decided to get to his feet.

Once upright, he blinked against the dizziness in his head and leaned against her because he needed to. He had a concussion, he thought. By the Thunder, he had a concussion! He blinked again and tried to focus on their two hobbled horses grazing on the riverbank.

"Nardo, are you all right?" Alane asked again. Her voice sounded anxious. Nardo turned his head and looked into her worried gray eyes. He attempted a grin.

They stood there, water dripping from their clothes and hair. Alane's arm was around Nardo's waist, but he was a full head taller and much too heavy for her to support. He tried to balance on his own feet and blinked against a new onslaught of dizziness.

"Oh, Nardo," Alane said. "I am so sorry."

He wasn't quite clear about what had happened, but he didn't think now was the time to ask. He blinked again. "Alane," he said. "You are going to have to help me get on my horse. I think I have a concussion."

"Oh."

"Just guide me," he said. "I can stay on my feet."

Moving very slowly, Alane managed to walk Nardo out of the river and over to where his mare was grazing. "Perhaps you ought to stay here, Nardo, and I will go and get help," Alane said.

"If I can just get on Snowflake I will be all right."

"I don't think I will be of much help to you," Alane said in a small voice.

"Find me something I can stand on," he recommended.

Leaving him leaning against Snowflake's flank, Alane ran to

her own mare, undid one of the pack baskets and dumped the plants she had so carefully gathered all over the grass. "This basket is very strong," she said to Nardo as she placed it upside down beside him. "I think it will hold you for a few moments at least."

It held long enough for Nardo to step on it and throw his leg over his mare's back. He grabbed her mane to secure himself and stared grimly at a landmark tree to stave off the dizziness.

"I will lead Snowflake for you," he heard Alane say.

"I'm afraid you are going to have to," he replied.

In a moment she appeared beside him on her own mare. He handed her Snowflake's reins, and they began to walk slowly along the river, heading for home.

Rune and Stifun saw Alane coming along the river and got Nardo off his horse and into Alane's tent. "Get those wet clothes off him," Alane said once they were safely inside.

Her brothers obeyed, efficiently stripping Nardo, who was conscious but not very focused. Alane had dragged out the sleeping skins while they were working, and the men put Nardo to bed for her. As soon as he was lying down, his eyes closed.

Rune looked at his sister. "You're as wet as he is," he said. "What happened?"

"Nardo fell in the river and hit his head on a rock," Alane replied.

"He fell? How did he fall?"

"Never mind," Alane returned stiffly. "But I am concerned about his having another head injury so soon after the last one."

Rune and Stifun exchanged a glance.

"Nardo is one of the most sure-footed men I know," Rune said.

"Well, he slipped," Alane retorted. "Now, will you ask Mother to come and look at him?"

Once more the brothers exchanged a look.

Alane saw it and glared. "Are you going to get Mother or do I have to?"

"We're going, Alane," Stifun said around a grin.

"Did you push him?" Rune asked mischievously, and ducked out of the tent before she could retaliate.

The shaman arrived before Adah. Alane could scarcely conceal her dismay as his tall, gaunt figure made its way into her tent. "I understand that your husband has been injured, Alane," Hagen said in his rich, deep voice.

Alane did not want him to touch Nardo, but did not know how to prevent it. After all, Hagen was the tribe's healer. "Sa," she said, her eyes on her hands folded at her waist, "but it is a little thing, Shaman. He hit his head on a rock and is dizzy. There is no need to trouble you."

She could feel Hagen's eyes on her. She felt her wet clothes sticking to her, her wet braid hanging on her neck, and she was afraid the shaman was coming to the same conclusion that Rune and Stifun had. She sought frantically to find a reason for Nardo's fall, but her mind was blank.

"If this marriage is distasteful to you, Alane," the shaman said, "it can be broken."

She was so surprised that she looked at him.

"This man"—he gestured contemptuously toward Nardo's recumbent form—"he is not of our blood. Worse, he has the stain of Norakamo blood on his hands. The tribal gods will rejoice if you put him away and take a mate from among your own people."

"Vili?" she asked, and was proud that her voice was so calm.

"Vili would be a good husband to you," the shaman agreed. "Is it not better to dwell in the tent of a Norakamo man who loves you than to live in exile among those of foreign blood?"

"Why are you saying these things to me?" Alane asked.

He smiled, and the creases along his cheeks deepened to knife-edge sharpness. "You pushed him in the river, didn't you, Alane? You don't want his big, dark hands touching you, do you, Alane?" He came closer and stared into her eyes. "You haven't lain with him yet, Alane. I can tell that just by looking at you."

His eyes, his repetition of her name in that mellow, musical voice, were strangely compelling. He was trying to put a charm on her, Alane thought. She must not let him do that. "You are wrong, Shaman," she said. "We *have* lain together, and I have found him very much to my taste. More so than I would ever find Vili."

Such an expression of malevolence came over Hagen's face

that Alane shivered and looked away. After a moment, "Very well," the shaman said. "If that is how you want it to be."

"It is."

Hagen held out a pouch. "These are herbs that will help a head injury," he said. "Give them to him in hot water."

Alane took the pouch. "Thank you."

As soon as the shaman was gone, she threw the pouch into the fire.

Nardo slept all night and for most of the following day. Alane kept watch over him the whole time, anxiously checking his color and his breathing, but both seemed normal. He woke in the late afternoon and said he was hungry. She fed him and made him tea, and then he went to check on his horses.

He had said nothing about how he came to be injured. Alane knew that he had not remembered the incidents that led up to his previous head injury, and she was hopeful that the same thing would happen this time and he would not remember the kiss.

It was growing dark by the time he returned to the tent. Alane frowned as he came in the door, turning toward him from the clothing basket she was rearranging. "You were gone for a longer time than was needful just to check on the horses."

"I was talking to Rune," he said.

Alane bit her lip. "Oh." She folded some shirts and put them in the basket. "What—what did Rune say?"

"I asked him how I came to hit my head, and he said he didn't know. He said you were the only one who was with me."

Hope flared in Alane's heart. "You don't remember what happened?"

"Not very clearly."

"You waded into the river to get a drink, and you slipped on one of the underwater rocks," she said firmly.

Nardo closed the doorflap behind him. Alane had lit the stone lamps earlier, so there was light in the tent. He said, "According to Rune, you were wet also."

"I got wet trying to help you up."

"I see."

Alane relaxed and finished filling the basket. When she turned she found him sitting on the hearth rug, staring pensively into the small fire. The flickering light from the flames made shadows on his unshaven face. "Does your head hurt?" she asked sympathetically.

"A little." He looked up and cocked an eyebrow at her. "You have been so tender with me, however, that I find I can't regret the pain."

She had been tender with him because she was feeling guilty about causing him to be hurt, but she wasn't about to tell him that. She looked around the tent to see if there was something else she could occupy herself with, and picked up the broom.

Nardo took off his headband, ran his fingers through his loosened hair and winced slightly as he touched the back of his head. Alane stopped sweeping. His head *was* hurting him.

"Would you like something cold to hold to your head?" she asked.

"Sa."

She took a piece of buckskin, dipped it in the water jar, and folded it into a compress. "Here," she said, holding it out to him.

"You hold it for me," he said.

He was perfectly able to hold it for himself. She almost told him so, but then she changed her mind, went to where he was sitting in the center of the tent, where the skins met high overhead at the smoke hole, tilted his head toward her, and gently pressed the buckskin against the tender spot on the back of his head. He leaned forward until his forehead was resting against her breasts. The weight of his head against her felt strangely pleasant, and she had to make a conscious effort to steady her breathing.

"Alane," he murmured. "Why did you throw the shaman's herbs in the fire?"

She stiffened in alarm. "What do you mean?"

"When the shaman came to see me, he gave you some herbs for my head. You threw them in the fire."

She stared down at the top of his head. "How do you know that?" she demanded. "You were asleep!"

"I was resting."

As she frantically tried to remember what else the shaman had said, she pushed his head away from her and began to back away.

Nardo let her go. "How is the shaman related to Vili?" he asked next.

Alane squeezed the wet cloth nervously between her fingers. "He is Vili's uncle."

He nodded. The lamplight was not strong enough to illuminate the high roof of the tent; it seemed instead to be pooled around Nardo's figure. "I see," he said. "And was he Loki's uncle as well?"

"Sa."

"So. Then he has no love for me. Is that why you threw the herbs into the fire?"

"Sa," Alane said again. Her heart began to slam. She had remembered the rest of the conversation.

Nardo's slippery black hair had fallen forward over his forehead. His eyes glinted through it wickedly and he said, "It is nice to know that you find me to your taste."

Alane had known that was coming and so she was ready. "If you really were listening to my conversation," she said coldly, "then you know perfectly well that I lied about that in order to irritate Hagen."

His head jerked up as if he had been slapped. Then, "You Norakamo women are more prickly than a fistful of burrs," he growled. "It is a wonder to me that there are ever any children born in this tribe!"

Alane was incensed. "Just because Norakamo women are not promiscuous, like the women of your tribe, there is no need to insult us," she shot back.

Now he was angry too. He surged to his feet. "You little shrew," he said, and his hand shot out toward her. Before Alane had a chance even to try to pull away, his mouth had come down on hers.

Alane went stiff with outrage. His body was hard against hers, with one of his hands pressing against her back and the other behind her head, forcing her face up to meet his kiss. She raised her hands to his shoulders to try to thrust him away, but as she did so the quality of his kiss changed. His hard, angry mouth softened, gentled, and sought for a response.

A warm, unexpected rush of feeling rose within Alane. Gradually her head stopped straining against his hand, relaxed, and fell back against his shoulder. The hands she had raised to push him away curved instead around the back of his neck. She leaned against him and her lips opened under the pressure of his. His body came farther over hers and she was almost lifted off her feet.

The intensity of their absorption in each other was interrupted by the sound of women laughing just outside the closed doorflap of the tent. Nardo raised his head, and they stared at each other out of dilated eyes.

"I am going to consummate this marriage tonight," he said in a voice that sounded as if he had been running for miles. "No more delays, Alane. Tonight."

She was quivering all over with a mixture of arousal and fear. What frightened her most of all was that she wanted to be back in his arms. But pride made her protest, "You said you would give me another week."

"I've changed my mind," he said, and reached for her again.

His kisses made her feel breathless and dizzy, and she clung to him for support. Then his hand came up underneath her shirt and his long, hard fingers touched her breast. Fire flickered in her loins. His fingers moved, circled, touched her nipple, and the fire burned hotter.

Suddenly Nardo put her away from him. Alane staggered a little and shivered. It was cold away from the heat of his body. "Wait here," he muttered, and she watched out of dazed eyes as he strode to the corner where the sleeping skins were kept, jerked them out and flung them to the ground. Then he was back again, lifting her to carry her to the bedplace.

Alane's brain ceased to function as her body responded to Nardo's caresses. She knew when he undid her braid because her hair was suddenly streaming around both of their bare torsos. She knew when all of her longings finally centered in one place, because she whimpered and arched upward toward him.

She heard him say in a strangely harsh voice, "Alane, this is

going to hurt you. You are a maiden and no matter what I do
to ease it, it will hurt."

Alane didn't care and when he positioned himself to enter
her, she arched her hips to meet him. She knew what it was she
needed.

He hit the barrier of her maidenhood and stopped, drew one
deep, shuddering breath, and drove.

Pain knifed through Alane. All the brimming, aching, wonderful tension was gone in an instant. She cried out in shock and
dismay and tried to pull away. She had not anticipated that it
would hurt like this!

Nardo's hands were hard on her shoulders, holding her
pinned to the bedskins. He drove into her again and again. After
her initial recoil Alane lay still, teeth clenched, eyes tightly shut,
enduring. It did not take long. She heard him groan, felt the
sweat that drenched his body, and then he was quiet, his face
pressed into her neck. She could feel the hammer beats of his
heart. After a long moment he lifted his head, looked at her, and,
with obvious reluctance, withdrew from her body.

She exhaled shakily.

He touched her cheek with a gentle finger. "I am sorry," he
said unsteadily. He waited a moment, then spoke more clearly.
"Alane. I am so sorry it had to hurt."

He was leaning above her, bracing himself on his hands,
spread on either side of her shoulders. He had lifted his weight
off her completely.

Along with the pain Alane felt a terrible disappointment. He
must have seen it, for he said confidently, "The next time it will
be better, Alane. The next time you will like it. I can promise
you that."

Alane heard the masculine arrogance in his voice. He had
gotten what he wanted, and she had made it easy for him. Too
easy. She snapped, "If there *is* a next time."

He loomed over her, broad and powerful, the muscles in his
arms rippling as they held his weight. He smiled as if she had
amused him. "There will be," he said.

With difficulty Alane refrained from reaching up and slapping
his too-satisfied face.

Chapter
Seven

A t the end of the summer the Norakamo changed camps. Nardo was amazed by how efficiently it was done. Within the space of a single day, all the tents were dismantled and packed upon the backs of horses. All of the tribe's household goods were similarly bestowed. Nardo had always wondered at the paucity of possessions in his wife's tribe. Now, when he thought of how many packhorses it would take to move all the items in his mother's hut alone, he understood why the Norakamo kept their lives so simple.

Autumn camp lay in the foothills on the east shore of the Big Crook close to one of the fords across the narrow, swiftly running river. The trip to autumn camp took three days: a day and a half to journey west along the River of Gold to the place where it joined with the Big Crook. Then it was another day and a half journey to follow the Big Crook as it veered south toward the high mountains, the Altas.

Scarcely had the new camp been set up when Tedric and a group of men set out to attend the Gathering which was held every autumn in a large meadow that lay between the rivers Aros and Dare. They took Nardo with them, since he had never attended this particular Gathering before, and as they came down a winding track between two small hills and approached the Gathering site, Nardo, who was riding beside Tedric, looked ahead curiously at the wide meadow which stretched out before them.

The meadow grass was heavily sprinkled with purple autumn crocuses, but the tents were less thickly spread than Nardo had expected. This impression was confirmed by Tedric, who said, "There are not as many tents as there were last autumn."

"Sa," returned Rune, "and last autumn there were not so many as the autumn before."

Tedric grunted, then turned to Nardo. "We always set up our camp near the stream over there." The stream Tedric indicated ran along the east side of the meadow; on the other side of the stream the land was hilly and forested. Nardo spent the remainder of the afternoon helping the men pitch the camp and unpack the baskets they had come to trade.

The following morning, Nardo and Rune set out together to explore the Gathering. Each of them carried several baskets on their backs; Rune's had been made by his mother, Nardo's by Alane. A display of goods for barter was arrayed in front of each of the tents spread across the meadow, and Nardo and Rune began to move from tent to tent, examining the wares.

The reception accorded them by the various traders was disturbing. *"Those are fine, fat horses you rode in upon"* was a typical comment.

And *"We have heard the reindeer still flourish in the mountains"* was another.

"I do not like this at all," Rune said to Nardo as the two young men turned back toward their camp, their untraded baskets still upon their backs. They were passing a display of clay pots when Rune's eye was caught by the girl who was sitting beside them. Her hair was the same fiery color as the coat of his favorite mare. Rune halted. "I think I will take a look at these pots," he said to Nardo. "You go ahead and I'll meet you back at camp."

Nardo looked from Rune to the girl and then back again to Rune. He said with amusement, "Certainly, Rune. I know how interested you always are in pots."

"My mother likes them," Rune said.

Nardo looked even more amused, but he moved off without saying more, leaving Rune alone with the girl. She was watching

Rune with frank interest, and when he approached her with a smile, she smiled back. Her teeth were even and white, except for a small chip on her left front tooth. Her eyes were neither brown nor gold, but a color somewhere in between. The bottom seemed to drop out of Rune's stomach.

The sun glinted on the reds and yellows and browns of her pots. He said, "I am thirsty." His voice sounded odd and he coughed to clear it. "Do you think you could give me a drink?"

Her slim, chestnut-colored brows wrinkled in puzzlement, and she said something in a language Rune did not understand.

"Thirsty," he said clearly. He cupped his hands and pretended to scoop up water. "Drink."

She laughed, a rich, rippling sound that sent a shock of delight up and down his spine. "Tirsty," she repeated. "Dink." Moving with indescribable grace, she went to a big brown clay pot that stood in the shade of the tent and dipped a horn into it. She brought the dripping horn to Rune and held it out.

He took it from her, in the process managing to touch her fingers. The seemingly accidental meeting of their flesh caused a shock to reverberate all through him. He stared at her in amazement and found her staring back. He thought in wonder, *She felt it too.*

He lifted the cup to his mouth and drank. When he had finished he held it out to her, and when she took it she let him touch her hand again.

"I am Rune," he said, touching his chest. "Rune."

"Nita," she replied, imitating his gesture. Then she pointed at the Norakamo camp and used a word he recognized as referring to his tribe.

"Sa." He repeated her word: "Horsemasters."

He was completely thrown off balance by this encounter. He had never in his life felt such an instant and powerful attraction to a girl. And, to judge by her response, she was feeling it too.

"Are you married?" he asked.

Nita frowned, obviously frustrated by her lack of comprehension.

Rune scoured his brain and came up with the Micos word for husband.

Her brow cleared and she shook her head.

He grinned. The unexpected thought crossed his mind that if Alane could marry outside the tribe, then so could he.

These pleasant thoughts were interrupted by a sharp female voice from behind Rune's back: *"Nita!"* The name was followed by a torrent of sharply spoken language. Nita, who was facing the newcomer, bravely raised her chin, but Rune could see the flicker of dismay in her eyes. She answered the woman, speaking emphatically and pointing first to Rune and then to the water pot.

The woman brushed past Rune, grabbed Nita's arm and thrust her into the tent. Then she faced Rune, hands on hips, and pointed toward the Norakamo camp.

Rune looked into Nita's mother's angry face and decided reluctantly that his wisest course for the moment would be retreat.

As he approached camp, Nardo came to meet him. "I have been waiting for you," he said. "Your father wants to see us."

They found Tedric standing beside his favorite mount, a short-backed, thick-necked mare who made up in stamina what she lacked in looks. The chief was holding the rope attached to the mare's halter while she grazed. "We are leaving," he said as soon as Rune and Nardo halted beside him.

"Now?" Rune asked.

"Tonight."

"You are afraid they will try to take our horses." Nardo made the words a statement instead of a question.

Tedric nodded and flicked a glance at the array of tents spread out under the benign sky. "Right now they are just angry because we have something they don't. In another day they may decide to do something about that anger. It will be best to get our horses to safety."

The mare pulled against the rope that was holding her, trying to move to a new patch of grass. Tedric walked with her. "They also know there will be no reindeer migration from the north this winter. Once the smoked fish and red deer meat are gone, they will be hungry."

"Hungry enough to attempt to hunt reindeer in our mountains?" Rune asked.

Tedric blew his breath noisily through his lips. "We will worry about that later. I am thinking the important thing now is for us to get away from this Gathering. There are too few of us and too many of them."

Both young men murmured their agreement.

"Let them think we are bedding down for the night," Tedric said. "Then, when the moon is at the top of the sky, we will take the horses and go."

"Shall we spread the word among the rest of the men?" Nardo asked.

"Sa," Tedric agreed.

Rune was surprised by the bitter disappointment that stabbed through him at the thought that he would not see Nita again.

By dawn, the men of the Norakamo were well within their own foothills. Each man was leading one packhorse and one spare mount, and the horses needed a rest, so they made camp and built a big fire for warmth and protection. The humans could have gone on, but a grass-fed horse had not the strength to carry a man fast or far. Tedric had not foreseen the necessity for haste in a simple trip to a Gathering, and so the men had not enough remounts to travel for more than four hours at a time.

During the entire ride, Rune thought about Nita. Never had he met a girl who so attracted him. He had cared for his wife, certainly, but they had known each other from childhood. There had never been the spark of instantaneous attraction between him and Tesa that he had felt ignite between him and Nita.

Forget her, he told himself. You will never see her again. But he lay awake for half the morning, tormented by the thought of rich chestnut hair and golden brown eyes.

Tedric had not been the only one to notice that there had been fewer people at this year's Autumn Gathering. Sagred, Nita's father, had been disappointed at the bride prices offered to him for his daughter, and he had decided to wait until spring before arranging her marriage. Nita was a particularly beautiful girl as well as being the daughter of a chief; he was not inclined to let her go cheaply. In the spring, he hoped, he would fare better.

Nita had not complained about the delay in making her marriage. She was finding it hard to set her mind on an ordinary boy when her thoughts were filled day and night with the picture of a golden-haired god. A number of the tribe's men spoke the Kindred language, and Nita teased her father to teach her some of the foreign words. It would be something to occupy her mind, she said guilelessly, while she waited for him to choose her a husband.

Nita's tribe was called the Micos, a word that in their language meant *people*. Their hunting grounds lay on the rolling plains between the Aros and the River of Gold, where many years before vast herds of buffalo and reindeer and aurochs and horses had grazed. The hunting grounds then had been largely open grassland, studded here and there with small stands of birch, poplar and oak. Nowadays, however, the land was slowly being covered by forest, and the large game animals that had fed the tribe were sparse and growing sparser. These days the tribe ate red deer and quail and fish, and the hunters were finding it increasingly difficult to bring in the quantity of smaller game they needed in order to survive.

But there were reindeer in the mountains. Reindeer and horses. Ibex and sheep. The high mountain pastures were still filled with rich, sweet grass in the summer, and the foothills had grazing enough for the colder weather. Other bands of the Micos had migrated north, but Sagred had a different idea, and on the night that Leaf Fall Moon was at its full, he called the men of his tribe together for a council.

"Men of the people," he announced, "there is not enough game left in our hunting grounds for us to survive the winter."

The silence was heavy as the men regarded their chief. The day's hunt had produced only two red deer. A band of a hundred people, such as theirs, needed four deer a day to eat properly.

Kau, one of the old men, broke the gloomy silence. "In the days of my youth, I have seen large herds of reindeer in our hunting grounds, but now they come here no more. They have gone back to the land of ice and snow. It grieves my heart to speak thus, but it is in my mind that we must leave the land of our ancestors and follow them."

"Such would be a long, hard journey," another old man said, "to leave our home in such a way. Hard on the women. Hard on the babes. Hard on the old ones, Kau, such as you and me."

Kau bowed his head. Then he looked up and spoke again in

his high-pitched, elderly voice, "We must have food, Zoti. It will be harder on us all to starve."

A young, robust voice was heard next. "You are right, my father, when you say that we must follow the game. But why must we travel so far when there are reindeer in the mountains?"

The silence vibrated. Finally Kau said, "We cannot go into the mountains."

"Why not, my father?" queried Sagred.

"You know why not." The old man cast an agitated look around the circle. "The Horsemasters dwell in the mountains!"

"That is so," said a different voice. "The Horsemasters are not likely to stand idle while we invade their hunting grounds, and there are too few of us to challenge them."

Sagred made the noise in his throat that everyone knew signified he was going to speak words of weight. All of the men looked at their chief, who folded his hands in front of his chest. Finally, when the air was almost singing with tension, he spoke. "While we were at the Autumn Gathering, I met in council with the other chiefs." Sagred's eyes moved slowly around the circle. "There was talk of combining our numbers and invading the mountains together."

The young men in the circle grinned with delight.

"Which chiefs did you speak to?" Kau, who had not been at the Gathering, asked in a quavering voice.

"Two chiefs of the Micos, and three chiefs of the people who dwell to the evening side of the Dare. All lead bands the size of ours."

"But the horses!" said Kau.

"We will kill their horses and eat them," Sagred replied. He lifted his head and looked down his proud nose. "That is what we will do with their horses."

The young men in the circle yipped their approval, and after more questions and answers, the old men agreed also. In the end, fear of the Horsemasters proved to be less than fear of the unknown north.

The first quarter of Reindeer Moon had risen in the night sky when the Norakamo first learned of the invasion. The tribe was at its winter camp, which was located on a promontory dominating both the Big Crook and the River of Gold, a position that afforded them vast views up both river valleys and over the lowland. Besides offering excellent grazing for the horse herd, the site allowed full control of any herds ascending or descending the River of Gold. At this section of the river, the animals were confined between the river and the steep slopes of the massifs, and could be corralled by the tribe at will.

It was Larz and Stifun who first discovered the invaders. The two young men had ridden northwest, toward the Gorge River, to check the grazing on the plateaus that flanked the steep and narrow ravine which had given that river its name, and they were stunned to find an immense camp of people occupying the land between the rivers Aros and Gorge.

"There are three times our number at least," Stifun reported to Tedric. "The tents covered the plain, Father!"

"Did they see you?" Tedric asked.

"I do not think so."

The following day Tedric himself went to investigate, taking with him Stifun, Rune and Nardo. After they had confirmed Stifun's information, they returned to camp, called the men together, and discussed what their course of action must be.

"They must be driven off." The words were Tedric's, and not a voice was raised in disagreement. The Norakamo lived a life of plenty in their foothills, but they numbered some two hundred people. There was not game enough in their hunting grounds to support the addition of six hundred more.

"We will all starve if they are allowed to remain," Tedric said, and again there was no disagreement.

Irek wanted to take the invaders by surprise, to fall upon their camp and kill as many as they could. "We did not ask these Horse Eaters to come here," he said. "Sky God has given us these foothills as our home. He has given us the grass for our horses, and reindeer, red deer, sheep and ibex and other game for our food. They have come here unasked. They want to take our land and kill off our game so that it will be hard for us to live. They must be driven back. Upon a trail of blood they must be driven!"

Irek's fiery speech ignited the hearts of many of the men. "Sa!" they shouted, and "Irek speaks true!"

As the noise began to abate, Tedric lifted his voice. "It is true that these foreigners must be driven from our mountains. But this is not just a hunting party, my brothers. They have their women and children with them. I say it is better first to talk to their chiefs, to give them the chance to withdraw before blood is shed."

One of the older men raised his voice in support of Tedric, and the discussion raged on.

It was past suppertime when Nardo finally returned to his tent. Alane was sitting by the fire, working on a winter tunic for herself, using reindeer skins that Nardo had taken several months before. The skins of adult females taken early in the fall before their winter coats got too thick provided the best combination of warmth and lightness for winter clothing. Late fall skins, like those of male reindeer, were too heavy to be comfortable, although they made excellent bedding. The skins of the reindeer young were used mainly for underclothing and boot liners.

As soon as Nardo entered the tent, he went to hang his fur tunic on the drying rack. As he approached his wife, his shadow flickered hugely on the tent wall behind him. Slowly Alane put down her sewing, and prepared to serve her husband his supper. The stew, thickened with reindeer blood, had been simmering in the fire pit for hours. She ladled it into a bowl and waited in silence while Nardo took off his boots. The tent, which was pitched against the overhanging shelter of a cliff, was too warm for boots.

Nardo grunted as he struggled with his footgear. It was not easy to get into or out of winter boots, for though they had plenty of room in the foot for warmth, they were made tight around the ankle to keep out snow. Nardo grunted again as the second boot finally came off. He dropped it and wiggled his toes comfortably in his socks, which were made of reindeer skin with the fur inside, unlike the boots, which had the fur on the outside.

"I like these socks," he said to his wife. The Kindred did not use socks inside their boots, but instead lined them with dried grass. Alane had made Nardo socks in the Norakamo fashion, and he liked the soft comfort of the new style. Alane handed him a bowl of stew, then rose to collect his boots and put them in their proper place beneath the drying rack.

"What did you decide to do about this invasion?" she asked Nardo as she returned to her place by the fire.

"The men decided to talk to the Horse Eaters before doing anything," Nardo said, chewing on a piece of meat. "They have women and children with them. It will be better to give them the chance to withdraw without bloodshed."

"Bloodshed," Alane echoed bleakly. "Will it come to that, Nardo?"

"It might."

"But . . . they are only looking for food."

"They are hunting the area around the Gorge River, Alane. When we move there to spring camp, all the game will be gone."

Alane did not reply, and after a moment Nardo stopped eating and looked at his wife. She was using her horn spoon to move around the meat in her dish, but she was not eating. She had been eating very little these past few weeks. Nardo thought he knew what had stolen Alane's appetite, and he had been waiting patiently for her to tell him she was with child.

"Are you feeling ill?" he asked gently, giving her an opening. "You are not eating."

She shook her head and continued to mush the stew in her dish. Nardo frowned.

She was a mystery to him, this wife of his. At night, when he held her in his arms, she was both yielding and passionate. Whenever he thought of those nights, as he was doing now, his phallus would harden and his heart would begin to pound. When they lay together like that, giving and taking, each feeling the beat of the other's heart, then he felt he knew her. But during the day her face retained its secrets.

He was certain she was with child. Why would she not tell him?

"You are too pale and thin," he said, refusing to give up. "Are you certain you are not ill?"

She stopped mushing her stew.

He pressed her gently. "Alane?"

She said, "I am carrying a child for you, Nardo." Her head was bent and she would not look at him. "That is why I am not hungry."

They were the words he had expected, but something in the way she phrased them hit him like a blow in the stomach. "I am carrying a child," she had said, "for you."

For the first time the full reality of this Norakamo marriage came home to Nardo, as he realized that this child would be born to *his* blood, *his* clan. Exhilaration pumped through him. He smiled at Alane and said, "I thought that might be the case."

Alane heard the jubilation in his voice and looked at him out of great, shadowed eyes. He tried to moderate his joy. "I am sorry you are not feeling well," he said.

"My mother says I will get over feeling sick," she replied in a cheerless voice.

Nardo was conscious of being annoyed. He *was* sorry she was ill, but she did not need to sound so dreary! "You don't sound very happy," he accused her.

She went back to mushing her stew. When finally she spoke her voice was low. "For me, this child means exile."

At first he frowned in puzzlement, but then recognition dawned. Once they reached the Kindred camp, he thought, she would have no mother or father or brother, no blood kin of any kind. All she would have would be a husband. Him.

He stared at his wife helplessly, not knowing what he could say to make her feel better. "You will have me," he said at last, feeling foolish and arrogant but not knowing what else to say to her. "I will take care of you, Alane."

"Will you?"

"Sa."

She put down her bowl and looked at him. "Dhu, Nardo," she whispered, "I am so afraid."

He moved instantly to her side and gathered her close. Some of the tension in her spine seemed to relax as he held her securely against him. He touched his lips to the smooth silvery hair on the top of her head, murmured foolish words of comfort, and realized for the first time that being a husband to Alane was going to entail more than he had ever thought it would.

Chapter Eight

The sky was low and gray with snow threatening on the day that Tedric and his tribesmen crossed the ford of the Big Crook River near the place where it veered abruptly to the south. To the north of the river stretched the plateau where the invading tribes were encamped.

Nardo and Rune were among the fifteen men riding with Tedric on this day. Each man led two remounts, and the horses' breaths hung white and foggy in the cold air. The men burrowed into their hoods to escape the keen wind that was blowing across the plateau from the direction of the Aros. The ground had been covered by a half foot of snow two nights before, and the horses' hooves kicked up a spray of white as they trotted toward the north.

The smooth crest of snow before the riders was untouched, save for here and there the dainty tracks of a deer, and the tents of the invaders loomed first as dark patches against the immaculate white landscape. The men of the Norakamo pulled up their horses and regarded the distant camp in silence. A group of hunters was returning from the direction of the Gorge River, carrying poles hung with baskets of still steaming meat.

Vili was the one to speak aloud the thought that was in every Norakamo heart: "That had better not be horse meat," he growled.

Nardo, whose eyes were as far-seeing as a hawk's, said, "Some of the men are carrying antlers. They must have taken reindeer."

A sound of inarticulate relief rose from the group.

"Come," Tedric said tersely. "Let us go and meet them."

Nita was filling the stone lamp in her parents' tent with the animal fat she had previously heated over the fire when she heard a sharp cry of warning from without. Her heart thudded as she ran to the doorflap, which, for warmth, was positioned to face south, and peered out. Outlined against the horizon, caught between the white snow under and the gray sky above, was a single line of horsemen. They were advancing on the camp.

Others in the camp had seen the horsemen, and from the other tents Nita could hear the high-pitched shrieks of women and the frantic questions of frightened children. Nita stood where she was and watched the horsemen come on.

They halted when they were a little more than a javelin's throw away from the nearest tents. Most of the riders were wearing their fur hoods, but one pale blond head was conspicuously bare. Nita felt her heart begin to pound as she recognized Rune.

It was a moment before she noticed that he was holding a stick of evergreen in his hand. A green branch was the universal symbol of peace, and the thought flashed through Nita's mind that Rune had come to ask for her in marriage. Her heart thudded even harder and color flushed into her cheeks. She was standing thus in the doorway of the tent when her father and two of the other chiefs came running up. The three leaders, each of whom was carrying a spear, halted a few feet in front of her tent. They had not stopped to pick up a green branch.

Sagred spoke first in his guttural Kindred Speak. "What do you want from us?"

Nita had realized even before her father spoke that Rune's party had not come to pay a wedding call. The horsemen might be carrying green branches, but their faces looked distinctly unfriendly.

The man in the exact center of the line of horses pushed back his hood, and Nita recognized the rugged features of the Horsemaster chief. His expression was harsh and forbidding.

"We bring you a warning," Tedric said. "You have entered our hunting grounds. If you do not leave of your own accord, you will force us to drive you away."

Nita did not understand all the words, but even from her half-hidden place at the tent flap she could see how her father's fingers tightened around his spear shaft. There was neither anger nor fear in Sagred's steady voice when he replied, however. "The reindeer come no more to the land of our ancestors. If we are to live, we must seek out new hunting grounds. Surely there is enough game in these mountains for all of our people."

Nita understood the gist of her father's words and looked back to gauge Rune's reaction. He was paying no attention to Sagred, however. Instead his eyes were moving around the camp, from tent to tent, as if in search of something. Nita's heart leaped in her chest, and she whirled away from the flap, ran to the drying rack, snatched up her furs, raced back to the door and stepped outside into the cold gray day. Her father was still talking and did not see her appear behind him. Rune saw her, however, and Nita smiled at him. He glanced quickly at Sagred before he shot her a quick grin in return.

". . . not enough game," Tedric was saying. "If you stay here we all will starve."

Rune looked so splendid sitting there upon his horse, Nita thought. Her mother said that the Horsemasters were hard, cruel people, but Nita could not think Rune was hard or cruel. He had smiled at her so sweetly. . . .

"Where are we to take our women and our children?" Sagred was demanding now.

"I do not care where you take them as long as you leave these mountains," Tedric returned pitilessly. "We do not want you here. You are Horse Eaters."

Sagred had drawn himself up to his full height, and his words, pronounced in his guttural accent, were fully as grim as Tedric's. "Then, if there is room in these mountains for only one of us, Horsemaster Chief, perhaps it is you who will be the one who must leave."

Rune abruptly returned his attention to the conversation between the two chiefs. Nita pouted in annoyance, but then she too concentrated on trying to understand what the men were saying.

"You are a fool if you think that," said Tedric.

Nita understood the word *fool* and looked nervously at her father. He did not seem to be angry, however, but replied in a quiet, even tone, "I know your numbers. You Horsemasters are not a large tribe. We have many more men than you do, and even though we have no horses, we know how to fight."

The enormous black-haired man on the lovely gray horse next to Rune spoke up for the first time. "The Norakamo are not the only tribe in these mountains," he said in a lilting accent that was different from Rune's. "We of the Kindred also do not want Horse Eaters in our mountains."

Nita understood the word *Kindred* and saw her father's back go rigid. Her eyes flew once more to the black-haired giant who must be of this legendary tribe.

"The Kindred?" The speaker was not Sagred but one of the other chiefs. "You are of the Kindred?"

"Sa." The black-haired man's eyes flicked briefly across Nita's face, then moved back to the chief's. "I am Nardo, son of the Kindred chief, and I have taken the daughter of the Norakamo chief to wife. Our two tribes have sworn a bond of kinship; if you encroach upon Norakamo land, then you encroach upon Kindred land as well." He paused. "And my tribe is not a small one."

There was a catastrophic silence.

"We have heard you," Sagred replied at last.

Tedric said, "If you have not left our lands by the dark of the moon, we will drive you forth upon a trail of blood."

A few flakes of snow began to fall as the line of horsemen wheeled their horses toward the west. Then, making a wide arc to allow their remounts room to turn as well, they cantered away toward the mountains. Before Rune turned his horse, however, he lifted a hand of farewell to Nita.

The horsemen rode until they reached the Big Crook River, by which time it was growing dark. It was still snowing, so they pitched their camp within the shelter of some trees. The men rigged a windbreak to protect the horses further and bedded down themselves in small tents, three men in each to share their warmth.

Nardo was in with Tedric and Rune. The three men spread their fur tunics on the snow, then put their winter sleeping bags on top of the tunics and crawled in. If the tunics had been dry they would have spread them on top of the sleeping bags, but if they did that when the coats were wet, they would freeze stiff before the morning.

Once they were warm and dry in their sleeping bags, the men took out the dried reindeer meat they each carried and chewed it for supper. Tedric was the first to break the silence. "You did not tell me you were going to say that about the Kindred."

Nardo's voice was rueful. "I did not know I was going to say it until I did. But the words I spoke were true ones, Tedric. The Norakamo and the Kindred *are* joined together in a blood bond now. And both our tribes are determined to keep the mountains safe from Horse Eaters."

"I am thinking that it will take more than a threat to bring the men of the Kindred to our aid," Tedric said. "The memory of Nevin's death is still bitter in their mouths."

Silence fell as they all recalled the hasty departure of Varic from the Norakamo camp.

"There are three of them to every one of us," Rune said at last. "And that is just counting the men. If we fall upon their camp, the women and children will fight also."

Tedric grunted.

"We could lie in wait for one of their hunting parties," Nardo suggested. "The one we saw today was perhaps four handfuls of men. We can match that number."

A wolf howled in the distance, and outside the tent the horses whinnied uneasily. Rune said, "Nardo speaks well, Father."

"He speaks out loud the words I was saying in my heart," Tedric replied. He coughed. "We saw today how they are hunting the area around the Gorge River. We shall hide a party of our own men, and when the Horse Eaters come hunting, we shall fall upon them. If we do this to every hunting party they send out, the rest of them will be forced to retreat, or they will die of starvation."

The single wolf had been joined by friends, and a symphony of howling was drifting through the cold night air. The men could hear the horses moving restlessly, could hear the voices of the men on horse guard trying to calm them.

"That is a good plan, Father," said Rune. "There is no need for us to attack the camp. We have only to keep them from hunting."

"Sa," Nardo agreed in an easy voice. "A very good plan. We shall hunt the hunters."

"But not until the dark of the moon," Tedric reminded the young men. "They have until then to withdraw from our hunting grounds."

"True." Nardo sounded faintly disappointed.

"I don't think they will," Rune said.

"We shall see," Tedric said. "We shall see."

"That was the girl with the pots," Nardo said to Rune the following morning as they rode side by side along the south bank of the Big Crook, heading for home.

Rune continued to look straight ahead between his horse's ears. "What girl?"

Nardo snorted. "The girl with the hair like Fire's. The girl who was smiling at you from behind Sagred's back. That girl."

Rune's finely chiseled features remained expressionless. "Oh. That girl."

Nardo tilted his head and squinted at the sky. The gray clouds of yesterday had lifted, and today the sun was shining on a pristinely beautiful world. The two rode for a while in silence. Finally Rune spoke again. "I have been thinking I would like to marry her."

He was staring once again between his mare's ears and so did not see the surprised expression on Nardo's face. "I did not think that the Norakamo took their women from other tribes," Nardo said cautiously.

"Nor do we usually marry our women into other tribes," Rune shot back. "Yet my father gave you Alane."

"That is so," Nardo agreed.

"I cannot get her out of my mind," Rune confessed.

"It is in my heart that she must feel the same way about you."

Rune turned to look at his brother by marriage. "Do you really think so?"

"The girl stood there in front of a whole line of hostile horsemen just to smile at you," Nardo pointed out.

"That is so." Rune sounded pleased. He ran his fingers through his bangs. "I am not quite sure how to approach Nita's father," he said next.

"That could be a problem," Nardo agreed. He sounded amused.

"It is not funny, Nardo! I am serious."

"Are you? Then think of this, Rune. You don't know this girl. You don't know any of her kin. You don't know what gods she worships or how she worships them."

"What did you know of Alane when you agreed to marry her?" Rune interrupted.

Amusement was back in Nardo's voice. "Exactly what you know of this Nita, I suppose. I knew I wanted to lie with her."

Rune grunted.

A horse squealed behind them, and both men turned to check that their remounts were behaving. One of Rune's horses had got too close to Bluebird, and Bluebird, who did not like this particular mare at all, had kicked her.

When the horses were once more in order, Rune returned to the same subject. "I have been thinking we might have to kidnap her," he said.

Silence. Then, "*We?*" Nardo said in surprise. "What do you mean by *we?*"

Rune shot him a look. "If you do not want to help me, you have only to say so."

Nardo scowled. "It is not that I don't want to help you, Rune, but in my tribe it is a woman's right to choose whom she shall marry."

"Nita stood up in front of all our men just to smile at me," Rune pointed out.

"That is so—" Another squeal came from Bluebird, and Nardo turned and shouted at her to behave. The mare he was riding, Snow Drop, bucked, and the mare directly behind her squealed. Nardo growled at both horses, and quiet was restored.

"I will help if the girl wants to go with you," Nardo said. "If she wants to stay with her own people, then I will help her to do that."

Rune scanned the dark face of his brother by marriage. Nardo was serious. "All right," Rune agreed. "The decision will be Nita's."

Sagred and his fellow chiefs met for several hours after the Norakamo visit, arguing back and forth what ought to be their next course of action. There was no doubt that the horsemen had intimidated them, although no one was willing to admit as much out loud. It was Sagred who made the deciding point.

"It is no more possible for a river to flow backward than it is for us to return the way we have come," he said. "Only emptiness and desolation await us in the land of our ancestors. Here in these mountains the game is abundant; the reindeer await the point of our spears. My brothers, if we must fight for this land, then I am for fighting."

In the end, the rest of the chiefs agreed. If the Horsemasters wanted them gone, then the Horsemasters would first have to kill them.

The fire was smoldering in Sagred's tent. The family, Sagred, his wife, and his only unmarried child, slept in a circle around its dying warmth. Outside, the stars were bright. The last sliver of the dying moon had yet to rise in the night sky. The camp was quiet.

Nita awoke to the sound of her name. She opened her eyes and sat up, bewildered and faintly alarmed. The glow from the stone lamp beside the hearthplace illuminated Rune's pale hair. Then Nita saw that he was holding the sharp flint point of a javelin to her father's throat.

Her mother stirred and also opened her eyes. Her father said calmly, "Be silent, Ralis, or he will kill me."

Nita stared with huge eyes at the tableau formed by the two men on the other side of the hearthplace. Rune had one arm around her father's upper body, and the other hand, perfectly steady, was holding the javelin.

"What do you think you are doing?" she demanded in a trembling voice. She spoke in her own language; every word of Kindred Speak had fled from her mind.

"It's one of the Horsemasters," she heard her mother say fearfully.

"Nita," Rune said again, and her mother's breath caught audibly at the use of her daughter's name. "Go outside," and he gestured with his head to make sure she understood.

Nita looked at her father. He nodded slightly. She crawled out of her sleeping skins, pulled on her boots and picked up the fur tunic that had been one of her covers. At the door she stopped, turned and looked at Rune. He gestured with his head once more, and Nita ducked outside.

There was a man there, holding two horses. Nita recognized the black-haired giant who had spoken during the Horsemasters' warning visit. He said something to her in that lilting voice of his and laid his finger on his lips in a command of silence. Then he put his big hands on her waist and lifted her to the back of one of the horses. Nita's mouth opened in astonishment, but she made no sound. Still holding her horse's reins in his hand, the black-haired man leaped onto the back of his own horse. They waited.

Half a minute later, Rune burst through the doorflap of the tent. Before Nita knew what was happening, he had leaped up behind her and taken his reins from his companion. Then, with both arms around her waist to support her, he urged his horse forward.

The two horses stretched out into a gallop almost instantly. From behind her Nita could hear her father shouting as he emerged from the tent with his spear.

Nita was stiff with terror. Not of Rune, not of being kidnapped, but of the horse. It was going so fast! She was certain she would be bumped off. She pressed against Rune, whose steadying arms were all that was keeping her from being thrown to the cold, hard ground.

Rune murmured something to her in a soothing voice. He was rocking to the rhythm of the horse's gait, and gradually, as Nita realized he was holding her securely, she let herself relax into the motion with him.

In the distance she saw the leaping flames of a fire. Rune and the other man shouted something to each other, and then the fire was coming ever closer. It was not until they were almost upon it that Nita saw the other horses.

The night was clear and very cold. When Rune lifted Nita from the horse, she went immediately to stand beside the fire. As the two men conferred behind her back, she rubbed her face and held out her cold hands to the welcome warmth.

"Nita." Rune put his hands on her shoulders and turned her so she was facing him. He scanned her face. She looked back at him and saw that his blue eyes were full of concern. He spoke slowly, using his hands to point, first to her chest and then to his, desperate to communicate: "Do you want to come with me?"

She understood his words, but she did not have the words to ask him what he would do if she did not wish to come with him. And she really wanted to know.

"I will take you back," he said, pointing again. "I will take you back if you wish to go."

The black-haired man came up beside Rune, and Nita looked at him in wonder. He was half a head taller than any man she had ever seen before. "Does she understand?" he asked Rune. "What does she want to do?"

"I don't know." Rune sounded frustrated. "She doesn't speak our words."

"I speak . . . little," Nita said.

The two men stared at her.

"You"—Nita pointed at Rune. "Me"—she pointed at herself. "What?"

"What?" Rune looked blank.

"She wants to know what you are going to do with her," the black-haired man said. He turned to Nita. "He wants to marry you," he said. "*Marry.*"

Nita knew the word. It was one of the words she had made it her business to learn. She bit her lip and looked indecisively in the direction of her father's camp.

"Nita." Rune took her cold hands into his warm ones. "Say you will come with me." He moved closer and gazed into her eyes; his thumbs moved up and down, caressing the chapped skin of her hands. "Nita?"

She had been attracted to him from the first moment she had seen him. She thought of the danger he had put himself in to take her away with him like this. He had known, of course, that there was no hope of winning her from her father. So he had resorted to . . . this. Nita smiled. "Sa," she whispered to him. "I go—you."

Excitement was running high among the men of the Nora-kamo. Their hunter's blood was up, and they waited with ill-concealed impatience for the dark of the moon. The women of the tribe were not as enthusiastic about the prospect of a confrontation.

"It's like preparing for a horse raid," Rune explained to Alane one afternoon as he came into her tent to collect Nita, who had been spending the afternoon with his sister. "We have all been missing horse raiding, and now we have something else to look forward to."

"This is far more serious than a horse raid," Alane said severely. "No one got killed on horse raids, Rune."

"We won't get killed, Alane," Rune assured her with a smile.

Alane gave him a level stare. "Why not?"

"Because we have the horses. We will surprise them, ride them down, and be away before they can even raise their spears."

"Perhaps that is the way it will be the first time you attack them," Alane agreed. "But the time after that, they will be prepared for you."

Rune shrugged and reached out to take Nita's hand reassuringly. "We have the horses," he repeated.

"You sound just like Nardo," Alane said disgustedly. It was clear she did not mean the comparison to be a compliment.

"You are alarming Nita," Rune said, squeezing his wife's hand.

"Nita would do well to be alarmed," Alane shot back. "It is her tribe that you are planning to attack."

Rune scowled. "They may decide to leave the mountains instead of fighting us."

Alane set her lips. "Well, we will know shortly, will we not, when Nardo and Stifun get back."

All during this conversation Nita had been looking back and forth from brother to sister. Now she said to Rune anxiously, "My father?"

Rune shot Alane an annoyed look, put a protective arm around his wife's shoulders and shepherded her to the doorflap. Nita went with him, after first throwing Alane a quick, apologetic smile.

The last trace of Snow Moon had disappeared from the sky. Soon the first crescent of Shadow Moon would rise, but for two days' time the sky would be dark. Nardo and Stifun, who had been keeping watch on the activities of the invaders, returned to camp to report that the tribes were still encamped upon the plateau. The deadline had passed. Tedric called the Norakamo men into council to plan their attack.

Alane sat alone beside her fire waiting for Nardo. Her fingers as usual were busy, this time with a basket she was weaving, but her thoughts were on her husband.

She had learned from Nita that the invaders greatly outnumbered the Norakamo. If there was fighting, it was extremely likely that some of the Norakamo men would be killed. And Nardo would be in the forefront of the fighting. It was not in his nature to be elsewhere.

If Nardo was killed, then she would not have to leave her home.

Alane had not allowed herself to think that way before. She had told herself that the tribes would surely withdraw, that there would be no fighting. Every time a thought of Nardo's possible death had begun to surface in her mind, she had pushed it back down. She would not think of it. There would be no fighting.

And now it was the dark of the moon, and the tribes had not withdrawn.

Alane's fingers worked the basket, weaving the weft through the warp, over one, under one, over one, under one, as her eyes gazed sightlessly at the fire and her ears listened for the sound of a footstep at the doorflap.

It was completely dark by the time he came. He ducked into

the tent and the stone lamps caught him in their glow. He was
so big, she thought as she looked at him. So big and so immensely vital. Even the lamps seemed to burn more brightly in
his presence. He gave her a grin as he crossed the dirt floor to
take his usual place by the fire.

I don't want him to die. Alane's mind formed the thought,
and then repeated it. *I don't want him to die.*

She shivered. What if by even considering the possibility of
his death she had ill-wished him?

He folded himself onto the rug, an economical and graceful
movement for so big a man. He looked at her, his large brown
eyes sparkling. "It looks as if we're going to have to drive them
off," he said cheerfully.

Alane scooped up dirt from the floor and threw it into the
fire to nullify any ill-wish she may have brought upon him. Then
she answered, "We are not talking about a horse raid, Nardo.
There are four of these people to every one of us!"

He looked surprised. "Where did you hear that?"

"From Nita."

"Nita? Are you able to talk to her, then?"

"I am teaching her to say our words. She is very quick to
learn."

He cocked one black brow. "And you are quick to ask
questions."

"Are the Kindred going to join us in this fight?"

He sniffed the air. "Is that supper I smell?"

In silence she scooped some stew into a bowl and handed it
to him. When he had put a spoonful into his mouth she said,
"Well? Are they?"

He was chewing deliberately. "Are they what?"

She hissed with exasperation. "Are the Kindred going to join
us? After all, that is the reason we married, isn't it? So that our
two tribes would help each other in case of invasion?"

"That is so," he replied amiably and took another spoonful
of stew.

"Nardo, if you don't answer me, I will dump this pot of stew
over your head!"

He sighed and rested the bowl of stew on his thigh. "Alane,

your father wants first to handle this with just his own men. If that is impossible, then we will send for the Kindred."

"Why doesn't he send for them now? Why take a chance on some of our men getting killed?"

"Because it will have to be very clear that this invasion is a serious threat before the Kindred are likely to come to your assistance," Nardo said bluntly.

Alane had not picked up her basket again after dishing out Nardo's supper. Now she took a wooden stick and began to stir the stew viciously. "What kind of a kinship bond is that?" she demanded. "Why should they need proof?"

"You are going to spill some of that on your hand and burn it," Nardo warned.

Some of the stew did indeed slop out of the pot. The fire sizzled. Alane glared at Nardo but stopped stirring.

Nardo said, "The death of Nevin still burns deep in the minds of my people."

"You have forgotten him," she said.

A shadow crossed Nardo's face and its expression became stern. "I will never forget my uncle," he said. "When I throw my spear, he is at my shoulder. When I say my prayers at dawn and sundown, I hear his voice. I have not forgotten him, Alane."

Silence.

Then, "I am sorry," she said. "That was a foolish thing to say to you."

He picked up his bowl and took another bite of stew. "The Kindred will come to our aid when it is clear that it is in their own interest to do so."

"If that is so," Alane said, "then what was the point of our marriage?"

He chewed slowly and reflectively, his eyes on her face. "Perhaps you are right," he said at last. "Perhaps it was not necessary."

Alane's eyes stretched wide.

Nardo smiled at her expression. He held out his hand. "Come here."

She lifted her chin and shook her head.

"All right," he said, "then I will come to you."

"Nardo . . ." she said warningly, but he was already beside her, his big hands hauling her into his lap. He bent his head and whispered in her ear, "I would have married you anyway. I would have kidnapped you, like Rune kidnapped Nita."

Alane tried to ignore the treacherous feelings his nearness was evoking. "I would not have been so willing a victim."

"I know." He blew softly into her ear.

She said bitterly, "You think all you have to do is smile and women will do whatever you want."

"How can you say such a thing?" He was deeply injured. His lips had moved to the delicate joining of her neck and shoulder.

"Well, it won't work with me."

"It won't?"

She stiffened her back. "Na."

His hands moved upward to cup her breast. "We'll see," he said.

The Norakamo winter camp was located at the confluence of the Big Crook with the River of Gold. There was a cliff at that location with a large, dry cave which the tribe used, and since both the cave and the tents pitched at the foot of the cliff faced west, they received sunshine for most of the day. The rivers provided not only fish and waterfowl, but also easy access to the uplands.

The Gorge River lay eight hilly kilometers to the north of the Big Crook. This river was well named, as it ran through the bottom of a deep ravine. The gorge was so narrow and steep that animal herds could not traverse it; they had to pass over the plateaus on either side. It was on the plateau to the west of the Gorge, called the Pasture Land by the Norakamo because of its excellent grazing, where the invaders had made their camp.

The Norakamo knew the Pasture Land well, and they knew the route that the herds passing up and down the River of Gold would follow on their way to the Big Crook and the mountains. When Tedric led a party of Norakamo men across the Big Crook ford on the morning of the first day of Shadow Moon, he knew exactly where the invaders would be most likely to send a hunting party, and exactly where he would set his ambush.

———

Sagred, chief of the Micos, was leading the hunting party that left the invader's camp on the morning of the second day of Shadow Moon. It was a cold day; the winter sun was hidden behind gray skies and the grass was hidden beneath white snow. Since they had encamped on the plateau the invaders had successfully hunted horses and aurochs and elk as well as red deer and reindeer. After the sparse hunting the tribe had struggled with over the past few years, Sagred felt as if he had returned to the golden age of his boyhood.

This was the first hunting party to venture forth from the invader's camp since the deadline issued by Tedric had passed. Sagred had scaled the number of hunters down so that he could leave behind a sufficient force of men to protect his camp. The kidnapping of his daughter had shaken him badly, and since that time he had made certain the camp was well guarded. He thought now with satisfaction that if the Horsemasters tried to attack while the hunters were away, they would be in for an unpleasant surprise.

A cold wind was blowing off the Altas from the south, and Sagred took one hand out of his reindeer fur mitten and held it over his face to warm it. The snow was about six inches deep, and the men's knee-high boots were sufficient to keep their feet dry. The hunting party did not have far to travel; herds of reindeer and horses crossed over the Pasture Land from the river valleys of both the Aros and the River of Gold, and the trails the migrating herds followed were not far from the invader's camp.

Sagred was hoping to take reindeer on this particular day, since they were considerably easier to kill than horses. In anticipation of sighting a herd, the hunters were wearing reindeer antlers tied over their hoods. This rudimentary form of camouflage made it easy for hunters to creep up upon the poor-sighted animals.

The chief put his mitten back on and sniffed the air. A golden eagle floated high above him, the finger ends of its broad wings spreading and narrowing as it hung like a black cross in the gray winter sky. Its head was turning from side to side as it searched the ground for grouse or hare.

Suddenly a herd of horses erupted from one of the clumps of birch trees that dotted the open grassland of the plateau. It was a startled moment before Sagred realized that the horses were carrying men. And that the men were carrying javelins.

Sagred shouted to his own men and tried to lift his spear, but the horsemen were upon them. One of the horses crashed right into him, knocking him to the snowy ground. He sprawled there for a moment, dazed, his spear loose on the ground beside him. His antlers had been dislodged by the force of the impact, and they hung over his forehead, obscuring his vision. He felt someone grab him by the neck of his fur tunic and drag him free of the struggling mass of men.

Once again Sagred was thrown to the ground. He jerked at the antlers that were blinding him, ripped them off his head, and looked up into the blue eyes of the man who had kidnapped his daughter. Sagred froze; once again the man was pointing a javelin at his throat.

The scene was now eerily silent. Beyond the blue-eyed man Sagred could see the men of his hunting party lying still on the bloodstained snow. A few horsemen dismounted and began to go among the bodies, quietly and efficiently finishing off those who were not yet dead.

The blue-eyed man spoke. "You are still alive because you are Nita's father. The next time you may not be so lucky."

Sagred lay in the snow, breathing heavily. The rugged-featured man whom he recognized as the chief of the Norakamo now moved his horse forward so he too could stare down at Sagred.

"I warned you," Tedric said grimly. "I told you to be gone from our hunting grounds by the dark of the moon. You did not listen."

"We have nowhere to go!" Sagred cried.

"That is not my concern" came the remorseless reply. "Bring this news to your people. No hunting party will be safe from us. You will starve to death here more quickly than you would in your own lands."

Sagred said nothing.

"We will kill all of you if we must," Tedric said. "Tell that to your people also."

"I will," Sagred said in a low, unsteady voice.

The two horses backed away from the man on the ground.

Then the Norakamo whirled around and galloped away, leaving Sagred alone with the corpses of his hunting party.

The Norakamo had received no injuries, either to men or to horses, in their encounter with the invaders. Tedric and his men made camp a mile away from the scene of the fight, hobbled their mares and turned them out to graze. They would wait to see what would happen next.

It was late in the afternoon when a large party of the Horse Eaters came to collect the bodies of their slain. Nardo and Rune watched them from the top of a small hill, making certain they were clearly visible to the unhorsed men below. They wanted the invaders to know that they were being constantly watched and to realize there was nothing they could do about it.

"I don't know how they think they are going to bury those bodies," Nardo commented. "The ground is still frozen and there are no caves in the area."

"They will probably burn them," Rune replied.

"Burn them?" Nardo shook his head in bewilderment. "I will never understand the ways of Horse Eaters."

Aside from the trip to collect the bodies, however, there was no sign that the invaders were packing up to leave the plateau. The Norakamo men gathered to discuss their next move.

"We need to plan a campaign of attack and run," Nardo said. "The horses are our great advantage. They have more men, but they cannot use their numbers to advantage if we refuse to engage them."

"A brilliant statement, man of the Kindred," Vili said with heavy sarcasm. "We know that the horses are what give us our advantage. What we need is a plan that will allow us to use them."

Tedric frowned at Vili. "I do not like your voice," he said. "Nardo fought for us this day, and you will address him with respect."

Vili scowled, but his eyes dropped before Tedric's piercing look. "I was just wondering if Nardo had any ideas," he said in a quieter voice.

"We can continue to attack the hunting parties," one of the older men said.

"We can do that," Tedric agreed.

"It is in my heart that we are bound to lose some men and some horses if we continue to attack their hunting parties," Rune said. "They will be looking for us now, and if we ride in among them as we did today, their spears will hit some targets."

"That is true," Tedric said. "I do not see any other way, though."

Nardo said, "We could attack the camp."

They stared at him.

"Is it your plan to kill all the Norakamo?" Vili demanded angrily.

Nardo ignored him and looked at Tedric. "I do not mean that we should ride into the camp," he explained. "We could wrap the tips of our javelins in skins, set them on fire and throw them into the invader's camp. If we are lucky, we will set fire to some of their tents."

Silence. Then the men began to smile.

"Sa," said Irek approvingly. "That is a good idea."

"Even if the fire does no great damage, it will make the Horse Eaters feel even more unsafe," Rune said. "What do you think, Father?"

"I think dawn is the time to do it," Tedric said. "They will be asleep and off guard. We can throw the torches and gallop away. There will be nothing they can do."

The smiles broadened.

"Do we have enough skins?" Nardo asked.

"We can use one of the tents if we have to," Tedric replied.

"We will lose all our javelins," Vili objected.

"We have more javelins back in camp," Rune said impatiently. "What is the matter with you, Vili? Don't you want to drive off the Horse Eaters?"

Vili shot Rune an angry look and did not reply.

The fire attack on the invader's camp was even more successful than the Norakamo had dared to hope. Two tents went up in flames, and the fire spread from them to others in the immediate vicinity. From a half mile away, the Norakamo sat on their horses and watched with immense satisfaction as the invaders struggled to contain the fires. The men in the camp could see the watching horsemen, but there was nothing they could do.

Once the fires had finally been put out, the chiefs of the invading tribes gathered for a council.

"If we stay here, we will lose half of our people," one of the chiefs complained. "We cannot fight men whom we cannot catch!"

"We outnumber them," another chief pointed out.

"The horses are more of an advantage than I had expected," Sagred said gloomily. "The Norakamo are not going to fight us face to face; they are going to pick away at us little by little."

"But if we leave here, where are we to go?"

That was the difficult question, of course.

"The Norakamo hunting grounds are not the only hunting grounds in the mountains," Sagred said.

"We do not want to anger the Kindred! They have horses too, and they are much larger in number than are the Norakamo."

"The Kindred hunt the mountains to the east of the Norakamo," Sagred said. "What if we move west?"

"We do not know the world to the west of the Dare."

Sagred shrugged. "We do not know the world to the north either, and that is our only other choice."

After several hours of talking, with the same things being said again and again, the tribes decided to follow the Aros River north and west until it reentered the mountains well to the west of the Norakamo hunting grounds.

At about the same time that the men of the Norakamo were celebrating their defeat of the Horse Eater invasion, far away to the west and north of the Pyrenees, in a land that would one day be called Britain, another tribe had learned about the place the traders were calling the Reindeer Mountains. This tribe was named the Redu, and their homeland was a peninsula that lay at the very edge of the southward migration of the reindeer herd. Even in good times the lives of the Redu were hard, and there had been no good times since the reindeer had ceased to come as far south as their hunting grounds.

Like so many other tribes faced with the changing pattern of reindeer migration, the Redu had reluctantly come to the conclusion that they must abandon their ancient homeland and follow the animals that were their life. The history of the Redu, however, was a long and sanguinary tale of feuds with the large tribe that lived directly to their north. The Tali were every bit as fierce as the Redu, as well as being considerably greater in number, and the Redu knew that it would be virtual suicide for them to attempt to migrate into the hunting grounds of their enemy.

The tribe had grown desperate by the time they learned of the mountains lying some three moons to the southeast of their own empty hunting grounds. It was the chief of the Redu, an eagle-faced man named Kerk, who made the final decision that the tribe must migrate.

The traders had told the Redu about the mountain tribes who rode upon the backs of horses, and Kerk was not foolish enough to assume that he would be able to move into another tribe's hunting grounds without a fight. But he also knew from the traders that the Redu had a weapon unknown in the world beyond Britain.

The mountain tribes might have horses and spears, but the Redu had the bow and arrow.

PART TWO

THE KINDRED

Chapter Nine

M ara was sitting in her usual place, holding in her hands the fawn's skin from which she was making a robe and a cap for her expected grandchild. The cap was made from the fawn's head, with the ears standing upright on either side. Mara had been stitching the small cut-out arms onto the robe, but for the past ten minutes her hands had been still.

The activity in the hut went on around her as usual. Tora, her younger sister, was calling some of the older children to come with her to the river for a bath. Riva, her elder daughter, was stirring the stew that simmered in the fire pit. Lora, Tora's younger daughter, was nursing her baby. Mara's younger daughter, Liev, was sitting gossiping with two neighbor women, and a noisy pack of small children were playing with an equally noisy pack of puppies in the corner. There were no men present; they were rarely home during the day.

A piercing shriek came from one of the children, and a puppy yipped excitedly. Mara spoke into the din, "Children and puppies, out of the house!"

With no diminution of sound, her grandchildren and her sister's grandchildren moved in a wave toward the open door of the hut. As they exited into the sunshine the big gray bitch who had been sleeping in the corner stood up and stretched. She yawned and scratched an ear. Then she too headed toward the door of the hut, stopping first to sniff one of the reindeer skin rugs. She looked over at Mara and whined piteously. When the woman said nothing, the dog continued on her way to the door.

Lora said softly, "Sabe misses Rorig."

Mara nodded but did not reply. Lora lifted her babe from her breast and held him to her shoulder. Mara stared blindly at the half-finished little garment she was holding in her hands.

She had scarcely finished grieving for her brother when her husband had been killed. It had been one of those foolish accidents that no one could foresee. Rorig had been riding his horse through the forest when a wildcat leaped from a tree branch onto the mare's rump. The horse had gone crazy and thrown Rorig, who had hit his head on a rock and never again opened his eyes. Four days ago a party of men had left for the Norakamo camp to fetch Nardo, who was now their chief.

I am like the old bitch, Mara thought bitterly, *sniffing around at the places where once they were, missing them and wondering when they will come again.*

The sound of horses' hooves came drifting in through the open door of the hut. Mara's whole body tensed to listen. A man shouted. Pounding footsteps sounded beside the house. Children shrieked. Then came a little girl's high, clear trill: "Nardo! It's Nardo! Beki, come quickly, Nardo is here!"

The other women in the tent all exclaimed and looked at Mara. Then they fell to talking in low voices.

Mara turned her eyes back to her work and forced herself to take a stitch, but all her nerve endings were straining toward the open door. There was no sound of steps to announce his coming, but her head turned the moment his great height filled the doorway. The other women in the room fell silent.

Mara put down her sewing. "So, Nardo," she said. "Finally you have come home."

"Sa, Mama," he replied in that well-known, well-loved voice. "Finally I have come home."

Mara watched as he crossed the floor, her heart swollen with love and with pride. His eyes were filled with concern as he looked searchingly into her face. No one had eyes more beautiful than Nardo, she thought. When he slept, his lashes were so long they almost touched his cheekbones.

He sat on his heels in front of her and took her rough, worn hands into his own much larger clasp. "I am so sorry, Mama," he said. Strength and sympathy flowed into her from the touch of his hands. "It is in my heart that you have had too much cause for grief of late."

"That is so, my son," she replied. Her voice quavered slightly and she paused until she could control it. "My heart has been lonely for you." She reached up to tuck a strand of his hair back into his headband and remembered how that glossy black hair used to cling to her fingers when she had combed it in his childhood. How long ago that seemed! "You have brought your wife with you?" she asked.

He shook his head. "She is due to give birth in one moon's time, Mama. I told her I would fetch her after the babe is born."

Mara smiled with relief. "That was well done, my son. She will want her mother by her when she gives birth."

"So I thought."

Mara reached out to run a gentle finger along one hard cheekbone, then smiled into his beloved face. "Everything will be well," she said, "now that you are home."

The Kindred tribe over which Nardo was assuming leadership held as its hunting grounds the territory from the River of Gold in the west to the Atata River in the east, and from the foothills of the Greatfish River in the north to the high pastures of the Altas in the south. This territory fell naturally into two regions, the region which was contiguous to the River of Gold and the Greatfish, and the region which lay along the Atata. These two great river valleys were separated by high mountains and joined only by the col known to the tribe as the Buffalo Pass.

Although the Greatfish and the Atata Kindred were led by different chiefs, they shared the same heritage and were composed of the same family clans. Intermarriage was common between the two villages, so the ties of kinship remained close.

There were two immediate actions Nardo needed to take as the new chief. First, he had to inform the Atata Kindred of Rorig's death and his own accession. And second, he had to change the rotation of horses in the summer camps.

The tribe had two main summer camps, a grazing camp and a hunting camp. The grazing camp, where the main part of the horse herd summered, lay in a rich mountain valley high in the Altas which was reached by means of a pass cut eons ago by the Greatfish River. The hunting camp lay on the Narrow River in the high country to the south and east of the permanent village on the Greatfish, not far from the Buffalo Pass. Most of the married men were usually assigned to hunting camp, while the unmarried men went to Bright Valley in the mountains—accompanied by most of the tribe's unmarried girls.

There was coming and going all summer between the village and the camps. Horses were rotated so that all of the herd would have a chance to spend two moons grazing on the sweet high mountain pasture of Bright Valley, and it was usually the chief who dictated which horses were to be placed where. As a courtesy, however, Nardo called together the clan council to tell them of his plans. He was unpleasantly surprised to find himself challenged by his cousin Varic.

The first part of the council meeting went smoothly, with the men agreeing with Nardo's suggestions about the embassy to the Atata and the rotation of horses. Then, as Nardo was about to dismiss the group, Varic spoke up.

"Why didn't you call upon the men of the Kindred to help turn back the invasion of the Horse Eaters?" he demanded. "I thought that was the whole purpose of that Norakamo marriage of yours, that the two tribes should work together to repel invaders."

Nardo stared in astonishment at his cousin, who was the last person in the world he had expected to be an advocate for helping the Norakamo.

To his further amazement, the rest of the council members agreed with Varic. "I would have called upon you if it looked as if the Norakamo needed help," Nardo explained to them.

Nat, council member for the Bear Clan, said disgustedly, "You should have called upon us immediately. Now the Norakamo will be so full of themselves they will be impossible."

"We could have pushed those people back in half the time it took the Norakamo," Matti of the Fox Clan agreed.

Nardo looked around the circle of animated faces and understood finally that the men were disappointed that they had missed out on the action. He said ruefully, "I did not call upon you because I thought that the memory of Nevin's death was too sharp to allow the Kindred to be overly anxious to lend any assistance to the Norakamo." He met the wide, childlike gaze of his cousin. "You made your feelings well known, Varic, when you came to my marriage."

"That was different," Varic said.

"Sa," Nat agreed. "In the future, Nardo, we would appreciate it if you would consult with the council before you make assumptions that are not true."

Once again Nardo looked around the circle of faces. "Very well," he said slowly. "I will remember that."

It was Rune who brought Nardo the news that Alane had given birth. Nardo had been helping a few of the old men who no longer went to summer camp to repair fishing nets when he saw the two riders coming from the west. Even from a distance he recognized the mares as belonging to Rune and Larz, and he went on foot to meet the visitors.

"Greetings," Nardo said as the horses halted on the river path but a few feet in front of him. "Welcome to my village."

Rune smiled. "Greetings, my brother. I have come to tell you that you have a son."

Nardo's eyes sparkled. "A son! That is good news, indeed. And Alane? She is well?"

"She is very well," Rune said.

"I am glad." Nardo turned politely to Larz. "You have brought me welcome news indeed."

Larz was looking curiously beyond Nardo at the village spread out upon the banks of the Greatfish. The Norakamo had often raided Kindred horses at their spring and winter grazing camps farther down the river, but none of them had ever seen the Kindred's main village. It differed considerably from the Norakamo home camps, and Rune too looked beyond Nardo to take in the view.

The village was located on the west bank of the river at the base of a cliff in which were set several large east-facing caves. There were at least two handfuls of big rectangular log houses spread across the site, and around each house was grouped a circle of huts, also made from logs. The village location looked to be pleasantly dry, and a hill on the opposite side of the river helped to shelter it from the wind. It was a perfect place for a village, Rune thought, but the surrounding woodlands did not offer much grazing for horses.

He said as much to Nardo, who agreed. "That is why we move the herd into mountain pastures for the summer and then back to the pastures east of the River of Gold for the winter." He gestured to a big corral made from logs on the far side of the river. There were two handfuls of horses in the enclosure, whose grass had long since been grazed down. "Those are all the horses we have in the village at present."

"Our own horses will need food and water before we return home," Rune said.

"There is good grass upstream, near the river Leza," Nardo reassured him. "I will have a few of the boys and older girls here in the village take your horses to graze. Meanwhile, you must be my guests."

Rune was impressed by the house which Nardo said belonged to his mother. The log building was at least forty feet wide and a hundred feet long, with a roof that was made of bark. Inside, the house was similar to a Norakamo tent in that it had a fire pit for cooking and racks for drying clothes and herbs. But this house also had a huge assortment of pots and eating utensils neatly stacked on a table made from split logs and rocks, and big covered clay jars held the fruits of the women's gathering. The dirt floor was covered with an assortment of fur rugs, and a big pile of buckskins lay against one wall, waiting to be sewn into garments. Another table held an array of scrapers and fleshers, along with sinew to be made into thread.

It was almost suppertime and the room was filled with women and children and dogs. The two Norakamo men checked on the threshold, startled by the noise.

Nardo seemed to find nothing unusual. "Alis, Beki and Mait!" he called over the din. "I have a job for you."

A little girl and a boy bounced up from the pile of children playing with the puppies. Another girl handed a baby to a young woman and approached the door at a more sedate pace.

"This is Rune, the brother of my wife," Nardo said to the three children. "And this is Larz."

The children stared at the newcomers. "They are Nora-kamo?" the boy asked.

"Sa. They are Norakamo and they are friends." Nardo turned to the men and said, "These are my sisters' daughters, Beki and Alis, and this is my sister's son, Mait."

Three pairs of large, speculative eyes regarded Rune and Larz.

Nardo said, "I want you to take their horses for some grass. They have ridden here today all the way from the River of Gold. Get Tor to help you."

"Sa, Nardo, we will do that," the eldest of the three, the girl called Alis, said.

The women in the house were silent, watching the door. Once Nardo had made sure the children had the horses in charge, he urged his visitors forward to where Mara sat enthroned on a pile of furs. Like a chief, Rune thought.

The men had supper with the women and children in the big house, but Nardo took them to sleep in one of the caves. It was the initiates' cave, he said, the place where the unmarried young men of the tribe slept together, where he had slept since his own initiation at the age of fourteen. It was deserted except for the three of them, since the rest of the young men were in Bright Valley with the herd.

"I will return to the Norakamo camp with you," Nardo told Rune as they spread out their sleeping skins for the night. "Then, when Alane feels strong enough, I will bring her and the baby home with me."

Alane had been enormously relieved when Nardo had proposed leaving her among her own people until after the birth of her child. The thought of having his haughty and hostile mother in charge of the birth filled her with dread. It was not until Nardo was gone that Alane had realized how dependent she had grown upon his presence in her life. She missed him more than she had ever dreamed she would, especially after her boy was born and he was not there to share her joy. When Rune left to ride to the Kindred village to bring the new father word, she hoped fiercely that Nardo would return with her brother.

She was nursing the baby in her tent when she heard the

sound of hoofbeats coming into camp. It was too early for the hunters to be returning, and her head tilted as she strained to distinguish voices.

"Will you help me see to the horses?" she heard her brother's voice ask. Alane held her breath, but the only voice that came in reply belonged to Nita. A sudden pang of loneliness struck Alane so sharply that she had to bite her lip to keep from crying out. He had not come.

She bent her head, closed her eyes, and rested her mouth on the top of the baby's fuzzy black head. She felt absolutely desolate.

"So, my wife" came a deep, familiar voice from the doorflap, "I hear you have borne a boy."

"Nardo!" She straightened so quickly that the baby lost the nipple. He howled indignantly until she gave it back to him. Then Nardo himself was kneeling beside her, his warm brown eyes scanning her face.

"You are well, Alane?"

"I am very well." She looked proudly at the baby sucking so steadily at her breast. "Here is your son, Nardo."

"All I can see at present is the back of his head." He sounded amused. "It is a very nice head, however."

"He was hungry," she said a little apologetically. "He will be finished shortly and then you will be able to see his face." She smiled. "He is beautiful."

"Then he must look like you." He touched the top of her head in a gentle caress. "I have had my mother and my sisters praying to the Mother that all would go well for you, Alane. You have been much on my mind."

The mention of his mother and sisters effectively diminished some of Alane's joy. She looked up into Nardo's face. His dark eyes looked so tender, she thought. His touch had been so gentle that it had not disturbed a single hair on her head. Her uneasiness went away and she smiled. "I have not named him," she said. "I was waiting for you."

He was silent for a long time, looking at her. Then he said, "In my tribe it is the mother who names her child."

The baby's nursing had finally slowed, and this time when Alane took him away from the nipple he was quiet. Her voice was firm as she answered, "That is because in your tribe a woman's child belongs to her clan. This child will be of your clan, Nardo, so you should have the naming of him." And she cradled the infant in the crook of her arm so that his father could see the small face.

Nardo gazed in astonishment into the baby's misty gray eyes. "But he has eyebrows!"

Alane smiled at his amazement. "Sa. He has eyebrows. He has fingers and toes too."

"None of the new babies I have seen before ever had eyebrows," Nardo explained. Cautiously he traced his forefinger over the fine arc of pale brown that gave the baby an endearingly questioning look.

"Would you like to call him Rorig?" Alane asked.

Still looking at the baby, Nardo shook his head. "Rorig is a name of the Eagle Clan." A note of pride crept into his voice. "This child will be of the Clan of the Wolf." He moved his forefinger to touch the baby's palm, and the tiny fingers curled immediately around the new object. Nardo looked delighted. "I would like to call him Nevin, if that is all right with you."

Alane frowned. "I am not sure if that is such a good idea, Nardo. Our shaman will not like it."

Nardo's eyes sparkled dangerously. "The Norakamo shaman has nothing to do with what I name my son."

Alane looked from Nardo to the baby and then back again to Nardo. "Since we are not going to live among my people, I suppose it will be all right," she said at last. "I don't dislike the name."

Nardo said, "Nevin is a fine name. A fine Wolf name for a fine Wolf boy." A little of the milk the baby had drunk dribbled out of his mouth onto his chin, and he burped. Nardo laughed. "Dhu," he said, "I am going to like having a son who belongs to me."

In the end, and somewhat to her surprise, Alane found that she was actually resigned to leaving her home to go with Nardo. All during this past year, and without her realizing it, the ties that bound her to her husband had slowly but surely been strengthening. The baby was just the final knot in the bond that held them together. When they left the Norakamo camp on a bright summer morning and turned their horses' faces east, Alane felt fear and apprehension about the new life she was going to, but she also knew that, given a choice, still she would go with Nardo.

Alane had never before been east of the River of Gold, and she looked around with lively interest as they traveled along the Greatfish River toward the main village of the Kindred. She was riding one of the mares her father had given her as a wedding gift, and she carried Nevin in a pouch snuggled between her breasts. The pouch was held by a harness of fur-lined buckskin that went across Alane's shoulders and crisscrossed down her back; it was the gear used by all Norakamo women to carry their infants.

Alane and Nardo were accompanied on this journey by Alane's brothers Rune and Stifun. All three of the men led an extra riding horse as well as a packhorse loaded with Alane's belongings. Their pace was necessarily kept to a walk because of the baby, so it would take them three days to reach their destination.

The Greatfish was not as wide as the River of Gold, but it was a bigger river than the Big Crook. Its banks were forested in many places, and Alane, who had been reared among pasture-land, was fascinated by the different sights and sounds along this river. She watched as ravens and eagles periodically swooped down into the trees in search of prey, then rose into the air again. When Nardo pitched their tent for the evening, the shrill *bri-bri-bri* call of marmots and the chattering of red squirrels from the forest at their back formed an unfamiliar accompaniment to her chores.

Alane started the cook fire and tended to the baby while the men took care of the horses. They had brought dried meat with them, but Stifun took his spear to the shallows of the ford which lay a few hundred yards downriver and managed to get two salmon. Alane cleaned them and cooked them, and they ate out-doors in front of the small traveling tents. There was little talk, but the silence was the comfortable sort that falls among people who know each other well.

After Nardo had finished eating, he took the baby from Alane with the easy competence of a seasoned uncle. As Alane took her turn eating, she watched a small herd of reindeer as they pranced across the ford, kicking up water like playful horses. When they reached dry land and shook themselves, the spray of drops was dazzling in the dying sunlight.

They did not go into their tents until the last ray of sun had left the sky and the cook fire was almost burned out. Alane in particular was in no hurry to reach the Kindred camp, where she would once again meet Nardo's mother, the formidable Mara. Soon enough she must begin to learn how to be a member of the tribe of the Kindred. She looked at her husband and her son and felt fierce possessiveness cramp her heart. There was nothing she would not do for them, she thought. Nothing.

The baby yawned, showing all his gums. Nardo chuckled and said, "It is growing late."

"Sa," Rune agreed. "We should be away at first light if we want to make your village by the following day."

The men arose and, reluctantly, Alane stood also. Nardo came to put the baby in her arms. "You are tired, little one," he said. "Go to sleep. We will see to the fires."

Let me hold on to this moment, Alane thought, looking up into his peaceful dark eyes. She had a premonition that once they reached the Kindred village, things between her and Nardo would never be so uncomplicated again.

Chapter Ten

By the end of the summer the Redu were ready to begin the initial phase of their great migration. All knew they would not last through another reindeer-less winter in their own hunting grounds, and even bad-weather travel was preferable to starvation.

Seven hundred people, Redu from five separate bands, had united to make this trek. Each of the Redu bands was led by a secondary chief, but Kerk was the chief of the whole tribe, and his leadership was unquestioned.

Before all else, the Redu were warriors, and the tribe's chain of command reflected this occupation. The initiated men of the tribe were divided into two main groups: the "right hand" men, who formed the secondary chiefs' council, were the most experienced hunters and the ones who had killed the greatest number of Tali enemies. This number could be seen at a glance by the thumbs which each warrior wore hanging as trophies from his belt. Kerk, the chief, had over six handfuls of thumbs dangling at his waist.

The younger, less experienced men of the tribe were called the "left hand." The left-hand men were always striving to collect enough thumbs to enable them to join the right-hand group.

Kerk had decided not to take the entire tribe on this trek. The very old and very young, as well as pregnant women and the mothers of young children, were left behind. The hunters of the tribe drew sticks, and the ones who drew short sticks stayed behind with the weak and the helpless. The proportion of hunters to mouths that needed to be fed was dangerously low, but Kerk wanted as many warriors as possible at his back when he invaded the Reindeer Mountains. When the mountains were gained, and the tribe was secure, then they would send for the ones they had left behind.

The late summer sky was hazy and mist hung low in the marsh on the day that the Redu set out from their ancestral homeland. Five hundred men went first, carrying their deadly bows made of strong yew and strung with sinew. Upon their backs they bore sacks of fire-straightened arrows flighted with the feathers of eagles and hawks. Behind the men toiled two hundred women and children, carrying tents, extra clothing and cooking gear.

Kerk had taken prisoner the four traders who were the source of his information about the Reindeer Mountains to act as guides. The Redu chief had given the traders into the charge of his son, Paxon, and made certain that the traders understood it was a matter of life and death to them that the Redu safely reached their destination.

"I want you to learn the language of these Kindred people," Kerk ordered his son. "You have some skill with words. You have learned the language of the Tali."

Kerk did not sound as if he admired this particular proficiency of his son's, but he would make use of it if he must. Paxon looked into his father's hard face and nodded obediently. Kerk had never thought much of any of the "softer" talents Paxon had inherited from his mother, which was why the boy had always worked so hard to excel in the warlike things his father did admire.

Kerk had calculated it should take five moons for the entire trek. The traders said it could be done in three moons, but the traders had not had seven hundred people to feed.

By mid-winter, Kerk calculated that the Redu should arrive at the Reindeer Mountains.

Alane stood at the door of the house, steeling herself to go in. After one moon of residence in the village, she was still appalled by the chaos of Mara's house. It was not that the household work did not get done. On the contrary, Alane had seen that with all the women in one family working together, there was little duplication of effort and everything was accomplished faster. But the number of people in the house overwhelmed her. The everlasting chatter of voices all talking at once set her teeth on edge. And the constant confusion of children and dogs was driving her insane.

She straightened her shoulders now and resolutely thrust aside the skins that were hung in the door frame for warmth. It was dim inside the big house, with the skins blocking the light from the door, but several stone lamps shed enough yellow light to illuminate patches of activity. Mara and her sister, Tora, were sitting by one of the lamps, softening some buckskin. Alis, the thirteen-year-old, was playing with a group of the younger children in a corner. Haras, Tora's son who was seeking temporary refuge from his mother-by-marriage's nagging, was talking earnestly to his sister Lora. Liev, Nardo's sister, was chopping up meat for the stew pot. The puppies were sleeping in a heap in the corner opposite the children.

Everyone looked up when Alane came in. Mara said, "There you are, Alane. We were wondering where you had disappeared to."

Alane had escaped to her own hut for a few peaceful hours with her baby. All of these women, with their constant awareness of everything she did, were rubbing her nerves raw. She did not trust herself to reply to Mara, but moved silently to join Nardo's cousin Lora, the only household woman she felt comfortable with. Lora was a pretty girl, with deep dimples in both cheeks and a lively sense of humor. She was just eighteen, the member of the household closest in age to Alane, and the two girls often worked together.

Alane began to lower herself to the fur rug, then frowned as she saw something stuck to the reindeer hide right in the spot where she was going to sit. She sniffed. There was a distinctly sour odor emanating from the spot. Alane straightened. "It looks as if one of the dogs was sick," she said in an expressionless voice.

Mara shrugged. "It happens," she replied. "You would understand better if you were accustomed to dogs, Alane." She made it sound as if this lack in Alane was a severe moral failing. "Alis, clean up the spot that is bothering Alane."

An uncomfortable silence fell as Alis bent to do Mara's bidding. Alane stood, erect and stiff, holding Nevin in her arms. Tora said in an obvious effort to break the tension, "I am thinking it is time those puppies went to the cave with the rest of the dogs. They are grown enough now to learn to hunt with the men."

A squeal of distress came from the children at these words. Alane was constantly amazed by the tolerance the Kindred accorded their children. They almost never reproved or disciplined them, and consequently none of them hesitated now to voice their disagreement with an adult's judgment about the puppies.

Mara waited until the children's protests had run down before agreeing with her sister.

Glum silence from the children.

Alis straightened from cleaning the spot and asked brightly, "Who wants to play a game of Hunt the Buffalo?" The children all shouted their enthusiasm, and Alane gritted her teeth. This game entailed every player but one closing his eyes while the one hid an item somewhere in the house. Then everyone had to search for it, the first to find it being the winner. It was an exceedingly noisy game.

Alane found a dry patch of rug, sat down and lifted Nevin from his pouch.

Lora reached over to straighten one of the baby's fawn ears. Then she looked curiously at the small, beautifully woven basket Alane had brought in with her. "That basket is lovely. I have never seen one quite like it. What is it for?"

"It is to hold tea," Alane said. "I would like to bring some tea to my own hut so I can brew it whenever I choose."

A startled silence fell. Then Mara's voice said, "The teakettle here is always full, Alane."

Alane turned her head to look at Nardo's mother. "That is so, my mother, but I would like to be able to make tea in my own home."

Mara's brown eyes regarded Alane with faint surprise. "This is your home."

"In my own hut," Alane said.

"It is not necessary," said Mara. "There is tea here."

Alane's face retained its perfect serenity. Her voice remained soft and reasonable. "It is not necessary," she agreed. "But I want to."

A faint frown crossed Mara's brow. Then she shrugged. "If you wish to take some tea, of course you may. The food here is for all the household." Her tone of voice said clearly that she thought Alane was being very rude.

Alane smiled gently. "Thank you, my mother. Then I will take some meat as well."

Nardo was surprised to find a cook fire going in his own hut when he returned from hunting late that afternoon. His face was ruddy from the chill wind that had been blowing, and he sniffed the air appreciatively. "Are you cooking stew?" he asked his wife.

She got up to help him with his furs. "Sa." She took the tunic he handed her and went to hang it on the dryer along the wall. "There is hot water if you want to wash."

He nodded and waited while she poured the water into a wide, lined basket. He pushed up the loose sleeves of his buckskin tunic and gratefully plunged his bloodstained hands into the warm water, scrubbing them together to cleanse them. Then he took the buckskin cloth she handed him and dried them. "We are eating here tonight?"

Alane added the damp buckskin to the wall dryer and replied, "I don't feel as if I've had a private conversation with you since I came to this village, Nardo. Every night we go to your mother's house to eat, and it is so noisy!"

"We come back here to sleep," he said. "We can talk then." He looked rueful. "Unfortunately, talking is all we can do until your time of impurity is up."

"You spend most of the evening in your mother's house talking to Haras and Dane," Alane pointed out.

"All right," Nardo said good-humoredly. "Then we will eat here tonight. Just wait while I go and get Samu. I left him at Mama's."

"Samu?" Alane said. "What do you mean, Nardo, you will get Samu?"

But Nardo was gone. In ten minutes he had returned, bringing with him a large, silver-tipped black dog whose vigorously wagging tail indicated delirious joy.

Alane's back stiffened. "Nardo, why are you bringing Samu here? He is supposed to stay with the other dogs in the cave."

Nardo fondled the dog's large, pointed ears. "He doesn't want to go to the cave," he said. "He likes me better than the other dogs." As if to emphasize this point, Samu rubbed his head against Nardo's thigh and whined for more attention. Nardo glanced up and said almost casually, "I'm going to have him sleep in the hut with us from now on, Alane."

Alane went rigid. He knew she did not like dogs. "Your mother does not let the dogs sleep in her house," she said.

"Sabe sleeps in the house."

"That is because she is old and needs the warmth."

He shook his head. "Sabe was my father's dog. She always slept in the house." Nardo sniffed. "That stew smells good," he said.

Alane glared. "Do not think you can distract me by praising my cooking!"

"Why are you making such a fuss?" he said. "This dog would never hurt you, Alane. He will protect you, in fact."

"I don't want to be protected by a dog."

Samu had moved into the hut while they were speaking, and now he padded over to the pile of fur where Nevin was sleeping.

"Nardo," Alane said urgently.

"He's all right," her husband replied mildly. He sat down on the hearth rug, obviously ready to eat.

Alane tensed, ready if necessary to defend her child from the dog's attack. The dog sniffed the baby's head. Alane said again, this time frantically, "Nardo." She was afraid that if she moved she would provoke the dog.

"He won't hurt Nevin, Alane. Just let him alone."

Samu rested his muzzle for a moment on Nevin's fuzzy black head. The baby continued to sleep. The dog wandered into a corner of the hut and lay down, his chin on his paws. Alane let out her breath.

"Alane," Nardo said, "if you are not going to feed me, then I will have to go to Mama's."

Alane thought bitterly that it was she who had put this

weapon into her husband's hand. She would have to keep the dog now, or he would go to Mara's, and her plan to keep him to herself would be foiled.

Her lips tightened. "I am coming," she said, and went to scoop the stew from the pot.

Alane also prepared breakfast for her husband the following morning, and after they had eaten, Nardo began to gather his hunting weapons while Alane got ready to go to Mara's house.

"And what will you be doing today, Alane?" Nardo asked with careful courtesy as he finished sticking two small bone-pointed javelins through his belt.

Alane was pouring fresh river water into the water pot. "I told Lora I would help her gather grains today," she replied. Now that the moment had come to face her mother-by-marriage after her act of defiance, Alane found herself distinctly nervous. She put down the water basket, looked at Nardo's cheerful, oblivious face, and felt resentment well up in her heart.

"That's nice," he said with obtuse male good humor. "I'm glad to see that you and Lora are getting along. Having a friend will keep away homesickness."

Alane said shortly, "It is not easy, Nardo, adjusting to a completely new way of life."

"I understand that, Alane," he said, reaching for his spear, "and I remember how having Rune as a friend helped me when I was dwelling among your people. That is why I am pleased about you and Lora."

Alane was galled by the easy words. He understood nothing, she thought. Never in all his big, strong, spear-wielding life, had he been made to feel as alien and unwelcome as she felt every time she set foot in his mother's house. She said with irony, "I am glad you are pleased for me."

He completely missed the sarcasm and came to drop a kiss on the top of her head. "I will see you at supper," he said. "We had better eat at Mama's tonight or she will be upset." And he was gone.

Nardo, in fact, was not unaware of the problems his wife was having with his mother, but he had convinced himself that the tension between the two women would be resolved more quickly if he kept out of it. He found himself in the uncomfortable position of understanding both sides. He understood his mother's difficulty in accepting as her daughter a girl from the tribe that had murdered her brother. And he understood his wife's difficulty in living among women to whom she was not related by blood.

Part of Alane's problem, he told himself, was that they could not make love because she was still considered impure from childbirth. That taboo would be lifted at the next full moon, and Nardo hoped that the resumption of sexual relations would help to reconcile his wife to her new life. In the days before her pregnancy had become too advanced, they had discovered together an intense, heady passion that Nardo had never known with any other woman. He had convinced himself that the trouble he sensed between him and Alane would lift once he could hold her in his arms again.

So Nardo was waiting with great impatience for the full of Stallion Moon. He made a quick trip to summer camp during the second week of the month, definitely planning to be home before the all-important day, but then he was held up by a visit from Rilik, chief of the Atata Kindred. Rilik kept Nardo in conference until darkfall, and when Nardo awoke early on the day of the full moon, it was pouring. Dismissing the objections of his fellow clansmen, Nardo set out for the village accompanied only by Lora's husband, Dane.

"I hope you appreciate what I am doing for you," Dane grumbled as the two men rode their horses through the knee-deep mud that flanked the Narrow River. He hunched his back fruitlessly against the drenching downpour. The raindrops drummed noisily into the rushing gray water of the river.

"You are a true heart-friend, Dane," Nardo said. "And if you had not accompanied me, I would have gone alone."

"That is exactly why I came," Dane retorted. He wiped the rain away from his eyes. "The tribe's rule is that no one should travel alone. Can you imagine what Varic would say if he learned that you—the chief—had broken one of the tribe's rules?"

Silence fell as the two men rode on, the rain dripping off their faces and soaking their hair and clothes. Finally Nardo said,

"I do not understand Varic, Dane. We were never close, but we were never unfriendly. Yet now he takes every opportunity he can find to undermine my authority with the tribe."

"He is angry that you married into the Norakamo tribe," Dane said.

Bluebird tossed her head, sending even more water into Nardo's face. He cursed. Then he said forcefully, "Nevin might have been Varic's father, but he was *my* mother's brother. If I was able to place the good of the tribe above my grief, then surely Varic could do the same."

The horses' feet were making sucking sounds as they plowed through the mud. Dane sighed. "It is not just Nevin, Nardo. I think that Varic is jealous of you."

"He is acting as if he wants to be chief," Nardo said grimly.

"I don't know what Varic wants," Dane said. "I don't think even Varic knows that. I just think he is angry at you, and jealous of you, and so he tries to make life difficult for you. Have patience with him, Nardo. He will get over whatever it is that is bothering him."

"I hope it happens soon," Nardo said, "because I will tell you now, Dane, that my patience is fast wearing thin."

The rain let up a little in the late afternoon, but it was fully dark by the time the two young men rode into the Kindred village. Dane volunteered to get a few boys to take care of the horses, and Nardo took his saddlebag and went to his own hut, where he built up the fire, lit the lamps, spread out the sleeping skins, and left Samu. Then he proceeded to his mother's house.

"Nardo! You are soaked through!" Mara cried as soon as he had ducked inside. "Whatever were you thinking of, to travel in such weather?"

But Nardo's eyes, narrowed and intent, were fixed on his wife and not his mother. "I will change right away, Mama," he promised. Then, his voice deepening noticeably, "Alane?"

She knew very well why he had made this ride through the rain, he thought, but her face gave nothing away. His loins tightened when he saw her rising to her feet. "I will come and find you some dry clothes, Nardo," she said. The lamplight glinted off her silvery hair as she bent to pick up Nevin. Nardo watched the movement of her slim, flexible waist with hungry eyes.

"Come back after you have changed, and I will have some hot food for you," Mara was saying.

"Alane will feed me, Mama," he said. "There is no need for you to bother."

Then Alane was standing before him. She glanced up quickly, saw the unmistakable look in his eyes, and looked away. "Come," she said. "You must be freezing." He held the door skins for her and waited while she covered Nevin completely with a fur rug. Then husband and wife ducked out into the rain.

Their small hut was cozy with lamplight and fire warmth. "I see you have been busy," Alane said. She was still refusing to meet his gaze and bent to put Nevin into his nest of skins. Samu was already asleep in his own bed in the back corner.

Nardo said, "I wasn't home yesterday because Rilik surprised me by paying a visit to summer camp, and I had to stay."

Alane tucked a robe around the baby. "You didn't have to ride through the rain, Nardo. You could have waited until tomorrow."

"You know very well why I didn't wait," Nardo retorted. "I have waited long enough, it seems to me. Too long. Forever, in fact."

Finally she lifted her head to look at him.

"I would have ridden through a blizzard, Alane," he said.

The faintest smile played around her mouth. Her gray eyes looked very large and very dark. "Would you?" she asked softly.

He felt something rumble deep in his chest, and without another word he stripped his soaked shirt off over his head and started toward her. She lifted her face to him, and then he was kissing her eyelids and her cheeks and her mouth. Her arms locked around his neck. "Dhu, but I have missed you," he groaned.

"And I you." Her breath tickled his ear. He straightened up so that her feet swung right off the ground. Her whole body was pressed against his as he walked to where he had spread the sleeping skins earlier. He laid her down, then paused a moment to strip off his wet trousers. Then he was kneeling beside her, and she reached up to smooth her thumbs along the hard line of his cheekbones.

He began to untie the leather thong that held her skirt at the

waist. It loosened, and he pulled the skirt downward. Alane lifted
her hips to help him. Then, with swift, economical movements,
he got her out of her shirt as well. Her breasts were very white
and looked very full against the narrowness of her rib cage and
waist. He kissed her breasts, her ribs, her waist, and then his
mouth moved lower. She buried her fingers in his hair and gave
a little sob deep in her throat, a tiny noise that effectively shattered his control. He slid his hands under her hips, lifted, then
sheathed himself in her warm moistness. She arched up to meet
his thrust, her body instinctively knowing his rhythm, the two of
them giving and taking, giving and taking, until the final explosion of the senses that harrowed their souls and left them to lie
together in peace.

"I almost forgot—I brought you a gift," Nardo said much
later as they were once more lying quietly wrapped in each other's arms.

Alane's cheek was pressed against his bare shoulder. He could
feel her jaw move as she yawned. "You did? A gift?"

"Sa. Wait here and I'll get it."

Reluctantly she released him, and he got up and went to
where he had dropped his saddlebag last night. He was naked
and when he looked up from extricating his gift from the bag,
he found her watching him with possessive eyes. He smiled and
brought the gift back to her. She sat up to take it from his hands.

"Oh, Nardo." Her voice was soft as she looked with delight
at the beautiful necklace of golden shells. "It is lovely."

He said with satisfaction, "I thought you would like it."

She held it up to the firelight to admire it better. "I love it."

He watched her. "Dhu, Alane." His brown eyes were brilliant.
"I thought this full moon would never rise!"

She lowered the necklace and looked down at it. At some
point during the night he had undone her braid, and her loosened hair covered her nakedness like a silver cloud. When she
spoke again her voice was quiet. "It has been . . . lonely away
from you."

He knelt beside her. "It has been more than lonely. It has
been torture."

At that she put the necklace carefully aside and reached up
to run her fingers tenderly through the hair at his brow. It was

so thick and smooth that it poured through her fingers like water. In the corner, Samu moved restlessly. He had awakened earlier and come over to see what Nardo and Alane were doing. Nardo had not appreciated the interruption and had pushed him away rather roughly. "You are so beautiful," Nardo said to her now.

Alane recognized the look in his eyes. "Nardo," she said in amazement. "Not again!"

He nuzzled her neck. "Why not?"

Her head tilted back. Her breasts seemed to rise of their own accord into his hands. "We'll both be exhausted in the morning."

"You can sleep," Nardo said. His mouth was moving lower. "I'll take care of Nevin for you."

Alane made a noise indicating disbelief. But when he gently began to push her back to lie upon the skins, she went.

Chapter Eleven

Alane watched in silence as Mara reverently removed the fur wrappings from the strange objects that apparently meant so much to the Clan of the Wolf. They were the sacred fire sticks, Lora had told her, important religious symbols to be used at the tribe's great winter feast, New Year Rites.

It was cold outside, but the big house was hot from the body heat generated by all the clan members who had crowded into its limited space. Alane stood close to the large, solid bulk of Nardo and felt suddenly and enormously comforted when his big, warm hand closed around her small, cold one and held it safe.

Mara finished unwrapping the last of the fire sticks and placed it carefully on one of the two separate piles she had made on either side of the fire. Then the matriarch looked up from her work. The firelight underlit her face and cast shadows under her high, sharp cheekbones and around her eyes and her mouth.

"The Spirit of Fire is now in the care of the Wolf Clan," Mara intoned. "What must we do to keep him safe?"

A child's voice piped the ritual reply: "We will plant our sticks and nourish them."

"We will dance the fire dance to show ourselves worthy" came a woman's voice that Alane recognized as belonging to Tora.

Nardo's deep voice filled the crowded room: "We will keep the flame always, in memory of our ancestor who first stole fire from the gods."

A small silence fell as the clan contemplated its responsibilities. Then Mara said, "Now I will give out the fire sticks."

She began to call out names, and as each name was called the person went forward, took his or her stick from Mara, then formed up on either side of the house, women on one side, men on the other. When Nardo's name was called, and he dropped her hand and walked forward, Alane felt suddenly very lost and alone. Then her own name was called, and she approached her mother-by-marriage, whose dark eyes regarded her with such stern disapproval. Alane held her own gaze steady as she took the wooden stick with the strange geometrical pattern carved upon it and went to stand among the throng of women.

Never had Alane felt these Kindred people to be more alien as she went with the women of the Wolf Clan to plant their fire sticks in the tent the clan had erected behind the big house. Nor was it just the religious ceremony that seemed so bizarre. Even more peculiar to Alane was the fact that she and Nardo were the only married couple who were participating in this rite. In true matrilineal fashion, the husbands of Nardo's sisters and cousins were not united with their wives in the preparation for this important festival, but went instead to the houses of their mothers. On the other hand, Tora's two sons, Haras and Mano, were present without their wives.

To Alane, child of a patrilineal tribe, these family alignments by maternal clan were completely foreign. Indeed, the whole of Norakamo society was more individual than was the communally oriented Kindred world. The Norakamo simply did not have large community festivals. Alane had been brought up to believe that religious life was intensely personal, something that transpired between the individual and the spirit world. When she tried to explain this to Nardo, however, she could see that he thought her people lacked reverence. This made her angry, but the more she tried to explain, the more bewildered Nardo had become. Finally she had given up.

So even though she felt like an imposter, she carefully

imitated the other women of the Wolf and dug a hole and planted her fire stick. When she looked up from her work, it was to find Mara watching her with a forbidding expression on her face.

During the past two moons the tension between Alane and her mother-by-marriage had tightened. Mara resented bitterly the obvious sexual attraction that bound her son to his Nora-kamo wife, and Alane, well aware of Mara's feelings, resented in turn Mara's excessive maternal possessiveness. Every other adult in the household was aware of the strain between Nardo's mother and wife, but, to Alane's relief, the rest of the family seemed more interested in keeping the peace than in choosing sides.

"It is always hard for a mother to see that her son cares for another woman," Lora told Alane one day as they sat together in Alane's hut, making baskets and watching their babies. "That is why a son leaves his mother's household when he marries and goes to the household of his wife. Nardo did not do that, and so it is harder for Mara. You must have patience with her."

"In my tribe, husbands and wives set up their own house-holds," Alane replied. "Their loyalty is to each other, husband to wife and wife to husband."

Outside, a chill rain was falling. The women could hear it drumming against the wooden logs of the hut. They had closed the skins at the door to keep the cold and the wet out, and the hut was faintly smoky from the fire.

Lora shrugged. "A husband's loyalty is not the same as a brother's, Alane. We Kindred women have a saying that hus-bands may come and go, but your brother is your brother for-ever." She plaited a strip of birchbark as Alane had shown her, her lips mouthing silently, *Over two, under two, over three, under one* . . .

Alane's fingers flew without any mental effort on her part. "In my tribe, husbands do not come and go, Lora. Once you are married, you stay married."

Lora's fingers stopped and she looked up. "But what if hus-band and wife do not agree?"

Alane put down her basket, got to her feet and fetched her

broom from its place in the corner. Then she turned it upside down and used its long wooden handle to poke at the smoke hole over the hearthplace. She answered Lora as she stood on tiptoe, moving the broom up and down in an effort to clear away whatever was blocking the hole. "If they agree before they are wed, why should they not agree after?"

Lora's eyes were on the smoke hole. "Sometimes they don't," she replied. "Only look at my brother Haras and his wife, Fara. Haras has been spending most of his time in our household of late because he finds his wife's home so unpleasant."

"It is in my heart that Haras cares very much for Fara," Alane said. "It is her mother that he cannot get along with." The smoke hole being cleared to her satisfaction, she put the broom back in its proper place and returned to her seat by the hearth.

"He does care for Fara," Lora agreed. A faint hiss came from the fire as some rain fell on it. "But if he cannot get along with Fara's mother, then he cannot remain married to Fara."

"Do you mean they can simply end their marriage?"

"Of course."

Alane had picked up her basket and now her fingers began their intricate weaving once more. "How?"

"The usual way," Lora said. "Haras will take all his belongings and move back with his mother and his sisters."

Alane was silent. At last she said, "So you're saying, then, that Nardo's first loyalty must be to Mara and not to me."

"I am not saying that at all," Lora said hastily. "Your case is different."

"Sa," Alane agreed in a deceptively pleasant voice. "I can see that it is different. Nardo is already living with his mother and his sisters, so if our marriage fails, then it is I who must be the one to leave."

Now Lora was alarmed. "I don't know how we ever got upon this subject! Your marriage will not fail, Alane. All can see how Nardo feels about you."

Sa, Nardo likes to sleep with me, Alane thought bleakly. *But there is more to marriage than that.*

She was far too proud to discuss such a private matter with Lora, however, and so she smiled and leaned over to show Nardo's cousin where she had made a mistake in her weaving. By mutual consent both women began to talk of something else.

New Year Rites were celebrated by the Kindred at the winter solstice during the time the Kindred called the Moon When the Reindeer Lose Their Antlers. This festival, which encompassed a variety of different ceremonies, had as its unifying theme the idea of rebirth. Each of the tribe's six clans traditionally performed a particular one of the six different ceremonies that composed the festival. The Tribe of the Wolf performed the Lighting of the New Fire; the Tribe of the Red Deer performed the fertility right of Winter Fires; the Tribe of the Bear performed the Ritual of the New-Born Sun; the Tribe of the Fox performed the Dance of the Birth of the World; the Tribe of the Leopard performed the Battle of Sky God with the God of the Dead; and the Tribe of the Eagle prepared and administered the Initiation Ceremony for the young boys who were of proper age.

This was one of the two times in the year when the entire tribe of the Greatfish Kindred came together. The different horse herds were all brought back to the main village and pastured in a valley to the east of the Greatfish River. When the men were not hunting or on herd duty, they were working with their clans on preparations for New Year Rites.

During the week before the festival the members of the Wolf Clan went every morning and evening to the tent behind Mara's house to sprinkle sacred ashes on their fire sticks. The ashes, Nardo told Alane, represented the death of the old fire while the fire sticks themselves were the means by which the new fire would be born. There was also a dance to be performed by the clan which told the story of how the Wolf Clan's ancestor first obtained fire for humankind.

Mara had wanted Nardo to play the part of the hero, but he had been deeply disturbed by some news the traders had brought of a large group of people migrating down the River of Gold, and, much to Mara's annoyance, he had insisted on riding through the snows of the Buffalo Pass in order to confer with Rilik, chief of the Atata Kindred, on this subject. In Nardo's absence, Mano, the Wolf clan's representative to the clan council, practiced the main part in the dance.

Nardo returned to the village two days before the start of the New Year rite. Alane, who had given up hope of his return once dark had fallen, had taken Nevin to the big house for supper. She was sitting with Lora and Haras, picking at her stew and listening to Haras' comments about his troubles with his wife's mother. The troubles were serious, but Haras could be very funny about them. He was careful, however, not to tell his stories in front of Dane, who was Lina's son.

"The woman must have been born at the dark of the moon," he concluded his latest installment, and Alane laughed.

Delighted by her response, Haras opened his mouth to continue his saga when there was a sudden draft of cold air from the door as the skins were lifted and someone came in. Everyone turned and there was Nardo, the doorway completely hidden behind his great height and breadth. It must have begun to snow, for there was a sprinkling of white on the shoulders of his fur tunic and flakes frosted the top of his bare head.

"Nardo!" Mara cried. "You have made it back in time after all!"

Across the heated, smoky room his eyes sought Alane's. Then he stepped farther into the room and answered his mother, "I told you I would be back for the festival, Mama. You should not have doubted me."

"Riva," Mara said, "get your brother some food. He is cold and hungry."

Haras was getting to his feet. "Do you need help with the horses, Nardo?"

"I put them in the corral and gave them some dried grass. They are all right."

Haras sat down again.

"Here, Nardo," Riva said, coming back from the cook pot with a bowl of steaming stew. "Give me your furs." She waited while he took his tunic off, then handed him the stew and went herself to the door to beat the snow off his fur parka before she hung it up on the drying rack.

Alane sat in silence, watching as Riva waited on her brother. Dane's voice came from his place by the hearth. "What did you discover from Rilik?"

Nardo carried his stew over to Alane, and Haras made room

so Nardo could sit beside his wife. "Rilik has heard nothing," Nardo replied. The children seated together in the corner began to chatter again, and Nardo raised his voice. "After the festival I will see if the Norakamo know anything more."

All of the men nodded, and at last Nardo was free to turn to his wife. Before he could say anything, however, a small boy crawled purposefully over his feet, sat in front of Alane like a hopeful puppy, and said, "Alane, will you tell us a story?" It was Gar, Riva's four-year-old son, a particularly beautiful child with large hazel eyes in a face like a flower.

Alane recently had discovered in herself a hitherto unknown talent for storytelling. She had begun by telling some Norakamo stories to amuse the children one rainy afternoon, and once she had run out of traditional material, she had started to make up her own tales. Most of these stories centered around a horse called Swift As the Wind and a boy called Namen and the various adventures they had in the Land of the Horse God. The children were not the only ones who adored these stories; the adults were more often than not listening with riveted interest while Alane was speaking.

"I don't think Alane wants to tell any stories tonight, Gar," Nardo was beginning to say when he was interrupted by his wife's distinctly cool voice:

"Of course I can tell the children a story, Nardo. You eat the supper your sister has brought you." She got to her feet, took Gar's hand and went with him to the children's corner, where she settled herself to spin a story about the time Swift As the Wind and Namen had to rescue a little girl who had been stolen by bears. Beki held Nevin while Alane talked, rocking him competently when he began to cry, then putting him on her shoulder and patting his back. By the time her baby was returned to Alane, he was once more blissfully asleep.

"Another story! Another story!" the children shouted when Alane had finished. But Nardo's giant shadow passed over them as he bent to lift his wife to her feet.

"Not tonight," he said, genial but firm. "I am tired and I want my bed."

The children subsided. While Alane had initially been

shocked by the latitude the Kindred allowed their children, she had also noticed that when an adult did actually issue a command to them, their response was usually obedient, prompt and cheerful. Nardo went to the drying rack to collect their tunics, and Gar said to Alane, "Tomorrow will you tell us another story?"

"Tomorrow," she promised with a smile. Nardo held Nevin while she put her furs on, then waited while she swaddled the baby in a buckskin blanket and popped him into his warm pouch. Together they went out through the fur-hung doorway.

Mara's house, like the other big houses in the village, was surrounded by its own compound of smaller huts, and Alane and Nardo walked the short distance through blowing snow to reach their own abode. On a cold night like this many of the household families would choose to bed down in the big house, where there were many bodies to generate warmth. Alane, however, always slept in her own hut, even if Nardo was away.

"It should be fairly warm; I built up the fire before I went over to Mama's," Nardo murmured as he held aside the doorway skins for Alane to go in. She felt herself stiffen at his words. She knew very well why he had built up the fire, but she had no intention of falling into his arms tonight until they had discussed a thing or two.

Samu came forward to greet them, and Nardo fondled his large, pointed ears. Alane was still not reconciled to the dog, but she was no longer afraid of him. She handed Nevin to Nardo and said, "Put the baby in his nest, Nardo," and went herself to get some wood from the neatly stacked pile near the door. Keeping the woodpile was a woman's job, and in the cold weather it needed to be replenished every day.

As Nardo tucked Nevin in, Alane began to stack wood on the fire, which had burned low. After she had laid the last log she looked up and saw Nardo still kneeling beside his sleeping son. There was such an expression of pride and love on his face that Alane's heart trembled with tenderness.

He looked up and saw her watching him. "Shall I put down the sleeping skins?" he asked.

Alane's tenderness vanished. "Not yet," she said. "Come and sit by the fire. I have a few things I would like to talk to you about."

He looked as if he scented danger. "Certainly," he said, his obliging comment at variance with his watchful look. "What do you want to talk about?"

She seated herself on the hearth rug. "Haras and Fara."

The wary expression lifted from his face. "Haras and Fara? What about them?" He came to sit beside her.

"Lora says that their marriage will not outlast the winter."

"Probably it will not." He reached over to take one of her hands and laced her fingers with his. His thumb gently caressed her knuckles.

"Lora says that if Haras cannot get along with Fara's mother, then Haras must go."

Nardo's thumb stilled. "That is so," he replied cautiously.

Alane looked down at their entwined fingers. "What will happen to our marriage, Nardo, if I cannot get along with your mother?"

"Alane." He sounded both irritated and helpless. "You have only lived among us for some four moons. You must have patience with Mama. Remember that she has lost her brother and her husband. It is not easy for her to lose her son to a Norakamo wife."

Deep down in her heart Alane felt a dull throb of anger that he could be so sympathetic to Mara's trouble and so blind to her own. "Well, it is even less easy for me, Nardo," she said. "Mara is surrounded by her family, while I only have you. And you are never here!"

Nardo's head lifted as if he had just had a revelation. "You are angry because I went to see Rilik," he said.

"You don't understand," she said. "It isn't just the visit to Rilik. It is all those other days and weeks when you are at summer camp, or herding camp, or at a Gathering. If you are home one week out of a moon, that is a lot!"

He shrugged. "That is the way life is among my people, Alane. The women stay in one place while the men follow the animals."

The shrug infuriated her. "And when you do come home," she accused him, "all you want to do is sleep with me."

He was beginning to get angry too. "Of course I want to sleep with you! You're my wife!"

"How can I feel like a wife if I never see you? Even when you are home you spend half of your time with your family."

"That is the way of our tribe."

She pulled her hand away from his. "It is not the way of my tribe, however, and I don't like it."

"What do you want me to do, Alane? Ignore my mother? Turn my back on my sisters?" His voice was low so as not to wake the baby, but it reverberated with outrage.

She did not answer immediately, and the only sounds in the tent were the sucking noises Nevin was making in his sleep. Finally Alane said wearily, "I can see that this discussion is pointless, Nardo. I suppose you had better put out the sleeping skins."

He didn't move. "I know this is hard for you," he said.

It was her turn to shrug. "I have just told you that it is."

He stared at her aloof profile. "I will try to be home more frequently, Alane."

She didn't look at him. "That would be nice."

He cast her a baffled look, then got up and went to pull the sleeping skins from their place along the wall. She did not help him but sat staring into the fire.

"I suppose there is no reason why we cannot take our supper together in our own hut," he said after the skins had been spread. "Would that make it better for you?"

At that, she looked up. "Sa," she said. "It would."

"Very well, then, we will do that."

"Your mother will not like it," she warned.

He sighed. "I know. But she will grow accustomed, Alane. You are right when you say that she has the rest of her family to support her." He gave her a crooked smile. "I am sorry if I have been a bad husband to you, Alane. I did not mean to be."

"I know, Nardo," she replied softly.

He held out his arms and she rose swiftly to her feet and went to him. They stood thus for a long time, locked together in a tight embrace. In his corner, Samu began to snore.

Alane stiffened. "Nardo," she said. "That dog is snoring."

He replied with his lips pressed to her hair. "If you want to see more of me, Alane, then you will have to resign yourself to seeing more of Samu."

Slowly the stiffness melted from her spine. She lifted her face. "I suppose I will get used to him," she said. Then his mouth came down upon hers, and Alane forgot about everything that was not Nardo.

Chapter Twelve

It was the deepest part of winter when the Redu arrived at the place called by the local tribes Big Rivers Joining. Here the Atata, one of the major rivers of the mountains, flowed into the River of Gold, commingling their waters for the remainder of their long journey to the sea. Soon the plain around the rivers was covered with the tents of the invaders, and the hunters went forth to bring in food.

It had been a hard trek, but the Redu were accustomed to hardship. The hunting along the River of Gold had, in fact, been better than the winter hunting in their own lands. A few of the children had died, and some of the women, but the tribe had actually survived the trek far better than Kerk had dared to hope. He had lost only one warrior and that had been to a hunting accident.

The tribes that dwelt along the river had scattered before them, evacuating their camps before the overwhelming numbers of the invading force. There had been fewer camps and fewer people than Kerk had expected, but the dearth of reindeer along the river was eloquent testimony as to why this was so.

There had been little snow to impede their progress, and the game they had taken was mainly red deer with some elk and some horses. They had been lucky to find a herd of buffalo the previous week, and the resulting kill had given them enough meat to last for quite some time. If buffalo had been plentiful along the river, there would have been little need to attempt the mountains. But last week's kill had been the first buffalo the Redu had seen. Kerk could not count on feeding his people with buffalo.

It had to be the mountains, then. He stood with his legs braced, facing south, his son at his side. The wind blew full into their faces, coming off the mountains. The sky above was hard and bright, with white clouds racing swiftly northward. Kerk flexed his fingers within his fur mittens. The traders had told him that either of these rivers would take him where he wanted to go.

They had said also that the horsemen who dwelled in the mountains were almost as numerous as the Redu. It was not likely that they would give over their land without a fight.

"I will wait until the weather is warmer before I move farther south," Kerk said to Paxon. "It is hard to pull the strings of a bow when your fingers are frozen." He turned his back to the wind and scanned the land to the east. "There is game enough here for now, and we have the buffalo meat if we need it. I will wait for one more moon. Then we will finish our journey."

Paxon put the weeks spent at Big Rivers Joining to good use, spending much of his time with the captive traders and learning their language. Kerk's son was fascinated by the fact that these mountain men rode on horseback, and looked forward eagerly to the possibility of capturing one of these tame horses and learning to ride himself.

It rained at the end of Shadow Moon, then it grew very cold, and a thick layer of ice lay over the land, making it impossible for the grazing animals to break through to the grass below. It was a good time for wolves.

"It is time to go," Kerk said to Paxon, and at the beginning of the Moon When the Bear Awakens, the Redu were ready to attempt the mountains. Kerk had chosen to follow the Atata, for the traders assured him that the numbers of horsemen dwelling on this river were less than those who lived along the River of Gold.

The full moon rode high in the winter sky, and the tribe's dogs sat on their haunches in front of their cave, their eyes half shut, their heads tilted toward the sky. Rogh, the leader, gave a single sharp signal cry, and then they all began to howl in chorus. It was a noise that started deep in the throat, a long, hoarse yowl that modulated through a variety of notes over a period of three to four minutes. Then all of a sudden it was over.

Alane had stopped what she was doing to listen to the eerie chorus. Tonight, after silence had fallen, she heard one of the puppies yelp again. He quickly fell silent, however, as he realized his mistake. The dogs howled only once.

This nightly song of the pack fascinated Alane. Was it a prayer? she wondered. A supplication to their god?

Soon they would all go back into the cave, where they would curl up to sleep. In winter the dogs all slept with their noses buried under their bushy tails to warm the air before it entered their noses. Nardo said they uncurled gradually as the year progressed, so that by summer they were sleeping stretched out, with their nose and tail as far apart as possible.

The winter had been good for Alane. True to his word, Nardo had braved his mother's displeasure and taken his meals in his hut with his wife. This sign of his concern for her needs had made Alane feel much more secure in her husband's love, and for her part she had done her best to fit in with his family. This had not been as difficult as she had feared. She liked the children. She got along with Nardo's sisters, and she had actually become good friends with his cousin Lora.

In fact, she was so happy with the improvement in her marriage that one day she advised Haras to ask Fara to try fixing him supper in their hut. Haras took her advice, and the result was that they saw him less and less in the Wolf household as he spent more time with his wife.

The winter passed and the days began to grow longer. During the day the hills behind the village resounded with foxes' harsh, piercing mating calls, and at night wolves howled with end-of-winter hunger. The bears were out of hibernation, thin and hungry from their long winter's sleep.

The animals knew that winter was ending, that the new life of spring was within their grasp. In the village of the Kindred on the Greatfish River, the tribe also felt the spring. The children, who had spent the cold winter days in the big house playing, the

boys with knucklebones and wooden horses, the girls with dolls
and miniature huts, moved outside to hold races and play ball
with an air-filled deer stomach. The frozen meat which had fed
the tribe all winter began to thaw, and the women dried what
was left over a wood fire, then pounded it up and preserved it
by pouring it over hot fat.

It would be another moon before the grass began to grow
again, before the waterfowl arrived on the river, before the
salmon began to run. But spring was coming, and anticipation
was in the air.

One chill, blustery day Nardo and Dane arrived in the village
with a train of packhorses loaded with fresh meat for the women
and children of the village households. The men were unloading
the horses to the accompaniment of a chorus of comments from
a pack of children when they all heard the sound of hooves coming along the river from the east. All heads turned in surprise;
the Kindred camps east of the village were unoccupied in the
winter. In a few moments a party of four riders, each of them
leading two remounts, cantered into sight.

Nardo recognized the lead rider's horse. "It's Rilik!" he said
in astonishment, and went forward alone to greet the chief of
the Atata Kindred.

"We have been invaded," Rilik said grimly, and jumped off
his horse.

Nardo looked instantly alert. "Invaded?"

"Sa. A strange tribe came down the Atata and settled at our
spring camp, Nardo. There are a great number of them."

Nardo called to the oldest children and told them to care for
the horses. The men who were unloading the meat had stopped
with the interruption, and Nardo told them to continue with
their work. He glanced around, hesitated as his eyes fell on his
mother's house, then said to Rilik and his men, "Come into my
hut and tell me about it."

The hut was bright with the light of two stone lamps, and a
fire burned in the hearth, giving off warmth as well as more light.
Alane was within, sitting by one of the lamps and sorting through
some children's clothing that Lora had given to her. Samu,
whom Nardo had sent out of reach of the smell of meat, was

curled up beside her. Alane looked up in surprise as Nardo came in followed by a group of strange men.

"Ah," said one of the younger Atata men involuntarily as he took in the picture before him, "this is nice."

Nardo looked around for a moment, trying to see his home through the eyes of this stranger. The hut, as usual, was immaculate: the fur rugs had been shaken out, the cooking utensils were lined up neatly on the stone hearthplace, the sleeping skins were rolled and stacked in the corner, and the drying rack was tidily piled with mittens and furs. All the household items not in use were stored in the beautiful baskets that lined the walls.

Samu came over to sniff Nardo. The light from the lamp fell on Alane's hair and illuminated her face. She was looking at him with a question in her eyes.

"These men have ridden all the way from the Atata, Alane," he said to her. "Do you think you could make them some tea?"

"Of course," she replied. She folded the small clothes back into a basket and moved toward the fire. All of the Atata men watched her, but Alane no longer found the gaze of strange men as unsettling as it had once been. "Perhaps you should take their furs, Nardo," she said gently. "It is warm in here."

As the men piled their fur tunics on the drying rack, Alane filled a big stone kettle with water from the water pot and hung it from a wooden frame so it was suspended over the fire. She began to set out some deerbone cups.

"Where is Nevin?" Nardo asked.

"Lora has him."

The men turned away from the drying rack, and Nardo invited them to sit down.

They sat as if they were very weary.

"So," Nardo said to Rilik. "Tell me."

Rilik rubbed his hand across his eyes. He was a powerfully built man of about thirty with a strong, intelligent face, steady hazel eyes and light brown hair worn to his shoulders. "It is as I said before," he answered. "A whole host of people came down the Atata. They have settled at our spring camp—have taken it over, Nardo, as if it belonged to them!" The hazel eyes were bright with indignation. "I rode up the river to see them for myself before I came to tell you. They have taken over all the caves and rock shelters of our camp, with many additional tents to house their numbers."

"I am thinking that these must be the people I heard of," Nardo said, "the ones who were traveling down the River of Gold."

"Perhaps. All I can tell you is that there are far more of them than there are of us."

"Did you try to talk to them?"

"Harl and I," Rilik gestured to the man beside him, "went to talk to them under a green branch. They have some traders with them who speak our tongue, and they told us that these people, who are called the Redu, have come from a distant land in the far west. The reindeer no longer come to their hunting grounds, and so they have decided to find new hunting grounds in our mountains. Their chief had the nerve to say, through the trader, that we must leave!"

Alane's low-pitched voice said, "The tea is ready."

She had made the mint tea of her own people, and the men of the Atata Kindred sniffed it inquisitively and then drank it with pleasure. "This is very good," the youngest of them said to Alane.

For a brief moment she met his eyes directly and answered, "I am glad you like it."

Nardo drained his own cup. "What are you going to do about these Redu?" he asked Rilik.

"I have heard that the Norakamo had an invasion such as this into their hunting grounds," Rilik said. "I have come to find out from you how they handled it."

Nardo told him. "Even if they outnumber you, the horses will make the difference," he concluded. "Men on foot cannot stand against horses."

"They outnumber us by almost four to one," the man called Harl said grimly.

"If you want the aid of the Greatfish Kindred," said Nardo, "you have only to ask for it."

For the first time since he had come into the hut, Rilik smiled.

"That is the other reason why I have come."

Mara was angry. At first she had not believed Beki when the child told her that Nardo had taken the visitors to his wife's hut. But then she discovered that Beki had spoken true. It did not placate Mara that Nardo had sent word that he was bringing them to her house for supper. Nothing changed the fact that they had first spent several hours in Alane's house, and that Nardo had also sent for Mano, her sister's son, to join them there.

Alane came in with the men at suppertime, and Mara closed her lips hard as she saw how the strangers all looked with covert admiration at Nardo's wife. Over the last half year Mara had learned to her sorrow just how dangerous that beautiful face could be.

He had taken the men to his wife's house. Not to his mother's.

It seemed like such a small thing. So small that Mara knew if she upbraided Nardo, she would sound petty and unreasonable. So she served supper to her guests and held her tongue, but all the while her memory was recalling the scene that had taken place between her and Nardo on the day she had reproached him for not taking his supper in the big house with the rest of the family.

She had deliberately sought an occasion to speak to him away from the house, and the opportunity had arisen late one snowy afternoon when she had seen him standing by himself along the river watching the small herd of mares and foals that had recently been brought to the village from one of the winter camps. Nardo had turned Bluebird loose among the horses so she could be reunited with her mother, and as Mara approached the corral, the pair had lovingly intertwined their heads and necks, all the while nipping each other and nickering ecstatically.

"Horses never forget their mothers," Mara said as she came up to stand beside her son. They stood together regarding the hobbled mares, who were quietly grazing on the sparse winter grass. Nardo smiled and put an arm around his mother's shoulders. Snow began to fall gently, and the flakes ignited a spark of adventure in the unhobbled foals, who started to race around with great excitement. Nardo and Mara watched in silence as the foals reared and whirled and kicked, squealed and raced, skidded to a stop, spun and then rushed off again. The wind was blowing off the Altas, and the air felt frigid. Mara leaned into the warmth of Nardo's side.

"I have missed you of late," she said at last. "You no longer come to my house for your supper."

He sighed. "Mama, you have to understand how difficult coming to live with us has been for Alane. You have been kind to her, I know, but she feels it very deeply that she has no blood tie to the women of our household. She has left her mother and blood kin behind, and in her heart she feels that Nevin and I are the only ones in this place who belong to her. She needs to have me to herself for a little. Do you see?"

"She will never feel herself a part of our family if she separates herself from us like this, Nardo," Mara said reasonably.

He gave her shoulders a gentle squeeze. "She will adjust, Mama. You must just give her time." He nodded at the horses in front of them. "A new mare always has a hard time when first she enters an established herd. You know that."

Mara frowned, trying to find the words to best express her fears. "It is not that I do not wish you to be a good husband, Nardo," she began, "but don't you see that such behavior is a challenge to the Mother's Blood way of our tribe? Alane's ways are the ways of a Father's Blood people. They are . . . dangerous to us."

"You exaggerate, Mama," Nardo said, and Mara could hear the impatience in his voice. "The fact that I am eating my supper in my own hut scarcely constitutes a challenge to the way of life of our tribe."

She did not back down. "I am greatly fearful that it does."

He dropped his arm. "Dhu, Mama, have you thought that if I had married a Kindred girl, I would never eat my supper in your house?"

"You would not be eating in my house, but in the house of your wife's *mother*," she replied logically. "Not in your wife's hut."

Silence fell between them. Two of the foals reared on their hind legs and struck out at each other in play. This time when Nardo spoke, his voice was dangerously quiet. "Mama, please do not put me in the position of having to choose between you and Alane."

Mara was sorely tempted to ask him whom he would choose if ever they should come to such a pass, but she was afraid of hearing his answer.

This scene was vividly in her mind as Mara regarded her son as he sat around her hearth with the household men and the guests from the Atata Kindred. As she watched, Dane leaned forward to say something to him, and Nardo grinned.

She remembered how, late on the night of her discussion with Nardo, the storm had increased. Inside her warm, dry house Mara had thought of the mares and babies outside. They would be standing with their heads lowered, shoulders hunched, rears turned to the wind, the foals pressed up against their mothers' sides. Suddenly, for a reason she couldn't explain, Mara had wanted to see them. Murmuring an excuse to her sister, she put on her fur tunic, pulled up the hood, and stepped outside.

The scene by the river was just as she had pictured it to be. As she watched, one of the foals thrust his head under his mother, seeking the security of warm milk. The mare turned her head, the wind blowing her forelock and long mane almost straight back, and rested her mouth on his haunches, protecting him as best she could from the storm.

Tears had stung Mara's eyes and frozen on her cheeks. She had pulled her tunic closer and hunched her shoulders. "You are an old fool," she had said to herself. But within, her heart had bled and bled.

She looked now at Nardo's grin, and her heart cramped with love and hurt.

He should not have taken these men to his wife's house, she thought. *He should have brought them to me.*

Chapter
Thirteen

Rilik and his companions remained in the village for two more days, sleeping in the initiates' cave and conferring with Nardo and his council. Each of the tribe's six clans were represented on this council: Varic for the Eagle Clan, Freddo for the Red Deer Clan, Mano for the Wolf Clan, Nat for the Bear Clan, Hamer for the Leopard Clan, and Matti for the Fox Clan. Nardo had sent to winter camp for these men, and they had ridden into the village at suppertime on the second day of Rilik's stay.

Nardo had been the only Kindred witness to the Norakamo defeat of the invasion of the Horse Eaters, and after supper he explained carefully to the others how that victory had come about. The men had eaten in the big house and then adjourned to Nardo's hut, where they sat, comfortably full and warm, around a small fire. Alane and the baby had remained behind at Mara's; Samu had accompanied Nardo and lay now with his eyes closed and his muzzle on Nardo's thigh.

"You never confronted all of the tribes together, then," Rilik said when Nardo had finished.

"That is right. We attacked their hunting party first, and then we attacked their camp with fire. They could not retaliate because of the horses. I am thinking that a series of quick strikes, such as the ones carried out by the Norakamo, would be very effective."

"You were greatly outnumbered, you say?"

"Sa."

"If your men will join with us," Rilik said, "we will be almost equal in number to these Redu."

"What is it you are thinking, Rilik?" Freddo asked. He was a tall, gaunt man, with small, dark, almond-shaped eyes that glittered like obsidian in his long, narrow face.

"I am thinking that these Redu will not be so easy to chase away as were the Horse Eaters," Rilik replied. "They have made a daring choice, to travel far from home to our mountains. It will take more than a few raids to turn them away."

Silence fell as the men contemplated that remark.

Rilik said bluntly, his eyes on Nardo, "I would like to strike one great blow against this tribe, and cut the heart out of them."

Nardo nodded and leaned forward to push a stick deeper into the fire. "We are bound to lose some of our own men if we do that," he said. Samu, whose resting place had been disturbed, lifted his head and blinked.

Harl said scornfully, "You can back us up if that is what you want. The men of the Atata Kindred are not afraid to take the burden of the fight."

The men of the Greatfish Kindred bristled, and Rilik frowned warningly at Harl.

Mano of the Wolf Clan, the twenty-eight-year-old son of Nardo's aunt, glanced sideways at Nardo, then said, "I like the idea of setting fire to their camp."

"This camp is not set up the way Nardo has described the camp of the Horse Eaters," Rilik responded. "That camp was pitched on open pastureland. The Redu camp has the river before it and behind it are cliffs. It is impossible to come at them in any numbers because there is too little space between the cliff and the river for many horses to maneuver."

Nardo grunted, picturing in his mind the scene as Rilik described it. "What about attacking their hunting parties?" he said.

"We could do that," Rilik agreed. "They seem to be mainly hunting along the river, however. Again, there would be little room to maneuver the horses. I do not think we could hurt them enough to cause them to retreat."

Varic spoke up for the first time. "What do you suggest we do then, Rilik?"

"They are arrogant, these Redu," Rilik replied. "Their chief stood beside the trader who spoke for him, and I could tell by the look on his face that he scorned us." Anger was audible in the Atata chief's voice, and his hazel eyes glittered with it. "I am thinking that if we challenged him to a battle, one tribe against the other, he would be foolish enough to accept."

Murmurs of excitement came from most of the men.

"I do not know if that is a good idea," Nardo said.

Varic blew out of his nose in noisy exasperation.

Rilik leaned toward his fellow chief, anxious to convince him. "The Redu chief will not know that we have increased our numbers," he said. "Those traders—may the Mother curse them!—have probably told him the numbers of the Kindred band that dwells along the Atata. He will not know that we have been joined by our kin from the Greatfish."

"Rilik has a point, Nardo," said Nat, a man of thirty-five who had the typical Bear Clan looks: a strong, square face with light brown hair and eyes. "If this chief is really that arrogant, he might discount the effect of our horses."

Varic said forcefully, "I like the idea."

The discussion continued, with the men becoming more and more enthusiastic as the minutes passed. All of the men of the Greatfish Kindred had badly missed the excitement that horse raiding among the Norakamo had once provided. Obviously they felt that this new venture promised to offer some of the adventure and challenge they were missing.

Nardo felt his own blood rising to Rilik's challenge, but his brain kept saying that it would be wiser to test the fighting skills of these Redu with a raid first. He said as much and was instantly accused by Varic of being overcautious.

"I am not being overcautious," Nardo said angrily. "I am being prudent."

But the rest of the men, who still resented Nardo's keeping them out of the fight against the Horse Eaters, agreed with Varic. Faced with such a united front, Nardo had no choice but to agree to Rilik's suggestion.

"We will need to decide the ground we want to fight on," he

said, trying to assert some leadership. "And we will need also to prepare a plan of attack, decide on our weapons and on how we will use our horses."

"We will do all that," Rilik promised. He looked around the council. "Can we depend upon your support, then?"

"Sa, the men of the Greatfish Kindred will stand with you, Rilik," Varic said grandly, and, as Nardo sat silent, the men of the council agreed.

After Rilik and his men had left the village, Nardo and the men of the council rode to the tribe's two winter camps in order to choose the men who would go with them through the Buffalo Pass and into the country of the Atata. The council had promised Rilik they would join him within the space of half a moon, and within a few days the village was filled with men preparing for a battle.

For the first time since Alane had come to the Kindred village, she and Mara found themselves in agreement. Neither of them liked Rilik's idea of issuing a battle challenge and neither was shy about voicing her skepticism. Nardo, who had doubts about the strategy himself, defended it stoutly against the female criticism. In this he was backed up by the other young men of the household.

"And what is Rilik planning to do?" Mara asked bitterly as they all sat together over supper the evening the men returned from winter camp. "Gallop full speed into a herd of men who are armed with spears and javelins?" She glared at her son. "It will not be like killing reindeer, Nardo! These men will fight back."

"I know that, Mama," Nardo said patiently. "But consider the weight of a horse. That alone is sufficient to knock a man down and render him incapable of defending himself."

"Can you count on controlling your horses under such circumstances?" Riva asked. Her four-year-old son, Gar, was sitting on her lap and listening with big eyes to the adult discussion.

"As Mama just pointed out," Nardo replied to his sister, "our horses are accustomed to hunting reindeer, which are much larger than men."

"Reindeer are quiet," Harlan commented.

A lamp was at Nardo's elbow, underlighting his face in a way that emphasized his cheekbones and lashes. He turned to his aunt's husband and replied evenly, "Our horses will obey their riders."

Alane had been staring at her husband's lamplit face. Since their marriage she had never criticized or disagreed with him in public, but now she bit her lip and said softly, "I fear this plan of Rilik's. It is too dangerous. Why do you not do what my people did when they pushed out the Horse Eaters? My father did not lose a single man, Nardo."

Mara said firmly, "I agree with Alane. The Norakamo successfully pushed back an invasion. Rilik should copy their tactics."

Alane turned to Mara. "And those tactics were Nardo's idea, my mother," she said.

Mara raised her level black eyebrows. "You never told me that, Nardo."

He waved his hand as if that was not important. "I did suggest to Rilik that he follow the Norakamo plan, but the situation faced by the Atata Kindred is different from that faced by the Norakamo. The land where the Redu are encamped is steep; it is not the open pastureland that made the invading river valley people so vulnerable to attack."

"How many of our men are you taking?" Riva asked. Her pensive face looked even sadder than it usually did.

"Most of the hunters," Nardo replied. He turned to his mother. "Do not worry, we will not be gone long, and I will leave at least one man to hunt for each household. The village will be fed."

Mara surprised everyone by saying, "You are thinking like Nevin in this, Nardo, and not like Rorig. That is a mistake."

Nardo's mouth tightened, and he did not reply.

The men spent the next few days choosing which horses they would take and readying their weapons. Once the decision to support Rilik had been made, Nardo cast aside his doubts and let his own enthusiasm for a good fight come to the fore. Citing his prior experience with the Horse Eaters, he was able to assert his leadership over the expedition, and one of his first orders was that every man must carry an ax.

"If they do not scatter and run after the horses hit them, there will be hand-to-hand fighting," he told his men. "It will be much more effective to swing down with an ax from horseback than to strike with a spear. A spear has to penetrate deeply in order to kill, and then it must be pulled back. A man's head can be smashed open with an ax. It will be just as deadly and much quicker." And he made them gallop up and down the river, practicing swinging the ax as they went. All of the men of the Kindred were superb horsemen, and even though they rode bareback, their seats were secure enough to enable them to wield their axes in the way Nardo wanted.

The night before the war party was to leave the village, Nardo sat in his hut changing one of the leather thongs that bound his sharp stone ax head to its short wooden handle. Nevin lay on a rug beside him, small rump in the air, working on getting his legs under him so he could crawl. Samu lay on his rug in the corner, watching Nevin with bright and curious eyes. Alane was repairing a tear in the small tent Nardo was going to take with him.

They would be traveling light, each man carrying but a small tent, a water bag made of salmon skin, dried meat which had been pounded and mixed with reindeer fat to preserve it, an extra shirt and trousers, a spear, a javelin and the ax.

Nevin crowed with delight as he was successful in pushing himself up on his legs, and Samu's ears pricked so far forward they almost touched. Alane said, "The tent is finished, Nardo."

"Good. Now I won't be dripped on while I sleep."

"Getting wet is the least of the things that may befall you on this adventure," Alane said bitterly. In the privacy of their home she had been far more disapproving than she allowed herself to be in the company of others.

"Da!" Nevin said in triumph. "Da, da, da, da!" Abruptly he fell on his stomach; his look of surprise was comical.

Nardo laughed and leaned over to scoop up his son with large, strong hands. "Stop nagging me, Alane," he said as he raised the delighted baby into the air.

Alane was incensed. "Do you know what makes me angriest about all of this, Nardo?"

"I am sure you are going to tell me." He shook the baby a little, and Nevin shrieked with excitement.

"You are going to make him sick," Alane said coldly.

"He likes it," Nardo said.

"He is like his father in that."

"In what?" Nardo gave her a puzzled look.

"In liking what is not good for him."

Nardo lifted the baby high once again. Nevin hiccuped and spat up some milk.

"I told you so," said Alane, and went to get a piece of buckskin to wipe her son's mouth.

Nardo relinquished Nevin to her and watched her gentle hands as she dealt with the overexcited baby. He felt a pang of guilt as Nevin spat up again.

Silence fell as Alane got Nevin ready for sleep. Samu closed his eyes. Nardo finished checking his ax and put it beside his other weapons, ready for the morning. Nevin finally fell asleep and Alane came back to the fire.

"I'm sorry I upset him," Nardo said.

She nodded without looking at him.

"Alane," Nardo said softly, "are we going to part in anger?"

Her chin came up. Her eyes were as darkly smoke-colored as her brows. "You are looking forward to this," she accused him. "That is what makes me so angry."

"Nonsense," he said.

"You are. Your eyes have been bright as stars ever since you launched this plan."

He grinned. "That is lust you see in my eyes," he said, and reached for her.

For a moment she resisted him, but then, as he knew would happen, her body softened, melted, and blended into his. She was so beautiful, he thought, and she always yielded to him with such heart-shattering sweetness. He did not think his passion for her would ever be satisfied. His hands pulled the velvet that tied her braid. He loved her hair, loved to touch it, loved to feel its smooth silkiness against his face.

"Nardo," she said. Her hands clutched him and her voice was constricted. "Dhu, Nardo, I am so afraid."

Poor little girl, he thought tenderly. She was afraid for him.

"There is nothing to be afraid of, little one," he said confidently. "Nothing is going to happen to me. I promise you that." And his mouth moved to find the smooth skin of her throat.

The Redu had settled around the large cave on the east side of the Atata River that the tribe of the Kindred used each year as one of its spring camps. The mountains were cliff-like in this area, running from east to west, and on its journey from the Altas to the River of Gold the river had cut a north-south gorge in the cliff wall. The cave that formed the Kindred spring camp was located high in this gorge.

The Redu had realized immediately that the cave was used as a hunting camp by one of the area tribes; the signs of recent human occupation were unmistakable. The reason why this cave had been chosen for a hunting camp was obvious also, for there were reindeer in the area. Large herds of reindeer, which moved up and down the river and were easy to corral and kill in the confines of the gorge. The Redu were ecstatic. They had not seen so many reindeer in years. Kerk, who had kept the captive traders alive while he needed their guidance, had them killed so they could not give information about the Redu to the neighboring tribes.

Paxon was on guard duty the morning that Rilik and a few companions approached the camp, and he stared in amazement at the men who sat so easily and naturally upon the backs of horses. Kerk's son had been upriver hunting the last time the horsemen had made an appearance, so he had not yet had a chance to see this phenomenon for himself. The horses stood so quietly and calmly under the weight of the men, controlled, it seemed, only by a leather strap around their noses. Amazing, Paxon thought. Amazing.

The horsemen were approaching from the south. The camp could be reached only by the trail along the river, for the cliffs on either side of the gorge made coming in from the east or the west impossible. This strategic location had been one of the reasons Kerk had chosen this particular cave as his base; the Redu chief was able to post guards to watch the north and the south entrances to the gorge and feel confident that no intruders would be able to slip up on him unaware.

Paxon took a moment to ascertain that each of the horsemen was carrying a green branch before he ran to inform his father about the visiting peace party.

Kerk was practicing shooting with his two closest friends, Madden and Wain, and three of their left-hand men when Paxon finally located him near the north end of the gorge. The men had set up the buckskin targets along the river, so they would have to shoot into the wind, and as Paxon approached he saw Kerk raise his long bow, draw back the plaited sinew bowstring, and let his arrow fly. It found its home in the dead center of the buckskin target one hundred yards away.

Paxon smiled. The horsemen coming up the river were carrying javelins, not bows. A javelin thrown with the aid of a spear thrower could go perhaps fifty yards. An arrow shot from one of the Redu bows, with the wind behind it, would go three times that distance.

"Father!" Paxon said, and once he had Kerk's attention he delivered his news.

The chief listened with a faint frown, then directed Paxon, Madden and Wain to come with him to meet the horsemen. The other three archers in the target-shooting party were ordered to gain the cliff, where Paxon had been stationed, in order to cover the river path. Once the archers were in position, Kerk and his party began to walk along the river path. On Kerk's orders they had left their bows behind and were carrying spears instead. Behind his back Paxon could hear the frightened voices of the women and children as they learned of the approaching horsemen and scurried up the cliff and into the shelter of the deep cave.

Kerk halted well within arrow range of the cliff where his bowmen were hidden, folded his arms across his chest, and watched the horsemen approach. The sun overhead burnished the taut copper-colored skin at the angles of Kerk's eagle face, and the wind blew his long black hair. The horsemen halted at a little distance, and the men regarded one another across the empty space between them. Then Kerk grunted impatiently, and Paxon raised his voice and spoke in a guttural but understandable Kindred Speak, "What you want?"

The horsemen stared at him in obvious surprise. Paxon understood. With his narrow, brown face, high cheekbones and thin, arched nose, he was clearly of Kerk's blood, and yet he spoke their language. "I learn your speak from traders," he said haughtily. "What you want?"

The big, powerfully built man with the light brown hair answered, "I am Rilik, chief of the Atata Kindred. This is our camp you have taken. I am here to tell you that you must leave this place. Leave our camp and leave our mountains."

Paxon translated for Kerk, all the while keeping his eyes on the horsemen and speaking out of the side of his mouth. The five horses facing them were all chestnuts, and the color of their shaggy winter coats blended with the buckskin trousers of the men who sat on them, making it difficult to see at first glance that man and horse were not one creature. Paxon was fascinated.

"Tell him," Kerk said, "that I grow weary of these pointless visits. We have no intention of leaving these mountains."

Paxon translated. The brown-haired man, who was riding the heaviest horse and who seemed to be their leader, replied, "Your presence here is both an insult and a threat. If you will not leave of your own will, then we will have to force you out."

When Kerk heard this, he laughed. Even with the distance between them, Paxon could see the veins in the other chief's neck cord with anger at that taunting laugh. His horse, sensing his rider's emotion, began to fidget. Kerk said to Paxon, "Ask him how he plans to accomplish such a thing."

"We are a tribe who follows the Way of the Mother," the Kindred chief answered. "We have not attacked your camp because we do not hunt women and children. I say to you now, let the men from both our tribes meet face to face in open conflict, and then we shall see who is left to call these mountains their home."

"Say again," Paxon said, to make certain he had understood. When the challenge had been repeated, Paxon relayed it to his father.

Kerk looked thoughtful. "Ask him where he wants this fight to be held," he told Paxon.

After Rilik had answered, Paxon said, "He says there is open grassland on the other side of the river to the south. He says that will be a good place for our tribes to meet."

Madden, who was on Kerk's other side leaning casually on his spear, said, "He thinks he can ride us down with the horses."

"Why don't we have our men on the cliff shoot their horses dead right now?" Wain said. "The fools are well within the range of our bows."

"They don't know that," Kerk returned. "The traders said these people have only small bows, good for shooting birds. They have no knowledge of bows such as ours. They use javelins for hunting larger game. See how careful they have been to keep themselves out of reach of a javelin throw."

Madden snorted with derision as he measured the distance between the horsemen and the Redu.

"I say it will be to our advantage to agree to this battle," Kerk said. "If we eliminate the local tribe, we will no longer have to watch our backs."

"That is true," Madden agreed.

"I also would like to capture a few of those tame horses they ride. Such horses would be extremely useful to us."

Paxon's dark eyes glowed as he assessed the mounted figures before him. How powerful it would make a man feel to ride upon the back of a horse!

"Say to these men that we will meet them in battle on the day of the full moon," Kerk instructed Paxon.

Paxon conveyed this message and waited while the horsemen conferred. After a short while Rilik announced his agreement. Soon after that the horsemen departed. The Redu watched the retreating figures with deep satisfaction in their hearts.

Rilik sent a messenger to Nardo asking him to make haste, and three days before the full of the moon, two hundred men of the Greatfish Kindred rode into the village, which was located in the deep and narrow valley of a tributary river of the Atata close to the Altas. The Atata Kindred, unlike their brethren, who dwelled on the lower-altitude Greatfish, had a magnificent view of towering snow-capped mountains all year round.

A number of caves dotted the cliffs of the valley, and the tribe used these as its principal shelters. The pasture in the area was limited, however, and Rilik directed his men to take the new horses across the river and beyond the cliffs, where there was still some grass to be found.

Nardo did not hear about the upcoming battle until he and Rilik, with several of their chief men, were having supper in the men's cave. Then Rilik told him of the agreement he had made with the Redu. "That is why I asked you to hasten to join us, Nardo. The battle is set for the day of the full moon."

For a moment Nardo said nothing, just continued to chew his ibex meat and look at Rilik. The Atata chief fidgeted a little under that level stare. "Well," Nardo said at last, "if the numbers are even, the horses will give us the victory."

Rilik looked a little relieved at Nardo's mild tone. He rubbed his nose and said, "There are more of them than we originally thought."

Nardo put the piece of meat he was about to eat back into his dish. "How many more?"

Rilik shrugged. "They outnumber us by perhaps twenty handfuls."

"Twenty handfuls!" said Mano.

"That was not the story you told us when you came begging our help," Varic said.

Harl leaped to his feet with a suggestion of menace. "Are you saying that we lied to you?"

"Varic did not mean to imply that at all," Nardo said soothingly. He sipped his tea and regarded the drawing of an ibex on the cave wall behind Rilik while he waited for Harl to resume his seat. When this had been done, Nardo said, "I would like to see the site you have chosen for this battle."

"Of course." Rilik was clearly relieved that Nardo was not going to pursue the matter of the numbers. "I shall take you there tomorrow. The place is only a morning's ride away for us, though it will be a day's journey for the Redu, as they must travel on foot." He looked at Varic. "Even with a difference of twenty handfuls," he said firmly, "the horses will prevail."

Six men set off early the next morning to travel north to the place where the tributary they were following would flow into the main river in this part of the mountains, the Atata. The battle site chosen by Rilik was just north of this confluence.

In this higher altitude the signs of spring that Nardo had noticed at home were not yet visible. The men and horses followed the river path that had been worn by thousands of migrating herds as they ascended and descended the river according to the seasons, and all around them the smell of resin and sharp pine needles rose from the great forest of evergreens that grew on the steep mountainsides. It was not a country overly suitable to horses, and Nardo imagined that the Atata Kindred had to take their animals up into the mountain pastures of the Altas as soon as the passes were open.

The two rivers converged in a small depression, and just north of this was the open meadow which Rilik had chosen to be the battle site. Nardo had seen that there was not a great deal of open land to choose from in the Atata territory, but he knew as soon as he saw the wedge-shaped meadow that Rilik had made a mistake.

"We will be hemmed in by the trees," Nardo said sharply, pointing at the cramped space between two woods that formed the southern part of the meadow, the place where the Kindred would form up. Then, as Rilik did not seem to understand the importance of this, Nardo, keeping his voice carefully controlled, explained. "The meadow is much narrower on our side than it is on theirs. We will not be able to spread our men as widely as theirs."

Still Rilik was unconcerned. "It is the charge of our horses that will break them," he said. "We do not need to spread out too widely."

Nardo slowly looked around. The day was clear and cold, an end-of-winter day. Three ibex had been grazing on the brown winter grass when the men rode in, but had disappeared in the direction of the river. The sky stretched above the patch of bleak grass like a great deep blue dome.

"The length of the line is important because we do not want them to be able to get around behind us," Nardo said in the same careful tone as before. He walked Bluebird forward a few paces and gestured to the two stands of trees. "See how cramped we will be."

Rilik was not pleased to be instructed by a younger man. "They will not get around us, Nardo. The power of our charge will splinter them apart. You have said yourself that men cannot stand against horses."

"If the men outnumber the horses, and the ground is in their favor, they might," Nardo said slowly, once more turning his head to consider the entire scene.

"What happened to the brave song you were singing when we spoke on the banks of the Greatfish?" Harl said nastily. "Are you frightened now that the spears are ready to be thrown?"

Varic began to answer hotly, but Nardo shook his head at his cousin and swung Bluebird around to face Rilik. "I have brought forty handfuls of men to this battle," he said. "That is two times the number the Atata Kindred will send. I would like to have been consulted about the ground before it was chosen."

"The ground *is* chosen," Rilik said angrily, "and it cannot be changed. Are you saying you will refuse to fight with us, Nardo?"

A huge griffin vulture glided across the sky, casting his shadow on the brown meadow. Nardo tilted back his head to watch the bird and thought of what would happen if he refused to fight. Either the Atata Kindred would go out to battle alone and be slaughtered, or they would back off and in so doing send a dangerous message to the enemy. Rilik had left him no choice. He turned to the Atata chief and said shortly, "Na. I am not saying that."

"The Atata Kindred will ride in the front of the charge," Rilik said proudly. "You of the Greatfish can ride behind us."

"We will be glad to ride in the front!" Varic was almost shouting in his outrage over the slight to his tribe's courage.

Nardo said firmly, "I would not take the honor of the front from the men of the Atata. We will ride behind." And, totally disregarding the chagrined faces of his men, he turned Bluebird and cantered back the way he had come.

Kerk also had made an excursion to investigate the battle site, and when he saw it his first thought had been the same as Nardo's. "They will be cramped between those two woods," he said.

Madden showed his teeth. "Once we surround them, they will be finished."

"Yes," Kerk said with pleasure. "They will be."

The Redu chief had learned strategy from his years of feuding with other tribes in Britain, and even if he had never before engaged in such a large confrontation, he understood the value of position. The Redu spent the night encamped near the battleground, and on the morning of the day of the full moon, Kerk disposed his five hundred men on the north side of the field. They outnumbered the men of the Kindred by two hundred, twice the number that Rilik had estimated to Nardo.

Kerk took full advantage of his breadth of ground and spread his line considerably wider than the enemy would be able to. The first line of Redu was composed of archers, their tall, deadly bows rising above their heads, their waists crammed with wooden arrows that had been carefully straightened by heat, flighted with eagle or hawk feathers and tipped by sharp flint points. The men stood three feet apart, to give themselves room to use their arms, and behind them, in the spaces left between the men of the front line, stood another line of archers, and behind them yet another. Arranged behind these three lines of archers were the hand-to-hand men, each armed with a spear and a short stone club. All of the Redu men proudly displayed the thumbs of their enemies on their belts and hoped this day to win some more.

Paxon stood in the first line of hand-to-hand men and looked at the horsemen who were forming up a quarter of a mile away on the other side of the meadow. The horses did not look so intimidating at such a distance, he thought. Like every other Redu on the field, all his senses were at high-pitch intensity as he watched the horses and listened for the sound of the horn that would be their signal to advance.

Finally it came, the sound they all were waiting for, the hollow booming of the war horn. Paxon's heartbeat accelerated as the men in front of him began to run lightly forward across the field. There was a shout of surprise from the horsemen as they realized the Redu were moving. What had they expected? Paxon thought in derision. That we would wait to receive the shock of their horse charge?

Once again the war horn boomed. They were just within bowshot now, and the Redu halted as the first line of their archers fitted their arrows into their bows. Then the air was filled with a sudden, rushing darkness, and shouts and screams came from the horsemen as men and animals were hit by the flying wind of death.

A voice from the enemy lines roared a command, and the frightened horses began to gallop forward, pushed on relentlessly by the voices and legs of their riders. By now the archers had fitted another arrow into their bows, and a second wind of death flew into the ranks of the charging horsemen. Horses fell, screaming with pain and terror. Those coming behind them had to leap over the thrashing animals on the ground to avoid being brought down themselves. Many of the animals began to rear and refuse to go on.

The first line of archers stepped back, and the second line let fly another shower of deadly arrows. The charge had been slowed by the first two volleys, and now the third slammed into the living flesh and blood of both animal and human, and the shrieks of the injured and dying rose to the heavens.

The third line of archers were ready now to fire. Paxon gripped his spear and club and did not even realize he was shouting. The archers would let what was left of the horse charge penetrate the Redu lines, and the hand-to-hand men would finish the rest of the Kindred men off and keep what horses were still alive.

"Back! Back! Turn back!" It was the voice that had urged the horsemen on before, close enough now for Paxon to recognize the words. He scowled and looked around for his father. They did not want the horsemen to retreat now!

But the riders were obeying the voice and wheeling their terrified horses around. The bowmen stepped forward for another volley, although this one was less effective as the retreating forces were weaving through the morass of the dead and dying left scattered on the field.

There would be no following them, Paxon realized. If horses were good for nothing else, they at least were good for escape. He relaxed his grip on his weapons, looked around, and realized that they had not lost a single man.

The screams of the injured and dying horses were terrible. Paxon looked at the bloody field before him and heard Kerk's voice, "See if any of those horses can be saved. If not, then put them out of their pain."

Madden asked, "What about the men?"

"The men are no good to us," Kerk returned. "Kill any that are still alive."

A party of men went to do the chief's bidding.

Almost all of the men of the Atata Kindred had been killed. That they discovered when the fleeing horsemen finally stopped long enough to count up who was left.

Nardo was heartsick. "When I let Rilik take the front, I never thought that this would happen."

"No one thought that this would happen," a bloodstained Nat replied. It was not his blood, but blood that spouted from the neck of the horse in front of him, he assured them all, his strong, square face grimmer than anyone had ever seen it. "You were afraid they would surround us. That was why you took the rear, Nardo, so you could counter a surrounding move. Rilik did not know that, but we of the Greatfish Kindred do."

"Dhu!" said Varic. "What kind of bows were they?"

"I do not know, but they shot almost three times the distance of a javelin!" said Mano.

"No wonder the Redu were so eager to accept Rilik's offer of a battle," Freddo said in a deeply bitter voice.

"How could Rilik have been so unaware of this weapon?" Nardo demanded. "Didn't he keep a lookout upon these people? Didn't he watch them hunt?"

"Apparently not," said Varic.

"We saw them carrying bows," said one of the few Atata men who had survived the charge. His voice was defensive. "We all use bows occasionally. We did not realize that this bow was different."

"It is twice as long as the one we use!" Nardo said.

No answer came from the Atata man.

"Get a count from your clans of whom we have lost," Nardo told the men of the council who surrounded him. "Then, Mother help us, we will have to tell the Atata women and children what has happened to their men."

PART THREE

THE DANGER

Chapter Fourteen

Paxon stood on the banks of the river and surveyed the narrow valley which, but a few short moons before, the Atata Kindred had called home. It was summer and the cliffs were brilliantly colored with the flowers that grew in the crags and crevices of their sheer heights: blue Pyrenean hyacinth, white and pale pink ashy cranesbill and the deep magenta of marsh orchids. In contrast, to the south snow-capped peaks rose to meet the sky. The young man felt a strange thrill at the beauty stretching before him. It was nothing at all like the flat country of his homeland. He inhaled deeply, then said to the friend who stood beside him, "The reindeer have got to be in the high mountains."

"Well, they certainly aren't here," Aven replied sourly, and he kicked the ground in disgust.

Paxon was in the valley because he had been sent on a scouting expedition by his father. The reindeer, so plentiful along the Atata in the spring, had disappeared with the summer, and the Redu were growing hungry. In the spring all the herds had been traveling south along the river, so Kerk had told Paxon to travel south also and find out where the reindeer had gone.

Paxon looked up at the high cliff walls that enclosed the valley. "These caves must have been the main campsite of the horse people we defeated in the spring," he murmured. "I remember that the traders described such a place to me: the river, the narrow valley, the caves high in the cliff. This is where they made their home."

"We didn't kill them all," Aven said. "I wonder where they went."

"The traders said that the tribe living along this river did not number more than three hundred people, including women and children. They must have been joined in battle by the horse tribe that lives along the river the traders called the River of Gold. I imagine that those who survived the battle took their women and children and fled west."

The two men stood in silence, their eyes on one particular cave halfway up the cliff. As they watched, a small herd of ibex picked their way daintily along the steep heights. Aven said, "The people of this camp must have lived on ibex and birds. There seem to be plenty of them in the area."

"Three hundred is not a large tribe," Paxon said. "If they could get reindeer in the spring and fall, as the herds migrated up and down the river, they could most probably live on ibex and birds for the rest of the year."

"We *are* a large tribe, however," Aven pointed out.

Paxon grunted. That, of course, was precisely why his father had sent him on this expedition.

"We might have to divide up into separate hunting camps, the way we always did at home," Paxon said. "This site can support three hundred people, and the site where we are presently encamped can probably support another two hundred."

A large golden eagle descended from the sky, alighted on a protruding rock near the top of the cliff, and surveyed the valley with lordly authority.

"If we divide up, that means we will need to find at least one other campsite," Aven said.

Paxon grunted. "Meanwhile, my father will want to know if reindeer really are in the mountains."

Aven scowled and looked southward toward the majestic white peaks. "You can't mean to try to climb up there, Paxon. We're not ibex!"

Paxon gave him a friendly smile. "Do *you* want to be the one to tell my father that we didn't bother trying to reach the mountains?"

The two young men looked at each other. The golden eagle left its perch and flew slowly south, its shadow reflecting in the glittering water of the river. The two Redu who had been exploring the cave appeared at its opening and waved excitedly.

Aven said, "No."

"Neither do I," Paxon said. "We'll sleep here tonight and tomorrow we'll head for the mountains."

"I am sure the reindeer are in the mountains," Paxon said to Kerk. "We saw a few small herds as we climbed up alongside the river, and I think there are probably pastures higher up. The problem is, the climb is too steep for the women and children."

Kerk grunted. "Then it is also too steep for men to bring down a decent number of carcasses."

"Yes," said Paxon. "At least the way we went is too steep."

"The traders said nothing of a pass?" Kerk asked.

Paxon shook his head.

Silence fell as Kerk thought. Paxon was fiercely proud that his father was turning to him more and more for information and advice. Once the Redu had left the familiar grounds of their homeland, Paxon had proved himself to be a scout with unusual abilities, and Kerk was not slow to make use of his son's talent.

Now Kerk ran his finger up and down the arrogant arch of his nose. "You say the Kindred camp was deserted?"

"Yes," Paxon replied. "Although there were signs that it had been fully occupied until recently—the hearthplaces were still full of bones and ashes." His voice took on a note of wonder. "The most amazing thing, Father, was that they had drawn pictures on the walls of the caves."

"Pictures?"

"Yes. Huge pictures of horses and bulls and ibex. They looked so real!"

"Riding horses and drawing pictures—they are a strange people," Kerk said. "Where do you think they have gone?"

"Probably to the shores of that other river, the one we did not follow into the mountains," Paxon said.

"The River of Gold?"

"Yes." Paxon watched a group of women as they hauled wa-

ter from the river. "The Kindred camp we found looked as if it
could support perhaps three hundred people," he added.

Kerk grunted. The men stood in silence, watching the women
toiling up the slope under their heavy burdens. Finally they
reached the lower cave and disappeared into its gloomy opening.

Paxon said, "The hunting around here can support another
two hundred."

Kerk stared up the river, his hawklike profile very somber. "I
do not want to divide us up into separate camps. It will make us
more vulnerable to attack."

"The traders said that the tribe that lived along the River of
Gold was a large one," Paxon said. "The hunting must be better
along the River of Gold."

"I have been thinking that," Kerk said. "I have been thinking
that next we should try that River of Gold."

Ever since their defeat in battle, Nardo had been trying to
convince the people of the tribe that they were going to have to
do something about the Redu.

"There are too many of them for the hunting along the Atata
to feed," he said again and again. "We are not safe."

But most of the clan council did not agree. They had been
horrified by the slaughter they had seen and, to Nardo's frustration, wanted no part of confronting the bow-and-arrow people
again.

"If indeed these people must move away from the Atata, they
could just as easily follow the reindeer into the Altas. Or move
east, toward Ripple River," Varic had said when the clan council
met one sunny afternoon inside Nardo's hut. The men were
alone since Alane was at the big house helping the women to
repair the clan's summer tents.

To Nardo's chagrin, his cousin's words counted for more with
the clan council than his own. Even Mano, the representative
for Nardo's clan, said, "I see no need for us to do anything to
attract their attention just now, Nardo. Better to wait."

"We have enough to do to feed the extra women and children
you evacuated from the main Atata village," Varic added, couch-
ing his words to make it sound as if the extra mouths were all
Nardo's fault.

"What would you have had me do?" Nardo replied angrily. "Left them to be captured by the invaders? Or starve?"

"No one is blaming you for taking in the Atata women and children, Nardo," Mano said soothingly.

"That is not the impression I received from Varic's words," Nardo retorted.

Varic's widely spaced eyes looked perfectly innocent. "It is not a matter of blame," he said. "I was just stating a fact. The addition of the Atata women and children has put a strain on our resources. We cannot spare men to go hunting the invaders as well."

And so, as spring softened the air and the reindeer began their annual migration from the mountains, the men of the Kindred followed their usual pastoral patterns and paid little attention to what was happening on the other side of the Buffalo Pass. Nardo had managed to convince Dane and a few of the young men who were at summer camp on the Narrow River to keep a steady watch on the pass, but he had doubts about their faithfulness to this task. Nardo knew well enough that Dane went along with him for the sake of friendship, not because he believed in the necessity of the surveillance. The whole situation fretted Nardo unbearably, but there was nothing he could do about it.

Then, early in the summer, word came from the Norakamo that Tedric was dead. When Alane expressed a wish to see her mother, Nardo, who wanted to speak to Rune about the Redu invasion, said that he would take her.

Mara was not happy with this decision. "Kindred women do not leave the village," she said to them both when told of this plan.

"You left the village to see your son married," Alane pointed out. "My father is dead. Surely you cannot deny that it is proper for me to make a visit to my mother?"

It *was* proper, and Mara knew it. Yet she could not help but think that this was one more occasion when Alane had subverted ancient Kindred ways. Nor did it help when she appealed to her sister and her daughters only to find that no one else in the household agreed. It was not a situation calculated to endear Alane any further to Nardo's mother.

Normally it was a two-day journey from the Kindred village to the Norakamo summer camp on the River of Gold, but since Alane and Nardo were burdened with a twelve-moon-old nursing child who had to ride in a cradle board upon his father's back, it took them almost three full days. Stifun and Larz, the messengers who had brought the sad news to Alane, accompanied them. At Alane's request Nardo left Samu at the village.

Alane had not fully realized just how confining she found the Kindred village until finally she was free of it. Not even the death of her father could destroy her pleasure in the feel of a horse beneath her, her husband beside her, the river path stretching before her, and the wonderful knowledge that soon they would be pitching their small tent for the evening and she would be cooking their supper under the open sky. Alane had spent her whole life making journeys and she missed them.

The sun was moving into the western part of the sky when Stifun moved his horse up to Nardo's other side and claimed his attention. Alane dropped back to let her horse walk beside Larz's. They had had no chance to speak privately before this, and now she gave him a friendly look and asked about his family.

He told her about his father and his sisters, then said a little constrictedly, "You look well, Alane. Living with the Kindred must agree with you."

Alane contented herself with saying merely, "Nardo is a good husband."

Larz looked at the sleeping baby strapped so securely to the broad back before them. Among the Norakamo the transport of children, like everything else pertaining to them, was left to the women. "He is a good father too, I see," Larz said.

"Sa." Alane smiled at the look of amazement on Larz's face as he regarded Nevin. "Have you married, Larz?" she asked.

"I am to be married shortly," he replied. "To Gurda."

Alane nodded approvingly. "She is a good girl. I am sure you will be very happy with her."

"Sa," he replied a little glumly. He changed the subject. "Your mother will be pleased to see you. Losing your father was a great blow to her."

Alane's face was grave. She knew that, and she supposed that was why she had felt this urgent need to go home. In truth,

Alane had not allowed herself to examine her own feelings about her father's death too closely. She had busied herself so much with her brother and Larz, had expended so much thought and energy on preparing for this journey, that she had managed to avoid confronting the issue of Tedric's death.

"My mother is a very strong woman," she said to Larz. *So strong,* she continued to herself, *that she could send her only daughter away to live her life among strangers.*

But for the first time the familiar accusation did not evoke the usual resentment. Since early childhood Adah's children had known that they came second to her husband. Adah would be bereft without Tedric, and suddenly Alane felt pity for her mother flood her heart.

She said as much to Nardo as they lay in their sleeping skins later that night, with Nevin asleep between them.

"Sa," he said. "I could see that your mother and father were close."

Alane sighed. "I am sorry now that I did not visit them sooner. It is in my heart that I would have liked to see my father again."

"It was not your fault you did not visit," Nardo pointed out. "I could not take you this spring; since the battle with the Redu we have been trying to adjust to all these new people in the tribe." He reached over the sleeping baby to take her hand. "Do not blame yourself, Alane."

"I suppose I am really blaming myself for the way I felt about him," she confessed. "I swore that I would never forgive him for making me marry you, and I didn't. And now it is too late."

Silence. Then, "I did not know I was so distasteful to you," he said. The hand that was holding hers had stiffened.

She raised his fingers to her mouth and kissed them. His calluses were rough against her lips. "I did not know you. And you were so big. You frightened me."

A horse squealed. They had put all of the horses together in a rope corral beside the two tents, and the Norakamo and Kindred mares were still arguing about the pecking order.

Nardo moved his hand from Alane's mouth and rested it on her breast. "I know I did," he said softly, and felt her breast rise and fall under his hand as she sighed.

"The fact that I have learned to love you very much didn't change my feelings toward my father." Her voice sounded sad. "I fear I am a very unforgiving woman, Nardo."

"You felt he had betrayed you and you were angry. That is very natural, little one. Don't have hard feelings toward yourself."

She sniffed. He gently brushed a finger across her buckskin-covered nipple. "Do you really love me very much?"

"Sa." She sniffed again.

"Very much?" He smiled in the dark as he felt her nipple harden under his touch.

She removed his hand and said, "Don't do that. The baby."

"He's asleep."

"He won't stay asleep, Nardo, if you start rolling around in here. This tent is too small."

He blew out his nose in frustration.

"Rune will be the chief now," Alane said, following her own line of thought. "How much things have changed since we wed two years ago, Nardo."

"Sa," he agreed grumpily.

"Sometimes you are worse than Nevin," Alane said, and she turned on her side and went to sleep.

Alane was surprised by how glad her mother was to see her. She was surprised also by Adah's looks; suddenly she seemed so old and fragile. What was left of Alane's resentment died the moment she saw her mother's worn and sorrowful face. The most alarming thing about Adah, however, was not her sorrow, but the fact that she seemed to have withdrawn from life. She sat in her tent and let Alane and Nita and Stifun's wife, Orel, do everything for her.

It was dangerous, Alane found herself thinking, to let your life become so dependent upon another person. All it took was an evil spirit in the lungs, such as the one that had killed her father, and two lives, not one, were destroyed.

For the first time ever, Alane's thoughts turned admiringly toward Nardo's mother. Mara was older than Adah, she had lost both her husband and her brother, but she had not given up on life. Her hand was as firmly upon the reins of her family as it had always been.

Alane mentioned her concern about Adah to Rune on the second evening of her visit, when she and Nardo were visiting after supper in Rune's tent. A pleasant breeze was blowing off the river, and the tent flap was open wide to admit the cool air. The four adults had finished drinking tea, and Rune's daughter, Kara, who at nine moons of age was just beginning to crawl, gave in to her fascination with Nardo and tried to pull herself up on his legs.

Nita, whose Kindred Speak was perfectly fluent by now, apologized to Nardo and tried to pluck her daughter away. "Na, na," Nardo said, waving his hand in dismissal. "Leave her be. She is not bothering me at all. She probably has never seen black hair before." And he lifted the baby, set her into the crook of his left arm and let her thrust her questing fingers into his hair, all the while continuing to talk to Rune.

Nevin, who was accustomed to sharing his father with a pack of cousins, evinced no jealousy of Kara, but toddled curiously around the tent looking at things. He had been walking for less than a moon and occasionally he would lose his balance and sit down hard, but he never cried, just got purposefully to his feet and started off again.

Kara got a good fistful of thick, shiny hair, shouted, "Da, da, da, da!" in triumph, and pulled hard.

"You wouldn't believe these bows," Nardo said to Rune as he reached up to disentangle the small fist from its trophy. "I wish I could see one up close. I would like to know what it is made of. It has to be very strong."

"Nita, take that baby from Nardo," Rune said in annoyance.

Nardo smiled good-humoredly at Rune's wife. "She likes me," he said. "She has very good taste." And he dandled the baby on his knees. Kara laughed delightedly.

"Nardo spends half his life at home covered with children," Alane said to Rune, amusement in her voice.

"Mama," said Nevin, "look!"

All the adults turned to see Nevin toddling toward them across the swept dirt floor. He was clutching the ivory centerpiece the Norakamo used to play their game of Sticks. Alane removed the game piece from her son's firm grasp and settled both children down with grain nuggets that had been dipped in honey.

Rune said to Nardo, "What are you going to do about these Redu?"

Nardo looked grim. "I cannot convince the tribe that we need to do anything about them, Rune."

Rune's blue eyes were grave. "From what you have told me, there is not enough hunting along the Atata to feed such a large tribe of people."

"There is not. They put at least seventy handfuls of men against us, Rune. That means there must be at least a hundred handfuls of women and children in their camp. That is far too many people for the Atata hunting grounds to feed."

"They will seek to move into your territory," Rune said. "If they came from Big Rivers Joining, then they know there are two rivers that lead into the mountains. I am thinking they will seek to explore along the River of Gold next."

Alane entered the conversation. "I think so too," she said to her brother. "And if they follow the River of Gold, Rune, they will be in Norakamo territory also."

Rune's thin face was grim. "I know." He turned to Nardo. "Are these bows truly so terrible?"

"They have three times the range of a javelin," Nardo said. "The front lines of our horses went down as if . . . as if they had stepped off a cliff." Nardo shook his head as if to clear it. "Dhu, Rune, sometimes in my dreams I can still hear them screaming."

Rune swore.

"I have been thinking and thinking about what we might do to counter that deadly bow," Nardo said.

"An open battle is obviously not the answer," Rune replied.

"Obviously," Alane agreed tartly.

"Why can't you attack their hunting parties?" Rune said. He glanced at Nita a little uneasily before adding, "As we did with the Horse Eaters."

"I can't do anything," Nardo said bitterly, "because the tribe will not listen to me."

Rune's eyes widened in surprise. "But you are the chief."

"A chief of the Kindred does not have the authority that a chief of the Norakamo does, Rune," Nardo replied even more bitterly than before.

A small silence fell. Then Rune said, "My life is not quite as easy as you seem to think, Nardo. I have a shaman to contend with."

"Hagen," Nardo remembered. "Is he giving trouble?"

Rune replied shortly, "Hagen always gives trouble. But I am dealing with him."

Alane said, "Nardo has convinced a group of the younger men who are at summer camp to keep watch on the Buffalo Pass."

"I do not know that one," Rune said.

"It is the only pass that connects the Atata valley with our territory," Nardo replied. "Our chief summer camp lies on high ground by the Narrow River, and the surrounding area is all enclosed pasture, except for the single valley that leads up to the Buffalo Pass. If they come through there, they will be in one of our richest hunting and grazing grounds." Nardo slammed his fist against the ground in frustration. "Dhu! I feel as if I am watching an avalanche come toward me, and there is nothing I can do to stop it!"

"If you are invaded, and you need help," Rune said, "you can call on me."

For the first time since the subject of the Redu had come up, Nardo smiled. "Thank you, my brother," he said. "I was hoping you would say that."

Chapter Fifteen

Kerk sent the two hundred Redu women and children to live in the camp Paxon had discovered close by the Altas, with fifty of his fighting men to hunt for them. The men were not happy with their assignment, but no one tried to argue with the chief.

This left the Redu with four hundred and fifty men in their original camp.

"Before we retrace our steps all the way back to Big Rivers Joining, I want someone to explore that small river north of the women's camp, the one that runs to the west," Kerk said. "It is possible that it leads to a pass into the next valley."

So once again Paxon found himself sent to scout strange territory. He and Aven were alone this time, and though the upward climb along the mountain river was steep, it was not nearly as difficult as their previous attempt at the Altas had been.

Paxon had made the discovery that he loved the mountains. Where the Redu had come from, the land had been flat, and in the summer there had been frequent mists and fogs. But here the air was so clear, and the sky seemed so close, that he found the whole atmosphere exhilarating.

He tried to express something of what he was thinking to Aven. "At home the sky is the roof of the world, but here in the mountains it is all around you, like a cave." His nostrils dilated

as he inhaled deeply. "I feel like I am living in the land of Sky
God."

Aven was puffing. "The air is hard to breathe when you are
so high." He looked up at the cliffs towering on either side of
the river path. "This is definitely a pass, Paxon."

"Yes." Paxon sounded pleased. "I think it is."

They were through the pass and descending toward the valley
on the other side when they heard the sound of horse hooves
approaching from the west. Fortunately, they had descended to
the point where the steep sides of the mountain were covered
with evergreen forest, and the two young men promptly dived
off the path and into the cover of the trees. From where Paxon
lay on his belly in a nest of fragrant pine needles, he watched
enviously as two men on horseback cantered up the path.

How different life must be for a man who could ride a horse!

Paxon felt the weight of his bow on his shoulder, and was
tempted to put arrows through both of the men when they returned down the path so he could steal their horses. His father
would be furious, however, if he warned the Kindred of the presence of a Redu scout.

The men continued up the pass, slowing the horses to a walk
as the grade became steeper.

"Do you think they are scouts?" Aven, who was flat on the
ground beside Paxon, asked softly.

"They may be. We are lucky they did not catch us farther
up the pass, where there is no tree cover."

"Well, now we know that the pass leads into the horsemen's
territory," Aven said practically.

"That is so," Paxon said. "We'll wait here until the horsemen
return. Then we shall continue to explore."

"The pass opens up into a wider valley," Paxon reported to
Kerk when he returned with his scouting report at the end of
the Moon of the Long Nights. "The valley appears to be where
the horsemen have their camp. And," Paxon paused for dramatic
effect, "we saw reindeer."

The two men were standing on the west bank of the Atata,
and as they talked a salmon arched into the air in the middle of

the river, then fell back into the water. Kerk's face became even more hawklike than usual. "Reindeer? In the summer?"

Paxon turned to look toward the south. The soft breeze from the Altas blew his black hair off his shoulders. "Yes," he said. "The land is considerably higher there than it is along this river, and evidently the reindeer don't migrate into the big mountains to the south."

The bright sun glinted off Kerk's head, which was still as black as his son's. The chief smiled slowly. "This pass. How dangerous would it be for our men to get through it?"

"It could be tricky, Father," Paxon warned. "The Kindred seem to be keeping some kind of a watch; it was sheer luck that we got through without being discovered. If there had been more of us, we would not have been so fortunate."

"You have no business relying on luck," Kerk snapped. Then, "What kind of watch?" he demanded.

Paxon refrained from trying to justify himself. His father had never been one to tolerate mistakes. "Two horsemen ride through the pass each day," Paxon said. "They would be certain to see us if we had all the men on the path to the top. And they would have time to go for reinforcements—the horses move much more swiftly than we do."

Kerk grunted. He had no desire to be caught by horses in the narrow confines of a mountain pass. Paxon stood in respectful silence while his father thought. "These riders merely ride through the pass during the day to see if it is clear?" he asked.

"Yes."

Kerk turned his proud profile toward the mountains west of the Atata. "So," he said with satisfaction, "then we will go through the pass at night."

Dark had fallen and supper had been eaten when the skins at the door of the big house lifted and Nardo and Alane came in. They crossed to where Mara sat sewing by the hearth. She looked up and Nardo said cheerfully, "We have come to say goodbye, Mama. We will be leaving for summer camp early in the morning."

"*We?*" Mara could feel herself go rigid. Surely he could not mean . . . ?

"We," her son replied. "Alane is coming with me."

Mara answered instantly, ignoring Alane, her eyes intent on Nardo's face. "Married women do not go to summer camp."

Nardo shrugged. He was trying to maintain his usual genial expression, but Mara could see he was uncomfortable. He had known she would object to this plan, she thought. Mara's eyes turned slowly to her daughter-by-marriage. Alane's face looked serene, but there was the faintest hint of challenge in the gray eyes that looked down into Mara's. That look told Mara immediately why Alane had accompanied her husband on this evening visit. She did not want to give Mara a chance to be alone with Nardo and perhaps make him change his mind.

Nardo answered Mara's objection. "Alane is not of our tribe, Mama. Norakamo women travel with their men from camp to camp. It is a way of life Alane is used to and she misses it. I cannot see the harm in letting her come with me. We will be gone for only a handful of days."

Silence had fallen in the house. It was as if even the children sensed something of importance was happening between Mara and her son. Slowly Mara rose to her feet. She was much taller than Alane, and she did not want to give away that advantage. "And what are you planning to do with Nevin?" Mara asked Alane directly. "Leave him with Lora?" Her tone implied that only an irresponsible and neglectful mother would do such a thing.

Alane did not betray by a flicker of expression that Mara's cutting words had found a target. "Of course not," she replied. "We will take him with us, my mother. He loved the trip to the Norakamo camp."

"It is not good for so young a child to make these journeys," Mara said.

"Norakamo children do it all the time," Alane replied.

"Nevin is not a Norakamo child."

"He has a Norakamo mother."

"You are a Norakamo no longer," Mara said. The battle was being waged openly now between the two women, with Nardo reduced to the position of onlooker. "We made you a member of our clan, Alane. It is in my heart that you owe it to us to live according to our ways."

"I am living according to your ways," Alane replied. "I am trying very hard to be a good Kindred woman."

"It is not the Kindred way for husband and wife to eat alone together in their own hut!"

Alane lifted one smoky brow as if amazed Mara could evince such passion over a little thing. Mara clenched her fists at her sides to keep herself from slapping the girl across her Norakamo face.

Nardo's voice dropped into the tense silence. "Come, Mama. We will be gone for only a handful of days. What is the harm in that, now?"

Mara stared bleakly into her son's splendid dark face. *You don't understand, Nardo, what this girl is doing to our tribe,* she thought. *She is separating you from the household of your Mother's Blood, and you are so besotted that you are helping her to do it.*

She knew he thought she was simply jealous of his affection for Alane, and she tried to explain that this was not so. "You are the chief, Nardo," she said, "and others will follow where you lead. If you make such a trip with your wife, then other men will want to do the same."

His face became suddenly very bleak. "Dhu, Mama, I wish what you say was true. But if my influence was as powerful as you seem to think, we would not have left the Redu unwatched in the valley of the Atata!"

Mara gave her beloved son a distinctly irritated look. This was not the time to be talking about the Redu.

Alane at least understood that much. She said, "What is so terrible about a woman paying a brief visit to a camp to visit her husband? Husband and wife are separated for so many moons in this tribe. If a wife's visit can give her more time with her husband, then I cannot see why you object to it so, my mother."

Mara could feel the other women in the tent listening intently to this conversation. Nardo might complain that he did not have enough influence among the men, but the same was not true of his wife's influence among the Kindred women. The young women of the tribe were watching how Alane was binding her husband to her, and some of them were beginning to imitate her ways. Already in Mara's own household Lora and Dane had started to eat sometimes in their own hut.

Then there were Fara and Haras, whom everyone had expected to be divorced by now. Instead Fara was distancing herself from her mother's household and turning more and more to her husband for the companionship she had heretofore found among her female relatives. Mara had gotten Nardo to send Haras to Bright Valley in the Altas this summer, hoping that in his absence Fara once more would draw close to her mother. But if Alane went with Nardo to hunting camp, what would stop Fara from deciding she wanted to make a similar trip to see Haras?

Danger. The Mother's Blood patterns of the tribe were in danger. Mara knew it. And it all stemmed from this young, grave-faced Norakamo girl!

"Who will do your work in the household while you are gone?" Mara asked Alane.

"You have many hands to help you, my mother," Alane replied. "This sharing of the work is one of the things I have learned to admire about the Kindred way of life. You won't miss me."

Lora, who was sitting on the far side of the fire, spoke up for the first time. "Alane is right, my mother. We can get along without her for a little while."

Mara's face was stony as she looked from her niece to Alane. Alane smiled, gracious in victory, and said, "We will not be gone for long."

Mara did not reply but sat down in her place and once more bent her head over her sewing.

One of the reasons Nardo was going to summer camp was to check that the watch he had ordered to be kept on the Buffalo Pass was still being implemented. Shortly after the battle, he and some of the younger men had cut logs and placed them where they would be easy to drag into position to barricade the pass. "If we can block the path high enough, where it is tightly enclosed by the cliffs, they will not be able to get through," Nardo had told Alane when first he had come up with the idea.

"That is so," Alane had agreed. "You can shelter from their arrows behind the logs, and throw your javelins at them."

Alane was well aware of Nardo's frustration at being unable to get the tribe to listen to him. She had listened to him often, and she did not think he was wrong to prepare for an invasion. She had been against his joining Rilik in an open battle, and the horror of how many men had been lost in that battle had made her a staunch advocate of any plan that featured the ambush tactics that the Norakamo had employed so successfully, and safely, against the invasion of the Horse Eaters.

Mara did not know it, but Alane's sympathetic ear was one more thing that was drawing Nardo ever closer to his wife. She was one of the few people with whom he could discuss what he felt was the inevitable conflict between the Kindred and the Redu.

It was early on a late summer morning when Nardo, Alane, Nevin and Samu set off on their journey. At the moment Alane was perfectly happy with her life. Accompanying Nardo on this trip had been a major victory for her, and both she and Mara knew it. The balance of power between them had shifted to favor the wife instead of the mother.

The well-worn path to the tribe's most ancient summer camp led south along the Greatfish to the place where the Narrow River fed into it from the east. At this confluence a traveler had a choice to keep going south along the Greatfish, a trip that led into the Bright Valley of the Altas, where the Kindred summered their horse herd, or one could turn east and follow the Narrow River to the Buffalo Pass, which led in turn into the valley of the Atata.

Summer camp lay about two-thirds of the way between the village and the pass. A man with a string of three remounts could easily make it in a day. Alane and Nardo, because they were encumbered with Nevin, had taken one remount each and would take two days to complete the journey.

They stopped once at the confluence of the Leza and the Greatfish, and then again at midday, to water the horses and so that Alane could nurse Nevin. Both the Kindred and the Norakamo nursed their children until they were three years of age, and most women did not have another baby until after the previous child had finished with the breast.

A very active child, Nevin had surprised his parents by how

patiently he traveled. When he grew tired of the cradle board, either Alane or Nardo would put him in front of them on the horse, where he would grab a fistful of long gray mane and smile delightedly.

Alane and Nardo ate some dried fish, and while Alane was nursing Nevin, Nardo took his spear and went off into the woods to a place where he thought he could get a bird for dinner. After Nevin's stomach was comfortably filled, he began to play with Samu, whom Nardo had left behind as protection for his wife and son. The dog had surprised Alane by how gentle he was with the small child, and instead of fearing him she had actually come to feel safer when Samu was around.

Dog and boy rolled around in the grass, one shrieking and the other panting, and then they both collapsed together in a heap and went to sleep in the heat of the noon sun.

Nardo came up behind Alane and dropped a quail onto the grass. "I thought I could get a bird," he said in a pleased voice. "We can have it later for dinner."

Alane picked up the quail and regarded it critically. It looked nice and plump.

"Nevin is asleep," Nardo said, his voice even more pleased than before.

She smiled up at him. "The quail will make a very nice dinner."

Nardo began to strip off his shirt.

"What are you doing, Nardo?" Alane asked.

"I'm hot and sticky," he said, "and I'm going to cool off in the river."

His bare brown torso did look sweaty. He bent to spread his shirt out on the grass to dry, and muscles rippled under the glistening coppery skin of his back. Two harriers circled in the hazy sky overhead. Nardo straightened up. His waist was so narrow that his trousers had slid down onto his hips. He looked into Alane's eyes and said softly, "Come and take a bath with me."

Her eyes flew to Nevin. "We can't leave the baby alone."

"He's all right. He won't wake for a while, and Samu will protect him."

Alane turned toward the water. The day was unusually warm for late summer, and she was hot and sticky also. "All right," she said, "but first make sure that the water isn't too deep." Alane could not swim.

Nardo stripped off his trousers, walked down to the river and waded in until the water was up to his ribs. He turned to call to her, "See! The bottom here doesn't drop down."

The horses Nardo had unpacked and hobbled were grazing peacefully and paid no attention to the man in the water. Alane began to take off her own clothes. The summer sun had tanned her face and arms to a delicate golden hue, but the parts of her that were protected by her clothing were still the color of ivory. She folded each item neatly as she took it off and laid it on the grass.

"Come on, Alane!" Nardo called. He ducked under altogether and came up, hair and face dripping. As Alane approached the water, he stood with hands on hips, watching her.

She stepped daintily into the water, and he took his hands off his hips and held them out to her. She waded slowly in until she was close enough to reach out and catch his fingers.

The cool water flowed all around them, and he lifted her against him and kissed her mouth. She put her arms around his neck and pressed the whole length of her body against his, feeling his erection. He slid his hands over her rib cage, her waist, and rested them on the gentle curve of her hips.

"Your bones are so small and light," he said. "I am always afraid I will squeeze you too hard."

"I won't break," she whispered and pressed her fingers against the back of his head, bringing his mouth down once again to hers. "Are you cooled down yet?" she murmured as his lips moved from her mouth to her chin and then to her throat. "If we tarry here too long, Nevin will wake up, and then you won't get a chance to do what you so obviously want to do."

He said, "I don't want to get out," and smiled into her surprised eyes. "Put your legs around my waist," he said. Her eyes widened even more, and he put his hands on her hips and lifted her. The water was high as her shoulders, and she felt almost weightless in his hands. "Open your legs, Alane," he coaxed. She glanced once over her shoulder to check on the sleeping baby. Then she did as he asked, and felt him slide inside her.

They were still for a moment, and she could feel his heart

pounding against her breasts. Then she tightened her legs, bringing him deeper into her, and heard him groan. He was holding her up, with his hands on her bottom, and now he began to move his hips. The expression on Alane's face narrowed and concentrated as she moved to meet him. The tension inside her mounted unbearably higher, then higher still, and her short nails dug into the skin of his shoulders as she approached the climax she needed. Then at last it was there, a tremendous explosion of pleasure, sending shocks of intense sensation shooting all through her, radiating outward from the center where he was. She cried out and then buried her face in his shoulder. Even though he was standing in cool water, his skin against her mouth was beaded and salty with sweat. His heart thundered against her own.

"Alane," he said. "Alane." It was as if he could find no other words to say, and she was satisfied.

The river flowed gently around them and the afternoon sun shone down on them. A group of ducks swam along the opposite bank, diving occasionally for fish. Farther upstream a deer and her fawn were drinking on the bank. Nevin and Samu slept in a tangle of silver-tipped fur and smooth brown limbs, and a butterfly fluttered around Samu's twitching black nose.

It was the first time Alane had ever been to the Kindred's summer hunting camp. It lay in the high country along the Narrow River, at the apex of an elongated triangular basin that was bounded on all sides by steep slopes formed by the confluence of several small valleys. The camp lay at a point where the river suddenly entered a narrow and winding gorge, and since all of the small valleys were cul-de-sacs, with the exception of the one which led up into the Buffalo Pass, the hunting camp was strategically located at the only possible exit from this large enclosed expanse of pasture.

The camp itself was centered around two large caves which overlooked the river, one at ground level and one set high into the cliff face. The men used the caves for storage and lived in the tents which were pitched on the river's bank. Their horses were pastured on the rich grass in one of the smaller valleys.

There were several unmarried girls with the men to help sup-

plement their diet by gathering grains and greens, so Alane
would not be the only woman in camp. It was mid-afternoon by
the time Alane and Nardo arrived, and after Nardo had helped
her pitch their tent, he rode up toward the Buffalo Pass to meet
the men who were due to be coming back from their patrol.

Dane and Crim, one of the few men of the Atata Kindred to
survive the battle, were the men who had ridden through the
pass this day, and Nardo met them on the river path a half hour
outside camp. Each man was leading a remount.

"Nardo!" Dane greeted him with a grin. "As you can see, we
have been faithfully doing our job for you."

"Sa," Crim said. An arrow had grazed his cheek in the battle,
and he still bore the scar. "There is no sign of anyone on the
other side of the pass."

Nardo turned the horse he had taken from the camp remuda
and walked back with the other two men. "I am thinking that it
is time to send a few men into the Atata Valley itself," he said.

"I will go," Crim volunteered eagerly.

But Dane was frowning. "Nardo, I fail to see what such an
expedition would accomplish. If the Redu come through the Buffalo Pass, we will see them in time to barricade their way. I agree
with you that it is wise to keep watch on the Buffalo Pass and,
as you asked, I have been making certain that someone does the
patrol each day. But if the Redu are not bothering us, I think
we are wise to leave them alone."

Nardo said, "They may have returned to Big Rivers Joining.
They may be coming down the River of Gold."

"If that is so, then the Norakamo will see them before we do
and get word to us. The Norakamo summer camp is right on the
River of Gold. Surely that is the reasonable thing to do."

Nardo let out his breath with noisy exasperation. "Sa, it is
reasonable. And it is all this reasonableness that I find so frus-
trating! What can I do to impress upon you the danger of our
situation?"

Dane shot him a glance but said nothing. After a moment
Nardo asked, "Do you patrol the Buffalo Pass at the same time
every day?"

"Sa," Dane replied. "We leave at midday, ride to the top of
the pass and through, to a point where we have a good view of

the surrounding territory." He smiled sunnily. "That way we are back in time for supper."

Nardo did not return the smile.

All night he could not get the pass off his mind. "They patrol it at the exact same time every day," he said to Alane for perhaps the seventh time in an hour.

"So you have told me," she replied patiently. "But surely that should be enough, Nardo. They have the entire afternoon covered, after all." Nevin was sleeping and they were talking in soft voices so as not to disturb him.

"What about the morning?" Nardo asked. He was pulling his shirt off over his head, so his voice was somewhat muffled.

Alane took the shirt from his hand and began to fold it neatly. "From the way you have described it to me, they would have to march all night in order to get through the pass before our men saw them." She laid the folded shirt on top of the cradle board. They were using the traveling tent, and space was limited. "Remember, these Redu do not have horses. They travel slowly."

"March all night," Nardo said in a hollow voice. "Dhu, Alane. Suppose that is exactly what they do—march all night."

She looked at him. His naked torso glimmered in the light from the lamp, but there were shadows on his face. "You cannot get through such a pass at night, Nardo," she said. "It is too steep to climb in the dark."

"But they don't have horses to worry about, only themselves. They can use torches. And we are approaching the full of the moon!" Samu, hearing the alarm in Nardo's voice, growled softly.

He was beginning to alarm Alane as well. She put a protective hand on the deerskin bundle that was Nevin. "Well, what can you do?" she asked.

He pulled a flint dagger from the waistband of his buckskin trousers. "What I want to do is send a few men through the pass to scout the Redu and find out what they are doing. That is our great advantage over them, Alane, the mobility given to us by our horses. And we are not using it!"

"The council does not want to do this?"

"The council says, *Wait*." His fingers clenched on the dagger. "If only I were not so young, then perhaps they would listen to me." His voice was inexpressibly bitter. "Even Dane doesn't listen. He is only keeping this watch on the pass to humor me. He doesn't believe anything is going to happen."

"I have never seen you this anxious before, Nardo," Alane said. "What is wrong?"

"I don't know." He stabbed the knife into the dirt floor of the tent so hard that the edge of the flint blade broke. Alane stared at the broken dagger and shivered, feeling the chill of an ill omen.

"I feel like a horse that scents a predator even though he can't see it," Nardo said. "I have felt like that ever since we arrived. I don't know why."

Alane shivered again.

"I want you away from here in the morning," he said.

Alane looked at Nardo's hard face and knew she would never convince him to come with her. Her eyes came to rest on her peacefully sleeping baby. "All right, Nardo," she said slowly. "If you think it is best, Nevin and I will leave in the morning."

The night was quiet, though Nardo lay awake for most of it, listening and thinking. In the morning he sent Alane and Nevin off, immensely grateful to his wife for her quiet acquiescence to his somewhat arbitrary order. Her arms clung tightly around his neck before he lifted her to her horse, and she whispered in his ear, "Be careful," and that was all. If only, he thought, the tribe would listen to him as well as Alane did!

That day he had the horse herd moved to a pasture closer to the camp. He got some complaints from the men about doing that, since it was not their usual routine, but in this at least he was able to prevail.

"I know they are all waiting for me to return to the village so that they can move the horses back," Nardo said grimly to Dane, "but I am not going. I am staying right here for as long as I smell danger."

Dane did not, but he obligingly accompanied his friend each evening when Nardo pitched a tent on the heights of the Kindred side of the pass, by a small stream at the very edge of an evergreen forest, and kept watch.

Four days after Nardo's arrival in summer camp, on the day after the full of the moon, the Redu crossed the Buffalo Pass.

It was Samu who first warned Nardo that something was wrong. When he heard the dog's anxious whining, Nardo awoke and crawled out of his sleeping skins and then out of the flap of the small tent he was sharing with Dane. He shivered in the cold of the high altitude, and looked up the pass. When he saw the torches, his heart dropped into his stomach.

They were coming. They were really coming. In spite of his warnings, in spite of his premonition, he could hardly believe it.

A quiet voice sounded at his ear. "Dhu. So you were right after all, Nardo."

Nardo looked to the sky to judge the time. The full moon was in the west, several hours past the height of its arc. In two more hours it would be light.

Samu whined again and Nardo hushed him. "We must get back to the camp for the rest of the men as quickly as we can," he said to Dane. "If we're fast enough we may have time to put up the barricade."

Without further discussion the two of them began to run toward the place behind the tent where they had hobbled their horses for the night.

Nardo cursed furiously to himself as they raced back down the pass as fast as they could go in the moonlight. If only the men of the tribe had listened to him, they would be moving the barricade into position right now!

Men and girls poured out of their tents when Nardo galloped into camp shouting for all to awaken, that the Redu were coming through the pass. His deep voice cut through the babble of higher voices. "I want these men," and he reeled off a list of ten names, "to take the horses that are here in camp and come back to the pass with me. We must get that barricade into place. The rest of you collect the horse herd and leave it here with the girls, then take one horse each and follow us up the pass. If we have been in time to get the barricade up, we'll try to force them to turn back. If we are too late . . ." He broke off, a very grim look about his mouth.

"What shall we do if we are too late?" said Nat, the Bear Clan council member and one of the chief among those who had accused Nardo of being an alarmist.

"Take all the horses and get back to the village," Nardo said.

"We have far too few men to challenge them outright, and we cannot take the chance of their capturing any of the horses." It was one of his deepest fears, that they would lose their chief advantage to the Redu if the invaders ever got their hands upon the trained Kindred horses.

"All right," Nat said, his face scarcely less grim than Nardo's. "Those of you who are to get the horse herd, come with me."

The men moved the horse herd by moonlight from its valley pasture to the campsite along the river. Then they mounted up and galloped for the pass, leaving the remainder of the herd for the girls to cope with. Since the mares were enclosed between the cliff and the river, they were not difficult to control.

"We had better get them all haltered and ready to leave," said Brina, a girl of the Leopard Clan who was the eldest of the girls and the leader.

"Sa," agreed another girl. "And it would be well to get as much of the camp packed as is possible. We can always unpack again if our men are successful."

"If only," said Annora, a girl of the Red Deer, "we had listened to Nardo!"

This was a sentiment the men were expressing also as they raced as swiftly as they dared up the pass.

"Perhaps they will have raised the barricade in time," Harlan said. But when they heard the sound of horse hooves approaching from in front of them, they knew that they had not been quick enough.

Nat, who was riding at the front of the line, raised his hand to halt the rest of them. A moment later, as the first light of dawn stained the sky, Nardo and his party appeared out of the gray morning light.

"They were too close," Nardo said to Nat. "We would have gotten only half finished by the time they were within arrow-shot."

"What next then?" Nat asked.

"First we must secure the horse herd. They already have the advantage in numbers and weapons. We do not want to give them the horses as well."

"That we do not," one of the men behind Nat said feelingly.

"Back to camp, then," Nardo said.

Once at camp they tarried long enough to finish packing their clothes and their sleeping skins and some of their more precious cooking utensils. They had to leave most of the tents, however, for there was not time to take down the larger ones. Then, with each man and girl leading a string of horses, they set off west up the Narrow River, toward home.

By mid-afternoon, the Redu were comfortably established in the Kindred summer camp. Kerk was delighted with the location. "The fools," he said to Paxon as they stood together by the river at the point where it opened into one of the small enclosed valleys of the basin. The afternoon sun shone down on thick flower-sprinkled grass and on a herd of peacefully grazing ibex and sheep. "They could have held that pass against us, and instead they ran away."

Paxon's thin brown face wore a smile of faint contempt. "They are not warriors," he agreed.

Kerk snorted.

"They do have one thing that we do not have," Paxon continued, "and that is the horses." His eyes blazed with enthusiasm. "Imagine, Father, how invincible we would be if we could only get some of those horses for ourselves!"

But Kerk did not agree. "We don't need them," he said, adding derisively, "The only thing these men use their horses for is to run away."

"We would find other uses for them," Paxon insisted.

Kerk shrugged and repeated, "We don't need the horses to defeat these cowards, Paxon."

Paxon looked unconvinced, but did not pursue the subject. He said instead, "Most likely they have retreated farther up the river."

Kerk grunted in agreement. "This settlement we have taken is obviously a seasonal camp. There were not enough tents to house the entire tribe. According to the traders, the main tribal camp is on that River of Gold."

"Perhaps we should try to find that camp," Paxon said, and both he and his father turned their eagle profiles toward the west.

"Not just yet," Kerk said slowly. "First I want to scout the area around this camp. We will look for the camp on the River of Gold, Paxon, but not just yet."

Paxon thought they should act immediately, but he had long ago learned the unwisdom of disagreeing with his father and held his tongue.

Chapter Sixteen

"Now perhaps they will listen to you," Alane said. It was very late and Nardo had finally come into their tent to sleep. The riders and horses from summer camp had arrived at the village after sunset, and the ensuing hours had been taken up with getting the herd out to pasture. "If not for you, the whole camp would have been ambushed," Alane continued. "It is in my heart that the men will see you now as the leader you are."

"Some leader," Nardo returned bitterly. "So far all I have done is lead them in running away."

"That is not your fault. If they had listened to you, you would have been able to keep the Redu from crossing the Buffalo Pass."

Nardo grunted and dropped to lie beside her on the sleeping skins. He flung an arm across his forehead and stared up into the darkness above. "I made a great mistake in letting them take the summer camp," he said. "I did not realize how great the mistake until it was too late. It is completely protected, Alane. A perfectly safe stronghold. The village will not be nearly as easy to secure as summer camp would be."

"It was not your mistake!" Alane was fierce in his defense. "You wanted to secure the pass, but the tribe would not listen to you!"

"I should have posted myself on the other side of the pass. That would have given us the time to put up the barricade." His voice was harsh with anger. "I stayed where I was because there was water for the horses, but I was wrong. I cannot afford to make those kinds of mistakes."

"If the tribe had listened to you and posted the number of men you wanted on the pass, the Redu would not have gotten through," Alane repeated.

He let out his breath in a long hissing sound. "Dhu," he said. "What are we to do now?"

"No battles!" Alane said quickly.

His laugh was bitter. "No battles," he agreed.

"Why cannot you do to them what the Norakamo did to the Horse Eaters?" Alane asked. "Ambush their hunting parties?"

"We could have done that while they were still in the Atata valley," he agreed. "But at summer camp they are protected. The only way into the area is by the river path, and I am certain the Redu chief will not be as stupid as I was about keeping watch."

"These recriminations are becoming a little boring, Nardo," Alane said tartly.

She felt him stiffen, and then suddenly he laughed. He reached over and picked up her hand. "You are right. I need to be thinking of what must be done in the future, not what I didn't do in the past."

He raised her hand to his mouth and held it there. Silence fell while he thought.

"You can send to Rune," she said tentatively. "He said he would help you."

"Mmmm," he said. Samu, who had come in with Nardo, was snoring gently on his bed in the corner. In his nest on the other side of Alane, Nevin slept the profound sleep of childhood. Except for the guards Nardo had stationed by the river, the village had settled for the night.

"If we cannot get into summer camp," Nardo finally said, "then that means that neither can the Redu get out." Alane lay quietly, feeling the movement of his mouth against her palm as he thought out loud. "If I send a party of men down the Atata to guard the Buffalo Pass from the other side, and if we guard the river path from this side. . . ."

Her voice was soft so as not to disturb the baby. "They will be trapped."

"They will be trapped. And the herds do not remain in the high pastures of the Narrow River during the winter. They travel up the Greatfish to the River of Gold." He pressed a hard kiss on her palm. "Dhu, Alane. We will have them!"

She smiled at the note she heard in his voice. "This time you can build barricades ahead of time," she said.

She saw the flash of his white teeth in the dark. "Dhu, instead of trying to keep the Redu out of summer camp, I should have been trying to lure them in!"

"I don't agree, Nardo. I felt much safer when they were on the Atata side of the Buffalo Pass," Alane said firmly.

"They would never have stayed in the hunting grounds of the Atata. There is not enough game in the valley to support such a large tribe." He put an arm around her and drew her close against his side. "You are the best counselor I have, Alane."

She turned her face into his broad shoulder so he could not see her smile.

Alane was right about the men's increased respect for Nardo's judgment. This time there was no objection when he proposed barring the two exits from summer camp. And when Mano said forcefully, "If the tribe had listened to you before this, Nardo, the Redu would not now be hunting game in our summer camp," the rest of the council agreed, with only Varic remaining conspicuously silent.

"You were right and we were wrong," Nat said. "If it is all right with you, Nardo, I will take the men of the Bear Clan and guard the Buffalo Pass from the Atata side." His strong, square face took on a grim expression. "And this time we will do it right."

"I will be glad to entrust that task to the men of the Bear," Nardo said. "I do not think that the Redu will try to leave summer camp until the herds begin to migrate, but it is wise to secure the pass now."

"I will not argue with you, Nardo," Nat said.

Nardo glanced at Varic's face before putting a brief, friendly hand upon Nat's shoulder. "Next," he said to the group of men sitting in a circle around him under the clear blue sky, "we must decide what to do about our own situation. There is not enough hunting around the village to feed us all."

Several men grunted in agreement.

"Nor is there enough pasture for the number of horses we have here now," Freddo said.

"I suggest that we send the horses, the women and the children to finish the summer at Bright Valley," Nardo said. "There is hunting and pasture in plenty in the Altas. We need to keep only enough men and horses here to bar the river path if it proves necessary."

Silence. The men looked at each other. Finally Varic said in a brittle tone, "The women will not like that. They never leave the village."

"If they want to eat they will have to move," Nardo said reasonably. "The Norakamo women change camps with their men all the time. If the Norakamo women can do it, surely the women of the Kindred can also."

At the mention of the Norakamo, Varic's lips tightened. The rest of the men once more exchanged looks.

"Nardo is right," Mano said at last. "If summer camp is lost to us, we will have to use the pastures of Bright Valley. And the Altas are too far away to keep sending food back to the village."

None of the men looked happy, but not even Varic disagreed.

Mara was not at all pleased with the idea of moving to the Altas for the remainder of the summer. "Why can't we live upon fish?" she asked Nardo when he first broke the news to her. "There is still plenty of salmon in the Greatfish."

"Not enough for the entire village," Nardo replied. "There are just too many people here, Mama, too many mouths to feed. Remember, we have all of the Atata women and children to care for as well as our own. Without the meat coming in from summer camp, there will not be enough to eat."

He did not make the mistake of holding up the Norakamo women as an example to his mother, and after much repetition of how difficult all of this was going to be, Mara finally agreed to the move.

However, for her to agree to leave the village was one thing. For her to choose what to take from the belongings of a lifetime was something else.

"You had better talk to your mother about her packing, Nardo," Alane said to her husband after Mara had been at work for almost an entire day. "She is taking far too many things."

Alane had caught Nardo as he and Nat and the men of the Bear were going to choose the horses that would make the trip to the Atata valley. Nardo frowned.

"Why are you bothering me with stories of Mama's packing, Alane?" he asked his wife irritably. "If she is taking too much, tell her so!"

Alane's look was ironic. "If I tell Mara she is taking too much, she will probably pack even more."

The irritated line between Nardo's black brows deepened, but he realized the justness of this observation. "Then have Tora talk to her. Or Riva."

"They are all as bad as she is, Nardo." She threw up her hands in exasperation. "Kindred women have so many possessions!"

Nardo looked at his wife's upset face and gave a resigned sigh. "All right, I will talk to her as soon as I finish with the horses."

When Nardo finally reached his mother's house near suppertime, he stared in horror at the immense collection of items Mara had piled together to be packed and said firmly, "No, Mama. It would take half the herd to carry the baggage you have collected here. You cannot take everything that is in the house to camp with you!"

"This is far from being everything that is in the house, Nardo," Mara replied haughtily. "I have taken only those things that I must have in order to run my household."

Nardo looked again at the belongings that were piled high against one of the walls of the house. "For example," he said, "why do you need three musk ox skull cook pots? One should be sufficient."

She scowled. "What if it breaks or gets lost? Then I will have nothing large enough to cook a meal for the whole household."

"It won't break or get lost, Mama."

"It may."

"If it does, I will send someone back to the village to fetch another one for you."

"Hmmm." Mara folded her arms and tapped her foot, clearly not convinced.

"And why are you bringing the winter sleeping bags?"

"It is cold in the Altas."

"Not cold enough to need winter bags."

"Old bones get colder than young bones do, Nardo," Mara said with dignity.

Nardo cast her a measuring look. "All right. Bring yours and Tora's, then, but my sisters are young enough to keep warm without winter skins." With a ruthless hand Nardo removed two cook pots and a pile of sleeping bags from Mara's stack. His eye lit on something else. "Now what about all these rugs? You will be living in a tent, Mama. You do not need all these rugs."

Two hours later, Nardo emerged from Mara's house with the items Mara wanted to pack cut in half. Alane was right, he thought as he went toward his hut, the women of his tribe did have a great many belongings. He supposed it made for comfortable living when you stayed in one place, but it was a decided nuisance when you had to travel.

Mara was not the only matriarch who was having trouble leaving her precious belongings behind, and consequently the packing took much longer than Nardo had originally anticipated. Loading a horse for mountain travel had to be done very carefully. First, the horse's back was protected by a buckskin rug; then on top of the rug came a kind of wooden cradle, which was held in place by wide cinches of twisted horsehair strapped tightly around the horse's stomach. Next, a wide strip of twisted horsehair went around the chest, and another strip was strapped around the quarters under the tail. These extra straps were to keep the load from shifting backward or forward. Then two large reindeer skin sacks were hung on either side of the cradle, and the sacks were filled and balanced. When the sacks were filled, sleeping skins were stretched on top of everything and tied down.

As all the Kindred knew, two things were absolutely essential when packing a horse for mountain travel. First, the load had to be balanced on either side of the horse and, second, it must be secured so firmly that it could not shift on even the roughest, steepest trails. If the load was unbalanced, the horse would be unbalanced, and the twisting caused by an uneven load would eventually cause injury to the animal.

Each horse was packed to its maximum weight, from a hundred and fifty to two hundred pounds depending on the strength of the individual animal, when the tribe finally set off toward the Altas on a clear, warm summer morning. They went slowly, stopping early in the afternoon so there would be time to set up tents for the oldest and the youngest. The tribe was aiming for the High Col, a pass that had been cut millions of years before by the Greatfish as it left its source in the Altas and began its journey to the sea.

It took the tribe four days to make the trip from village to valley, following the path taken by herds since time immemorial as they too sought the summer richness of the mountain pastures. The going was particularly slow on the last day, for the path climbed steadily upward into the heights of the Col. The mountainside on either side of the path was filled with a breathtaking array of columbine, mountain lilies and narcissi, and Alane, who had never before been in the Altas, was transported by the beauty of the flowers. When the pack train finally emerged from the High Col into the valley, the afternoon sun was a brilliant blue, the lush mountain pasture before them was ablaze with flowers, and in the distance two glittering snow peaks soared up into the breast of the cobalt blue heavens. Alane's breath caught in her throat.

"This time of summer, our grazing camp is west of here," Lora said.

"Have you been here before, Lora?" Alane asked reverently.

"Before I was married. I came one summer to help the men." As Alane turned to look at Nardo's cousin, Lora's dimples appeared. "That was the summer when Dane and I first came together."

"You married him after the summer?"

Lora's dimples deepened. "When I learned there was a babe on the way."

Somewhat to her surprise, Alane was not shocked by such a revelation. Instead she laughed.

"You would be amazed how many children are conceived in this valley," Lora said mischievously, and Alane laughed again.

It was another hour before they came within sight of the Kindred camp. Nardo had sent ahead to tell the men that he was moving the village, and there was plenty of food awaiting the tired travelers when finally they alighted from their equally weary horses. By the time they had all eaten it was growing dark. The grazing camp tents were turned over to the oldest women and the youngest children, and the rest of the tribe crawled into their sleeping skins and slept under the intensely brilliant mountain stars.

Mara sat on a sun-warmed rock that was tucked cozily inside a rocky niche in the mountainside. A fat marmot sat upright beside his burrow not far from her feet, unconcerned by her quiet presence in his world. Above her on the mountainside two snowcocks cackled as they stripped the rich grass heads to eat. The smell of mint perfumed the air.

The mint reminded Mara of Alane, and she frowned.

Earlier this morning Mara had walked alone up the valley, and when she had seen this protected place a little way up the cliff, she had climbed up to it. She had been sitting here for some time, long enough for the marmot to grow accustomed to her, and now she pressed her hand flat against the sensuous warmth of the rock and looked down at the valley floor, at the sprawl of tents in the distance that was the Kindred's summer home.

They had been in the Altas two weeks. Two weeks and already the damage was beginning, already the ancient Mother's Blood living patterns of the tribe were beginning to change. For here in the valley, the matriarch's big house, which served as the heart of the family when they lived in the village, was no longer an entity. No tent could accommodate the number of people the big house could. Mara's daughters and son, and her sister's daughters and sons, were all living with their spouses and their children in their own tents.

A breeze blew down the valley, stirring the hair at Mara's temples and rippling the buckskin of her skirt.

At home the women often did not sleep in their huts because

for most of the year their husbands were not there to share the hut with them. The way Kindred life was organized, a man spent at least three quarters of the year at either a hunting or a grazing camp. One of the reasons the women held together so closely was the prolonged absence of their men.

This was not something Mara had thought about before. It was not something she enjoyed thinking about now. But she had to understand the winds of change that were battering her family if she was to be successful in withstanding them.

Meltwater from the snows above had made the slope directly across from Mara's perch intensely lush and brilliant with flowers. She stared at the beauty blindly, her eyes focused inward on her thoughts.

Of course, not all the men were present in Bright Valley either. Six handfuls of men were guarding the Buffalo Pass, and six handfuls more were watching the Narrow River exit from summer camp. Nardo had said he would change these men periodically until the end of summer, when the herds began to leave the mountains.

Still, many more women had their husbands beside them than usual. And Mara could see that the women liked this. Nor were most of them finding the easygoing camp life of Bright Valley at all unpleasant.

"We really do not need all the things we have accumulated at home, Mother," Mara had heard Lora saying to Tora yesterday. "They only make a clutter in the house. It is in my heart that the Kindred women should imitate the women of the Norakamo and follow their men from camp to camp. Such a life could be great fun."

Lora's words had lodged like a stone in Mara's heart. Her greatest fear was that her niece was merely voicing out loud the thoughts of many of the younger women of the tribe.

I must do something, Mara thought. *The Mother's Blood is in danger.*

It was bitter gall to her that her beloved son was the one most to blame in what was happening. It was he who had brought the Norakamo stranger into their midst. It was he who had taken the tribe's women from their ancestral village to this male camp where life was turned upside down.

Even with all the extra Atata women and children, every-where Mara looked there seemed to be a group of men!

Mara comforted herself with the thought that they could not remain more than another moon in the Altas. Summer was coming to an end. Nardo would take the tribe back to the village, and the men would go to the winter camps as they always had. Life would once more return to normal.

Mara's eyes swung toward the camp and lighted on a a figure that was lifting a water basket to rest on silvery pale hair.

The Norakamo woman. There was where the true danger lay, Mara thought. Sooner or later she was going to have to do something about Alane.

At the beginning of Ibex Moon, Kerk at last sent out a scouting party to explore the territory to his west. Paxon and the rest of his party had traveled several miles along the Narrow River when they found themselves entering a narrow and winding gorge. Their progress was abruptly halted by the sight of a seven-foot-high log barricade looming ahead of them on the track. The scouting party stopped abruptly.

"What is it?" Aven asked.

Under his breath Paxon muttered, "I knew we should not have given them so much time."

"It's a barricade, Aven," a young man called Jorde said sarcastically.

Paxon frowned at Jorde, then said, "I wonder if it is manned."

The five men stood in the bright sun and surveyed the barrier before them. There was no sign of human presence, just the huge log edifice that stretched across the path from the sheer cliff to the river.

"There is only one way to find out," Jorde said with bravado, and he made a sudden dash toward the barricade.

"Come back here, you fool!" Paxon shouted. But it was too late. Before the Redu could move to ready their bows, two heads appeared above the barricade and two javelins were thrown, both of them hitting the surprised Jorde squarely in the chest. The thuds were clearly audible, and Jorde went down like a stone.

Paxon scowled and cursed. Then, "I'll go for him," he said to his men. "Cover me."

Aven reached out to put a hand on his friend's arm. "Leave him, Paxon. There is no way only three of us can protect you, even with arrows. Those bastards are quick."

The straight, thick lines of Paxon's brows drew together as he regarded the barricade. Then he looked at Jorde's motionless body. "I can't leave him there," he said. "He might not be dead."

"He took two javelins in the chest!" Aven protested.

"I can't leave him," Paxon repeated. He shook off Aven's arm and started forward slowly. The three Redu left behind quickly raised their bows to their shoulders, fitted their arrows, and trained their sights on the top of the barricade. Paxon glanced back, saw they were ready, then darted forward the ten feet that had put Jorde inside javelin range, seized the fallen man by his shoulders and dragged him back toward safety. No heads appeared above the barricade and no javelins were thrown. The Kindred apparently were content to let the Redu retrieve the body.

"By the thunder, but he is heavy!" Paxon grunted as he released Jorde's body.

Aven bent to feel for a heartbeat. His hand came away covered with blood. "He is also dead," Aven said grimly.

The four Redu looked from the lifeless body of their comrade to the huge log wall.

"Our arrows still have a longer reach than their javelins," Aven said. "They can't rush us."

"They don't want to come in," Paxon said. "They want to keep us from getting out."

"How many of them do you suppose there are behind that thing?" Aven asked next.

"I don't propose we try to find out," Paxon said grimly. "I think we had better bring this news to my father."

Kerk was astonished by the existence of a barricade. "I did not think these people had so much resistance in them," he said, and next sent scouts up the Buffalo Pass. Paxon was not greatly surprised to find that blocked by a barricade also.

Kerk made one attempt to win through the barricade at Narrow River, but ended up retreating when he realized that he would not be able to break through without a tremendous loss of Redu lives.

The deer were still plentiful at summer camp during Ibex Moon, so Kerk was under no necessity to act immediately. For the moment he decided to settle down in comfort while he turned his mind to what his next move would be.

Chapter Seventeen

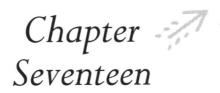

Ibex Moon died and Leaf Fall Moon rose in the sky. Snow began to fall on the higher mountain pastures, and in Bright Valley the temperature at nights regularly fell below freezing. It was time for the Kindred to leave the Altas.

Alane was reluctant to turn her back on the mountains. She did not think she had ever been as happy as she had been these past two moons. Away from the suffocating atmosphere of the big house, she had been free to run her own household and care for her husband in the way she wished.

Life in Bright Valley had the further advantage of stripping Nardo's mother of most of her power. In camp, each small household was a unit unto itself. Alane was afraid that once they returned to the village, Mara would be able to reassert her authority, something Alane was not anxious to see happen.

But it was autumn. True, there were still flowers in the Altas—late-blooming gentians and primroses brightened the crevices of the rocky mountainsides with their vivid blues and yellows—but new snow dusted the lower slopes and the upper ones were solidly white. The deer were returning to the lower altitudes for the breeding season, and the mountain sheep were already in rut.

Frost covered the grass on the morning the tribe began its trek back to the village, and the ground crackled under the horses' hooves as they moved across alpine meadows toward the High Col. Alane rode beside Nardo, and as they passed a scree of rocks, a flock of pheasants were flushed from their cover and fled, cackling wildly. Bluebird shied and Alane's heart dropped into her stomach. Nevin was sitting in front of Nardo, completely unstrapped. Nardo had the mare under control almost immediately, however, and Nevin was still in place when Bluebird began to walk forward once more.

Nevin laughed and clapped his hands.

Alane said, "Nardo, perhaps Nevin ought to ride in the cradle board."

"He'll be fine, Alane," her husband replied. "I will keep him safe."

Alane did not agree. "I think the cradle board would be wiser," she said.

Nardo looked annoyed. "You cannot keep him a baby forever, Alane."

"He is only a year old, Nardo!"

"Big boy," Nevin said proudly, turning to look at his mother.

Nardo smiled and patted his arm.

Boom! The sound came rolling through the air like thunder, and, distracted, Alane looked up. *Boom!* She narrowed her eyes against the sun, scanned the peaks, and then she saw them: two rams on a high, narrow ledge overhanging the sheer rock wall that led to the pass. As Alane watched, they backed off from each other with lowered heads, stood perfectly still for a moment, and then charged. Their horns met and the *Boom!* resounded from rock to rock. The rams backed away again, waited, and charged once more.

Beside her, Nardo halted his horse. Like Alane, his eyes were raised to the battle being waged on the narrow ledge high above them.

The charging had stopped; the rams had locked horns and were straining against each other, each trying to push his opponent back. At last one of the rams began to win. Even from her observation place far below, Alane could see that the other one was weakening.

Then he was down. Alane watched as the other ram followed up his advantage, and the two great horned sheep struggled together desperately on the narrow ledge. A body came hurtling through the clear mountain air.

Nevin cried out in dismay.

Head raised, the victorious ram stood like a conqueror surveying the domain he had just won.

Alane said disgustedly, "All male animals are alike. All they know is rutting and fighting and death."

"They both wanted the same territory, Alane, and neither one would give it up," Nardo replied. She turned and met his grave dark eyes. "Sometimes a man has to fight to keep the things that are his," he said, and his big hand lifted to ruffle the smooth black hair that hung on Nevin's brow.

Alane's eyes fell, and she did not reply.

By the end of Leaf Fall Moon, Kerk realized that he could not stay where he was for the winter. The big herds of reindeer and red deer that had fed them all summer had migrated either east or west along the Narrow River, into the territories of the Atata or the Greatfish and the River of Gold. All that was left in the Redu hunting grounds were ibex and sheep and birds— not enough game to feed over four hundred men.

"We must break out of here," he said to his council of secondary chiefs as they met in the big upper cave on a chill and overcast autumn morning. "We may lose some men in the trying, but we will lose even more to starvation if we try to spend the winter in this camp."

The council of thin-cheeked men looked grim.

"They have a very strong position at both exits," Madden said heavily. "We may lose half our men and still not be able to break through."

Wain was nervously drumming his fingers on his knee. "If only we could get some archers into the heights above them!" he exclaimed.

"Impossible," Madden returned, shaking his head with reluctant slowness. "The walls above the barricades are sheer stone."

Kerk stroked the arch of his nose and regarded his men. "I think they are probably feeling very safe behind those barricades," he said. "What they do not know, however, is that all of our men are not at this camp."

Madden's breath caught audibly in his throat as he realized what Kerk was talking about.

Wain grinned. "That is so," he said triumphantly. "I had forgotten about Cuch and the fifty men you sent with him to hunt for the women. If they could come up behind the Kindred men guarding the Buffalo Pass . . ."

Kerk raised his narrow black eyebrows and said, "Yes."

"But how are we to get word to Cuch of what he must do?" one of the chiefs asked angrily. "We are trapped here!"

"I will send Paxon," Kerk said. "He has the agility of an ibex. If anyone can climb out of this valley, he can."

Kerk was not speaking out of mere fatherly pride, and all the other chiefs knew it. The gloom disappeared from the council like magic.

"This is a good plan," Madden said enthusiastically. "If Cuch and his men come up behind the men at the barricades while we are attacking them from in front, we will have them."

"Yes," said Kerk again, "we will."

Safe behind their barricades, the men of the Kindred watched with satisfaction as the reindeer migrated westward by way of the river. But as the days grew steadily colder and the herds passed in increasing numbers into lower altitudes, Nardo began to worry. He knew that the Redu would not remain in the camp all winter and starve without first making a serious attempt to break out.

What would I do if I were the Redu chief?

This was the question Nardo asked himself as he stood on the river path late one afternoon, staring eastward toward the camp of the penned-up Redu. *I cannot afford to make another mistake,* he thought. *If they get by us here, the village will be doomed.*

"What are you scowling about, Nardo?" Dane said. Nardo did not turn his head as his friend came to stand beside him on the path. "I am thinking it is the Redu chief who should be wearing that frown, not you."

"He will be planning something," Nardo said. "I am just trying to imagine what it is he will do."

"He'll try to break out again," Dane said with certainty.

Nardo grunted, then raised his head and scanned the sheer rock walls of the gorge.

"There is no way the Redu can scale those heights, Nardo," Dane assured him. "They cannot get behind us. It is impossible."

"That is what they must do," Nardo muttered. "Get behind us."

"They can't," Dane said flatly. "The whole tribe is neatly caught in our trap."

"The women too?" Nardo asked suddenly.

"What do you mean?"

"The women." Nardo swung around and fixed a hard, alert stare on Dane's face. "They did not bring their women when they made that march through the Buffalo Pass."

Dane was puzzled. "That is true. They probably sent for them after they had secured the camp."

"We had barricades up at the Buffalo Pass within days, Dane. They could not have had time to send for their women!"

Dane frowned. "I don't understand what you are saying, Nardo."

"I am saying that if they left their women behind, they must have left some of their men also. No chief would leave his women and children completely unprotected."

"That is so . . ." Dane still did not understand.

Nardo said, "Don't you see? Nat has the enemy behind him as well as before him, and he doesn't know it!"

Finally Dane understood. "Dhu." He stared at Nardo in horror. "What can we do?"

"Send some men to find the Redu women. And pray to the Mother that we are not too late!"

It took Paxon a week to reach the women's camp. There were times when he thought he would not make it at all. His nails were torn, his hands were bleeding and his feet were bruised from scaling the rocky cliffs that enclosed the valleys of summer camp. The majority of the Redu men would have never been able to make that climb, he thought. They *had* to break out of that cursed camp by way of the Buffalo Pass!

Cuch, the secondary chief who was in charge of the women's

camp, was horrified by Paxon's state when he came staggering in. He was picked up along the river by some of the men and almost carried up the steep path to the big cave that had once served as the men's meeting place for the Atata Kindred and was now living quarters for the Redu.

It did not take Paxon long to explain the gravity of the tribe's situation. "Kerk says we must come up behind the men who are barricading the pass," he ended. "Kerk will be ready on his side of the pass, and when he hears our war horns and knows that the attack has been launched from the rear, then he will attack the front."

"What of the women and children?" Cuch asked. "Do I leave them here unprotected?"

Paxon nodded, his young face set into unusually grim lines. "They can fend for themselves for a short while, and we will need every man we can muster."

"All right," Cuch agreed. "I'll call the men together and tell them."

"If we leave tomorrow afternoon, we will reach the bottom of the pass by nightfall. We can get a few hours' sleep and be ready to climb the pass and attack with the dawn. It is vital that we take them by surprise."

"That is Kerk's plan?"

"That is Kerk's plan."

"Very well," said Cuch. "Then we will follow it."

Nardo and the men of the Kindred were waiting for the Redu at a place just south of where the Narrow River fed into the Atata. A high, sloping hill dropped to the river path there, and it was on the heights of this hill that Nardo had posted his men. The day before he had discovered where the Redu women and children were camping and the number of men who were with them.

"What if they don't come this way?" Varic asked when Nardo first made his dispositions. "There cannot have been any communication between these men and the men in summer camp. How will they know that the rest of their tribe is caught in a trap?"

"They cannot know that, of course," Nardo replied. "But I am thinking they will be wondering why they have heard nothing from their chief. They will send men to contact him. In fact, I am surprised that they have not done so already."

The men of the Kindred had only two days to wait before Dane came galloping up with the news that he had seen the band of Redu archers coming down the Atata.

Nardo heaved a sigh of profound relief. He was not too late.

"We cannot give them the opportunity to use their bows," Nardo said emphatically to his men as they gathered around him. "If we use the formation we practiced this summer and smash into the middle of their ranks, we will be in too close quarters for them to use their bows, and we will be in good position to use our axes."

It was late in the afternoon, and a chill wind was blowing off the Altas and funneling up the river. The men of the Kindred blew on their fingers to warm them as they arranged their horses into the arrow-shaped formation that Nardo wanted. They had practiced this kind of charge again and again on the stony hills of Bright Valley, and both horses and men knew what they were expected to do.

They waited, Nardo at the apex of the inverted V shape, fifty horses and riders exactly in position, waiting for the signal to begin their precipitous descent.

Nardo could feel Bluebird's excitement and knew she was reacting to the tension she sensed in him. He patted her shoulder, murmured soothingly and breathed slowly, trying to relax his own muscles.

Wait, he told himself. *Wait. It is vital not to commit to the charge too soon.*

The horses, trained since first they were ridden to stand quietly while hunting reindeer, stood like statues behind the concealing juniper bushes on the hillside. The close formation had been very carefully planned so that each horse was surrounded by friends and thus would have little temptation to kick or bite.

The line of Redu, marching four abreast, their huge bows slung over their shoulders, came around the curve of the hill and directly under the eyes of the poised horsemen. Still Nardo waited. Varic, who flanked him immediately on the left in the wedge, hissed furiously, "How much longer do you mean to wait?"

Nardo ignored him, waited a few more nerve-shattering seconds, then raised his hand. A golden eagle, its feathers ruffling in the cold wind, rose into the gray sky from its nest in the rocks on top of the hill. Nardo's hand dropped, and fifty men and horses surged forward.

Their furious downhill descent gained momentum with every stride. The hill was so steep that the horses were almost sitting on their haunches, but they held their formation and hurtled forward.

The Redu were taken utterly by surprise. Heads turned in alarm as they heard the thundering noise of the charge. Paxon, at the forefront of the line, was one of the first to realize what was happening and reached for his bow. But it was too late. The horsemen crashed into the line of Redu with shattering impact.

The entire center of the Redu line of march went down under the onslaught. Paxon watched in horror as the huge black-haired man on the gray horse who had led the charge raised his arm and brought his ax down on Cuch's unprotected head. Blood spurted, Cuch went down, and the black-haired man began to force his horse through the splintered ranks of the Redu, swinging his ax in a figure-of-eight motion that felled men all around him. The horsemen began to surge along the river path, all of them now using their axes in the manner of their leader.

They would all die if they stayed on this path. "The river!" Paxon shouted to the men nearest him. "Try to get across the river!" And he scrambled off the path and down the bank toward the cold gray water of the Atata.

He was in up to his ankles when he heard the thunder of hooves behind him. Cursing, he waded farther, needing enough water to submerge himself. Instinct made him turn just at the moment that an ax was descending toward his head. He ducked, the ax missed his head and hit him on the shoulder, sending excruciating pain down his arm. He whirled, not wanting to die with his back toward his enemy. The brown-haired man on the horse towered above him, ax raised high.

"Coward," Paxon shouted in Kindred Speak. "Get off the horse and fight me face to face!"

Dane's arm was arrested halfway through its descent. "You speak my language!"

"Sa," Paxon spat, "I speak your language." The water was only up to his knees. Curse his luck that this part of the river shelved off so gradually. The mare's nostrils were flared as she sucked in air, and Paxon could see the veins standing out on her sweaty gray neck. Her rider had lowered his ax. Paxon measured the distance between himself and the man on the horse's back. If he could push the man off and mount the horse himself . . .

Paxon jumped for the man. The horse leaped almost as soon as he made his move, and Paxon fell to his knees in the cold water. Instinctively he raised his arm to protect his head. The mare was snorting and kicking up water as she danced in excitement. The man on her back spoke coolly, "I think my chief will want to talk to you. Drop your weapons into the river and come with me."

Nardo was at the center of a laughing, triumphant group of victorious warriors when Dane approached with his prisoner. The laughter stopped abruptly when the Kindred men saw the Redu.

"Have you gone moon-mad, Dane?" Varic demanded. "What are you doing with him?"

Dane ignored the Eagle leader and said to Nardo, "He speaks our language, Nardo. I thought you might find him useful."

Nardo came forward to stand before Paxon. The Kindred chief's height and breadth dwarfed the slim young Redu, but Paxon stared haughtily at the bloodstained giant before him and showed no sign of fear.

"Do you understand me?" Nardo asked.

"Sa," Paxon replied through his teeth. "I understand you."

Nardo looked at Dane. "We can use him to communicate with the Redu women," he said. "You did the right thing in keeping him alive."

Paxon's expression sharpened at Nardo's words. "You go next for our women?"

"I cannot just leave them," Nardo said a little grimly. "If I do they will starve."

Paxon's face said clearly that he thought starvation would be preferable to a visit by the men of the Kindred, but he held his tongue.

The men found the Redu women and children in the main campsite of the Atata tribe. The Kindred huts were perched on the top of a high cliff that gave good views down the valley, and so the women had ample warning of the horsemen's approach. When Nardo and his men first rode up the cliff path and into the camp they found the huts deserted, but then the sound of a wailing child told them that the inhabitants were hiding in the big cave.

"Tell them to come out," Nardo instructed Paxon, and the Redu reluctantly did as he was told.

Slowly, fearfully, the Redu women and children crept outdoors again and gathered in the big open space before the cave. Some of the women were moaning aloud in terror, and all of the children were huddled close to their mothers, pressing their faces into the comfort of soft maternal bellies and breasts. The picture vividly brought back to Nardo's mind an almost identical moment when, in this very place, he had had to tell the women of the Atata Kindred that their men had been killed in battle. His face very grim, he turned to Paxon and commanded, "Tell them what has happened to their men."

A bleak-faced Paxon obeyed, and the wailing of the women rose to the heavens.

Nardo had to raise his voice to make himself heard over the noise the women were making. "Tell them not to be afraid. Tell them that the Kindred do not make war on women and children. We will not hurt them."

Paxon gave him an incredulous look. He had little illusion about the fate of the Redu women. At home, rape had been one of the time-honored spoils of war.

Nardo said sternly, "Tell them."

Paxon drew a breath and spoke again. When he had finished, the women in front of him looked as incredulous as he did.

Dane muttered to Nardo, "What a sorry-looking sight this is."

"I know," Nardo replied. "It makes you wonder what their men would do to our women if the situation was reversed."

Paxon listened to this exchange, and a puzzled frown came to his face. He looked around at the obviously under-control group of Kindred men, then asked Nardo with genuine interest, "What you do with them?"

"I cannot leave them here," Nardo replied reluctantly. "They will starve without men to hunt for them. Nor can I take them back to my own village. We have already taken in the women and children of the Atata Kindred whose men fell in battle against you. I will have to send them east, out of the mountains to the plains. There are many tribes there who trade over the sea. Extra women will be useful to them."

Anger ripped through Paxon. "You give Redu women to other tribes to *trade*?"

Nardo's dark stare was as unflinching as his voice. "Would you prefer me to kill them now? That is the choice you have given me, man of the Redu. I will not leave them here to die slowly by starvation. Either I finish it quickly, or I send them to the plain."

"The choice I have given you?" Paxon flared. "This not my choice, Kindred man!"

There was a moment's silence during which it occurred to the Redu that this young chief was every bit as intimidating as Kerk. Then Nardo said, "It was you who put them in jeopardy when you brought them here to a land that was not yours. It was you who have forced me to make a choice about women and children that I never wanted to make, and that I hope the Mother will forgive me for."

Paxon could find no answer to this, and so he turned to the women and told them what would be their fate. The women wept and wailed some more but in a subdued fashion, and Paxon knew that in their hearts they had realized that things could have been far worse.

Nardo sent thirty of his men to escort the two hundred women and children safely over the mountains to the plain. Hoping to conciliate Varic, he put him in charge and gave him most

of the remounts, so only twenty Kindred men rode up the river
path and into the village on a cold late-autumn afternoon.
Twenty Kindred men and Paxon.

They were greeted a quarter of a mile from the village by
what looked like a wildly ecstatic wolf. The Redu did not keep
dogs, and Paxon thought at first that they were being attacked.
It was not until Nardo laughed, jumped from his horse and bent
to give the creature a rough embrace that Paxon realized the dog
was tame.

"Samu missed you," Dane, who rode on Paxon's right, called
to Nardo.

Paxon stared with astonishment at the man and dog before
him. The dog was so excited he couldn't keep still, but kept
circling around and around the man's legs, and Nardo kept patting whatever quivering part he could get his hands on.

"Let us hope our wives missed us as much as Samu missed
Nardo," another man said, and everyone laughed.

Nardo gave the dog one last pat and straightened up. Then
he leaped once more onto Bluebird's back, and the party of
twenty-one men, forty-two horses and one dog moved forward
again. As they rounded a bend in the river, Paxon saw a welcoming group of women, children and puppies bounding toward
them. The yipping of the puppies and the shouts of the children
were deafening. Paxon looked with amazement at the oncoming
throng, his eyes passing curiously over the joyful faces of the
women and children.

He spotted a girl a little distance behind the pack, running as
gracefully and lightly as a deer. A shimmering flag of wheat-gold
hair streamed behind her, and when Paxon saw her face he
stopped breathing. Her eyes were fixed on a point somewhere to
Paxon's left, and just as he realized he needed air, she halted. In
front of her was a heaving, noisy crowd of families being reunited, but the girl stood apart, waiting.

Paxon did not even see the man who was making his way
toward her through the crowd. He simply sat on his horse and
looked at her, until all of a sudden she disappeared into an enormous embrace.

Nardo, Paxon thought blankly. She belongs to Nardo.

His eyes were glued to the pair, but all that he could see at the moment was Nardo's broad back. It seemed forever until the man loosened his arms and raised his head and the girl appeared again. Paxon saw her look around at the diminished number of men who had ridden in, then up at Nardo. Her lips moved. The man shook his head in response, then turned to the crowd behind him.

"All of our men are safe." Nardo's raised voice managed to carry over the din of people and puppies. "I have sent Varic and most of the men who rode with me to escort the Redu women and children out of our mountains. The Redu men who were guarding the women are dead, and the rest of them are still trapped in summer camp. The village is safe."

Women and children cheered. Nardo draped his arm across the shoulders of the girl who must be his wife and began to walk toward Paxon, the only man still horsed. The thought flitted through Paxon's mind that now was his chance to escape. But his hands were tied, and he could not drag his eyes away from Nardo's wife. They stopped a little distance from him, and the girl glanced in his direction.

"Is that one of them?" Her voice was deeper than he would have expected. Her hair lifted in the breeze, and several long silvery strands caught on Nardo's stained buckskin sleeve.

"Sa. He speaks our tongue, Alane. That is why I have taken him captive. He was useful in communicating with the Redu women, and he will be useful again if ever we have to communicate with the Redu men."

Paxon realized that they did not think he could hear their voices. "He looks so young," the girl said.

"He's dangerous," Nardo returned, and suddenly realized that Paxon was unguarded. "Too dangerous to be left alone like that." Nardo strode forward to grasp the halter of Paxon's horse. The girl followed behind her husband. "Mano!" Nardo shouted, and a man came running. "Hold Graystone until I can make arrangements for keeping this Redu safe," Nardo ordered.

The girl had caught up with her husband, and from the safety of his side she looked up at Paxon. Her eyes were gray and clear as a mountain stream between long, dark lashes. Paxon knew he would never again see a face as beautiful as this one. He smiled at her.

The gray eyes widened. Faint color stained her cheekbones. She looked away from him and said to her husband, "Is it necessary, Nardo, to tie him up?"

"Sa," he replied grimly.

A gust of wind came down the valley from the west, and the girl's hair blew into her face. She pushed it away. "I was drying my hair in the sun when I heard you were back," she said. "I didn't even stop to braid it."

Nardo slid a big hand into the silky length. "I like it like this."

She wrinkled her nose. "You have no sense of what is proper."

His eyes sparkled and he grinned. Paxon stared at the Kindred chief's suddenly transformed face.

"What do you want us to do with this Redu, Nardo?" Mano said.

Reluctantly the chief turned his attention from his wife. "I'll see if we have an empty hut."

"We do not have an empty hut," the girl informed him emphatically. "The addition of the Atata women and children has filled up all our houses."

Nardo's eyes raked the village. "We'll put him in Nessa's hut, then," he decided. "Adun has gone with the Redu women and children, and Nessa and the children can sleep in Mama's house for now."

"All right," Mano said. He looked up at Paxon and barked, "Get off."

Paxon slid off the horse and felt his knees buckle as his feet hit the ground. A soft voice said, "Poor boy."

"He is not a poor boy, Alane," Nardo said impatiently. "He is a Redu. He probably killed a handful of Kindred men in the battle."

Paxon couldn't resist. He turned his arrogant nose in Nardo's direction, showed his teeth, and said, "Two handfuls."

Nardo made no reply but handed over the short javelin that was stuck through his belt. Mano pointed the javelin at Paxon and gestured. Paxon turned his back on the Kindred chief and his wife and began to walk in the direction of what looked like a permanent village.

Her name, he thought, was Alane.

Days passed and then weeks. The weather became colder and the Redu grew hungrier. Finally Kerk was forced to admit that Paxon had not gotten through to the women's camp.

"He must have fallen," Madden said. "Paxon was a good climber, but even he was not an ibex."

Madden's use of the past tense said more clearly than anything else what he thought had happened to Paxon. Kerk felt a sharp stab of grief and stared intently at his crossed legs to hide his face.

"Something has happened to him," he admitted at last. "Otherwise he would have returned here, or Cuch would be attacking the Buffalo Pass." He paused, his eyes flicking from one secondary chief's face to another. "It looks as if we will not be able to rely on assistance from the outside."

The men were meeting in the upper cave, whose elevated placement in the cliff gave them a good view of the cold gray ribbon that was the Narrow River and of the mountains that rose on the other side of the valley. They had a fire roaring and the skins they had hung at the cave opening were pushed aside to let the smoke out. "We have made it through hungry times before," one of the chiefs said stoutly.

Kerk shook his head. "We don't have any stores of grain and dried fruits. We have almost gone through our stores of dried fish and smoked meat. There is not enough game here to keep us alive until the spring. It is not a hungry time that is facing us—it is starvation."

"What are we to do, then?" Wain asked in angry despair.

"We must climb out of here," Kerk replied.

The men stared at the hard-set eagle face of their chief.

It was Madden who broke the silence. "How?" he demanded. "If Paxon could not make it, Kerk, how are we to scale those heights?"

"Paxon went to the south," Kerk returned. "We will try the mountains to the north."

"It's snowing," one of the council members said softly, and

all the men turned to stare out the cave opening. This was the first snow that had fallen on their camp.

"Do we have a choice?" Kerk asked his council. "Either we stay here and starve, or we take our fate into our hands and try to get out of this trap."

"It might be better to try to break out through the Kindred barricades," Wain said.

"They will cut us to pieces," Kerk replied. "I would rather chance the mountains."

It was a freezing, overcast morning in the middle of the Moon When the Reindeer Lose Their Antlers when Kerk led his men north into the untrodden wilderness of the mountains that enclosed the Kindred summer camp. They had no food except a little ground-up dried meat mixed with fat, but they were extraordinarily tough men who had lived most of their lives in the shadow of hunger and death. There were no complaints as they shouldered their bows and turned their faces into the north wind. They knew they must scale the mountains or die.

The tribe crossed the Narrow River at a ford a little to the west of their camp and began to ascend out of the valley. The first part of the climb was not too bad. They had to scramble to find their footing in some places, but the snow on the lower slopes had not as yet risen beyond a few inches. As the day grew dark, the tribe was able to pitch camps on several ledges, and each man unrolled his sleeping skins and got some sleep.

They woke in the morning to the sound of the wind howling through the upper branches of the pines with a harsh, angry sound. As they ate their meager breakfast, it began to snow.

Kerk knew there was no choice but to go on. With their eyes half closed to protect them from the stinging, blowing snow, the men staggered ever upward. The slope they were ascending grew steeper, the snowdrifts deeper, and the going was desperately hard. Before long the only way they could progress was to crawl on all fours. The greatest burden fell on the leaders, who, in addition to the exertion of the climb, had the job of breaking a trail through the ever deepening snow. Those who crawled exhaustedly in the leaders' wake at least had a path to follow. Kerk had to change leaders every fifty yards, the toll on the ground breakers was so great.

It was sheer luck that the slope Kerk had chosen led to a pass. They stood at the top, and the wind roared through the cliffs and the snow beat against their faces in hard, stinging particles, but Kerk knew that whatever god had directed him along this route had saved their lives. If they had been met at the top with an impassable rock barrier, they would have perished.

Once through the pass, the downward haul was almost as difficult as the ascent had been. The drifts were deeper on this side of the mountain and the men were exhausted. Every half hour Kerk called a halt, and the men collapsed in the snow to recoup their energy. They limped and lumbered down, stumbling and slipping. By the time they had descended below the snow line onto a slope of grass and scree, they had reached the limit of their endurance. They unrolled their sleeping skins almost blindly and slept where they dropped.

Two days later, the Redu scouts reported to Kerk that they had found a small river. As all hunters knew, where there was water there was likely to be game. Kerk and his hungry followers shouldered their bows and headed for the River Volp, the location of the Kindred women's Sacred Cave.

Chapter
Eighteen

This year the Kindred's great winter religious festival, New Year Rites, was severely hampered by the absence of nearly half the tribe's men. The thirty men Nardo had sent to escort the Redu women and children out of the mountains were not present, nor were the two bands of fifty that were guarding the exits to summer camp. The shortage of males was further complicated by the fact that the tribe had taken on nearly a hundred additional women from the Atata Kindred.

Nardo suggested that the tribe forgo the Winter Fires ceremony altogether this year, but Lina, the Red Deer matriarch, would not hear of such a thing.

"The women of the Red Deer have been holding Winter Fires since the time when Earth Mother first made the world," she reprimanded Nardo. "It is not for any male chief to interfere with such a sacred thing."

Nardo shrugged his broad shoulders. "I am only thinking that there will not be enough available men for a fertility rite."

"Bring back the ten handful of men who guard the exits to summer camp," Lina said. "Then there will be men enough."

"Impossible."

"It is not impossible," Lina retorted. "They need be away from their posts for a mere two days. The Redu have done nothing in all this long while that our men have been watching those wretched exits, Nardo! Two days will make no difference to their vigil."

When Nardo continued to refuse, Lina went to Mara. Nardo's mother agreed with the Red Deer matriarch, and the two of them united to confront him on this issue.

"You have brought back from guard duty the men who play the principal roles in the dances put on by the clans of the Fox, the Bear and the Leopard," Mara argued. "*You* will be here for our own rite, the Lighting of the New Fire. It is not fair to the Red Deer that theirs is the only ceremony that will be canceled."

"Lina has said that she will not cancel it, Mama," Nardo returned with careful patience. "Certainly the women's part of the rite can go forward as usual. And I will release from duty any particular man whom you feel you need, but he will have to be replaced by someone else."

The Red Deer matriarch was furious. "With half the men gone, that means half of our women will not be able to participate in the Sacred Marriage! And I am not even counting all of the husbandless Atata women who have joined us."

To which argument Nardo replied stoically, "I will not leave the exits unguarded."

It was not only the women who grumbled at this decision. Winter Fires was the most looked-forward-to of all the New Year Rites. The high point of the Winter Fires ceremony was the mating of god and goddess to ensure the fertility of the tribe and the herds the tribe lived upon. This mating was emulated by all the male and female participants in the final dance. It was a time when sexual juices flowed hot and eager, when the pounding of the drums woke an answering pounding in the blood, when man and woman came together with an urgency and abandonment that was rarely if ever equaled in the day-to-day world. The men did not want to miss this highlight of the long, cold winter, and it was a measure of the respect that Nardo had gained when, at his command, they remained in their places at both the exits to summer camp.

The opening ceremonies of Winter Fires were not held in the Kindred village but at the Sacred Cave of the Mother on the

Volp River. In the days when the tribe had been much smaller, the whole ceremony had been held inside the cave, but these days it was only the opening rites that were held at the site on the Volp.

This was the first time Alane would join the other women in these secret rites. Nevin had been too dependent upon her milk last year to be left for any length of time. This year, although he was still nursing, Nevin could eat enough other foods to last the day, and so on this sunny, dry winter morning, Alane was part of the worshipers going to the Sacred Cave of the Mother for the women's part of Winter Fires. The women led no remounts, for the journey from village to cave was under three hours each way and the horses would have time to rest in between. Each carried a stone lamp, which would be needed to light the darkness of the cave.

Alane was looking forward with great curiosity to the day's ritual. Lora had told her that they would go deep into the cave, to a chamber which contained the most sacred mystery of life. There the women of the Red Deer would perform a sacred dance to Earth Mother. "It is hard to explain," Lora had said. "You have to be part of it to understand. Never will you feel so close to Earth Mother, Alane. Never will you understand more fully how holy it is to be a woman."

Alane was reflecting upon these words as Snowdrop picked her way along the path that went north and east through the hills. During this past year Alane had slowly begun to realize that women had a value among the Kindred that they did not have among the Norakamo. For one thing, in this tribe women had a spiritual life that was separate from the men's. The initiation of a young girl, celebrated when her moon blood first began to flow, was a more important moment to the Kindred than was the initiation of a young boy. Moon blood meant continuity to the Kindred, for it was a woman's blood that carried the life of the clan and the tribe.

This was an aspect of life among the Kindred that Alane found herself liking very much. In her own tribe women had value solely in relation to their fathers and their husbands. By themselves they were nothing. On the other hand, marriage among the Kindred was not the close bonding that Alane had grown up with. Kindred women seemed to be independent of all men, even their husbands.

Was it possible to have both? Alane wondered as Snowdrop picked her way over the rocky trail. Did it have to be one or the other?

Up ahead the ground rose more steeply. "The river is beyond the hill," Lora called softly from behind Alane. "We are almost there."

The long line of riders crossed the hill, descended into a narrow valley and turned north, following the river. Ten minutes later, the river disappeared into a hole in the limestone hillside. The women had reached their destination.

To the Tribe of the Kindred the Sacred Cave represented the womb of Earth Mother, and it was here the tribe celebrated her mysteries. Here it brought its young women when the menstrual blood of life first began to flow; here it brought its young men when they first became of age to worship the Goddess by having intercourse with a woman; and here the women of the Red Deer Clan made their twice-yearly dance to ensure continuation of the tribe's life.

Alane felt her scalp prickle as she looked at the mysterious dark cavern into which the river ran. There was just enough dry land on either side of the ribbon of water to allow entrance. "In the spring," Lora said, "the river is so high that we have to use boats to get into the first chamber."

All around Alane women were sliding off their mares, who stood quietly, not tossing a head, not stamping a foot. It was as if even the female horses sensed they were in the presence of something sacred, Alane thought.

Suddenly a woman's voice, sharp with fear, violated the quiet: *What is that? Across the river, on top of the hill!*

Alane's eyes jerked up and there, silhouetted against the clear blue of the winter sky, was the figure of a man with a bow slung across his back. As the women all stared upward, the figure was joined by another bearing an identical bow. The two men's faces turned toward the women crowded around the cave's opening. For a breathless moment the two parties stared at each other across the river. Then the men turned away and disappeared from the women's sight.

"By the Bear," Alane said, unconsciously using her father's favorite oath, "they were Redu!"

"They can't be." Lina, matriarch of the Red Deer, shaded her eyes with her hand and looked to the now-empty heights on the far side of the river. "The Redu are trapped in our summer camp!"

"Perhaps they climbed out," said Mara grimly. "They knew they could not get by our men and so they went over the mountains."

"All of them?" a girl asked fearfully. "Do you think all of them climbed out?"

Alane, who had not yet dismounted, said, "If the whole Redu tribe is about to descend upon us, we need to know it. I will go and take a look. Snowdrop is still fresh."

Alane had been looking at Mara when she spoke, and Mara nodded briskly. "If you follow the path that begins next to that boulder"—Mara pointed at a large rock that partially blocked the path downriver—"you will gain the top of the hill. From there you should have a good view of the entire valley."

Alane gathered her reins.

"I'll go with you," Lora offered.

"And I," said Fara, Haras' wife.

The three girls reached the boulder Mara had indicated, picked their way across a slide of scree, and began to make a zigzag ascent following a rough sheep track. It was difficult going, but the mares were mountain horses and before long they had gained the crest of the hill. From this vantage point they had a good view of the Volp valley, good enough for them to see the massed numbers of men who were moving briskly northward in the direction of the Sacred Cave. The men were all carrying bows and, worst of all, the first of them had already reached the place where the path from the village entered the Volp valley. It was too late for the women to retrace their steps and run for home.

"What are we going to do?" Lora's fist was pressed to her mouth. "They have us trapped!"

"Let us get back to the rest of the women," Alane said. "Whatever we decide to do, there is little time."

Snowdrop slid on her haunches all the way down the hill, and

Alane urged her on, fervently hoping she wouldn't cut a leg on a rock.

"It's the Redu!" Lora called as soon as they had cantered into the cleared opening in front of the Sacred Cave. "All of them!"

A babble of female voices greeted this remark.

"*Silence.*" Mara's authoritative voice cut through the noise. When the voices had obediently quieted, she asked Lora, "How far away are they?"

"They are between us and the way back to the village," Lora replied grimly. "We cannot go back the way we came."

A subdued murmur of dismay rustled among the women. Most had thrown their horses' reins over their necks so that the mares could graze, and the women's soft voices mingled with the tearing sound made by the mares' teeth on the grass.

"We can hide in the Sacred Cave until they are gone," Lina said. "Earth Mother will protect us. If they are fools enough to try to follow us, they will lose themselves in the many chambers."

A number of women turned to look at the cave's entrance, so dark and mysterious in the clear winter light.

"That strategy might have worked if they did not know we were here," Mara said. "But they do know, Lina. They won't follow us into the cave. All they will need to do is wait. We have no food. We cannot hide for long in the cave."

"I say we should ride north," Fara called. "We can outrun them to the River of Gold and then return to the village by way of the Greatfish. Even if we have to stop to rest the horses, still they are on foot and won't be able to catch us."

This suggestion met with enthusiastic approval from the rest of the women.

Alane opened her mouth to object, but Mara was before her. "When we are not back at the village by sundown," she said, "Nardo will send a party of men to the Volp to look for us. And they will run right into the Redu."

An appalled silence fell as the women realized the truth of Mara's words.

"If we cannot hide from these men, or run away from them, then what are we to do?" Lina demanded, using anger to mask her fear.

Alane looked at Mara, but Nardo's mother was grim-faced

and silent. Alane drew in a long breath. "We must return to the village the way we came," she said calmly. "It is the only way to keep our men from running into certain death."

The women around Alane turned to her with incredulous stares. "Alane, you have just told us that the Redu are between us and the way home," Riva said impatiently.

"That is right." Alane raised her voice so she could be heard by all. "I am saying that we should ride through them."

This time the silence was thick with disbelief.

"Are you serious?" Lora said at last.

"I am serious." Alane had dismounted earlier and now, still holding Snowdrop's reins, she moved to step up on a rock so she could make herself seen by all. The winter sun glinted off the crown of her head, and her cheeks were flushed, her eyes glittering with the challenge she was about to issue. "Nardo and the men spent all summer teaching the horses to hold together and charge. We can all ride. There are almost as many of us as there are of the Redu." Her eyes swung across the sea of female faces upraised before her. Her chin lifted. "Why can't we ride these men down ourselves?"

Stunned silence. Then, "What about their bows?" someone called.

"They won't be expecting us," Alane returned. "We will be upon them before they can fit an arrow."

The Wolf women looked at Mara, but she was silent, staring at Alane as if in a trance.

Fara stepped up on the rock beside Alane. "I think Alane is right," she said. "We will leave these bowmen behind in our dust!"

A group of the Red Deer girls, who were standing in the midst of the crowd of women, cheered. Then one of them said, "I watched the men practicing all summer. All we must do is put the horses into an arrow formation and gallop as fast as we can."

"The river path is too narrow," Lina objected.

"It widens just before it turns around the bend at Owl Rock," Mara said, asserting herself at last. "We could wait until they reach that place, then gallop around the curve and straight into them. There would be room there for us to ride eight abreast."

A hum of excitement began to rise from the gathering of women. "We don't have much time," someone shouted. "We had better decide quickly what to do."

Before Alane could speak again, Mara turned to Lina. "You are the matriarch of the Red Deer, Lina, and this is the day of Winter Fires." Mara's voice was clear and strong, audible to all who were gathered there in front of the Sacred Cave. "What would the Mother have us do?"

Lina, who at one time had possessed the same red-haired beauty as her daughter Fara, proudly drew up her aging body. "It is in my heart that the Mother would not want us to lead our men into certain death," she said firmly. "I say that we ride these Redu creatures down."

Alane grinned. "Snowdrop is used to going first," she called. "I will lead the way."

Mara stepped forward, gesturing imperiously to Alane and Fara to vacate their rock, which the Wolf matriarch then ascended. "Snowdrop can go first, but you, Alane, will ride in the middle," Mara said. She raised her voice. "All nursing mothers will ride in the middle. Those of us whose children are grown will ride on the outside."

There were some cries of disappointment, but no one disputed the intelligence of Mara's decision.

"Give me Snowdrop, Alane," Mara said next. "I will ride the point."

It took what seemed like forever to Alane for the horses to get into formation. At Mara's direction, the nursing mothers were in the center of the wedge-shaped formation, the mothers of younger children formed the layer after them, then came the young unmarried girls and the matriarchs. Finally they were ready, nearly three hundred strong, Mara sitting tall and straight on Snowdrop at the point. Alane looked at the gray head of Nardo's mother just before they began to ride forward, and felt an unexpected flash of fierce pride.

The girl who had been posted up ahead came galloping back to say breathlessly, "They are coming! The first of the line is almost at Owl Rock!"

"We'll wait for a few minutes more," Mara said.

The wait seemed endless. Alane's heart was hammering so

hard her whole head throbbed with it. Up in front, Mara raised her arm. Alane tensed. The arm fell and Snowdrop surged forward. The rest of the mares followed.

The path at this point was almost too narrow to keep in formation, and Alane's knee crashed into Lora's, who was riding beside her. Both girls ignored the pain and urged their horses on. They reached the bend, swung around, the path opened up, and they were face to face with the enemy.

The Redu were stunned. The ones in the front of their line of march hesitated, checked by the sight of that thundering charge. Mara, at the point of the formation, never hesitated. "Faster! Faster!" she shouted, and Snowdrop, now in full gallop, crashed into the front line of the Redu.

The rest of the women, knowing that loss of momentum would be fatal, urged their horses on with knees, heels and voices. Men were screaming and going down under horses' hooves. Others were leaping for the safety of the river. In front of Alane, one of the mares stumbled to her knees as she tripped over a man on the ground, and the girl on her back lost her seat and slid off. She scrambled to her feet, miraculously unhurt, but the mare had regained her balance and galloped off. By now Alane was beside the girl on foot. "Get on with me!" she shouted and tried to hold her mare to a slower pace. The girl made a tremendous leap, landed, wobbled, and clutched Alane around the waist. For a moment the two of them rocked uncertainly, then settled into the motion of the mare's gallop. A moment later, they were past the men and galloping down the river toward the path to the village.

Kerk still could not believe what had happened. Who would have ever believed that women would have the courage to do something like that? They had ridden through his men with all the ruthlessness of a summer storm ripping down a valley.

The Redu leader would have been more furious and less amazed if his men had suffered any lasting damage from that astonishing charge. The only injuries were from the hooves of the horses, and while these numbered several broken ribs and arms and a quantity of bruises, there was nothing that would not heal. Once the women had passed, Kerk collected his stunned men and herded them toward the cave where the women first had been discovered by his scouts.

They had interrupted some sort of religious ceremony. Kerk had known that must be what so many women were doing by themselves so far from their camp, and he was certain of it when he saw the stone lamps that they had left behind. They had been going to hold a ceremony in the cave.

As the men made camp and tended to their wounds, Kerk picked up a lamp, lit its wick from one of the cook fires, and went to stand at the edge of the cave. Then, walking very slowly, he began to follow the stream as it wound its way into the depths of the mountain.

It was warmer in the cave, although the damp smells of earth and stone and river were strong in Kerk's nostrils. After a little while the passage through which the river was traveling widened, and Kerk found himself in a large chamber. He walked along the walls, examining the pictures of buffalo, reindeer and horses that were engraved upon the limestone. A sign he did not understand appeared again and again. He stood for a while, frowning at this mysterious P, before he continued his exploration.

A small gallery led from the first chamber, and Kerk followed it cautiously, watching the walls to make certain that he would be able to retrace his way. The gallery ended and Kerk stepped into the next chamber of the cave. This room was vast and white and hung all over the ceiling and the floor with glorious milky white stalactites and stalagmites. The glittering chamber was utterly silent save for a ghostly drip-drip of underground water somewhere in the distance.

Drip, drip, drip went the water. The air was perfectly still. The hair on the back of Kerk's neck rose, and he knew suddenly that this was not a place for men. Slowly he began to back up, step after step, the white floor hard under his boots. He turned when he reached the gallery and, holding the lamp high, made his way back as quickly as he could to the first chamber.

The river roared in its underground channel. The animals on the wall stared at him in silent reproach. His mind said, *Get out, get out, get out.*

Kerk found the river path and made his way as quickly as he could toward the light of day.

The women galloped triumphantly into the village and poured out their tale to the men who were there.

Nardo was holding his wife's horse and listening to her tale when Fara called to him, "It was Alane's idea!"

Nardo looked thunderstruck. "Alane's?"

"Sa," said Lora, who was standing close by. "We were going to outrun them to the River of Gold, but Mara said we could not do that, since the men would be sure to come after us. Then Alane said we should put the horses into the arrow formation you practiced all summer, Nardo, and ride the Redu down."

Alane's cheeks were pink and her gray eyes shone. She cast a glance at Mara's stony face and said quickly, "It was Mara who rode the point." She looked up at her husband, laughing and generous in her triumph. "She kept shouting, 'Faster! Faster!' and we all just galloped after her."

Nardo grinned for the first time since he had heard the news of the Redu presence on the Volp. "You must have stunned them."

Lora giggled. "They didn't know what had happened to them, Nardo."

He turned to Mara. "Are you certain you are all right, Mama?"

"I am fine," she returned. None of the triumph that the other women were experiencing was present on Mara's face, however. Nardo gave her a puzzled look, and she forced a smile. "It is in my heart that the Mother did not like her rites being interrupted by men."

"Sa," Lora said fervently. "She was watching out for us, I think."

Mara looked around the group of women standing by their horses. The feeling of power emanating from them was unmistakable. She raised her voice. "I am thinking that only Kindred women, who follow the Mother, would have been capable of such a deed as we did this day."

Fara laughed and said, "The idea came from a Norakamo woman, Mara!"

"Alane is Norakamo no longer," Lora protested. "Since her marriage she has been a woman of the Wolf."

"She has the heart and courage of a wolf," Nardo said, regarding his wife with obvious admiration.

Alane's face glowed with youth and gladness, and Mara felt a knife twist in her heart.

Chapter Nineteen

Nardo immediately sent for the men who were engaged in the now-useless duty of guarding the exits to an empty summer camp. Then he sent a party of horsemen to the Volp to watch the Redu and report back if the enemy showed any signs of turning toward the village.

Paxon was greatly relieved to learn that his father had escaped from summer camp. "He will probably continue north along this Volp hoping it will lead into the River of Gold," Paxon assured Nardo. "Kerk's chief aim at the moment will be to feed his men, and he will hope there is game in the region of the River of Gold during the winter."

In the weeks since Paxon had come as a captive to the Kindred village, he had reached an accommodation with Nardo. It had soon become clear to the Redu that it was virtually impossible for him to escape. Even if he managed to capture a mount, his own unsure horsemanship would doom any attempt to outrun pursuit. When he pointed this out to the Kindred chief, and offered to give his word not to attempt an escape, Nardo had agreed to allow him the freedom of the village. In truth, the logistics of keeping the Redu confined had been a nuisance, and Nardo had been happy to find a way to resolve what was becoming a troublesome situation.

To the great relief of the Kindred, Paxon proved to be correct about the actions of his tribe. Instead of turning to follow the women, the Redu continued up the Volp until they reached the River of Gold. There they showed signs of settling in for the winter. Nardo ordered a guard put in place to keep the Redu camp in sight and report on their doings, and he himself took the first rotation of guard duty.

Ever since Paxon had been allowed the freedom of the village, he had shown a decided penchant for Alane's company. For her part, Alane saw in the young Redu a strong resemblance to her Norakamo brothers, and so she was more indulgent toward him than she might otherwise have been. In truth, she found herself rather enjoying the way she could shock his notions of male dominance with her newfound female pride.

One cold, overcast day the Redu as usual trailed after Alane as she went to the river to fetch the household water. He stood on the frozen shore, arms folded, and watched while she filled her two baskets from the icy waters of the Greatfish. When she had filled the second basket, she glanced up at his face, and her eyes sparkled with mischief. "Would you mind carrying one of these baskets back to the hut for me, Paxon?" she asked.

His look of absolute astonishment almost made her laugh out loud. "Hauling water is women's work," he announced.

Alane said, "It is women's work among the Kindred also, but if my husband is nearby, he will often help me." She gave the Redu a look of great innocence. "He is clumsy but strong."

"I not clumsy," Paxon said instantly.

Alane raised her brows in disbelief.

Paxon scowled.

"Do not worry, I understand," Alane said. "It is not easy to carry a full basket of water. I'll do it myself."

"It easy for me," Paxon said haughtily, and bent to pick up one of the baskets from the icy ground. Some water immediately spilled. Alane's lip quivered.

Fierce black eyes stared into hers, but Alane did not have any difficulty in meeting them. Just so would her youngest brother look when his male dignity had been ruffled. "Nardo spills all the time," she said.

Paxon grunted, balanced the basket more evenly, and began to walk forward. Water dripped in his wake. Alane swung her own basket to her head and followed, trying not to smile.

Mara's look was brooding as she watched Paxon and Alane enter Alane's hut together. In the weeks since their brave charge against the Redu, Alane had become something of a heroine in the eyes of the young Kindred women, and in Mara's mind this had only increased her potential danger. The young women not only admired Alane, but they sought to imitate her.

It must be stopped, Mara thought. *She must be stopped. If she is not, the whole Mother's Blood way of the tribe will be lost.*

As Mara stood there, the skins of Alane's hut were pushed aside again, and Paxon and Alane emerged into the sunlight. As Mara watched, Paxon bent his head toward the girl and said something that made her laugh. The boy's whole attitude was so obviously possessive that Mara's eyes suddenly narrowed.

She thought, *Perhaps this Paxon is a weapon I can use to get rid of Alane for good.*

Alane was much happier this winter than she had been the one before. She felt more secure in her marriage, and she was even beginning to enjoy the busy life of the big house. She had grown fond of Nardo's sisters, Riva and Liev, and Lora was like a sister.

Ironically, it was the presence of Paxon that figured largely in Alane's growing reconciliation to life among the Kindred. The young Redu's attitude was a constant reminder to her of the way the men of her own tribe regarded their women, and there was no question that Alane preferred the attitude of the Kindred men to that of the Norakamo.

This major difference between the two tribes was made very clear one night when the whole household, including Paxon, was having supper in the big house. Nardo had come in from winter camp that afternoon, bringing with him six packhorses carrying the roughly dressed carcasses of three reindeer. Mara had supervised the unloading and bestowal of the Wolf Clan meat, with Nardo and Dane obligingly following her commands.

Nardo and Alane had joined the family for dinner and everyone was eating heartily and talking noisily when Paxon, who had been staring at Nardo with ill-concealed jealousy, suddenly leaned forward to ask him a question. Nardo could not hear him and, raising his voice to make himself heard over the noise, he asked Paxon to repeat what he had said.

Paxon's eyebrows drew together. "I not understand how these women are allowed to make so much noise," he said.

Nardo looked at the Redu in astonishment. "What do you mean?"

"I not understand the men of this tribe," Paxon announced. "If I not see myself how good you hunt, I think you were women yourselves."

The Redu's voice was particularly nasal, and it cut through what was left of the household conversation. Silence fell in the warm and smoky house.

"This house belongs to the women of the family," Nardo said in the sudden quiet. His large eyes had begun to sparkle with anger, but his voice was very soft. "It is their right to talk all they want in their own house."

"Nothing belong to women in my tribe," Paxon said grandly.

Alane glanced at Mara and waited to hear how Nardo's mother would handle this young upstart. For the moment, however, Mara was content to let her son answer. "In this tribe," Nardo said, "the home is made by the women. It is they who cook the food, they who scrape the skins, they who sew the clothes. It is the women who bear the children, the women whose blood carries the life of the clan and of the tribe. They make the home, and the home belongs to them."

Paxon scowled. "The women of my tribe do these things also."

Dane entered into the conversation, asking with genuine amazement, "Then how can you say that nothing belongs to them?"

"They are women," Paxon said.

"Dhu," said Dane, clearly at a loss.

Finally Mara spoke. "It is true that the men of the Kindred are fine hunters," she said. "You see for yourself, Redu man, how well we live in this tribe. Our men hunt. They take care of the horses. They train the dogs. No Kindred woman would try to tell her men how to kill reindeer, or where to graze their horses. And no Kindred man would tell his women how to cook his dinner or sew his clothes. That is how life is lived in this tribe."

Paxon looked warily at Mara, considering his answer.

Alane could resist no longer and entered the fray. "I am thinking that that is how life is lived among the Redu also, my mother," she said, "but among the Redu no honor is given to the work done by the women. That is the difference between the two tribes." She turned to look at Paxon. "Is that not so?" she said.

His black eyes glittered. That was exactly so. He knew it, and he was having a hard time defending it. He said, "Women's work is not as important as men's."

Mara said coldly, "Would you like to spend the night out-doors without the clothes on your back, which were made by women?"

Riva added, "You did not seem to find that reindeer stew unimportant. You certainly ate it fast enough."

Dane chuckled.

Paxon's scowl was ferocious.

"What harsh lives you Redu men must live," Nardo said sym-pathetically. "No mother and sisters to fuss over you and make you feel important." He reached out to drape an arm around Alane's shoulders. "No loving wife to welcome you home after a long stint in winter camp."

Paxon's face paled. His eyes were glued to the arm that was encircling Alane as he said, "We have mothers and sisters and wives."

"Not like we have mothers and sisters and wives," Nardo re-turned with certainty, and he drew Alane close against his side.

Alane looked at Paxon's face and was surprised by the rage she saw there. Poor boy, she thought. Everything here was so strange to him. Just so would Fenris look if he were flung down amidst the Kindred in such a way. From within the circle of her husband's embrace, she sent Paxon a reassuring smile.

The night air was icy, and Alane shivered and clutched her fur tunic close as she and Nardo walked from the big house to their hut. Nevin was asleep on Nardo's shoulder and did not wake when his father laid him down in his warm nest of furs for the night. Samu padded quietly to his rug against the back wall and lay down, grunting with satisfaction as he curled up in the familiar, safe place. Alane knelt to trim the wick of the stone lamp, returned it to the flat hearthside stone, then turned to look up at her husband.

He had taken off his fur tunic to spread over Nevin, and was standing beside the sleeping child, legs slightly spread, watching her. In the confines of the small hut he looked enormous. Her heartbeat accelerated and she remembered with amazement how once she had feared him, had actually feared the strength and the power and the male sexuality that was making her blood run so hot just now.

He said, "That Redu has very strange ideas."

"They are not as odd as you may think, Nardo," she replied. "Norakamo men are very much like Paxon."

"That is your measure of a man, then?" he asked in a voice that was unusually harsh.

She gave him a puzzled look. "What do you mean?"

He shrugged. "You were brought up among Norakamo men. Perhaps in comparison Kindred men seem womanish to you."

Alane stared at him in astonishment. "My measure for a man is very simple."

"And what is it?" he asked.

She replied softly, "You."

They looked at each other, and then he came, quick and silent as a cat, to kneel beside her. He reached out and with his big hands began to remove her fur tunic. She knelt up straight, watching him.

His eyes were very dark, his face serious and intent. It was a look she knew well, and a familiar tingling sensation began to grow in her loins. She reached up, slid her hands under his hair and cupped the nape of his neck with her fingers. He had been at winter camp for three weeks, and the touch of his warm flesh was making her dizzy.

"Did you miss me?" he asked.

His voice was deep and dark. Alane shivered and ran her tongue around the inside of her parted lips. Her loins were throbbing now. He bent his head and kissed the hollow of her throat. His lips felt warm and hungry. "Did you?" he murmured against her skin.

"Sa." Her voice was husky and unsteady. Her legs felt too weak for her to continue kneeling. She wanted to lie down, to stretch out on the bedplace, to let him touch her and please her. His hand came up under her buckskin shirt and cupped her breast. Alane sank against him and together they toppled onto the hearth rug. The big branch in the hearthplace had caught and was beginning to smoke and the kindling was beginning to go out. Nardo rolled so that Alane was beneath him. He kissed her mouth and at the same time began to fumble with the draw-string at her waist. Alane kissed him back and moved her hands to help him with the string. In short order the rawhide waist tie was loosened and Nardo began to pull the trousers off of her. Alane lifted her hips to help.

The air was cold as it touched her bare skin, but then his big body was covering her. "You are hotter than the fire," she murmured as she ran her fingers through his hair.

"I have been heating up for a long time now," he growled. His hand swept down her body, along the dip of her slim and flexible waist, along the sweet curve of her hip. He caressed the pale, soft skin of her thigh, and then he touched the quivering part of her that was calling to him. Alane whimpered and moved to meet his touch.

"Dhu." He felt the evidence of her readiness, and his hands went to the waist of his own trousers. In seconds he had stripped them off and was looming once more over Alane. She looked up at him, all of her mind and her feelings concentrated on that one place at the core of her being where she needed him to be. She reached out her hand to put him there.

He filled the aching emptiness. Completely. She closed around him and the intensity of the sensation was all-encompassing.

"Alane," he muttered. "My beautiful girl. Sa. Sa. That's right, that's the way. . . ."

His hips moved, driving him into her. She wrapped her legs around his waist and moved with him. The climax when it came was shattering for them both and, still joined, they collapsed sideways on the skins of the hearth rug, Nardo careful to relieve her of his weight.

Nardo's heart was hammering. Alane slid her hand inside the neck of his shirt and felt sweat on his bare skin. She pressed her cheek against his shoulder and closed her eyes.

No two people could be closer than this, she thought. It was not possible.

They lay together quietly, and then she felt Nardo's lips on her temple. "You are mine," he said.

She opened her eyes in wonder. He had sounded so fierce!

Life among the Kindred was a constant wonder to Paxon. Not only had these people tamed horses, but they lived with dogs. The tribe that had been the Redu's ancient enemy had used dogs for hunting also, but those dogs had been ferocious beasts kept in line by whips and other forms of intimidation. The Kindred dogs were friendly animals who lived in the initiates' cave with the young men. A number of them even lived in the houses with the women and children.

The Kindred men kept Paxon at a distance from the horses, but the dogs he could get close to. They fascinated him. Samu, Nardo's big wolflike dog, was gentle as a woman with Nevin. And he would follow Alane like a vigilant shadow whenever Nardo was gone and had left him behind.

"Nardo says that dogs are like wolves," Alane explained to Paxon when he commented on the unusual good nature of the Kindred animals. "Wolves are very loyal to their pack, he says, and the dogs probably relate to us the way a wolf relates to its pack."

Paxon looked at Samu, who was lying before the fire with his nose propped on his paws. "I not know that wolves was loyal to their packs," he said.

"They are. Nardo says that wolves live in a family group, just like we do. There are usually a mother and father, uncles and aunts and siblings all living together. They know how to get along in a group, and that is one of the reasons dogs can learn to get along so well with men."

"How Nardo know so much about wolves?" Paxon inquired skeptically.

Alane bristled at his tone. "He is of the clan of the Wolf," she informed the Redu. "One of the initiation tasks for a boy of the Wolf Clan is that he must spend two moons living with wolves."

Paxon's slim black brows soared with disbelief. "Live with wolves? I not believe it."

Nevin had picked up the piece of reindeer hide with bird wings tied on it that Nardo had been using to teach Samu to pick up birds in his mouth. The dog pricked his ears and watched the child attentively.

"Perhaps they don't precisely live with the wolves," Alane admitted as she watched her son bring the dummy to Samu. "I think it is more that they keep close to the pack and observe its habits. When the boy comes back, he must answer questions put by his elders. Nardo says that only if he knows the answers will he be allowed to undergo initiation." Alane smiled slightly. "When first I came to dwell among the Kindred, I was afraid of the dogs," she confessed. "But I have grown quite fond of them."

The ways of the Kindred were certainly strange, Paxon thought as he watched Nardo's beautiful wife going about her household chores. Most strange of all to Paxon was Nardo's permissiveness in allowing him to spend so much time with Alane. No man of the Redu would have allowed his wife such freedom. Yet Nardo went off for days on end and never seemed to give a thought to the fact that his wife was spending a great deal of her time in the company of another man.

It was insulting, Paxon finally decided. Nardo did not think he was worth worrying about. Nardo, Paxon thought angrily, was a fool.

Chapter
Twenty

Snow Moon ended and the first sliver of Fox Moon rose in the night sky. On the second day of the new Moon, Nardo rode into the village. He had been gone for several weeks, making the rounds of the winter hunting and grazing camps, checking on the watch being kept by the tribe on the Redu. Paxon stood in the doorway of the initiates' cave, where he slept with the few boys who were not away at camp, and watched the greeting the Kindred chief received from his family.

Alane came running. Paxon watched broodingly as Nardo scooped her up in his arms and kissed her soundly. He was so big that her feet completely left the ground. She emerged from the embrace with her cheeks flushed and a smile on her face.

Next came Nevin, reaching up his arms to his father and crying, "Dada, Dada, Dada!" Nardo swung the child up and deposited him on his broad shoulders. Nevin clutched his father's black hair and shrieked with delight.

After Nevin came a flock of nieces and nephews to take Nardo's horses and ply him with dozens of questions in the process.

"You're back, Nardo!" It was Riva, standing at the door of the big house and calling to her brother. "Come inside and have something to eat. You must be cold and hungry after such a long ride."

Paxon watched Nardo walk toward his mother's house, his son on his shoulders, his arm around Alane, and felt such a stab of jealousy that the pain was almost physical. At that moment he hated Nardo bitterly, hated him for having all the things that Paxon was just beginning to understand that he wanted for himself.

Paxon waited in the initiates' cave, watching, and finally when he saw Nardo leave the big house, accompanied by Dane, the Redu went to take his place. As he walked in he saw Alane telling a story to the children in the corner. Paxon sat down at a short distance to listen and to watch the play of expressions on her face.

It was a while before Paxon realized that he himself was being watched. He glanced over his shoulder and encountered Mara's unfathomable dark gaze. It was not the first time that he had found Nardo's mother looking at him thus, and he wondered anew why Mara, who was so careful of her son's welfare in every other way, did not object to Alane's friendship with another man.

Alane finished the story, rose to her feet, and took Nevin's small hand in her own. Paxon got up immediately. "You go home?" he asked her.

She nodded. "I must get the water in for supper."

"I will help you," Paxon offered, and he fell in beside her as she walked toward the door. He could feel Mara's eyes boring into his back the whole time he was crossing the floor.

The two adults walked through the late afternoon sunshine with the child running ahead of them. Paxon waited while Alane collected her water baskets, and then they walked down toward the river, this time with Nevin trailing behind.

Alane stood on the shore and watched while Paxon competently filled her baskets. She was secretly delighted with the changes in the young Redu, for which she took full credit. Until she married, she had been unaware of the potency of her beauty. She had learned about her sexual power from Nardo, and it was not until he had shown signs of jealousy that she had begun to perceive the true nature of Paxon's feelings for her.

It had been fun to exert her power a little, to count her small triumphs as the edges of Paxon's male-dominated mentality softened under her influence. But recently Alane had begun to worry that she had encouraged the Redu too much, that perhaps she had ignited a fire she would not easily be able to put out.

Consequently, she felt guilty when Nardo told her she was letting Paxon follow her around too much, and to avoid finding herself on the defensive, she attacked. It was late one evening and they were in their hut preparing for bed. Both Nevin and Samu were already asleep, and the two adults were speaking in low voices so as not to disturb the child.

"He is perfectly harmless," Alane said as she watched Nardo put a slow-burning log on the fire for the night. "There is nothing he can do to me, Nardo. It is not as if I go off alone with him. I am not a fool, you know." She had loosened her hair from its braid, and now she began to comb it out.

"I know you are not a fool," he replied, "but neither are you familiar with the kind of man that Redu is." He stepped away from the fire and turned to look at her. "He is not like the men you know, Alane. A man like that has no respect for women."

"I know that kind of man very well," Alane retorted. "I grew up with that kind of man, Nardo."

He frowned. "You cannot seriously compare your father and brothers to that Redu! It is true that the Norakamo are a Father's Blood tribe, but you yourself have often told me how close your mother and father were. Your mother has not been the same since his death. And Rune certainly loves Nita!"

"What you say about my mother and father is true, Nardo." Alane's face was very earnest in the midst of its silver cloud. "But their closeness was a private thing. In public my mother had no honor. She sat in her corner quietly and served tea when my father asked for it." Her head tilted back as she gazed up at him. "Why did she have to be so reticent? Why was it not possible for her to join in the conversation of the men? My mother was a very astute woman. My father certainly sought her counsel in private. It was not right that she had to hide herself away the way she did."

Nardo's eyes were on his wife's hair. "I will not disagree with you, Alane," he said.

"And Rune," Alane went on relentlessly, "he may love Nita, but he kidnapped her!"

He came to sit beside her on the skins. "She was willing to go with him. I asked her. If she had not been willing, we would have returned her to her father."

"*You* asked her," Alane said. "Not Rune." She separated out a strand of hair that had a knot in it and ruthlessly plied her ivory comb.

Nardo watched her and did not reply.

"So you see," she said, "I do know something about men like Paxon."

"It is not the same thing." Nardo's voice had taken on a grim note. "I do not like the way he looks at you, Alane. I know what is on his mind, and I do not like it."

She stopped combing her hair. "Do you think I am looking back?" she demanded.

He shook his head slowly. "Na, I do not think you are looking back. But I think you perceive this Redu as a harmless boy, and he is not that. He is older than you are, Alane. And I do not think his dealings with women have been gentle ones."

"Perhaps that is so." She tried not to sound defensive. "But he is learning about women, Nardo."

"And you think you are teaching him?"

"Sa," she replied defiantly, and once more began to comb her hair.

Silence. Alane worked at another knot, waiting to see if he would order her to stay away from Paxon. If he did that, she thought angrily, then everything she had thought about the men of the Kindred would be wrong. He would be as bad as her father.

"I cannot live your life for you, Alane," he said at last. "But I think you are mistaken in this boy."

The relief Alane felt was startling in its intensity. She gathered her hair in one hand, pulled it off her face, and gave him a radiant smile. "I have heard you, my husband, and I will be watchful," she promised.

"I don't know why I didn't kill that Redu when I had the chance," Nardo grumbled. "He has been nothing but trouble for the tribe since I captured him."

"You could kill him now," Alane said. "You don't need him, Nardo. You know you don't."

He stared at her incredulously. "Am I hearing you right?"

She reached up and began to untie the strings at the neck of his shirt. "He is not a faceless enemy any longer, is he?" she asked softly. "Now he is Paxon. He is a nuisance, and you don't trust him, but you can't kill him."

"I can't kill a man who has eaten meat in my mother's house!"

Her smile was tender. "I know."

He slid his hands into her loosened hair and bent his head. "Forget that Redu," he ordered, "and concentrate on me."

That was not hard to do, Alane thought as her body sank against his. Slowly she moved her hand from his shirt strings to caress the warm column of his throat, feeling with her fingers the place where the pulse beat so steady and so strong. He lifted his head and whispered, "I missed you."

"I missed you too," she whispered back. "I always miss you when you're gone."

The door hangings kept the cold of night at bay. The skin bared by the open neck of Nardo's shirt gleamed warmly golden in the light of the small fire. He radiated heat and sexuality, and Alane pressed her lips to the pulse beat where her fingers had been, then tilted her head to smile up at him. Her hair streamed down her back, covering his hands in a silvery waterfall.

He groaned. "When you look at me like that, Alane, I could go mad."

Her smile deepened. He bent, lifted her, laid her down upon the bed skins and began to loosen her clothes, his lips following where his hands first led. Alane felt his mouth on her waist and her breasts, the warmth of his breath replacing the warmth of the buckskin that he was removing. Then he was slipping down her trousers, his mouth following again, first on her belly, then down to the soft inner skin of her thighs. Her breath caught in her throat, and the tension at the core of her being began to mount, a tension that rose higher and higher under the touch of his skillful fingers.

When she had begun to clutch him, he moved his hands to cradle her hips, lifting them as he reared above her, parting her for his entry. She raised her legs to encircle his waist and took him in deeply, her body a sheath into which he plunged with irresistible power. Alane met him, her passion flaring as wildly as his, her fingers digging through the buckskin of his shirt into the strong muscles of his back. So they took possession of each other,

until finally the shuddering ecstasy of the flesh was finished and
they lay at rest together.

Alane's promise to be wary of Paxon allowed Nardo to leave
for a visit to the Norakamo with a lighter heart than he would
otherwise have done. Winter would soon be ending, and it was
time to alert Rune to the danger that lay encamped to his north
on the River of Gold. Nardo had deliberately held back from
informing his brother-by-marriage any sooner of the Redu menace, but he could not keep such news to himself any longer.

Rune received Nardo's words with a grim face. "Time was
when we welcomed any visitor who brought us news," he said.
"I fear that is not the case any longer."

The two men were sitting in Rune's tent, located in the Norakamo winter camp just south of the Big Crook River and west
of the River of Gold. The River of Gold here was deep and wide,
a major barrier to both animal herds and to men. The Norakamo
were in no immediate danger even if the Redu should come
down the river as far as the Big Crook confluence, for they would
not be able to get across to reach the Norakamo camp.

"Perhaps we ought to attack these invaders immediately,"
Rune suggested. "We can hardly expect them to go away on their
own."

"Na, we cannot expect that," Nardo agreed heavily. "But
they are not like the Horse Eaters, Rune. These men are accustomed to fighting. And they have those bows! If we try to attack
their hunting parties as we did with the Horse Eaters, they will
be ready for us."

"What about attacking their camp?" Rune asked.

"It is the same—they will be ready for us. Perhaps we would
prevail, but the loss of men and horses would be tremendous."

It was silent outside the tent. Supper had been eaten and
early winter darkness covered the camp. All the tribe were within
their shelters. After supper Nita had taken Kara and gone to visit
the tent of a friend, so Nardo and Rune were alone.

"Then what do you suggest that we do?" Rune asked with
some exasperation.

Absently Nardo stroked the fur on Samu's neck. The dog had
caused a great deal of commotion among the tribe when first

Nardo had ridden in. With his fingers buried in Samu's fur, Nardo answered Rune thoughtfully. "They have two advantages over us: their numbers and their bows. But we have two advantages over them: our horses and our knowledge of the mountains. It was our use of the horses and the mountains that enabled us to defeat the Redu men who were going to the assistance of the men trapped in summer camp. We need to find a way to use those advantages again."

Rune ruffled the long bangs on his forehead. "How?" he asked bluntly.

Nardo grinned ruefully. "I am still thinking about that."

"And in the meantime they are camped upon the River of Gold taking our reindeer."

"Sa," Nardo said.

The doorflap lifted and Nita and Kara came in. The little girl immediately toddled toward Samu, who was sleeping with his chin propped on Nardo's thigh.

"Kara!" Nita said urgently. "Leave the dog alone!"

"She will be all right," Nardo said easily. "Samu is used to Nevin."

Kara, who had stopped at her mother's command, now proceeded more carefully toward the dog.

"Samu," Nardo said, running his hand over the dog's head, "wake up."

The dog opened sleepy eyes.

"I touch?" Kara asked.

"Come here and I'll show you how," Nardo replied.

Both Rune and Nita watched with contained nervousness as Nardo took the child's small hand and stroked it up and down Samu's neck. The dog closed his eyes again and settled his muzzle more comfortably on Nardo's thigh.

"He may look like a wolf, but he certainly doesn't seem very ferocious," Rune said with a small smile. "What use is he to you?"

"All the dogs in our tribe have learned to herd reindeer," Nardo replied. "They are useful in driving a herd into an enclosed pass, where we can take the ones that we need. They are also good at driving ibex up the mountain and into our traps."

"If only the Redu were reindeer," Rune said, "and we could set your dogs on them."

"That is exactly what we must do, Rune," Nardo returned slowly. "We use the land and the rivers to our advantage when we hunt animals; we must do the same when we hunt the Redu. We must choose the place where we can be most effective, and then drive the Redu into it."

Rune grunted. "In the meantime," he said, "we will help you to keep watch on the invaders."

Nardo replied cautiously, "I am thinking that it might be more beneficial to us if you did not."

Rune frowned. "What do you mean?"

"It is in my mind that we have one other advantage over the Redu, Rune. They do not know that there is a tribe of horse people dwelling on the evening side of the River of Gold. It would be wise for us to keep them in ignorance of that fact."

Silence fell as Rune considered this comment. "Is this why you waited until now to tell me of the Redu camp?" he asked bluntly.

Nardo shrugged. "I did not want to make a winter journey if it was not necessary."

Rune stared at him in open skepticism.

"The men of the Norakamo are easily distinguishable from the men of the Kindred," Nardo went on. "Your horses are short-maned and brown while ours are long-maned and gray. The Norakamo are fair and wear their hair differently from the men of the Kindred. If we want to keep your presence a secret, you will have to keep out of sight of the Redu."

"That will leave us dependent upon you for our news," Rune said a little stiffly.

Nardo leaned forward, anxious to persuade. "You may trust me to keep you informed."

After a long moment Rune nodded slowly. "All right. We will do things your way. For now."

Her husband's warning had made more of an impression upon Alane than she had allowed him to see, and while Nardo was away visiting the Norakamo, Alane decided to make a concerted effort to divert Paxon's attention away from herself.

I do not like the way he looks at you, Nardo had said. *I know what is on his mind, and I do not like it.*

For the first time Alane allowed herself fully to realize what was probably on Paxon's mind, and consequently she was growing very uncomfortable in the presence of the Redu. Paxon had probably fastened on her, Alane reasoned, because she had shown herself sympathetic to him. What she needed to do now was to redirect Paxon's interest to another sympathetic girl.

There were many young girls in the Kindred village that winter. Too many young girls, in fact, for the presence of the women of the Atata Kindred had pulled the man-woman ratio of the tribe completely out of balance.

It did not take Alane long to decide that Dane's sister Pettra, one of the Red Deer girls, would be the perfect solution to her problem. Pettra had lately been making excuses to visit Mara's house, and Alane had several times caught her bright eyes regarding Paxon with frank appreciation. One sunny afternoon, when the tang of spring was in the air, Alane made her move.

Paxon was a little surprised when Alane suggested that he take a walk along the Greatfish in the direction of summer camp, but when she said that he would find a nice surprise waiting for him, he went eagerly, thinking she meant to join him herself.

The rays of the sun were warm on Paxon's head, and all around him the valley birds were enjoying the beautiful afternoon. Yellow and red-billed choughs busily performed their aerobatic antics in front of the cliffs, all the while calling to one another in their distinctively mellifluous voices. A wallcreeper worked its way up the rock face of the cliff on the far side of the river, its crimson wing patches glowing brightly as blood against the gray stone. As soon as it reached the top of the cliff, it flew back down to the bottom and started to climb again.

Paxon was scanning the path ahead of him, searching for Alane, when he heard his name being called by a different female voice. He turned in surprise and saw Dane's sister Pettra coming toward him along the river path.

He glanced at the path behind her and saw no one else. "Are you alone?" he asked as she drew near him.

She shook her head. "Tosa and Mira came with me."

He felt a flash of bitter disappointment. Once again he looked up the valley and saw no one.

"They are waiting back there with the horses." She gestured to a place beyond the curve in the river.

He was instantly suspicious. "Why?"

Pettra smiled. She was a pretty girl, with long, faintly slanted greenish eyes and brown hair that shone with a reddish glow in the brilliant winter sun. Paxon had noticed her of late, for she seemed to be in his vicinity more and more often. "Can't you guess?" she asked, amusement mixed with something else in her voice.

Paxon had realized by now that the unmarried Kindred girls were not held to the same sexual code that bound the girls of his own tribe. In fact, he had been profoundly shocked when he discovered that unmarried men and women of the tribe were allowed to lie together. "I have been watching you, Paxon," Pettra went on, "and it is in my mind that we would agree well with each other."

Paxon stared, afraid to believe what he thought she was saying.

Pettra approached until she was standing right before him. "There is a small cave a short way down the river," she said. "We could build a fire for warmth."

Paxon cleared his throat. "You want lie with me?" he said, careful to make certain he was understanding her correctly.

"Sa," Pettra said. She smiled.

"Your friends?"

"They will wait." Her green eyes gleamed. "They know why I wanted to see you alone."

"Why?" Paxon's whole body was now fully aroused, but caution had not yet deserted him. "I am enemy," he said.

In answer Pettra reached up and drew his head down to hers. Paxon had never been kissed on the mouth by a woman before. It was a stunning experience. Pettra drew away and said softly, "We are not enemies, Paxon. We are a man and a woman. Why don't we do what it is that men and women were born to do with each other?"

"Sa," Paxon croaked. All his thoughts of Alane had fled. In

silence he let Pettra take his hand and lead him into the shelter of the cave.

That evening Paxon sat in the corner of the big house and looked broodingly at Alane. She was seated between Lora and Riva, working on a basket. Riva's and Tora's husbands were the only men beside himself in the house this night. Tyr and Adun were away at winter camp, and Nardo and Dane were paying a visit to the Norakamo.

What had happened between himself and Pettra this afternoon had been a revelation to Paxon. The encounter, far from distracting Paxon from thoughts of Alane and refocusing them on Pettra, had served only to feed the Redu's lust for Nardo's wife. Before his afternoon with Pettra, Paxon had ached to have Alane in his power, had dreamed of driving between her legs and pumping the juice of his body into her. It had been a fantasy that had replayed itself in his mind over and over again during these last weeks.

But now the fantasy was so much more detailed! Paxon had never imagined it was possible to do the things with a woman that he had done with Pettra this afternoon. The first time had been quick, but Pettra had been as hot for him as he had been for her, and for the first time Paxon had felt what it was like to have a woman enjoy him. They had not left the cave immediately either, and in the course of the next two hours Paxon had learned things that the men of his tribe had never even dreamed of.

And now he dreamed of doing the things that he had learned with Alane. He looked at her face, looked at the delicate line of throat revealed by the open neck of her shirt, looked at the sweet curve of her breast. He felt his phallus hardening and tried to get a grip on his thoughts. He forced his eyes away from Alane and they encountered Mara's.

The matriarch had been looking at him again. Her face was enigmatic, but Paxon had no doubt that she had seen the hunger in his. He struggled to control his expression, to control his body. The tension inside him was so great he felt as if he would explode.

"I have to go outside," he said to Pier, who was the closest person to him. No one commented as he made his way to the door. Everyone assumed he was going outside to relieve himself, which he certainly was, if not in the way that the family expected. Only Mara's eyes followed the Redu until he had pushed the skins aside and ducked out into the cold air.

Mara had indeed read the expression on Paxon's face, and she thought the time was just about ripe for her to take action. Nardo was away and not expected back for a week. The tribe had grown accustomed to the Redu, and he was not watched as closely as he once had been.

The Norakamo woman must go.

This had been Mara's determination for over a year, and she told herself that she could not weaken now that the time to act was upon her. It must be done. She would give Paxon a horse and a spear, and tell him to be gone and to take Alane with him.

Mara had managed to convince herself that even if Paxon did join up with his people, it would not matter if he told them about the location of the Kindred village. Nardo was keeping an eye on the Redu, she thought. Nardo would be able to stop them if they began to move in the direction of the Greatfish.

Of course, the Kindred would know that someone had helped Paxon, but they would naturally assume that someone to be Alane. She had been foolishly allowing the Redu to follow her about like a shadow for almost two moons now. Mara had seen that Nardo was not overly happy about his wife's penchant for Paxon's company. Under the circumstances, even Nardo would be forced to the conclusion that Alane had abetted the Redu's escape.

Chapter Twenty-One

It was three hours before dawn when Alane was awakened by the sound of someone calling her name. She opened her eyes, checked to see that Nevin was sleeping peacefully beside her, then, without moving, looked cautiously toward the glowing light of a stone lamp. To her astonishment she saw that the person holding the lamp was Mara.

"My mother!" Alane said. She sat up. "What are you doing here?"

"Dane has just ridden in with word that Nardo is hurt," Mara replied.

Alane sucked in her breath audibly. Her hands clenched. "Badly?" she asked.

"Dane was not sure. They were coming home early from their visit to the Norakamo, and the accident happened an hour's ride down the Greatfish. A rock slide. Dane left Nardo in a cave and came for help. I am going to go to him, and I thought perhaps you would want to come with me."

Alane was already scrambling to her feet. "Of course I will come! Let me first bring Nevin to the big house."

"There is no need for that," Mara said. "Alis is coming down here to stay with him. Let him finish his sleep undisturbed."

"That will be better," Alane agreed. She was at the drying rack by now, and Mara watched as she thrust her feet into her boots and bent to tie the rawhide laces. She straightened, took down her fur tunic, and turned to Mara. "What medicines shall we bring?"

"I have already packed what we will need," Mara replied. "And the horses are waiting for us."

Without further speech Alane hurried after her husband's mother as the two women left the hut.

Outside, the village was bathed in moonlight. Alane glanced around, expecting to see other people, but the moon showed only the black outlines of the big houses and the smaller huts. It was very quiet.

"This way," Mara said softly, and she began to walk toward the river. Alane saw that four horses were picketed by the shore, two riding horses and two packhorses, already roped together nose to tail, ready to go. "Let us not delay," Mara said.

Alane frowned, looking at the two riding horses. "But where is Dane?" she asked. "Is he not coming with us?"

"Dane was slightly hurt in the accident also. Lora is seeing to him and then he will get some of the other men and follow. I did not want to wait for so long."

Alane's puzzled frown deepened. "Then why cannot Pier come with us, if Dane is hurt? We cannot move Nardo by ourselves, my mother!"

Mara gave Alane a scornful look. "I have said that they will come after. If you fear to venture forth without a man for protection, then wait for the men," she said. "I am going on." And, leading her mare to a rock, Mara threw her leg over its back and mounted.

Fear ran like ice water in Alane's veins. How badly Nardo must be hurt for Mara to be acting like this! Without replying, Alane rested both her hands on Snowflake's withers and vaulted onto the mare's broad back. Mara picked up the first packhorse's lead line, and the four horses moved off.

As they rode west along the Greatfish, Alane pressed Mara for details of Nardo's accident.

"I do not know any more than I have told you, Alane" was all that Mara would say. "Dane just said that Nardo was hurt, that he dragged him into a cave, left Samu to guard him and came to the village for help. We will have to wait until we get there to see just how badly off Nardo is."

Paxon waited, his shadow stretching like a giant before him on the moonlit path. He stood perfectly still, listening intently, but there was no sound of hoofbeats approaching from the east. He had been standing thus for two hours, having been promised by Mara earlier in the evening that she would meet him at this place with weapons and gear.

And with Alane.

"I will help you to leave if you will take her with you," the Wolf matriarch had told him, her large brown eyes steady with determination. "I will give you horses and spears and sleeping skins. If you are any kind of man at all, you will be able to make good your escape."

At first Paxon had been skeptical. It did not seem possible to him that the old woman could be serious. He suspected her of plotting against him in some way. But after he had listened to her for a while, he became convinced that she was sincere. She was so desperate to separate Alane from Nardo that she would even stoop to helping him escape.

Once convinced, it had not taken Paxon long to agree to Mara's terms. To gain his freedom and Alane both! It scarcely seemed imaginable that the gods could look upon him with such favor.

So Paxon had followed Mara's orders. He had managed to leave his companions of the initiates' cave by using the excuse of an assignation with Pettra. The boys, who had roused with a hunter's alertness when he first moved, had grinned and gone back to sleep. They had heard the news of his encounter with Pettra from the girls who had accompanied her, and so his excuse had seemed reasonable. They would not miss him until the morning, when it would be too late.

"Alane will not want to go with you at first," Mara had warned. "But she is from a tribe where women do what men tell them to do. She did not want to marry Nardo, and see how fond of him she has grown. It will be the same with you. You must just give her time."

Paxon had smiled. "I will know what to do with Alane," he had said.

"If you force her, she will never forgive you," Mara had warned. "Give her time, Redu, and she will come around by herself."

You old bitch, Paxon had thought. *You're ready enough to put her into my hands, but you don't want to think about what will happen to her there, do you?*

In a smooth voice Paxon had said, "I hear you, old woman, and I understand what you say."

So now he stood here, alone in the moonlight, listening. Finally the sound of hoofbeats came from the path to the east. *At last,* Paxon thought, *they are here.*

Alane was stunned to see Paxon standing on the path. Mara rode right up to him and came to a halt, and Alane said in bewilderment, "What is he doing here?"

Mara said to Alane, "Get off and I will explain."

Alane could see no cave in the cliff. "Where is Nardo?" she demanded next.

"First get off, Alane," Mara said irritably. "I have said I will explain."

It was the irritability that reassured Alane; had Mara spoken sharply, Alane would have balked. By now it was obvious to her that something was not as it should be. Slowly Alane slid from Snowflake's back.

As soon as her feet were on the ground, Mara said to Paxon, "Take hold of her." And this time her voice was sharp.

For the first time Alane sensed danger. She backed away from the approaching Redu. "What is going on here?" she demanded.

Paxon reached out and closed his fingers around her arm. Alane pulled against his hold. "Let me go!" She pulled again.

His grip did not relax. "Not fear, Alane," he said to her. "Just to stand quiet."

He was a slim young man, but his fingers were very strong. Alane stopped struggling and looked at Mara. "Where is Nardo?" she repeated.

"At the Norakamo camp," Mara said. "He is not hurt. It was just a trick to get you to come with me."

"Not hurt," Alane repeated in relief. Then, as the full extent of Mara's perfidy dawned upon her, "A trick? What do you mean, a trick? And why is Paxon here?"

It was the Redu who answered her. "You to come away with me. We to find my people and you to be my woman."

Alane looked at him in amazement and dawning anger. "I will go nowhere with you," she said.

The Redu tightened his grip, letting her feel his strength. "Alane," he said. "You must."

As she finally realized what was happening, absolute rage swept through her. Never in all her life had she felt such anger. But it was a cold fury that possessed her, one that left her mind as sharp and clear as an icicle. She looked at Paxon. "Try to take me with you," she said, "and I will kill you."

Paxon looked startled, then he scowled and turned to Mara.

"Don't be a fool. She can't kill you," Mara said.

"Make no mistake about this, Mara," Alane said. Her voice was very quiet and very scary. "I will kill him. And then I will come back to the village and tell Nardo what you have done."

Mara stared at her son's wife. Alane's gray eyes were glittering and her moon-bleached face looked absolutely pitiless. She was not in the least afraid, Mara realized. She was enraged. The two women faced each other in the moonlight, both knowing that the struggle was between them, that the man was extraneous.

Paxon had not realized this as yet. "I not hurt you, Alane," he said. "I be good to you. This I promise."

Alane glanced at him as if she were surprised he was still there. "I will never lie with you, Paxon," she said. "Do you understand me? I am a married woman, and I would never so dishonor my marriage as to lie with another man." Her eyes went back to Mara. "Unlike the women of the Kindred, I was brought up to revere my marriage vow."

"Perhaps you not have choice," Paxon said.

Alane did not even bother to look at him. "Force me, and I will cut off your phallus," she said.

Paxon stared at her in shock.

His silence caught her attention as his words had not. She turned to him and her gray eyes were blindingly clear, like winter ice on a mountain lake. "I mean what I say," she said. "You would never be safe from me, Paxon. One night I would do it."

Paxon looked into those eyes and believed her. Very slowly he opened his fingers and released her arm.

Mara stood there on the path and said nothing. The two women looked at each other, the silence between them taut. Finally Alane said, as if they had come to a decision, "You will have to let him go. I do not think either of us is capable of returning him to the village just now." Her voice was full of contempt.

Still Mara said nothing.

"Nardo will be furious, but there is no help for it." At last Alane turned to Paxon. "You cannot have the horses. You know nothing about taking care of horses, and I will not trust them with you." She walked over to the packhorse that was carrying the spears and removed them. Over her shoulder she said to Mara, "Get him a set of sleeping skins and a knife."

Still silent, Mara turned, went to the other packhorse, removed the items Alane wanted, and put them on the ground. Alane went over to Snowflake and vaulted easily onto her back. With her eyes on Paxon she ordered Mara, "Get on your horse."

Once Mara was mounted, and had taken up the lead line of the packhorses, Alane gestured to her to start down the path toward home. "Canter," she said tersely.

Mara set off down the path, and Alane regarded Paxon. He looked very young and forlorn standing by himself in the moonlight, and her rage abated enough for her to feel a pang of pity for him. He was as much a victim of Mara's plot as she was, she thought.

"You are man enough to get a woman without having to kidnap her," she told him. She threw down the spears she was holding, and the flint points banged together as they hit the ground. "Farewell, Paxon," Alane said. Then she turned Snowflake and galloped down the path after Mara, leaving Paxon staring after her in the moonlight.

Mara sat back and obediently her mare slowed her pace. The packhorses followed, and soon all four horses were walking along the river path, striding forward eagerly as they realized they were heading home. The two women were silent. The only sound in the chill night air was the soft four-beat thud of horse hooves on the dirt path.

The world had a different appearance by night, all looming shadows and white moonlight. After an hour's walking the cliff walls fell away from beside the path and forest appeared. An owl hooted and Mara heard the heavy flap of its wings somewhere within the tall trees.

Never had the Wolf matriarch thought that her scheme would end in such ignominious defeat. Never had she dreamed that the Norakamo woman would have it in her to so face down her would-be kidnappers. While part of Mara was deeply apprehensive about what would happen when Nardo heard the tale of this night's doings, another part of her was filled with reluctant admiration for Alane.

She had vanquished the two of them. Mara and Paxon had held Alane in their power, and she had bested them. With words! Mara thought back on what had been said during that moonlight encounter, and she shook her head.

They were but ten minutes from the village when Alane finally spoke. "It still lacks an hour until dawn. If we are lucky, we can return the horses to the corral and no one will know that we have been gone."

At that, Mara turned to look at the younger woman. "You are not going to expose me?" she asked in amazement.

Alane was riding behind the two packhorses, and Mara could not see her face clearly enough to read it, but her answer came with crisp authority. "I am too angry right now to know what I should do. It will be best if we do not have to make any explanations right away."

The relief Mara felt was staggering. She said, "I think we will have time to return the horses and get to our bedplaces before our absence is discovered."

Alane did not reply, and after a moment Mara turned to face front once more.

Mara's return to the village went far more smoothly than the earlier part of her evening had. She and Alane rubbed down the

four horses and returned them to the corral. Then they shouldered the remaining gear and took it to Alane's hut for temporary storage.

As soon as they entered the hut and Alane saw her son
sleeping in peaceful solitude, she whirled to face her mother by
marriage. "You left Nevin alone here!" she accused.

"He was perfectly safe," Mara replied.

Alane's anger flared more hotly than it had all night. "What
if he had awakened and found me gone? He would have been
frightened!"

"He would have gone to the big house to look for you," Mara
returned.

Alane looked once more at her sleeping child. "You told me
Alis was coming to stay with him!"

Mara shrugged. It should be obvious to Alane, she thought
irritably, that she could not possibly have sent Alis on such an
errand—not with the plans Mara had had in mind.

Evidently Alane saw the foolishness of her accusations, for
she broke off abruptly, walked to the back of the hut and
dropped the set of sleeping skins she had removed from the packhorse to the floor. "Put the rest of the things here," she said over
her shoulder. "We will return them to their rightful places in the
morning."

Mara did as she was told. Without looking at her husband's
mother again, Alane went over to her bedplace and dropped to
her knees. Nevin was sleeping on his stomach, and she reached
out and touched his cheek with a gentle finger.

The gesture was so eloquent that, abruptly, Mara felt her
throat close down.

I was going to part her from her son, she thought.

For a moment longer she remained, watching Alane and
Nevin, and then she turned and pushed her way out of the hut.

No one stirred when Mara entered the big house. Nessa and
her children were sleeping within this night, as well as Tora and
Harlan, and they all knew one another's footfalls so well that the
sound of Mara's steps did not disturb their sleep. Mara was able
to crawl undetected into her sleeping skins and lie there until
dawn woke the household to greet the new day.

There was a great outcry when the tribe realized that their Redu captive was gone. The young men who had shared the initiates' cave with him immediately sought out Pettra, only to learn that Paxon had not been anywhere near her that night.

"None of the horses are missing," Tyr reported next. "If he has gone, he has gone on foot."

"We must get him back," Harlan said. "He knows where the village is. We do not want him to bring that news to the Redu!"

The rest of the men agreed, and after a hasty breakfast they mounted up to go in search of the missing man. "He has heard from us that his tribe is wintering on the River of Gold north of the Volp," Tyr said. "I am thinking that if we follow the Volp, we will find him."

It was late in the afternoon, when the sky had clouded over and the air had grown bone-chillingly damp, when Mara finally sought out Alane. She found her in her hut telling a story to a group of children gathered around her fire. Mara sat down near the door and waited.

"And that is how the horse lost his wings," Alane said finally. The children sighed with a mixture of rapture and sorrow—rapture with the story and sorrow that it was over.

"Another one!" Gar cried. His big eyes sparkled in the glow of the fire. "Tell us another one, Alane!"

But Alane shook her head. "Go on back to the big house now with Alis," she told her disappointed audience. "You see that Mara wishes to speak with me."

Mara stood up as the children obediently filed out. The door skins fell closed after the last one had gone, and she and Alane were alone. The small hut was redolent with the smell of burning wood, but little smoke hung in the air. Most of it was efficiently drawn out the hole in the roof above the hearthplace.

"They will find him," Mara said.

Silence fell as the two women regarded each other over the footprints that the children had left on Alane's meticulously swept floor.

"Why did you do it?" Alane said at last. "I have been asking and asking myself that question, and I cannot find an answer. I know that you have never liked me, but to do such a thing!" She drew a ragged breath. "I cannot understand it."

There were shadows like bruises under Alane's eyes. The Wolf matriarch saw them and felt her own weariness hit her like a blow. She straightened her back automatically. "I was afraid of you," she said steadily. "I was afraid of what you were doing to the tribe."

"What I was doing to the tribe?" Alane said in bewilderment. "What do you mean? I have done nothing to the tribe."

Slowly Mara moved toward the fire. "I am tired, Alane," she said. "May I sit down?"

Alane gestured to a rug. "I will make tea."

Mara lowered herself wearily to the hearth rug. "Tea will be good," she said.

Once both women were seated, with steaming cups of tea in their hands, Mara tried to explain herself. "This is a tribe that has always counted kinship by Mother's Blood," she said. "You are trying to change that, and I sought to stop you."

Alane was astounded. "I am not trying to change the way of this tribe. How could you think such a thing?"

"You seek to wean Nardo from the women of his blood and bind him to yourself," Mara said. "You know this is true."

Alane looked at her and said nothing.

"This would not be so bad," Mara went on, "if it only involved you and Nardo. But your influence is affecting the other young wives of the tribe. They too are seeking to strengthen the tie that binds them to their husbands, and in doing so they weaken the ties that bind the men and women of the same Mother's Blood."

Alane carefully took a sip of her tea. "There is no danger in closeness between a husband and wife," she said.

"There is no danger for the man," Mara agreed. "There is much danger for the woman."

A faint line appeared between Alane's smoky brows. "I do not understand you."

"I will tell you what I see," Mara said. She put her teacup on a flat hearthstone and leaned a little toward Alane. "I see that if a wife cuts herself off from the brothers and sisters who share her blood, if she becomes completely dependent upon her husband, then she is in danger of being exploited."

Silence fell. Mara once more took up her tea, blew on it to

cool it, and sipped. Alane frowned thoughtfully and gazed into the fire.

"Is this not what has happened in your own tribe?" Mara said at last. "When a woman marries, she gives up her own blood and becomes part of the blood of her husband. She has nothing that is hers. She is . . . property."

Alane's eyes lifted from the fire. Mara's dark eyes flashed as they met that clear gray gaze. "You were brought up in this way," Mara said, "so you do not see what I see. You are trying to bring the ways of your own people into this tribe, and I have not been able to stop you. Nardo does not understand. He thinks I am jealous of his affection for you." Mara's mouth twisted. "Perhaps he is right. Perhaps I am jealous. But this thing between us, Alane, is not about Nardo. It is about something far greater than just one man."

"If what you say is true, if these have been your concerns, then why have you never spoken of them to me?" Alane asked. "I do not understand why you would resort to such a terrible thing as kidnapping without even talking to me!"

"I did not think it would do any good," Mara said. She added, with a discernible trace of bitterness, "You have never shown yourself overly receptive to any words of mine, Alane. Particularly if they concerned your relationship with Nardo."

Alane bent her head. There was truth in what Mara said, and they both knew it.

"I will tell you something now that may surprise you," Mara said. "I am sorry that you were not born to this tribe. You are a daughter to be proud of, Alane. I am amazed that a tribe such as the Norakamo could bring forth so strong and valiant a woman."

Color flushed into Alane's face at Mara's words. Mara finished her tea and put down the cup. "You asked me why I did what I did. Well, that is why." And she folded her strong, workworn hands in her lap and waited.

Slowly Alane lifted her head. Flags of color still flew in her cheeks, but she met Mara's gaze, and when she spoke it was with calm deliberation. "If it is true that I am strong and valiant, it is because the Tribe of the Kindred has taught me to be so. It is in the Tribe of the Kindred that I have learned the worth of a woman, my mother. You are right when you say that among my own people, women are scarcely more than property."

Mara's brown eyes opened wide. Alane smiled faintly. "You are surprised to hear me say that?"

"Very surprised," Mara admitted.

"Most of what I have seen in this tribe, I have come to admire very much," Alane said. "The one thing I have not liked is the lack of closeness between husbands and wives. It is in my heart that marriage is one of the most deeply intimate of all human ties. Husbands and wives are bound together in ways not possible between brothers and sisters."

Mara's face was set. "Husbands and wives do not share the same blood," she said.

Alane's voice was soft. "Perhaps not, but their bodies become as one, my mother. The whole future of the tribe depends upon that, depends upon husbands and wives mating and having children. Is that not so?"

After a moment, "Sa," Mara agreed a little reluctantly. "That is so."

"A man can love his wife and still honor the ties that bind him to his mother and his sisters." The fire was burning low, and Alane reached out to poke it with a stick. A spray of burning embers fell from the log she had pushed. She put down the stick and continued in the same careful voice as before. "Because Nardo eats and sleeps with me, does that mean he does not care about Riva and Liev? Do you think he would refuse to come to their aid should they ever need him?"

Mara let out her breath. Without speaking, she shook her head.

"I would never try to stand between my husband and his duty to his family." A trace of some unidentifiable emotion sounded in Alane's voice. "In truth, I would like very much to feel that my own brothers would stand behind me the way I know Nardo will always stand behind Riva and Lora."

"I never dreamed that you felt like this, Alane," Mara said.

"I did not feel like this when first I came here," Alane admitted. "I was so lonely, you see. And I was jealous of Nardo's love for you and for his sisters and his cousins. He was all I had and I did not want to share him."

"He understood that," Mara said. "He told me to have patience with you, that you would come around when once you became more comfortable among us."

Alane's mouth curled. "Nardo is a man. His life is different. It is easy for him to give advice about being patient."

Mara's lips formed the same rueful shape as Alane's. "That is so."

The two women regarded each other with perfect comprehension.

"Now," Alane said, briskly changing the subject, "about this matter of Paxon."

Mara said, "Alane, I am sorry."

Slowly, and with great dignity, Alane bowed her head and accepted the apology. "I am sorry now that I did not give him a horse," she said after a moment. "If he were horsed he would have a chance to escape. On foot as he is, our men are sure to catch him."

Mara disagreed. "You were right about the horse. He would only abuse it."

"He is not a bad boy," Alane said excusingly. "He would not abuse the horse intentionally; it is just that he does not know its needs." She wrinkled her nose in a charmingly mischievous gesture. "In many ways he reminds me of my brothers."

"Is that why you have been so kind to him?"

"Sa. I have been trying—a little—to teach him things."

Mara sighed.

Alane leaned forward. "If Paxon tells the story of what happened last night, we must deny it."

"Deny it?"

"Sa. We will say that he is lying. If we back each other up, who will take the word of a Redu over ours?"

"They will suspect something," Mara said. "Why should Paxon say such a thing if it is not so?"

"Let them suspect," Alane said grandly. "If we deny it—if *I* deny it—there will be nothing anyone can say."

Silence. When Mara finally spoke there was an odd note in her voice. "I do not understand why you should be willing to do such a thing for me when I tried to do such a terrible thing to you. You have every right to want vengeance."

Alane shrugged. "Vengeance is the way of men," she said. "I am thinking that women are wiser."

Mara smiled crookedly. "Now indeed you are sounding like a woman of the Kindred."

"But you see, I am a woman of the Kindred," Alane replied. The hairs on the edge of the rug upon which she sat were ruffled, and absently she smoothed them down with her hand. "My mother and my father severed my blood ties to the Norakamo when they married me to Nardo. I have no other tribe but his."

Mara watched her face and said nothing.

"At the time of my marriage, I was very angry with my parents," Alane confessed. "As you said earlier, a Norakamo woman gives up her blood ties when she marries. But she does not give up her tribe! I thought it was a terrible thing they were doing to me. I did not want to marry Nardo at all." She smiled faintly and watched her fingers as they smoothed the rug hairs. "I have since changed my mind."

"Nardo can be very persuasive," said his mother.

Alane's smile was very private. "Sa." She looked up from the rug. "It would pain him unspeakably if he knew that you had tried to do this to me. It would divide the family. It would divide the clan. It would not be good for the tribe. For all these reasons, Mara, we will deny Paxon's story."

The lines in Mara's face seemed to have deepened. "What will we say happened?" she asked.

"That he escaped on his own. That he is trying to avoid punishment for breaking his word by putting the blame on us. I am thinking that the men will accept our word over the already broken word of a Redu captive."

"Sa," Mara said, "I think you are right."

PART FOUR

THE REDU

Chapter
Twenty-Two

One small but ugly incident marred the friendliness of Nardo's visit to the Norakamo camp. He had taken Dane and Nat with him, both even-tempered men, and the visit had gone very smoothly until two days before they were due to leave. On that day the three Kindred men rode out with Rune and Stifun to view the horses that had been given as Alane's bride-wealth. The horse herd was pastured on the big plain that lay on either side of the Big Crook River, and the Kindred men had been pleased to see the excellent condition of their mares. When they returned to camp, however, Nardo discovered that one of his remounts was sick.

"What happened here?" he demanded angrily as he viewed the obviously distressed mare.

"She was foolish enough to eat grass that did not agree with her," one of the Norakamo men replied.

Rune was furious. "Why did you take the horses to graze in a place where the grass was not good for them?"

"Our horses are wise enough not to eat grass that will make them sick" came the quick reply. "How were we to know that these horses were different?"

Nardo stared at the man who had spoken. "Were you the one who grazed this horse, Vili?" he asked.

A dozen heads swung around to look at Nardo. His voice had been very soft and very, very dangerous.

"Sa," said Vili, cousin to Loki, the man Nardo had killed. His eyes dropped from Nardo's face and he turned to Rune. "I was doing as you asked, Rune. I helped to take the Kindred horses to graze."

"And you did not watch what they were eating?" Rune asked coldly.

Vili shrugged. "I do not know what they are accustomed to eating at home. How was I supposed to know what would or would not agree with them?" He cast a quick look at Nardo, then looked away.

Nardo turned back to Snowdrop. She was a pathetic sight, her thick winter coat wet with sweat even though the air was cold. She kept swinging her head around to look at her stomach and pawing the ground in a way all horsemen knew and dreaded.

"She wants to lie down, but we have kept her walking," Larz said to Nardo.

"Cover her with a rug or she will take a chill," Nardo said grimly. Someone ran to do his bidding. Snowdrop pawed the ground and tried once more to lie down. Nardo went to her head, took the lead rope from Larz and said, "I will walk her." As the horsemen of both tribes knew, horses with a bellyache could not be allowed to roll. If they did, they usually died.

Five hours later, Snowdrop finally seemed comfortable enough for Nardo to relinquish her to someone else. It was dark; hours ago the Norakamo had built two fires around whose perimeter Nardo had been walking the suffering mare. He came now into Rune's tent and dropped gratefully to the rug by the fire. Samu, who had been following faithfully at his heels for the whole time he had been walking Snowdrop, grunted loudly and collapsed beside him.

"Here is your dinner, Nardo," Nita said, and she scooped red deer stew out of the pot she had kept simmering on the stove and brought it to Nardo. Samu whined.

"There is meat for the dog also," Rune said.

"I get it, Dada," Kara said excitedly, and she went immediately to a small basket near the door, reached in and took out a chunk of deer haunch. Samu quivered all over, but he waited until the child had set it down and Nardo had dismissed him before he went over to the meat and wolfed it down.

"This is very good, Nita," Nardo said, eating with scarcely less speed than Samu.

Nita smiled. "You are hungry. I am sorry your horse was sick, Nardo."

Nardo smiled back at her, then turned to address himself to Rune. "Vili is trouble," he said.

Rune frowned. "What he did today was stupid, certainly. But you cannot think he deliberately took your mare to grass that was not good for her."

Nardo chewed slowly. "Once he tried to push me off my horse during a reindeer hunt."

Rune's head came up like a stallion that has scented danger. "When was this?"

"When I was living among you after Alane and I were first married."

"Did you tell my father?"

Nardo shook his head. "If you remember," he continued, "it was Vili who got into a fight with Varic. Varic told me Vili called him an unspeakable name."

"I remember that fight," Rune said slowly.

"I do not trust him," Nardo said. "He bears ill will toward me and my people for the death of his cousin."

Nita said, "Wasn't it Vili who wanted to marry Alane? He is probably jealous of you, Nardo."

Rune's blue eyes were cold. "There was to be no blood feud between our tribes over the deaths of Nevin and Loki. Vili knows that."

Nardo said slowly, "What does Hagen say about your helping us with the Redu?"

Rune's eyes became if possible even colder. "Hagen is the shaman. His job is to see to the tribe's religious and medical needs. He has nothing to say about my decisions." The ice blue eyes narrowed. "I am the chief of this tribe," Rune said, "and Hagen will have to learn that I mean to rule it."

Nardo took another bite of stew, chewed reflectively, and did not reply.

Even though Paxon was on foot and they on horseback, the men of the Kindred almost didn't capture him. In the end it was

topography that gave them their victory. Paxon's downfall was a
gorge on the upper Volp, a deep canyon with only one way in
and one way out. The men of the Kindred, who had not been
able to pick up his tracks, rode ahead to the gorge, through which
he would have to travel, and waited.

Once Paxon was surrounded on the narrow path, he stood
quietly, accepting defeat. When he had left Alane and Mara, he
had not had great expectations of a successful escape, but as the
day had gone by his hopes had begun to rise. It was bitter to
have made it so far only to be caught. As he stood with dignified
resignation amidst his angry captors, Paxon knew that he was
facing death. No one among the Kindred would take lightly his
attempted kidnapping of Alane.

To his surprise, however, the men who captured him said
nothing of either Mara or Alane.

"I don't know how you came by these weapons," Pier
growled as he removed them from Paxon's grasp, "but you won't
get the opportunity again. We have learned how to value the
word of a Redu!"

"Sa," agreed one of the initiates who was with the party of
men. "And don't expect to fool us again with a story about going
to visit a girl."

Paxon said nothing. He continued to say nothing as they tied
his hands and boosted him onto the back of a horse. He listened
to the men talk as they traveled back along the Volp and made
camp for the night. Not once was there a mention of Mara or
Alane.

Could it be that Alane had held her tongue? Two days ago,
Paxon would not have believed such silence possible from a
woman, but now there was little he would put beyond Alane.

Paxon's spirits began to rise. Perhaps they would not kill him
after all. If Alane had kept silent, then Paxon would keep silent
too. He was not a fool. He knew it was in his own interest to
keep Mara's secret, and for as long as it was possible, that was
what he was going to do.

Nardo returned from his visit to the Norakamo at nightfall a
few days later. He and Dane gratefully handed their horses over

to the boys who came running from the initiates' cave, and the two turned their weary steps toward the big house, where they expected to find their wives. Warmth and noise struck Nardo's senses like a blow as soon as he lifted the door skins.

"Nardo!" a young female voice screamed. "Look, Alane, Nardo is here!"

Nardo narrowed his eyes, adjusting to the smoke and the dim light of indoors. A small boy began to run toward him, calling, "Dada! Dada!"

"Dane too!" the same female voice screeched. "Look, Lora, Dane is here!"

"Stop shrieking, Beki," Mara said calmly. "We have eyes. We can see for ourselves who has just arrived."

Nardo smiled, lifted a gleeful Nevin high in the air and gave him a hug, then moved toward the fire and Alane. Samu went to his usual place by the door and curled up to watch.

"Beki, your voice would frighten away an enraged bear," Dane said good-naturedly as he followed behind Nardo.

"We have told her that often enough," said Nessa, Beki's mother.

Nardo had reached Alane. Alis and Elexa, who had been sitting beside her, got up to make room for him. He gave them each a grateful grin, then lowered himself to the rug beside his wife. Nevin crowded in on his other side. Alane smiled at him. "Hungry?" she asked softly.

"Very," he replied, the look in his dark eyes giving an additional meaning to the word. She patted his knee, then frowned as she felt how damp the buckskin was.

Alis, who had not gone very far, said, "I will get you some stew, Nardo."

"Is it raining?" Alane asked.

"We ran into some rain an hour ago."

Nevin imitated his mother and touched Nardo's knee. "Dada wet," he announced.

Alane said, "You should have stopped to change your clothes, Nardo. It's too cold to be wearing wet clothing."

"Alane is right," Lora said, testing Dane's trousers the way Alane had tested Nardo's.

Nardo took the steaming bowl of stew from Alis.

Dane said, reaching for his bowl, which had been brought by Elexa, "We had our fur tunics on. Stop fussing."

Nardo looked around the house. When he had swallowed the stew that was in his mouth, he said, "Where is Paxon?"

The quality of the silence told him something was wrong. He put down his stew and looked toward Harlan. "Has something happened?"

Harlan's long face seemed even longer than usual as he looked back at Nardo. "Everything is all right now," he said. His moist eyes glittered in the lamplight. "The Redu tried to escape shortly after the full of the moon, Nardo, but we caught him and brought him back. Since then we have been keeping him confined to one of the huts. Evidently his word is not to be trusted."

Nardo scowled. "How far did he get?"

"To the Volp gorge above the Sacred Cave."

"Dhu!" said Dane.

"He went on his own?" Nardo said incredulously. "With no weapons?"

Pier joined the conversation. "He had weapons. We still have not determined how he got hold of them."

Nardo swore.

Alane said, "There is no need to be angry, Nardo. No harm was done. Eat your stew before it grows cold."

Nardo gave her an impatient glance. "If he had reached his tribe on the River of Gold, there could have been a great deal of harm done. He knows the location of our village. He knows our numbers." He turned back to Pier. "Dhu, it was a good thing that you caught him!"

"Sa," Pier said.

"Tell me how it happened."

As Nardo ate his stew, Pier recounted the tale of Paxon's escape.

"Pettra?" Nardo said inquiringly when the story was finished.

Alane said, "Evidently she is quite taken with him, Nardo. She has been bearing him company during these last days while the men have kept him confined to his hut."

"The addition of the Atata women has left the tribe with

more young women than young men," Mara said. "And the Red Deer girls have always liked a challenge."

Alane took Nardo's empty bowl. "Would you like some more?"

He shook his head.

Dane said, looking at Lora, "I should get out of these wet trousers."

Her dimples showed. "You have worn them the whole day without complaint."

"They are growing stiff as they dry," he said.

"I am thinking it's not just Dane's trousers that are growing stiff," Pier said with a laugh. "He's been away for over half a moon now, Lora."

Lora made a witty retort and everyone laughed. Nardo looked at Alane. She had been appalled by such frank talk when first she had joined the Kindred, and the family had respected her obvious discomfort by never teasing her and Nardo the way they were now teasing Lora and Dane. Alane's eyes were downcast, but there was the faintest of smiles upon her lips. He bent over and whispered in her ear, "Dane is not the only one suffering from stiffness."

To his delight she chuckled.

Lora said to Tora, "Can the children sleep in here tonight, Mama?"

"Of course," Tora replied.

"Me too!" Nevin said. Lora's son, Crim, was two years older than Nevin, and Nevin adored him. "I stay Crim."

Nardo said promptly, "An excellent idea."

To his surprise, his mother asked, "Alane? Is it all right with you if Nevin spends the night here?"

Alane smiled. "That will be fine," she said.

It had begun to rain when Alane and Nardo left the big house to make their way to their hut. Nardo sniffed. "I can smell grass in the rain," he said. "Spring is almost here."

Alane, who was carrying a stone lamp, ducked into the hut first. "I can smell wet buckskin," she said. "I will have to resoften those trousers tomorrow."

He was right behind her, with Samu on his heels. Alane went to the firewood stacked beside the door and began to pile it on the hearth. "How is my family?" she asked Nardo as she arranged the kindling.

"They are well," he replied. "Your mother is looking older."

Alane lit the fire, watched while it caught, then turned to face him. "I would like to see her, Nardo," she said a little forlornly.

"I will take you as soon as we are safe from these Redu, Alane. I promise."

She sighed, nodded, then asked, "Did you have any trouble with Hagen?"

He began to walk toward her. "Nothing serious."

Alane frowned. "You did have trouble. Tell me about it, Nardo."

"I'll tell you later," he said softly. "Just now I have other things on my mind."

"It is still cold in here," she protested weakly.

He reached out to draw her into his embrace. "Don't worry, little one. I will keep you warm."

Alane yelped as she came into contact with his clothes. "You won't keep me warm by pressing me into those wet buckskins, Nardo! Take them off."

He grinned. "Gladly."

She looked up into his face and her heart melted. He was so big, so immensely powerful, and yet she knew with utter certainty that he would never use that power to force a woman against her will. He stripped off his shirt and she reached up to rest her fingers on his muscled upper arms. His strength was her joy; never would it become a threat.

I cannot live your life for you, Alane, he had said. Every other man she knew had wanted to live her life for her. Only Nardo was willing to leave her free.

He cursed. He had been struggling with the string that held his trousers at the waist, and now he said fretfully, "I cannot get this string undone!"

"Let me. My fingers are smaller." She used her nails to try

to loosen the knot in the leather tie. It was stiff and difficult to move. "Nardo, even this tie is wet!"

Her fingers touched his flat, hard abdomen, and he said wickedly, "You can touch even lower if you like."

She smiled. Next to Nardo, she thought, Paxon was nothing but a selfish, skinny boy.

Chapter Twenty-Three

Vili flung his tunic to the ground and said, "Rune is much mistaken if he thinks we are going to help those Kindred bastards do anything."

"They did nothing to help us when we fought the Horse Eaters," Noli agreed. He looked at his uncle. "It seems to me this famous alliance between our two tribes is all to the benefit of the Kindred and none to us."

The two cousins had come directly to the shaman's tent from the tribal meeting held by Rune, and now Hagen himself spoke in his softest voice. "I fear that Rune is too much under the influence of this Kindred chief. Who is the chief of the Nora-kamo, I wonder. Rune? Or Nardo?"

Vili said with hatred, "Nardo."

Hagen looked at his nephew with hooded eyes and said nothing. It was cold outdoors, but the shaman's tent was always warm and stuffy.

"These Redu have been camping on the River of Gold for the whole of the winter," Noli said indignantly, "and Nardo has waited until now to bring us the news?"

"Nardo thinks of us as a subordinate tribe, to be used however he wishes," Vili said. "Well, we shall prove him wrong."

"And Rune too," said Noli.

"Softly, softly, my nephews," Hagen said. "It will be well for us to bide our time and not make our move too quickly or else we will lose everything. Too many of our men have been fooled by promises of Kindred aid."

"What would you have us do, Uncle?" Vili asked eagerly.

"The Norakamo have never been fond of inactivity," the shaman said with a thin smile. "I am thinking that playing a waiting game will start to pall very quickly."

"That is so," Noli said, nodding emphatically in agreement.

"We will wait until that happens," Hagen said, "and then we will make our move."

Nardo had spent the entire winter thinking about what he might do to defeat the Redu. Unfortunately, it had not proved feasible to duplicate the firepower of the enemy by making replicas of the Redu long bow. It was not that the construction of the bow was so complicated. It was much larger than the Kindred bow, of course, but the Kindred bow and arrow makers were able to copy the backing of sinew that reinforced the wood and made it so strong. However, it had soon become evident that making the bow was one thing, but learning to shoot with it was something else. If the Kindred wanted to learn to be effective with such a weapon, it would take intensive training over a long period of time. And time was something Nardo feared they did not have.

What advantages did they have to counterbalance the Redu bows?

They had horses.

They had their knowledge of the mountains.

They had the Norakamo.

All Nardo had to do was find a way to combine these advantages, and by the beginning of spring he thought that he had.

In the spring the reindeer would leave the low altitude of Big Rivers Joining and move toward the mountains. The herds would travel south along the River of Gold, and the Redu would doubtless follow them. And if the Redu did that, they would run right into the Norakamo summer camp near the Big Ford.

The first step in Nardo's plan was to ask the Norakamo to use another location for their summer camp this year, and this necessitated yet another trip to see Rune.

Somewhat to Nardo's surprise, Rune suggested that they ride

away from the Norakamo camp in order to hold their discussion. The two men rode to the Gorge River, picketed their horses to graze, and stood together gazing down into the deep canyon while Nardo explained what he wanted Rune to do.

Rune balked. "How can I tell my men that we are simply going to back away and let these strangers use our camp place?" he demanded angrily.

"I want to trap them, Rune," Nardo replied, "and to do that I need you. I want to lure them into a place where they will be vulnerable from the back, and then I want you and the Norakamo to fall upon them. They must not know of your existence!"

Rune looked at Nardo. "Where do you want to trap them?" he asked.

Nardo told him the whole plan.

"It is a good plan," Rune admitted when Nardo had finished speaking.

"Will you help?" Nardo asked.

Rune looked a little grim. "Sa, Nardo, I will help you. But it is not going to be easy to convince the tribe to give up our traditional summer camp."

Nardo regarded the fast-flowing river as it rushed through the deep canyon it had worn in the rock. "Hagen?" he said.

Rune nodded. The breeze blew his blond bangs back from his forehead, and Nardo could see in his clear-cut profile a resemblance to Alane. "The shaman is making trouble as usual." He looked at Nardo. "He wants to be the chief."

Nardo said bleakly, "I have been having the same problem with my cousin Varic."

The two young men looked at each other.

"We need to make this plan work," Nardo said at last. "A series of small raids might succeed in reducing the Redu numbers somewhat, but we would also be bound to lose men. And there are more of them than there are of us.

"We need to get rid of them all," Rune agreed, "and the only way to do that is to slay them the same way we slay a large herd of reindeer. Trap them and kill them while they are helpless to defend themselves. If your plan succeeds, we will do that."

"Then you will go along with me and keep the tribe from summer camp?" Nardo asked.

"Sa," Rune said. "I will keep the Norakamo encamped upon the Gorge so that the Redu may pass unimpeded down the River of Gold."

At the beginning of Salmon Moon, the first moon of spring, Nardo called the clan council to a meeting in his hut. As the men settled down, Nardo looked at the familiar faces and remembered how recalcitrant they had proved last year when he had asked them to keep watch on the Buffalo Pass. He did not know what he would do if they refused to listen to him again. He would do something, though, he vowed. Never again would he allow himself to feel as helpless as he had last year.

It was raining outside and the men's wet buckskin garments steamed gently in the warm air of the small hut. When Nardo finally began to speak, his calm voice gave no hint of his inner tension.

"It is Salmon Moon," he said, "and the reindeer will be beginning their spring migration. They will want to be in their mountain pastures in time for the fawns to be born. I am thinking that soon the Redu will have to move from their camp at Big Rivers Joining."

Hamer, council member from the Leopard Clan, grunted in agreement. The other men nodded, their faces grim.

"They tried the Atata last spring," Nardo said. "This time they will try the River of Gold."

Again the men nodded in grim agreement.

Varic looked at Nardo and said with seeming casualness, "If they follow the River of Gold, they will run into the Norakamo summer camp."

Nardo met his cousin's widely spaced brown eyes and knew he was in for trouble from Varic over the Norakamo. He cursed inwardly, although he let none of his frustration show upon his face.

Matti took Varic's bait eagerly. "Will the Norakamo fight the Redu for possession of their camp?"

Nardo said calmly, "I have asked their chief, who is my brother by marriage, not to use their summer camp this year, and he has agreed."

Varic's lip curled with scorn. "The Norakamo are only brave when they are fighting one man," he said.

Nardo gripped his anger hard. "Nevin was my mother's brother and I mourn his loss as much as you do, cousin. But now is not the time to let old grievances stand in the way of our tribes working together. We need the Norakamo if we are to defeat the Redu, and they need us."

"Old grievances!" Varic flared. "My father's death is no old grievance!"

Nat leaned forward and spoke in measured tones, "Do you have a plan, Nardo? What is it that you want us to do?"

"This." Nardo looked slowly around the circle of men, carefully measuring their responses. "I want to take the whole tribe to the Altas, as we did last summer. But this year we will go to Bright Valley by way of the Eagle Pass and the River of Gold instead of going through the High Col from the Greatfish."

He paused. It had begun to rain harder outside; they could hear the drops beating on the bark that covered the roof. Some rain came down through the smoke hole, and the fire hissed as the water hit it.

"Why?" Hamer demanded. "If we know the Redu are going to be on the River of Gold, why should we place our women and children within their reach?"

"Because I want the Redu to follow us," Nardo replied.

A startled silence fell.

"You will have to explain yourself, Nardo." Varic's gaze flicked quickly around the faces in the hut. "We are obviously too stupid to understand."

Nardo ignored the deliberate provocation. Instead he looked at Nat's strong, square face and spoke to the leader of the Bear Clan. "This is the way I see the situation," he said. "We have three advantages over the Redu: our horses, our knowledge of the mountains, and the Norakamo. If we are to defeat these intruders, then we must exploit our advantages."

Varic said bitterly, "I would not count the Norakamo as an advantage."

"We will have to," Nardo said quietly, "for they are the key to our victory."

Varic's protest was drowned out by Nat's deeper voice: "What are you planning, Nardo?"

"This." All the men but Varic leaned imperceptibly closer to Nardo. "I want to take the tribe through the Eagle Pass and into Bright Valley, and I want the Redu to know where we have gone. As you all know, the Eagle Pass is but three horse widths across at its widest place, and it is hemmed in by the mountains on both sides. It would be very easy for the Redu to hold the Eagle Pass, and that is what I want them to do. I want them to think they have us trapped into Bright Valley as neatly as we had them trapped in summer camp last year."

Freddo's slanting, obsidian eyes gleamed in the firelight. "But we can always leave Bright Valley by way of the Greatfish," he said.

"The Redu know nothing about the pass to the Greatfish," Nardo returned.

Matti thrust impatient fingers through his hair. "But what is the point of all this?" he asked. "Why do we want them to think they have us trapped in Bright Valley?"

"I imagine that Nardo wants the Norakamo to come up behind the Redu while they are concentrating on us," Hamer said. "Then we will have them between us."

Nardo nodded. "Between us, and at our mercy. If we do our work well, we should be able to kill them all."

Nat shook his head. "This is all very well, Nardo, but the chief of the Redu is not a fool. He will keep guards posted on the River of Gold to watch his rear. The Norakamo will not be able to sneak up on him unaware."

"The Norakamo will not come up the River of Gold," Nardo explained. "They will come up the small river that breaks away from the River of Gold when it reaches the Altas. There is a sheep track that they can take across the mountains that will bring them right to the place where the Eagle Pass begins."

"The mountains on either side of the Eagle Pass are too steep for horses," Nat objected.

"That is so," Nardo agreed patiently. "But the sheep track will bring them onto the path *before* it narrows to go through the pass."

"That will give the Redu time to see them," Matti said.

Nardo answered, "Here is where the horses are to our advantage. The Norakamo will come too fast for the Redu to be able to organize a defense."

"I do not know this small river or this sheep track," Freddo said with a frown.

"I scouted it one moon ago," Nardo replied. "If Dane and I could cross the mountains in the snow, then the Norakamo should be able to make the climb in better weather."

Mano said quietly, "The Norakamo horses are not mountain horses like ours are, Nardo. Can they make the climb?"

"Their horses are good enough," Nardo replied.

"I do not trust the Norakamo," Varic said. His face was wearing a stubborn look. "I do not think it is wise of us to base the whole success of our plan on the Norakamo. What if they don't come?"

"Why wouldn't they come?" Nardo spread his hands expressively. "It is as much in their interest as it is in ours to be rid of these intruders. The Norakamo are a smaller tribe than we are. It is only sensible for them to join with us in this endeavor."

"Rune may think it would be clever to let the two larger tribes fight it out," Varic said. "Then, when we are both mortally wounded, he could step in and take over our hunting grounds."

Nardo looked grimly at his cousin. Varic's eyes were glitteringly bright as he returned Nardo's look. He was out to scuttle his cousin's plan, and he wanted Nardo to know it. Nardo felt his anger beginning to rise.

Hamer was the first to waver. "Varic may be right," he said. "I am thinking it would be better if we left a group of our own men to make the surprise march upon the Redu rear."

"The Redu outnumber us," Nardo said. His voice was a little too quiet, his face a little too still. "If we add the Norakamo to our number, however, we will be evenly matched." He looked from face to face around the circle, pausing fractionally longer when his eyes met Varic's. "I want this fight to end things forever. The longer these people stay in our mountains, the harder it will be for us to get them out."

"Nardo is right," said Mano. "I think this is a good plan."

"Of course Mano thinks it is a good plan. The Wolf clan always sticks together," Varic said sarcastically.

Mano scowled and opened his mouth to reply. Nardo held up his hand. "Enough," he said pleasantly, and everyone looked at him with sudden wariness.

"I have told you my plan," Nardo said, still with that dangerously pleasant voice. "Does anyone else have a plan to offer?"

"I think we should follow your plan, but instead of the Norakamo I think a group of Kindred men should fall upon the Redu rear," Varic said.

Hamer and Matti grunted in agreement.

"That is not your plan, Varic," Nardo said. "That is my plan with your variation. I do not like the variation. If we follow my plan, we will follow it as I presented it."

There was silence in the hut.

"I repeat," Nardo said, "does anyone else have a plan to offer?"

The men dropped their eyes. The silence was heavy.

"I take it we are all in agreement that we must do something?" Nardo asked.

"Sa," Mano said strongly. "We must do something."

Nat nodded.

"Varic?" Nardo asked. "Do you think we should just ignore the Redu and hope they go away?"

Varic was looking sulky. "Na. I do not think that."

"Then, since there are no other suggestions, I propose that we follow my plan," Nardo said.

Nat turned toward Varic. "Nardo was right last year when he wanted to guard the Buffalo Pass, and we were wrong. I am thinking that he proved then that he deserves our trust." He turned back to Nardo. "I am in favor of your plan," he said.

"And I," Mano said.

"And I," said Freddo and Hamer and Matti.

"Varic?" Nardo asked, still with that intimidating softness in his voice. "How stands the Eagle Clan?"

"Oh, I suppose I will have to go along with you, Nardo," Varic said sullenly. "But I will be making my prayers to the Mother that you are not wrong about the Norakamo."

"If the Norakamo should prove unfaithful, we can always leave Bright Valley through the High Col," Hamer said practically. "We are not trusting them with our lives, Varic."

"Do you not see?" Nardo said. "This is the very reason why my father made a marriage between me and Alane. Rune is my brother by marriage. He will not fail me."

"Let us pray that he does not," Nat said grimly. "For if he does, he may cause the destruction of both our tribes."

Chapter
Twenty-Four

Shortly after Nardo's return to the village, Paxon found himself being given more and more freedom. At the beginning he was allowed to leave the hut to take some exercise, and during the first week of Salmon Moon he was once again permitted to take his meals with one of the tribe's households.

He did not return to his old place at Mara's house. Besides Alane, Mara was the only person who knew what had really happened on the night Paxon had escaped, and it made him distinctly uneasy to be around her. He was uncomfortable knowing that she had seen him back down before a woman. And there was no hiding the fact that, on that miserable night, he had backed down.

At first he tried to excuse himself for his cowardly behavior. Alane had surprised him, he told himself. Never had he dreamed that so lovely and soft-spoken a woman would prove to be such a virago. She had shocked him so much that for a moment he had not known what to do, and his momentary confusion had allowed her to seize the initiative.

Mara had seen this happen. It did not matter that Mara also had backed down before Alane's fury. Mara was not a man.

Oddly enough, Paxon was not embarrassed to be with Alane herself. The reason for this dated back to the week after he had been recaptured, when Alane had come to see him in the hut where he was being held prisoner.

It was a small hut, furnished only with two hearth rugs, a set of winter sleeping skins and one stone lamp. Paxon had been idly throwing a set of knucklebones, given to him by a kind-hearted Pier to alleviate boredom, when he had heard her voice assuring whoever was on guard that she would be all right. He jerked his head up and looked warily toward the door. If it had been within his power to refuse to see her, he would have.

The door skins rippled, were pushed aside, and there she was. The sun behind her made a silver halo of her hair. Slowly Paxon got to his feet, all the time staring at that flawless face. She did not look even remotely ferocious as she stepped into the hut and regarded him out of perfectly clear eyes. He thought: *Is it possible that this beautiful creature actually said such terrible things to me? Or did I dream the whole thing?*

It was Alane who first broke the silence. "You have been wise to hold your tongue about Mara's part in your escape," she said approvingly. "We would have denied it, of course, but it is much better not to have it mentioned at all." She dropped the door skins behind her and stepped into the hut.

He answered carefully, "When they capture me, the men ask me how I get the weapons. I know then that you say nothing, so I say nothing too."

Alane smiled. It was not possible to look more delicately feminine than she looked at that moment. "When Nardo returns, he will be angry to learn that you broke your word and tried to escape, but if he knew that you had tried to kidnap me, Paxon, I am thinking that he might well kill you. You were wise to say nothing."

"Sa," Paxon agreed, her smile already making him feel more comfortable. "It wise for me to keep quiet. But you—it is you I not understand. That woman want you gone! She give you to me, and she not care what I do with you, Alane." He took a step closer to where she stood by the doorway. "Why you keep her secret? Why you not tell your husband what kind of woman his mother is?"

Alane sighed and moved farther into the hut. For the first time Paxon noticed that she was carrying a kettle. "Sit down," she said. "I have brought you some of my tea."

He had become very fond of her mint tea, liking it better than the sage tea usually brewed by the Kindred. Slowly, with his eyes still on her, he sat on one of the hearth rugs. She knelt on the other and set out two bone cups, which she took from a buckskin sack she wore over her shoulder. Then she poured them each a cup of tea.

As she handed it to him, he said, "I not understand you at all. You not tell about Mara, and you bring me tea." He shook his head and sipped the hot drink. It was very good. "Why you not hate us?" he asked.

"It was all a misunderstanding," she replied serenely. "Mara was afraid of me when there was no cause for her to be. She realizes that now, and we are friends."

Up until a week ago, Paxon would not have believed that anyone could possibly be afraid of Alane. He felt differently now.

"You not hate me?" he asked in amazement. "I try to steal you away, to make you my woman."

"I don't hate you, Paxon," she replied in the low-pitched voice that was so lovely to listen to. "You were wrong to do that, and I think you knew you were wrong. After all, you didn't steal me, did you? When you saw how I felt, you let me go." She smiled at him. "You have a good heart, Paxon. It is just that being brought up among the Redu, you have not learned how to treat women."

Paxon much preferred Alane to think he had backed down because of his good heart than because he was afraid of her, and so he said, "Maybe it is so."

They sipped their tea.

"Still," she said, "the men are angry. You broke your word and they will not trust you again."

He shrugged. "It my first need to return to my father if I can. No word is bigger important than that."

"Our men do not agree with you, and I am afraid you will be made to suffer." She looked sad.

He gave her his haughtiest look, his pride restored by her generous understanding. "I strong," he said.

She smiled at him. "Perhaps they will let Pettra come to visit you. She likes you, Paxon. Would you like to see her?"

He thought of the afternoon he had spent with Pettra in the cave, and his pulse began to race. "Sa," he said hoarsely. "I like Pettra too."

"Finish your tea," Alane had said, "and I will see what I can do."

Pettra came to visit often, and they both enjoyed themselves very much. When Nardo had returned and the restrictions on Paxon began to be loosened, he began to take his meals with Pettra in her mother's household.

Lina, matriarch of the Red Deer, was surprisingly agreeable to the relationship that had developed between her daughter and the captive Redu.

"There are not enough men in the tribe now that we have added the women of the Atata Kindred to our households," she said to Bria, a matriarch of the Leopard clan, as they drew water together at the river one spring morning. "The Atata girls have drawn the interest of many of the young men, and our girls are lonely." She shrugged. "This Redu boy is better than no boy at all."

"It is a problem," Bria agreed. "I also have two girls of my household who lack boys. It does not help that two of the girls who joined us are walking with two boys of the Eagle clan. And these boys had previously shown an interest in the girls they are now ignoring!"

Lina sighed. "It is understandable, I suppose. The Atata girls are new and so seem more interesting than the girls the boys have known all their lives."

"That is so. But it does not make it any easier for our girls."

"Na," Lina said gloomily. "It does not."

Alane was surprised by Nardo's willingness to give Paxon back so much of his liberty. She herself was sympathetic toward the young Redu because she knew how Mara had maneuvered him into making his abortive escape attempt, but Nardo knew nothing of his mother's intervention. Alane had suggested allowing Paxon the freedom of the camp without really expecting Nardo to agree, and she had been surprised by her husband's positive response.

The horsemen Nardo had posted to keep watch on the Redu camp at Big Rivers Joining reported at the end of Salmon Moon that the tribe was beginning to make its move down the River of Gold. Nardo ordered the Kindred to get ready for their trek to the Altas.

There was a great deal of protest from the women when first they learned they were going to take the River of Gold pass to Bright Valley. "It makes no sense," Mara fumed to Nardo. "If we go by the Greatfish we can go directly south and through the High Col. To get to the River of Gold we have to go north first! It is two times as long as the Greatfish route."

Nardo tried to make light of the change. "We can make a few stops along the way, Mama," he said pleasantly. "Our winter camps lie along the route, and we can use the caves and huts there to rest for a few days before moving on. It won't be so bad."

But Mara would not be placated, and it did not take Nardo long to realize that Paxon was most certainly going to hear about the women's discontent. The young Redu would learn there was a second pass into Bright Valley, and Nardo did not want him to know about that pass.

Nardo said to Mara, "I rode up to the High Col last moon, Mama, and there was a rock slide during the winter. The pass is virtually closed. There is no way we will get the tribe through it."

"A rock slide?" Mara said.

"Sa. All across the narrowest part of the pass."

"Why did you say nothing to us about this slide?"

He tried for an injured look. "I suppose I thought that the tribe would take the word of its chief as to the best route."

"It would not have taken many words to tell us about the slide," Mara said mildly. "Now it is clear why we must take the River of Gold. I will tell the rest of the women."

"Do that," Nardo said, and went immediately to inform the rest of the council members of the tale that he had just spun.

Two nights before the tribe was due to depart, Nardo and Alane were alone in their hut, talking in soft voices so as not to disturb Nevin, who was sleeping.

Nardo had discussed his plan with Alane even before he had presented it to the council, and she was aware that his story about a rock slide in the High Col was untrue. He had told her that he did not want the rest of the tribe to know about the plan because he was afraid the women would worry overmuch. Alane had not agreed with him, but she had followed his wishes and held her tongue. It was a source of considerable pride to her that she was the only person besides the council in whom he had confided.

"The packing is going better this year than last," Alane said now. She had spent the entire day helping the household women to pack up the big house. "Mara even relinquished her second-favorite teapot." There was warm amusement in her voice.

"That is good."

"There were a good many complaints about the rock slide that is making the trip so inconvenient for us." She gave him a sideways glance.

"That rock slide was a good thought of mine," he said imperturbably. "It has saved me many arguments."

"I still don't think that the women would panic if they knew your true reason for using the Eagle Pass."

He shrugged. A short silence fell, then Nardo spoke in the soft voice that usually sent shivers down her spine. "Why don't you let me loosen your braid?"

But Alane was not yet ready to give up the conversation. "One thing is worrying me about this plan of yours, Nardo," she said. "I understand that we are going by the River of Gold because you want the Redu to think that the Eagle Pass is the only way into Bright Valley. I understand that you want them to follow us. What I don't understand is how they are going to know where we have gone! They can't keep watch on us as we do on them. They don't have any horses." She turned to look at him, her smoky brows drawn together in a frown. "If they don't know we have gone to the Altas by way of the River of Gold, then how can they come after us?"

Nardo cocked an eyebrow and looked thoughtful. "Good question."

She knew immediately that he had a plan. "A good question indeed," she replied steadily. "Does it have an answer?"

The fire had gone out, but he poked it with a stick anyway. "Perhaps."

Her face set and she stared at the ashes in the hearth. "If you don't wish to tell me, just say so."

He shivered and said, "Brrr. A cold wind just blew through this hut."

Alane was furious. "There is no need to say any more. I understand that I am just a woman and not to be trusted." She crossed her arms over her chest and refused to look at him.

"Alane," he said coaxingly, "you know I trust you. You are the only other person besides myself and the council who knows about this plan. Would I have told you if I didn't trust you?"

"Apparently I am not to be trusted with the whole of your plan, though," she said stiffly.

"It is not that I don't trust you . . ."

She turned to look at him. His dark eyes were regarding her with a rueful expression. "I might have known you would perceive the one piece of the plan that was missing." He sounded resigned.

He was going to tell her. She leaned forward and kissed the side of his jaw. "I didn't think of it until this morning," she said. "What are you going to do?"

"I am going to take Paxon with us to the pass, and then I am going to let him escape."

"Oh, Nardo, na!" Alane said softly. "That is too cruel."

"That is why I did not tell you. I knew you would not like it."

"If your plan is successful, you will be sending him to his death."

"He is a Redu, Alane. His allegiance is to his own tribe, not to us."

"Pettra loves him."

"You are the one who has fostered that partnership. Not I."

"This is the real reason why you have kept your plan from the tribe," Alane said suddenly. "Now I understand the need for secrecy. You do not want Paxon to know that there is another pass into the valley."

"Sa."

"Nardo . . ." Alane leaned toward him. Her voice was persuasive. "He is a good boy."

His mouth was hard. "There may be many good boys among
the Redu, Alane, but that does not change the fact that they are
our enemies. It does not change the fact that they are the ones
who invaded our mountains. We did not seek them out, remember. They are the ones who came to us."

"But we have come to *know* Paxon, Nardo! He is not 'an
enemy' anymore; he is Paxon."

Nardo met her eyes. "He does not feel the same loyalty to
you that you do to him, Alane," he said. "He has tried to escape
before. And you can be certain that if he had not been recaptured, he would have told his tribe all about our village. So you
can stop being so softhearted about this 'boy.' "

Alane felt a pang of guilt. She really did believe that Paxon's
good heart had triumphed over his lust on that memorable night,
and she felt she owed him a debt. She thought now that Mara
had trapped him into that escape attempt as surely as Nardo was
planning to trap him again. Poor Paxon.

"I am not so certain that Paxon would have betrayed us," she
began cautiously.

Nardo said, "Don't be stupid, Alane. Why else was he trying
to escape?"

Never before had Nardo called her stupid. Alane's temper
began to rise. "You don't know everything about that escape
attempt," she retorted unwisely.

Nardo's face went very still. Alane saw it and bit her lip.
"What do you mean?" he asked, his voice so quiet it was
intimidating.

Alane looked away from him. His hand shot out and circled
her wrist. "Look at me, Alane. What do you mean, I don't know
everything about that escape attempt?"

Unwillingly she raised her eyes to his and knew she would
have to tell him. She dropped her eyes to the big hand that was
clasping her wrist, and in a low, expressionless voice she related
the tale of Mara's treachery.

He dropped her wrist halfway through the telling, and there
was a long silence when she had finished.

"Your mother feared that I was changing the Mother's Blood

pattern of the tribe," Alane said in further explanation. "She thought this was something she had to do. She and I discussed this thoroughly, and she understands now that I would never want to change the Kindred ways. We have settled things between us, Nardo. I do not want you to let her know that I have told you this story."

Nardo was looking more baffled than angry. "I cannot believe that Mama would do such a thing."

"It was not well done of her," Alane agreed.

"Not well done of her." He stared at her. "Dhu, I would call it more than that!" His expression hardened. "If Paxon had been successful, do you know what I would have done to him when I caught up with him?"

Alane repressed a shiver at what she read on his face. "Well, you did not have to catch him," she said. "When he saw how distressed I was, he let me go."

His eyes glittered. "I should kill him for even thinking about laying his hands on you."

Alane said austerely, "I seem to remember that you once assisted in a kidnapping, Nardo. You were not so nice in your thoughts then."

It took him a moment to realize what she was talking about. Then, "That was different," he snapped. "Nita wanted to go with Rune."

"He did not know that until he kidnapped her," Alane pointed out.

"If she had wanted to stay with her tribe, I would have returned her."

"Which is exactly what Paxon did," said Alane.

Nardo scowled. "Nita was not married!"

"That is so," she agreed. "There is a difference there."

Nardo pushed a finger under his headband, as if he were finding it too tight. Then, impatiently, he pulled it off and ran his fingers through his hair. Released from confinement, it slid forward across his forehead. "Do you have any other secrets you would like to confide in me?" he asked sarcastically.

"That is the only one, and I only told you because you are planning to do the same thing to poor Paxon again."

"Stop talking about him as if he were a child, Alane! He is a full-grown man. I am certain his thoughts about you when he was agreeing to kidnap you were not those of a child!"

"Perhaps not. But he was persuaded into that escape, Nardo. Mara dangled me in front of him the way you would dangle a honeycomb in front of a child. She promised him weapons and horses. Would you have refused to escape under such circumstances?"

He shoved his fingers ruthlessly through his hair. "What happened during Paxon's first escape attempt has nothing to do with my plan, Alane. As you yourself said, I need a way of letting the Redu know where we have gone. I need to let them know about the Eagle Pass. Paxon is the answer to those needs. I have to use him."

He meant it.

"Nardo . . ."

He shook his head. "It's late," he said and turned toward their sleeping skins. After a few moments Alane removed her moccasins, lay down with her back to him and curled on her side. His mind had been on love before, but he had enough sense not to reach for her now. It was not long before the even sound of his breathing told her he was asleep.

Alane lay awake for a long time, thinking.

The following day Alane went back to the big house once again to help with the packing, and at mid-morning Pettra stopped by with the news that her sister Iva had put away her husband.

"Well," Mara said after a short pause, "I cannot say I am surprised."

The rest of the women of the Wolf murmured softly in agreement. It was well-known that lately Bram had taken to walking out with Orel, one of the Atata women.

"When did this happen?" Riva asked.

"Early this morning. When he came home from making his morning prayer by the river, Iva had put all his clothes outside the door of their hut."

Alane was listening to this with wide eyes. "What did Bram do then?" she asked.

The women looked at her in surprise. "He took his clothes

and went home to his mother and sisters, of course," Mara said. "Iva does not want him for a husband any longer."

"And this is the end of the marriage?"

"Unless someone can get Iva to change her mind," Lora said.

"Bram's mother came to talk to her," Pettra volunteered, "but Iva is furious with him for disgracing her in front of the tribe. She says everyone knows about him and that Atata woman. Evidently Iva told him a while ago that unless he stopped seeing Orel, she would divorce him. He did not stop, and so she put his clothes outside her door."

"I do not see why all the men are so interested in those Atata women," Lora said angrily. She could speak freely on this subject because there were no Atata women present; Mara's household had been the only one in the tribe with no kin to absorb.

"Bram did not get on that well with Mama," Pettra said. "I am thinking that Orel gave him a sympathetic ear."

"Her ear was not the only thing about her that was sympathetic," Riva retorted. In the case of a divorce the members of the tribe usually tended to side with the party of their own sex, and Riva's empathy was clearly with Iva.

"My brother Haras also has had his problems with Lina," Nessa murmured. "I am thinking that perhaps the Red Deer matriarch is too hard on her daughters' husbands."

"Whatever his problems, Haras did not go walking with another woman," Pettra pointed out.

Alane stood by the cook pots she had been wrapping in a deerskin rug for protection and listened. She too had been aware of Bram's interest in Orel, but she had not thought that Iva would have any recourse but to accept it. Male infidelity was not unknown among the Norakamo, but a wife's only means of dealing with it was to pretend ignorance.

"What will Bram's clan do?" Alane asked curiously. "Will the men of the Bear really allow Iva to end the marriage?"

Riva looked surprised. "What has Bram's marriage got to do with the men of the Bear, Alane?"

It was Mara who understood the reason behind Alane's question. "Remember, Alane, unlike in your tribe, there is no bride-wealth given when a Kindred girl marries," she explained. "Since no property was exchanged, neither Iva's clan nor Bram's will be the losers if the marriage dissolves. The only ones affected will be Iva and Bram themselves."

What Mara said was true, Alane thought wonderingly as she finished wrapping the pots. Not even Iva's children would be greatly affected. They were of her clan, and would still have their uncles and aunts and cousins as well as their mother. Nor would Iva's life change that much. She would remain in the same household where she had lived since childhood. She would be entitled to the same share of the household food as she had received when she had a husband hunting with the rest of the men. It was Bram, who must return to the house of his mother, whose life would be affected most.

Evidently Riva did not agree with Alane's conclusion, for as Alane bent to put the securely wrapped pots on the floor beside the rest of the things to be packed, she heard Nardo's sister say, "Iva will be affected more by this divorce than Bram. He will probably marry Orel, but men to marry Iva are in short supply."

"That is the fault of those Atata women," Lora said bitterly. She had caught one of the Atata girls of the Bear Clan flirting with Dane the other day, and she was still furious about it.

Mara sighed. "Nardo did not do the women of this tribe any favor when he brought ten handfuls of Atata women and children for us to house."

Alane sprang immediately to her husband's defense. "There was nothing else he could do. Their men were dead. He could not leave them to fend for themselves."

"Maybe he should have," Lora muttered. "They certainly show no gratitude."

"The tribe needs more men," Pettra said, and Alane stared at her as if she had just heard the answer to a very important question.

Chapter
Twenty-Five

As Nardo had suspected, Paxon had heard about the rock slide only hours after Nardo had first concocted the story.

"It is a great nuisance," Pettra told the Redu when they were fishing one afternoon in the river. "It means we will have to take the River of Gold into the Altas, and that way is much longer than the Greatfish route."

"Does Kindred usually summer in the Altas?" he asked her. They both were standing on the bank of the river; Paxon had already speared a dozen salmon and they were taking a break.

"Na." She gave him a faintly ironic look. "The women usually remain here in the village, while the men split the herd between summer camp and Bright Valley. Your tribe knows about our summer camp, however, and Nardo does not want to get trapped in there the way we almost trapped you last year. And the village is too close to summer camp—the Redu might find us. That is why we are all going to Bright Valley this year."

It was over supper in Pettra's mother's big house when Paxon first heard the men discussing the fact that his father was moving the Redu up the River of Gold.

"Are you not afraid you meet my tribe if both are on this river?" Paxon leaned forward to ask Haras, who was sitting on the other side of Pettra.

Haras shook his head. "Your tribe is yet far downstream of

the Big Ford. We will be long gone before they reach our part of the river."

Pettra obligingly sat back so the men could see each other. "What if also Redu keep going along river to this valley you speak of?"

"They won't," Haras said confidently.

Paxon's black brows drew together in a straight line. "Why not?"

"There will be no necessity," Haras explained. "There is more game on the River of Gold during the summer than there is on the Altas. The Redu will have plenty of food."

"You will hide away in mountains and let my tribe have your hunting grounds?" Paxon asked incredulously.

Haras looked angry. "We will not be hiding."

Paxon began to reply, but Pettra abruptly leaned forward, effectively cutting off his view of her sister's husband. She put her hand on Paxon's arm and asked him a question about something else. He hesitated a moment, then, with unusual discretion, sat back and kept his opinions to himself.

It was strange, Paxon thought as he rode along in the midst of the Red Deer household on the first morning of their journey to the Altas, how comfortable he had grown to be with these people and the kind of life they led. He thought of how fond he had grown of Pettra, with her flashing smile and her green eyes; how he liked it when she teased him; how she could make him laugh.

Suddenly, "I ride with Paxon," announced one of the Red Deer children, who had started out the day riding with Pettra.

She glanced at Paxon with a smile. "Do you mind?"

He shook his head and she dismounted, lifted Iva's three-year-old son from her horse and plunked him down in front of Paxon. Instinctively Paxon put an arm around the child to secure him. The Redu was finding it much easier to ride at the slow pace necessitated by the heavily laden packhorses.

The little boy tilted his head to give Paxon a sunny smile. "I too big to ride with a girl," he said. "I ride with you."

Paxon smiled back. "Good."

An hour later, the little boy was asleep. Paxon felt the warm, trusting weight of the small body snuggled against him and bent his head to brush his chin against the soft curls nestled against his chest. A strange warmth flooded all through him, and he looked at Pettra. She could be carrying his child, he thought.

She turned her head as if she had felt his glance and gave him a faint, intimate smile.

I like it here, Paxon thought suddenly. *I wish I could stay.*

Usually when the men of the Kindred went to Bright Valley in the summer, they were driving before them a large herd of mares. There was no herd to drive this year, however, since all the horses were either being ridden or being used to carry the tribe's household goods. Hundreds of horses followed one after the other as they went along the ancient track that lay beside the Greatfish and then the River of Gold. Each rider had from two to six horses, tied together nose to tail, following behind. Some of the horses were remounts, some were packhorses. All walked sedately in line, save for the foals, who frisked and romped at their mothers' sides.

The tribe stayed two separate nights at large caves that overlooked the valley and which, Petra told Paxon, the men used as winter camps. "The grazing is good here, and the low altitude makes for mild winters," she said. "There are many reindeer along the river during the winter."

Amazingly, there were no other tribes living along the River of Gold. Paxon regarded the wide, salmon-filled, fast-flowing river and the lush meadows for grazing that lay along its banks, and wondered if the Kindred knew how incredibly rich they were.

The River of Gold went ever southward, first winding to the west and then curving widely to bear back toward the east. It was when it finally turned directly south that Paxon first saw the snowy peaks of the Altas.

He had been in these mountains once before, when he had tried to climb them from the valley of the Atata, so the sight of that great wall of precipitous slabs rearing up against the cobalt sky should have come as no surprise to him. In truth, however, he was astonished anew by their height. It did not seem possible to him that all of these women and children and heavily laden horses could make the ascent into that cold, inhospitable universe of stone and snow.

The closer the caravan drew to the mountains, the colder it grew. The River of Gold ran swiftly here, fed by the vast snows of the Altas. The river was narrow and lay deep in the stony gorge it had cut ages past in the mountain rock. When they began to climb in earnest, Paxon inhaled the clear, cold air, and his nostrils flared with pleasure as he savored once again the exhilaration of the high altitude.

They were climbing into the very heart of the Altas, yet as he looked at the immense wall towering above him to the left of the path, it seemed to him that all their hours of climbing had not reduced the size of the mountains at all. The horses constantly amazed him as, surefooted as ibex, they scrambled up the steep, snow-covered path.

Then the horses in front of the line began to turn off the path, seeming to disappear into the side of the mountain, and Paxon realized they had reached the pass.

Pettra had not been able to describe the Eagle Pass to Paxon since she herself had never seen it, so the dark and narrow crack between the huge slabs of mountain rock came as a complete surprise to the Redu. It stretched before him, a long, steep-sided corridor through the mountain, a barren, rock-lined funnel, sided with unbroken stone cliffs that soared upward and ever upward into the sky. Directly above them, beating its golden wings in lazy rhythm, soared one of the birds that had given the pass its name.

"Dhu," Paxon said. He looked at the walls that enclosed them. There was room for perhaps four horses to go abreast where he was riding, but up ahead the pass narrowed even further. The Redu looked at that narrow, strangling gorge and said almost to himself, "This place is a death trap."

Next to him, Pettra shivered. "I don't like it. It is so deep that the sun can't get in."

"Are you cold?" Paxon asked. There was a chill wind blowing up the pass, and it was much colder in the sunless depths of the gorge than it had been on the river path. The snow was over the horses' hocks.

She shook her head. Then she changed her mind. "Sa, I am cold. But not from the weather."

He nodded in somber understanding. The thought crossed his mind: *This is a dangerous place. I hope Nardo knows what he is doing.*

"This pass is the only way into this Bright Valley of yours?" he asked Pettra.

"Now that the High Col is closed by a rock slide," she agreed. She forced a smile. "Wait until you see Bright Valley, Paxon. It is a paradise in the summer. The grass is better than anywhere else in the world."

"In the summer. And in the winter?"

"Nothing stays in the Altas for the winter," Pettra returned. "Except the eagles." She looked up, and once more she shivered.

The pass ran for almost a full mile, and then it widened and the ground began to descend. As Paxon emerged from the gorge, he saw an immense valley stretching away below him. There was snow on the surrounding hills, but the entire floor of the valley was a vast sheet of rich, flower-sprinkled grass. Paxon's mare raised her head and whinnied.

"She knows where she is," Pettra said with a smile.

The descent to the floor of the valley from the pass was steep, and Paxon had time to observe the small herds of ibex and sheep and reindeer that flowed over the thick grass.

So this was where the animals went when they left the rivers during the warm weather, he thought. Bright Valley. It was well named.

Not until several hours later did the caravan finally halt. The horses were unpacked, tents were set up, and cooking fires were lit. The Kindred were in their summer home.

The weather grew warmer and by the time the first crescent of Horse Foal Moon appeared in the night sky, the Redu had reached the Norakamo summer camp on the River of Gold.

Kerk had been aware that he was being watched over the winter; he had seen the horsemen in the distance. But there had been no surveillance since he had left Big Rivers Joining. It was beginning to make him nervous, this lack of vigilance on the part of his enemies. Kerk could not make himself believe that the

Kindred chief was willing to give him free access to the riches of the river.

He discussed this absence of the enemy with his council of secondary chiefs. "Perhaps they have gone back to the valley where they were last summer before we drove them out," Madden said. "There was fine hunting there during the warm weather."

Kerk could not believe that the Kindred chief would be so stupid. "Better than anyone, he knows that valley is a trap."

"In order to close the trap it is necessary to have men at both ends of the valley," Madden pointed out. "They may think that because we do not have horses, we will not be willing to put so much distance between us."

"Then they would be thinking right," Kerk retorted. "I am not willing to be caught by these horsemen when half my men are a six-day march away!"

"Remember," Wain said, "they did not have their whole tribe in that valley last year. They must have some other place where they spend the summer. Perhaps they have gone there."

"They have all those horses to feed," Madden pointed out. "They will need a place where there is plenty of grass."

"There is plenty of grass here," Leam said, looking around. "On both sides of the river."

"I know," Kerk replied grimly. "And the circle of hearth-places indicates that not so long ago this place was a camp. A summer camp too, I would guess. Yet there is no sign of anyone in the vicinity. I don't like it."

"Perhaps they went south, into the high mountains," Wain said.

"What I want to know," said Madden in the tone of voice that indicated he was getting down to serious business, "is where are they keeping their women? From what Paxon told us about the high mountains, they are no place for women and children."

"Nor could they have had all their women in that summer camp last year," Leam put in. "There must be some other place where they keep them."

Kerk grunted. A winter without women had not left his men in the best of tempers. "The first thing we need to do," he reminded his secondary chiefs, "is to find and destroy the Kindred men. Once that is done, it will be easy for us to take their women."

"But where are these men?" Wain demanded. "How can we find them if they continue to hide from us? They can move so much faster than we are able to."

Kerk's thin mouth tightened. "It is not in battle where those horses give them an advantage over us," he said. "It is at times like now that they are so valuable."

"Do you think we should send some scouts into the mountains to look for them?" Madden asked.

"Not yet," Kerk said. "There is fish enough in this river and game enough on its banks to feed us easily for the next moon. I will send scouts to the valley where we found them last summer, just to make certain they are not there. Then we will keep watch and give the Kindred a chance to find us first."

"And if they don't?" asked Wain.

"Then," promised Kerk, "we will go looking for them."

Chapter
Twenty-Six

For as long as anyone could remember, summertime in Bright Valley had been a time of courtship for the young men and women of the tribe. Traditionally it was the unmarried men who took the horse herd to the valley, while the married men stayed closer to home in summer camp on the Narrow River. And to Bright Valley also had gone the unmarried girls, to gather and to cook for the men, and to play the sweet games of courtship that most of the time would culminate in marriage.

This summer the entire tribe was camped in Bright Valley, and all was not harmony.

"We were all together in Bright Valley last year," Nardo complained to Alane one evening as they walked together in the deepening twilight along a little stream that ran through the thick, flower-carpeted grass. It was alive with butterflies, grasshoppers and crickets, all flying and mating and calling to each other. The tents of the camp were a mile behind them, hidden by a curve in the valley wall. "I do not remember any of these arguments among the women last year. What is so different now?"

"Last year when we came to Bright Valley, the Atata women were still grieving for the loss of their men," Alane replied bluntly. "This year they are looking for new husbands to replace the ones that have been lost. Our girls also are looking for husbands. But there are not enough men to go around, Nardo, and that is why there is so much discontent."

They walked in silence for a while. In the rocks above them a spectacular display of irises splashed their deep purple color against the rugged mountainside. Nardo said quietly, "I don't know what I can do about it, Alane. I had to bring those women and children into our tribe."

"Of course you did," she agreed. "No one is saying you should have done anything else. But this predominance of women is a problem, my husband."

He nodded gloomily.

"Nor is it just the unmarried women who are being affected. Look at what happened to Bram and Iva."

He looked even more gloomy than before. "I know."

The hum of the insects was loud in the slowly fading daylight. Butterflies rose from a patch of yellow Turk's cap lilies on the far side of the stream. Alane said, "When I first came among you, it seemed to me that the Kindred made too light of the severing of a marriage, but I have seen from this affair of Iva and Bram that this is not so. There is ill feeling between the clan of the Red Deer and the clan of the Bear because of the divorce, Nardo."

He grunted. "I had to separate Bram and Dane today. They had gotten into a fight over the horses, which wasn't about the horses at all but about Iva. Dane thinks Bram has treated his sister badly."

"And Nat was rude to Pettra this afternoon, saying the divorce was all her mother's fault, that his brother could not bear Lina's nagging," Alane said. She looked at Nardo. "The tribe does not need any more divorces."

"I agree," Nardo said fervently. "But the problem remains, Alane. As you said, there are not enough unmarried men to go around."

There was the sound of rushing water, and a few moments later a waterfall came into view, pouring down the mountainside into the stream which Alane and Nardo were following. "The flowers are so lovely," Alane said in a pleased voice, looking at the dazzling blue drifts of hyacinth that grew along the rocks beside the falls.

"I don't suppose the women would agree to let the men have two wives," Nardo said tentatively. "I have heard that some tribes do this."

"*What?*"

Nardo looked at his wife's outraged face and his mouth twitched. "You don't think so?"

"If you think you have trouble now, just make that suggestion and see what happens," Alane said dangerously.

He shrugged. "Then I don't know what I can do about the situation, Alane. I suppose we will just have to live with it."

"Nardo." Alane's voice was suddenly very soft, and she reached out to put a hand upon his arm to halt him. "Look," she said.

Lying there among the grass and the rocks, not four feet from where they were walking, was a red deer fawn. It was curled up and lying very still. It did not move when the two humans looked at it, but merely looked back, blinking its big brown eyes. After a moment Alane and Nardo moved quietly onward.

The light was fading fast now, and Nardo said, "We should be getting back to camp."

Alane did not slow her steps. Instead she said, "I have been thinking, Nardo, that Pettra seems to have solved for herself the problem of the shortage of men."

"What do you mean? I know that Pettra is walking out with Paxon, but she can't *marry* him, Alane. She may have a man for now, but he will not be staying and then Pettra will be alone again."

Alane said, "Why can't she marry him?"

Nardo halted and stared at her in utter stupefaction. He said, "She can't marry him because he is a Redu. An enemy. He is not, and never can be, a member of this tribe."

"Why can't he be?" Alane asked, halting also and facing him with just the faintest hint of defiance in her stance.

He was beginning to get angry. "Because of all the things I have just said. He is a Redu and an enemy. Probably he is a Horse Eater. Dhu, Alane, have you lost your reason, to ask me such a question?"

She shook her head. "I have not lost my reason, Nardo. In fact, I think I am looking at things very reasonably. We have a problem in this tribe—there are not enough young, unmarried men. Paxon is a young, unmarried man. Furthermore, I am quite certain that there are other young, unmarried men among the Redu. Now, instead of killing all these men, as you have planned to do, why don't you ask them instead to join our tribe?"

He spread his legs and stared down at her. "You have to be born to the Kindred to be a member of this tribe."

"I was not born to the Kindred, Nardo. Are you saying that you don't consider me a member of the tribe?"

"You are different."

"I don't see how I am any different from Paxon."

"The Norakamo were not our enemies!"

"Well, you certainly made a good pretense of it, then," she retorted.

"We played games with each other, Alane. It is not the same thing, and you know it."

"Well, perhaps it is not. But it seems to me to be a sad waste to kill a whole host of young men when we are in need of young men ourselves. There is nothing wrong with Paxon, Nardo. It is not his fault if his tribe was starving and had to seek out new hunting grounds. What would you have done if the same thing had befallen us? Would you just have stayed in your empty homeland and watched your people starve to death? Or would you do as the Redu have done, and seek out a better place?"

"*My* people have not offended the Reindeer God," Nardo said, "so such a question does not arise." He narrowed his eyes. "And I am growing a little weary of hearing you singing Paxon's praises to me. Have you forgotten that this is the man who wanted to kidnap you?"

"Na, nor have I forgotten that he is the man who let me go," she retorted angrily.

He began to get that dangerously still look on his face, and Alane forced down her rising temper. She would get nowhere with him if he got angry. "Nardo." She rested a light hand on his bare forearm. "If Paxon once had thoughts of me, he thinks of me no longer. It is Pettra whom he wants now. And she wants him."

He stood perfectly still under her touch, his arm hard as stone under her fingers, his dark eyes unreadable. He said, "He may have Pettra in his bed, but who do you think he pictures in his mind when he drives his spear into her?"

A year ago, she would have flinched from such frank speech. Now she answered positively, "He doesn't think of me."

Nardo's face looked as if it had been carved from granite. "He did."

"Well, he doesn't anymore." She ran her fingers up and down his arm, ruffling the crisp black hairs. "I think I scared him," she confessed. "First I told him that if he kidnapped me, I would kill him. Then I told him that I would cut off his phallus."

He stared down into the beautiful face that was lifted to his. "You told him *what?*"

She repeated what she had said.

Very slowly the hard, still look she dreaded lifted from his face. The corner of his mouth quirked. "I see now what cooled his ardor."

"I think I shocked him."

His eyes glinted. "You certainly would have shocked me."

"I would have done it too," she said. "I have never been so angry in all my life."

"You had cause to be, little one." He began to grin. "I wish I could have seen his face."

"Once he understood that I was serious about not wanting to go with him, he let me go. I think you should remember that, Nardo."

"Mmmm." He bent his head to kiss her lightly on the lips. Then he put his hand over hers on his arm, turned her and began to walk back toward the camp.

"You could still follow your plan," she persisted as she walked closely beside him. "The only difference would be that when you had the Redu securely trapped, instead of killing them you would offer to let them join us. They have no women of their own anymore. I am thinking they would be happy to accept your offer."

"They would be happy to accept any offer made under those circumstances," he murmured dryly.

"But . . ."

She stopped talking as once again he halted and swung

around to face her, dropping the hand that covered hers and pulling his arm from beneath her fingers. "Understand this, Alane. Even if I do as you ask, there will be many deaths. The Redu are going to have to be beaten into the ground before we can afford to make them any offers. There must be no doubt at all in their minds that they cannot rise against us again."

Swallowing, she nodded.

His face was stern. "There is no guarantee that Paxon will not be one of those who fall."

"I understand."

"I can tell the men not to kill him, but in the heat of a battle it is not always possible to be . . . temperate."

She nodded again, her gray eyes dark and huge.

He frowned. "We will need him, however. He is the only one who can speak both our tongues."

"I am certain that the men of the Red Deer will watch out for Paxon," Alane said. "They have seen how Pettra loves him."

He grunted.

"So you will do it?" she asked breathlessly.

He blew out through his nose. Then, "I suppose it is worth a try," he agreed.

She gave him a radiant smile.

"I foresee one major problem, however," he warned.

"What is that?"

He cocked an eyebrow. "What do we do if all of the remaining Redu men are old?"

Alane put an arm around his waist and, leaning into his body, began to walk with him again. "If a man is strong enough to fight a battle, he is strong enough to mate with a woman," she said.

He draped his arm across her shoulders. "I suppose that is so."

She rested her cheek against his shoulder. "It will work. I know it will."

"I see it had better," he replied humorously, "or I won't sleep at night wondering what you might do to me."

She chuckled and he tightened the arm that lay across her shoulders. "Of course, I can think of a few things I would like to do to you," he added in a deep, soft voice.

"Good," she said serenely, and pressed even closer into his side.

The Norakamo were growing restless. For the first time in anyone's memory they had not made their usual summer migration but had remained upon the Gorge and continued to graze their horses on the plateau instead of on the rich meadows of the River of Gold. No one was happy. The women complained because they did not have access to the different variety of gathering that was available along the River of Gold, and the men complained about having to move the herd farther and farther from camp in order to find pasture that had not yet been grazed down.

"I know it is a hardship on the tribe to remain here," Rune said as patiently as he could when the men met around the campfire one evening to air their problems. "But I have shared with you the reason for our doing this. It is vital that the Redu be kept in ignorance of our existence, and since the Redu will be traveling down the River of Gold, we must stay away from it."

"We know your reasons, Rune," Hagen said. "I am not so certain that we agree with them."

"That is so," Vili put in belligerently. "I for one cannot understand your love affair with the Kindred. By all the blood laws of our tribe, we should be demanding vengeance from them, not acting as their friends!"

Stifun said dismissively, "Vili, you are like a man who knows only one song."

Vili's face got red, his fists clenched, and he started to surge to his feet. Hagen laid a hand upon his nephew's arm to restrain him. "Vili has deep attachments for those of his blood," the shaman said softly. His strange, lightless eyes moved around the circle of men's faces, evaluating the reactions he saw to his words. "My own fear is that Rune is going to make us dependents of the Kindred, and as your shaman I would strongly object to the rule of a tribe that counts its kinship by the blood of women."

The men of the Norakamo growled in agreement with this statement, and Hagen looked with concealed triumph at Rune.

Rune returned the look, his blue eyes like ice. "I have no intention of putting this tribe under the rule of the Kindred," he said. "I am the chief of the Norakamo, and I intend to keep my authority." He leaned forward a little, his eyes boring into the shaman's. "Is that clear, Hagen?"

The shaman's smile was sharp as a knife. "Perfectly clear, Rune," he said. "If you can do it."

Under Hagen's direction, Loki began to talk to the men whom the shaman had singled out as most likely to be disaffected by Rune's present policy and so most likely to succumb to Hagen's lures. As the summer went by, the shaman drew into his snare eight restless and dissatisfied young men, all of whom were bored with the inactivity of camp and were chafing at the loss of their favorite sport.

Horse raiding had always been more important to the men of the Norakamo than to the men of the Kindred. For one thing, it was vital to a Norakamo man that he own a large number of horses—if he did not he would not be able to afford bride-wealth—and the surest way to increase the number of horses in one's herd was to steal them from the Kindred. Then too, Norakamo society was more aggressively male than Kindred society, and one of the main ways a Norakamo boy could gain prestige was by success in horse raiding. Without the renown to be earned in horse raiding, Norakamo boys were finding it more difficult to gain the honor they craved.

Such young men were fertile material for words of revolt.

"What we must do is very simple," Hagen told his recruits as they met one morning in the shaman's tent. "Nardo has said that he will send a messenger to tell Rune when we must march to the Kindred's assistance. All we will need to do is keep watch for the Kindred messenger, then intercept and kill him before he can get to Rune. This plan of assisting the Kindred is mad.

Let the Kindred and the Redu slaughter each other, and then we can move in to finish up the job."

"*And* collect the remaining Kindred horses," Noli said with a grin.

Smiles and laughter greeted this sally.

"Very well, then," Hagen said. "We will keep watch in turns. I have made up a plan."

Chapter
Twenty-Seven

Paxon had never been so content as he was that summer in Bright Valley. Occasionally on the cool, fragrant mountain nights, as he lay awake in the tent at night after making love with Pettra, thoughts of his father and of his lost tribe would intrude on his tranquillity, but he would do his best to banish them. There was nothing he could do for the Redu, he told himself resolutely. All he could do for the present was to live each day as it came.

When first he arrived in the valley, he had been careful to keep close to the camp. He was grateful not to be penned up in a hut any longer, and he did not want to do anything that might signal danger to his captors and cause them to confine him once again. But as the weeks went by, the camp, with its disorderly bustle of women and children, began to seem like a cage. Paxon would watch the men as they rode in and out of camp, so in harmony with their horses that they seemed to be one creature and not two, and a yearning so strong it hurt would sweep through him. How magnificent they were, these horsed men! How he longed to be one of them!

One afternoon, after the men had ridden in from hunting, Paxon was standing beside the small rope corral that held a group of the riding horses when Nardo joined him. The Redu drew himself up when he saw who was at his side. "I just watch horses," he said defensively. He looked back at the mares in the corral, and a wistful note crept into his voice. "They are very beautiful."

Nardo turned his eyes toward the corraled horses. The sun was a ball of fire on the horizon, and their gray coats and proud aquiline heads had taken on a reddish hue from the crimson sky. A current of air was blowing down the valley, and the long, straight manes and sweeping tails stirred in the gentle breeze. The odor of horse and manure mixed with the fresh scent of grass and flowers drifted on the summer air. Nardo turned back to Paxon with a look that was almost friendly. "You like horses, I think," he commented. "Would you like to learn to ride better?"

Paxon felt his mouth drop open. "Sa," he croaked when he was finally able to speak again. "I like very much."

"I'll ask Pettra's brother Dane to teach you," Nardo said. Bluebird, who was one of the mares in the corral, heard his voice and came over to greet him. Nardo reached up to scratch the crest of her neck in the exact spot that she liked best.

Paxon could not believe that Nardo had just offered him his heart's desire as casually as if he were offering him a drink of water. The thought flashed across his mind that if Nardo knew what he had been planning to do to Nardo's wife, the Kindred chief likely would be murdering him instead.

"Thank you," Paxon managed to get out in a choked-sounding voice.

Nardo gave him a genial smile. "The women of my tribe are wonderful, but a man needs to do a man's work. Is that not so?"

Paxon nodded speechlessly and watched as Nardo ducked into the corral to run his knowledgeable hands down Bluebird's legs. The Kindred chief straightened up, and the mare, feeling an itch, began to rub her bony face vigorously up and down against his shoulder. Nardo braced himself and let her do it.

"Did she hurt leg?" Paxon asked.

"It is always a good idea to check your horse's legs after a day's work, that is all," Nardo replied.

Paxon nodded, finding himself hungry for knowledge about these beautiful creatures that fascinated him so.

To learn to ride! To be able to fly like the wind on a horse's back as these men of the Kindred did! Paxon felt a grin split his face, and he inhaled deeply the horse-scented evening air. There was nothing in the world he would like better than to gallop on a horse across the thick grass of this magnificent valley.

The following day after breakfast, as Nardo had promised, Dane arrived to take Paxon out riding. Dane, who had been told about Nardo's plans to let Paxon escape, was both a competent and an encouraging teacher.

They went riding every day for two weeks, and each day Paxon felt more secure on the horse's back. By the second week his muscles didn't even ache anymore.

"I think maybe I should be insult," Paxon said to Pettra one evening as she spread the sleeping skins out in their small A-shaped tent. "Nardo think so small of me that he does not care what I do."

"I don't think that's the reason Nardo is letting you learn to ride, Paxon." Pettra was on her knees, smoothing out the skins, and now she looked up over her shoulder at him. He was standing near the doorflap under the highest part of the roof—the only place in the tent where it was possible for a grown person to stand erect. Petra continued, "It is in my heart that he thinks that one of these days you will be part of our tribe, and if that should happen, then you must know how to ride."

He stared at her in astonishment. Pettra was not a beauty like Alane, but the light from the stone lamp fell softly on her chestnut braid, and her face with its tanned golden skin and flashing white smile were vivid with life. "What you mean?" he demanded.

"Well." She bit her lip and her eyes dropped from his. Nervously she twitched a corner of the skins. "I suppose he thinks that someday we will marry." Once the words were out she bravely raised her eyes once more.

He struggled to keep his face impassive, not wanting her to see the stab of joy that had knifed through him at her words. After a moment, "I am Redu," he said sternly. "I cannot be Kindred."

"Perhaps you cannot," she agreed. Her face looked anxious in the soft yellow lamplight. "But in our tribe the children follow the blood of the mother, Paxon. Our children would belong to the Clan of the Red Deer, and as my husband you would be expected to live with my family anyway. So, you see, it really would not matter if you are a Redu."

"You . . ." Pause. His eyes flicked around the small tent, so warm and cozy-looking in the soft light. "You *want* marry me?"

"Sa," she said. She nodded vigorously. "I want very much."

Moving slowly, he came to kneel beside her. He lifted his hand and touched her cheek with hard fingertips, callused by years of pulling a bowstring. Then, "I want too," he said.

She put her hand over his and moved it until it rested lightly against her lips. His body was roused, but his voice was husky with tenderness as he asked, "Sleeping skin is ready?"

She kissed his hard fingers. "Sleeping skin is ready."

It was mid-summer before Paxon realized that he might be able to steal a horse at night and escape through the Eagle Pass. Under Dane's instruction, his riding had improved dramatically, and on this particular day Nardo had actually allowed him to ride out hunting with some of the men. The small hunting party he was accompanying had taken seven red deer near the pass, and then Dane said, "It is growing late and I am tired. We can butcher these deer tomorrow morning and take them back to camp."

Paxon, whose thoughts were on Pettra, said, "Is light for a few more hours. Why we not do deer now?"

Paxon's suggestion was not unreasonable. The Kindred did not fully butcher the game they had killed until they got it home. Instead they would "field dress" the animal—that is, remove the entrails and visceral organs to ensure the preservation of the meat until they could get it back to camp. There was certainly enough hours of daylight left for the men to field-dress the deer they had killed, load them onto their packhorses and make it back to the main camp. They would not even have to divide the carcasses, for a packhorse could carry a single red deer. If the men had taken reindeer, they would have had more work to do because it took two packhorses to carry the meat of a reindeer.

So Paxon's suggestion was certainly reasonable. For some reason, however, the rest of the men agreed with Dane, and the hunting party pitched a small camp for the night.

At first Paxon was merely disgruntled. It made no sense to

him to be sleeping on the hard ground when he could have been home sleeping with Pettra. It was not until the snoring of the other men told him they had gone to sleep, and his own eyes had begun to close, that he realized he was within a mile of the Eagle Pass. With horses available.

I could escape. The thought was there, whole and intact in his mind, and there was no evading it. He knew his father and the men of the tribe were encamped upon the River of Gold. All he needed to do was ride through the pass and down the river, and he would find them.

An image of the pass came into his mind. A death trap, he had called it. And if the Redu blocked off that narrow stone corridor and penned the Kindred up within this beautiful valley, when the snow came, the tribe of the Kindred would die.

The night air was chill, but Paxon felt sweat break out all over him. He didn't want the people of the Kindred to die. He didn't want Pettra to die. But if he did not take this chance, if he stayed in the valley, then he might be condemning his own people to death. His father. The friends he had grown up with.

Slowly, cautiously, Paxon sat up. The rest of the men were sound asleep, lying in a circle around the fire they had built for warmth and protection. Paxon stared at the red gold sparks as they flew upward into the black sky, and in his agony he almost groaned aloud.

What was the matter with these men of the Kindred? he thought furiously. What was the matter with Nardo? Didn't they realize their danger? Did they indeed hold him so lightly that they couldn't believe he would try another escape just because his first attempt had ended in failure? They deserved to be betrayed for being so stupid.

The scent of the fire was in his nostrils. He told himself that it was the smoke that had brought the moisture to his eyes.

What to do? What to do?

Never in his young life had Paxon felt so torn. He did not know what he was going to do, but this he did know: whatever path he chose, he would be the loser.

Nardo had sent Paxon out with Dane and the men who composed the clan council, the only men in the tribe who knew of his plan, and when the hunting party awoke in the morning they fully expected to find that the Redu had gone. Consequently they were both surprised and dismayed when they opened their eyes and discovered that a distinctly haggard-looking Paxon was still in camp.

"He just didn't go," Dane said to Nardo much later in the day, when the two of them were walking through a fine, misting rain ostensibly to check on the horses in the corral.

"You are sure you gave him the chance?"

"Nardo, we could not have made it plainer to him. We camped a mile from the Eagle Pass. We left the horses within reach. We went to sleep and snored loudly. He didn't leave."

Nardo kicked disgustedly at the wet grass under his feet.

"He thought about it, though," Dane said. "He looked terrible in the morning, as if he had not slept at all. He knew he could escape, all right, but he chose to stay."

Nardo did not reply. They began to descend the slope toward a flat stretch of ground where the corral was pitched. The grass was wet and slippery under their moccasined feet. The mist was so thick that the horses in the corral were only indistinct shadows, a slightly darker gray than the foggy air.

Dane said, "This morning after we returned, Pettra spoke to me of marrying Paxon. I am thinking that perhaps Pettra is the reason he did not leave, Nardo. She is very fond of him, and she says he feels the same way about her."

The two men had come to the bottom of the slope, where the mist was even thicker and carried in its heavy wetness the distinct smell of horses. Nardo said grimly, "He has to leave, or the Redu may never find us and we will not be able to spring the trap."

Dane glanced sideways at Nardo, his sleepy hazel eyes gleaming in the mist. "I understand that," Dane said. "But Pettra is my sister and I do not like the idea of sending the boy that she loves to his death. Nor do I think it is fair to Paxon. He *didn't* leave, Nardo. He *didn't* betray us."

They had reached the corral, which held a small group of two-year-old fillies who were just learning to wear a halter and to lead. The men watched the youngsters for a while, commenting back and forth about particular characteristics and personality traits they had noticed during the training sessions, and then Nardo said, "This shortage of marriageable men in the tribe is becoming a problem." Then he proceeded to describe Alane's idea about bringing some of the Redu men into the tribe.

"It is true that the shortage of men is a problem," Dane agreed, "and not just for the unmarried girls. Look at what has happened to my sister Iva's marriage."

One of the fillies had been inching closer and closer to the two men, and now she was within reach of them. Nardo smiled faintly and slowly extended his open hand, which had a treat resting on its palm. "Nor is it just the women who are affected," he said to Dane. "There is bad feeling between the men of the Red Deer Clan and the men of the Bear Clan over that divorce."

"Bram embarrassed and insulted my sister," Dane said stiffly.

A dainty muzzle was extended, soft, velvety lips touched Nardo's palm, and the root was gone. "I know he did, Dane," Nardo replied in a quiet voice.

The mist was now so thick that the men found it hard to see each other's features. The only sounds were those the filly made as she munched the root between her strong, young teeth. "Neither Pettra nor Iva are women who want to live the rest of their lives without a man," Dane said at last.

The filly finished her treat and once more extended her muzzle, looking for another. Nardo obliged. "I take it, then, that you would not be distressed by a marriage between Pettra and Paxon?" he asked.

"He is a little arrogant perhaps, but he is young." Dane rubbed his nose thoughtfully. "I would not be upset."

Nardo nodded, withdrew his empty hand from the corral, and turned to Dane. "The tribe has need of more men," he said, "and if the rest of the Redu are like Paxon, we could do much worse." Through the mist Dane could see the gleam of Nardo's teeth as he smiled. "I am thinking that they could teach us to use those bows of theirs."

Dane thoughtfully puffed out his lips. "That is so," he agreed.

"Well, then," Nardo said as he began to walk back in the direction of camp, "if we are to bring all of these plans to completion, we must get Paxon to leave."

"I do not know what more we can do," Dane said as he followed his chief. "Believe me, if ever a man was given a chance to escape, we gave it to that Redu last night!"

Nardo frowned into the swirling mist. "We need to give him a greater incentive than mere opportunity. We need to make him think his tribe is in danger."

Dane skidded a little on the slick grass, then righted himself. "And how are we to do that?"

Nardo spoke slowly, thinking aloud. "We could let him overhear pieces of talk about a plan we have to destroy the Redu. Not the actual plan, you understand. Just letting him realize that we have one should be enough." With the back of his hand Nardo wiped away the drops that were clinging to his eyelashes. "If Paxon thinks the decision is between the survival of his tribe or ours, then it is in my heart that he will choose his own people."

Dane grunted. "Under those circumstances, I do not think that he will have a choice."

"We don't want him to have a choice," Nardo said flatly. "We want him to go."

Dane followed Nardo's orders, and during the following two weeks he made certain that Paxon heard the tag end of two separate conversations pertaining to a Kindred plan to annihilate the Redu. Then, at the end of two weeks' time, Nardo once more sent Paxon with the same hunting party as before to look for red deer in the vicinity of the Eagle Pass. This time when the men of the Kindred awoke in the morning, the Redu was gone.

Chapter Twenty-Eight

Four days after Paxon's escape, a large party of Redu appeared on the mountain side of the Eagle Pass. Nardo led a group of his own men into the pass, to a point just outside arrow range, and then, followed by the taunting cries of the Redu, the Kindred men and horses hastily retreated. Once they were safely within the valley walls, Nardo grinned. He had them.

Early the following morning, Mano and Dane left camp to ride through the High Col and down the Greatfish to seek out Rune and the Norakamo. Their message was simple: on the day of the full of Butting Bull Moon, by two hours after dawn at the latest, the Norakamo were to be at the Eagle Pass. They were to cross the mountains from the west and come in behind the Redu, thus penning the bowmen between the two tribes. Meanwhile, in order to lure all of the Redu into the pass, Nardo would spend the two days before the full moon acting as if the Kindred were preparing a major assault on the Redu position. If the Redu chief wanted to keep the Kindred trapped, he would have to call on all his men to reinforce the pass defenders. Then, on the day of the full of Butting Bull Moon, the men of the Kindred would indeed make their assault, and the men of the Norakamo would have to be there to do their part in closing the trap.

———

Varic was still opposed to Nardo's plan, and had not hesitated to say so within the council when they had met the morning after the Redu appearance to plot their next move.

"Do you really expect the Norakamo to come to our assistance, Nardo?" he asked scornfully. "I am telling you, nothing would please that tribe more than to see the people of the Kindred destroyed."

"I expect Rune to honor his word," Nardo returned. "He has said he will come, and come he will."

Nat's light brown eyes rested on Varic's face. "I understand your feelings, Varic, and I honor them. The Norakamo killed your father, and you have cause for your distrust. But the reason why Rorig made a marriage between Nardo and the daughter of the Norakamo chief was for just such a moment as this. Working together, we can destroy this tribe. Working alone, we cannot."

"Nevin was your mother's brother," Varic said bitterly to Nardo. "I cannot understand your thinking in this."

A muscle jumped in the corner of Nardo's mouth, but otherwise his face did not betray any reaction to Varic's remark. "The blood of Nevin has been avenged," he said. "It does not make sense to carry on a feud that has been resolved." Varic scowled and opened his mouth to reply, but Nardo held up a commanding hand. "Rune is my wife's brother and I would trust him with my life."

"You are doing more than that," Varic shot back. "You are trusting him with the lives of all the tribe!"

"Not quite," Freddo put in. "If things should go wrong, if the Norakamo do not come, the High Col into the Greatfish valley is always there for an escape route."

The grass was still wet with morning dew, and the men of the clan council were sitting on a circle of rocks below one of the valley walls, a short distance away from the encampment. Samu sat beside Nardo, his chin propped on Nardo's thigh. On the cliff walls above the men, a herd of agile mountain sheep leaped from ledge to ledge, looking for the particularly tasty morsels of lichen that grew between the rocks.

"Perhaps it would be wise to send the women and children out of the valley before the full of the moon," Nat suggested.

"If for some reason the Norakamo do fail us, there is a possibility that the Redu might break through the pass and into the valley."

Nardo's hand absently stroked Samu between his upright ears. "If the Norakamo do not come, then we will not fight," he said. "I have told Rune to send a smoke signal when he is in position to attack. If there is no smoke signal, we will not charge."

The mountain air was chilly, as it had begun to be in these late-summer mornings. The men all wore their long-sleeved shirts, and a few of them had their arms crossed over their chests for warmth. Above them, a ridge of high gray-white clouds passed over the sun, making it seem even colder.

"Nardo is right," Freddo said. "If we send out all the women and children, then we will have to send along men to hunt for them and to take care of the horses." He made a comical face. "The women will not leave without their belongings, Nat, and that means they will take most of the herd to carry them."

Matti and Hamer laughed and Nat said ruefully, "That is so. The women and children had better remain."

Varic's slender body was strung as taut as a bow. "I still think you are wrong," he said to Nardo.

"Well, since you are the only one who is against the plan, Varic," Nardo returned in his most pleasant voice, "you are out-counted." The last of the cloud bank floated by, and the sun streamed down once more. Nardo said, "We will depend upon the Norakamo."

It was late in the afternoon of a warm, hazy day when Dane and Mano at last crossed the Big Ford and turned up the forest track that headed north and west in the direction of the Gorge River.

"It looks as if it's going to storm," Dane said, glancing up at the rapidly darkening sky.

Mano agreed. Then, a moment later, as the dimness of the forest path flashed into brightness, "Dhu. Was that lightning?"

One of Dane's two remounts squealed and threw up her head. The mare he was riding bucked. "It was," Dane said grimly.

The dark sound of thunder rumbled in the distance. "There are cliffs along the river south of the ford," Mano said. "Perhaps we can find a cave to shelter in."

Dane shook his head. "By the time we get there, the storm will be over."

The wind had begun to whip up, blowing the horses' forelocks and manes, swaying and snapping the branches of the oak and beech forest that flanked the path on either side. "Perhaps we ought to get under cover of the trees," Dane said, raising his voice to be heard above the noise of the moving branches.

Suddenly the sky lit up, bright and yellow as a fire when the kindling catches all at once. Summerdew, Dane's mount, reared and the horses he was leading scrambled backward to get out of her way. Mano's mare rolled her eyes and danced on the path. Then the rain began to hammer down.

It was Summerdew's rear that saved Dane's life, lifting him out of range of the javelin and substituting instead her own beautiful curved neck. Mano was not as lucky. The javelin that had been aimed at him found its target, and he slid slowly to the ground, the spear still lodged in his breast.

Dane's mare crashed over sideways, Dane managing to throw himself clear of the massive falling weight. Summerdew hit the ground and began to thrash about in agony, in the process kicking Dane in the ribs. He gasped, and through the haze of pain saw two men riding toward him from the trees to the south of the path. Then the sky lit up once more. The crack of thunder that followed immediately sent all the horses, including those ridden by the attackers, into a frenzy. While his attackers were attempting to control their terrified mounts, Dane raced for the forest to his north. Bent over, holding his midsection, sobbing with pain, he ducked into the concealing trees. Behind him Summerdew screamed once more in agony.

A man's voice rose above the sound of the storm. "One of them is getting away!"

"I'll go after him," Vili shouted back "You stay here and put that mare out of her pain."

Dane plunged ahead, dodging trees and jumping over fallen branches, not worrying about making noise, knowing that the rain and thunder were his allies. There was no way his pursuers could hear him over the sound of the storm.

They had spoken the language of the Kindred, but not with the right accent. They were Norakamo, Dane thought. And they would be expecting him to go north and west, toward the Gorge River and the Norakamo camp. Without a second thought Dane veered east. He had to cover as much ground as he could while the storm still concealed him. It seemed to him forever that he scrambled through that steep forest, climbing up rocks, sliding into wet and muddy gullies, getting scratched in the face by low-hanging branches. After about twenty minutes, the storm subsided and Dane too lay quietly, listening.

It hurt to breathe. Summerdew must have broken his ribs when she kicked him. He felt dizzy and sick, and he lay on the muddy ground and said his prayers of thanksgiving to Sky God for sending his thunder. And then he fainted.

On horseback Dane and Mano should have arrived at the Norakamo camp during the first week of Butting Bull Moon. This would have given Rune at least another week to gather his men and get them to the Eagle Pass. Dane, however, not only lacked his horse, but he was badly injured himself. Starving, filthy and pain-wracked, he finally crawled into the Norakamo camp two days before the full of the moon, where he gasped out his story to Rune.

"If you were so certain these men were Norakamo, then why did you continue to come here?" Rune asked.

"They were Norakamo. I recognized the accent." Dane was lying flat on the floor of Rune's tent, with Nita gently washing the dirt from his face. He had eaten voraciously when first he arrived, and now exhaustion was setting in. "I came because I figured that you did not need to ambush Nardo's messengers if you did not mean to keep your promise to him, Rune. You simply did not have to respond to his call. Therefore, I decided, these men must have been acting on their own."

Rune did not reply, but his blue eyes were hard on Dane's weary, pain-filled face.

"Nardo had no doubts about you," Dane added, "and Nardo is a good judge of men."

Rune ran a hand through his long bangs, the gesture effectively hiding the expression on his face. "Would you recognize the men?" he asked after a moment.

"Na. It happened too fast." Nita finished washing him, and Dane flashed her a grateful smile. Then he stared up at the high, pointed ceiling of the tent, despair etched into every weary line of his face. "I came as fast as I could, but I am too late."

Rune said, "Perhaps not. The Norakamo can travel fast."

Dane's fist opened and closed. He shook his head. "The full moon is the day after tomorrow. If you ride hard, perhaps you can make it down the river by nightfall tomorrow, but it will take another six hours to cross the mountain. The sheep track that Nardo found is long and winding on the afternoon side of the mountain, although once it reaches the ridge it descends quickly. My instructions were that on the day before the full of the moon, you were to camp overnight on the track just before the top of the ridge, and then you were to attack at first light the following day." Dane closed his eyes. "We need one more day, and we do not have it."

Rune said, "I can be over the mountain by noon on the day of the full moon."

"It's no good," Dane said hopelessly. "The breeze through the pass dies down two hours after dawn, and Nardo must have that breeze."

Rune's thin face did not change. "Then we will have to cross the mountain at night. The moon is full; as long as there are no clouds there will be light enough."

"With men and horses that have had no rest? It's a treacherous path"—Dane slammed his fist down on the skins that lay beneath him—"and I am not in the best condition to lead you."

"We don't need you," Rune replied. "I know the track."

Dane stared. "Nardo said you did not know the track, that I would have to show you."

Rune bared his teeth in a smile that was not good-humored. "Since you are hardly in a condition to show me anything, Dane, isn't it a good thing that I scouted that track myself?"

"You were not supposed to" was all Dane could mumble. "You were supposed to keep out of the Redus' way."

Rune looked at his wife, who had retired to a corner of the tent. "Give him some of your red flower medicine, Nita. He is hurting."

Dane tried to sit up and did not make it. Rune bent down and put a reassuring hand on his shoulder. "Rest. You have done well, Dane. You can leave the rest to me."

Dane looked up into the cold blue eyes of Alane's brother, and thought that perhaps he could.

As soon as Rune heard Dane's tale, his thoughts turned to Hagen. He had known the shaman was hungry for power, but he had never dreamed Hagen would resort to such treachery as this.

The sun was going down, streaking the long, thin clouds on the horizon with red and violet, when Rune summoned all the men of the tribe to their usual meeting place before the big cave that looked out over the plain. Speaking in a flat, unemotional voice, Rune told them what had happened. He knew that Hagen must have involved more men than Vili in this conspiracy, and all the while he was speaking his eyes looked shrewdly around the circle of men. At least three of the more youthful faces looked distinctly suspicious.

Rune finished, "Such an action as this has dishonored the whole tribe."

Tense silence reigned around the campfire. Rune pushed a little harder. "I gave my word to Nardo, and now it will look as if I am forsworn."

It was too much for Vili. "You have more love for Nardo than you do for the men of your own tribe, Rune!" he burst out.

"*Vili*," the shaman hissed, but his nephew was beyond hearing him.

"If you were a true chief of the Norakamo, you would have seen that the best thing was to let the Kindred and the Redu kill each other," Vili rushed on. "Why should we involve ourselves in their battle?"

The whole sky had turned the same blood red color as the setting sun. All the men of the tribe looked at their chief. Rune's pale hair glowed with a fiery stain as he answered Vili in measured tones. "Don't you understand that without us to come in upon the Redu rear, it is only the Kindred who will be slaughtered? Then the Redu will be free to turn and fall upon us."

"We don't need the Kindred!" Vili cried. He looked around the tribal circle, making his plea to the men who were watching him so somberly. "We got rid of the Horse Eaters by ourselves. We can do the same with these Redu!"

"The Horse Eaters did not have the weapons that this other tribe have," said Irek.

Stifun spoke next. "Nardo stood with us against the Horse Eaters. How can you expect us to desert him when he has asked for our help."

"*Nardo killed my cousin!*" Vili almost screamed.

"Your cousin killed Nardo's uncle first," Irek reminded him. He turned to his chief and added in a heavy voice, "Vili could not have acted alone, Rune."

Most of the men looked at Hagen. Rune, however, fixed his eyes upon one of the youngsters he had picked out earlier. "Mal," he said.

The sun was now a ball of fire above the horizon.

"Who was the leader of this conspiracy, Mal?" Rune asked.

The boy flicked nervous eyes at Vili.

"It wasn't Vili," Rune said. "He hasn't the intelligence to come up with a plan such as this."

Hagen sat in silence, his gaunt face revealing nothing.

"I don't know what you mean, Rune," Mal said breathlessly. "Why are you asking me?"

"Because you were involved," Rune said. "You were involved, and by your actions you have disobeyed and dishonored your chief, as well as endangered the whole of this tribe. You deserve to die." Mal's Adam's apple bobbed visibly as he swallowed. "You are young, however," Rune went on, "and I might be inclined to give you a second chance. If you will name your leader."

Scarcely anyone seemed to breathe. Then, "It was Hagen," Mal said forcefully. "It was all Hagen's idea!"

"Ah . . ." said Rune, turning his head. "Hagen."

The shaman's face was livid in the light of the dying sun.

"Someone had to do something," he said contemptuously to Rune. "Your plan would be a disaster for the tribe."

"I am thinking that it is you who are the disaster, Hagen," Irek said. "We all have seen how you constantly try to undermine Rune's authority. You are the shaman, not the chief, but you do not seem to understand that."

"What good to us is a shaman who does not want to be shaman?" Stifun asked.

"No good," said one of the men.

"I consulted the spirits and they told me what to do to save the tribe," Hagen said. But for the first time he was beginning to look uncertain.

"The only spirit you consulted was your own hunger for power," Stifun said angrily.

Rune looked slowly from face to face. "Hagen is our shaman," he said. "If we put him to death, then who will protect us from evil spirits?"

At the words "put to death" Hagen went pale.

"Hagen is the evil spirit we most need protection from," Irek said bluntly.

"My mother is as good a healer as Hagen," Stifun said. "And young Veden has passed the beginning tests to be a shaman. I am thinking he will be a better advocate for us with the spirits than such a one as Hagen."

The men rumbled in agreement.

"Put him to the death, Rune," Irek said. "He is a traitor to the tribe."

Hagen suddenly leaped to his feet, but Stifun was as quick. The shaman halted, panting, when he felt the point of Stifun's javelin sticking in his ribs.

"What of Vili?" Irek asked.

Rune looked at Vili. "Hagen has used you, Vili," he said.

Vili bared his teeth at Rune. "I hope the Redu tear you to pieces," he snarled.

Rune's face set like a stone. He said to Irek, "Vili too."

"I will take care of this, Rune," Irek said, and gestured for men to take Vili as well as Hagen in custody and come with him.

———

Rune spent half the night collecting the horses and gear that he would need for the upcoming trek. At first light the following morning, the Norakamo set off to follow the River of Gold south to the place where the river forked. The tribe's plan was to take the southwest fork, then follow a sheep track across the mountains to join up with the main branch of the River of Gold just before the Eagle Pass. Riding hard, Rune and his men managed to make it to the sheep track before the last of the daylight had died.

"We will rest until the moon has risen high enough to light our way," Rune said. "Then we will cross the mountain."

There was not enough time to sleep, but the men lit cook fires and ate while the horses tore hungrily at the grass that sprouted amongst the rocks of the hillside. There was a stream pouring down the mountainside into the river, which Rune said ran all along the track, so they would not have to worry about watering the horses. Finally, when the full moon was high enough in the western sky, the men of the Norakamo, each riding one horse and leading one remount, turned in to the mountain.

The track was steep, narrow and treacherous. The horses, which had been going since dawn, were worn out. It was a grim-faced Rune who finally made the decision to halt when they were yet two hours from the ridge.

"If we stop now, we won't be able to attack by the time Nardo wants," Stifun said to his brother.

"If we don't stop, the horses will be useless," Rune returned. "The men too. None of us will be any good to Nardo if we don't have rest."

Looking at the men and horses behind him, Stifun had to agree. At Rune's word, the exhausted line of men and animals stopped. The horses stood where they were, heads drooping low, ears flopping, eyes closing. The men wrapped themselves against the cold mountain night, lay down on the rocks of the precipitous path, and slept like the dead.

It was more than two hours past dawn, and still there was no smoke signal to say that Rune had come. Nardo and his men stood on their side of the pass, eyes straining toward the place in the sky where they expected to see a tower of black smoke. The only thing moving in the deep blue vault of the heavens, however, was a single eagle making graceful circles above the steep walls of the cliff. It hovered in the air for a few moments and then descended out of sight.

"I told you he would not come," Varic said. He and the rest of the clan council were standing with Nardo at the head of the narrow funnel of rock that was the Eagle Pass. "You were a fool, Nardo, to place your trust in a Norakamo."

"The breeze is still holding," Nardo said. "We have yet some time."

Nat said, "Perhaps we ought to attack without them. If we follow Nardo's plan we should get safely through the pass. Once we do that, we will be able to fight them on equal terms, man to man."

Nardo shook his head emphatically. "We would be fighting in too confined a space. The Redu have the advantage in numbers, and they have merely to hold their ground to win. We must break through them, and we cannot do that without great loss of Kindred lives. Na, if the Norakamo do not come, we will not attack."

Silence fell as the men continued to watch the sky. The breeze they were so dependent upon stirred Nardo's hair and blew a black strand across his cheek. He brushed it away.

"My greatest fear is that they were held up and will try to attack later in the morning," Freddo said grimly.

Nardo's face was strained. "I told Mano and Dane to make it very clear to Rune that he must be here by two hours after dawn."

"It is beyond that time now, and they have not come," Varic said.

Nardo set his jaw and turned, squinting into the low morning sun, to look at the flanking rows of men behind him at the head of the pass. They had left their horses behind today; the men of the Kindred would fight this battle on foot.

Where are you, Rune? he thought urgently. *This breeze is not going to hold for much longer!*

The only sound in the valley was the calling of birds. No one spoke. All eyes were lifted to the sky.

"Nardo." Freddo's fingers clasped his forearm imperatively. "Nardo, look!"

Nardo turned back to face the pass, raised his head, and there, staining the clear blue of the morning sky, was a single black cloud. Only it wasn't a cloud. Nardo's fists clenched and for a moment he shut his eyes. When he opened them again, the cloud was still there.

He said, too softly to be heard by the others, "*Thank you, Rune.*" Then he swung around to face his men.

"The Norakamo, my brothers! The Norakamo have come! And the breeze still holds! They are in time!"

The men of the Kindred were grinning. Nardo grinned back and shouted, "Let us advance to the barricade!"

Paxon stood in his position at the front of the Redu ranks, a quarter of a mile into the Eagle Pass. His father thought that Nardo was going to try to break out of the valley today, and Paxon very much feared that Kerk was right. During the past week the Kindred had managed to build a barricade about half-way through the pass, and the Redu chief was convinced that they were going to launch an attack from behind this wooden structure.

It was hopeless, of course. Nardo must know that. If the Kindred used their horses, the Redu bowmen would kill the front-runners and their bodies would clog the pass so that those behind would not be able to climb over, would be themselves easy targets for the long bows of their enemies. If they came on foot, there would be ample time for the arrows to find their targets. The Kindred forces would be so depleted by the time they came to hand-to-hand fighting that they would not have a chance.

They did not have a chance anyway. Paxon understood perfectly what Nardo had said earlier to Nat: in a situation like this one, the advantage was always with the men who had merely to hold their line.

All my fault, Paxon thought. It was a refrain that had been running through his brain ever since he had returned to his people and told them about the pass. Then, inevitably, followed the thought that was almost more painful. *How Pettra will hate me.*

It was a moment before the shouts of surprise intruded upon

Paxon's bitter reverie. He turned and looked up, following the direction of the men's heads around him. There, floating high in the vast blueness of the sky, was a single black cloud.

"Name of the Thunderer!" he heard Madden shout. "That is a signal. They must have someone coming in behind us!"

Paxon frowned.

"Paxon." It was Kerk's voice at his shoulder. "Who is this?"

He shook his head in bewilderment. "I don't know, Father. I could swear that all of the Kindred tribe was within the valley."

"Well, someone is sending them a smoke signal."

Kerk pushed back through the ranks of his men, and shortly after Paxon learned that he had ordered a contingent of Redu bowmen to advance a short way down the river to prepare to stop whoever might be coming up the path.

Paxon looked through the long, dark stone corridor that lay before him. "Here they come," the man next to him muttered.

Nardo was in the lead. Even at this distance it was impossible to mistake that tall, broad-shouldered form. Paxon felt his stomach contract as he watched the line of Kindred men approach the barricade they had built a quarter of a mile away from the Redu position.

If Paxon could have changed sides at that moment, he would have chosen to die with the Kindred. For he knew they were going to die. Even if Nardo had been clever enough to arrange to have a contingent of men attack the Redu rear, still it would not save the men of the Kindred. They reached the barricade and halted.

It was cold in the pass. The breeze that blew early every morning from the east was whipping through the pass into the faces of the Redu, and Paxon shivered.

His nose caught the scent of burning before his eyes saw the flames. Then the smoke overwhelmed him, a great billowing cloud of smoke, growing thicker and thicker as it swept through the pass on the easterly wind.

Name of the Thunderer! Nardo must have packed the wooden barricade with dried grass and fired it! Acting as a great flue, the Eagle Pass was funneling the smoke directly into the faces of the waiting Redu!

Concealed from his comrades by the thick smoke, Paxon grinned.

"I can't see!" Cries were coming from all the men around Paxon. His own eyes were streaming, and he had to raise his arm to protect them. He knew Nardo would be coming under cover of the smoke. This evening of the odds raised his spirits enormously. Now he could act with a free heart.

"Just shoot!" he called, and raised his bow and let loose an arrow. "It doesn't matter if you can't see, shoot anyway! We're bound to get some of them!"

Curses rose from the Redu line, but then a few more men began to fire.

Nardo and the men of the Kindred snaked through the pass on their bellies, their sore eyes streaming. Overhead they could hear the whine of arrows as the Redu shot sightlessly into the smoke. By the time the bowmen realized what was happening, Kindred javelins were raining into them.

The two tribes came together with a clash and began to fight each other hand to hand, crammed within the stone walls of the narrow pass. The Redu, who had the smoke full in their faces, were at a disadvantage, but they struggled valiantly to hold their position. Both sides knew that if the Kindred could force their way out of the pass, the battle would belong to them.

For what seemed like ages the two tribes were locked together in mortal combat. The Redu were not as good with javelin and ax as the Kindred men, and they lost some ground; but it was clear almost instantly that the Kindred were not going to be able to push them back a quarter of a mile.

It was Rune and the men of the Norakamo who broke the impasse. Using Nardo's V formation, they galloped headlong down the mountain path and smashed into the contingent of men whom Kerk had sent to watch for them. The Redu had been expecting the reinforcements to come down the River of Gold, not from the other side of the mountain, and Rune's charge took them completely by surprise.

Next, Rune led his men up the path and, before the Redu realized what was happening, his horses galloped into the pass, directly into the rear of Kerk's force. The Redu, penned in the narrow pass between Nardo and Rune, faced both ways and began to fight desperately for their lives.

Paxon was taken quite early in the fight. He was pushing forward, yelling like a fiend, when the line of Kindred in front of him abruptly opened up. Without thinking, he rushed forward and found himself surrounded. Someone struck him a vicious blow on the arm, and his javelin fell from suddenly numb fingers. He narrowed his streaming, swollen eyes, looked into the equally filthy, red-eyed face of Pettra's brother, and prepared to die.

To his utter astonishment Freddo grinned, teeth flashing in his smoke-blackened face. "Thank the Mother, we've got you," he said. "Pettra would flay me alive if anything had happened to you in this fight."

They were standing in the midst of the Kindred lines, with men pushing forward all around them. No one made any attempt to touch Paxon.

"You are not going to kill me?" he said. Shouted, actually, above the noise of the battle.

Tyr, who was on his other side, shook his head. "Keep safely out of the way, Paxon. We will need your tongue later to talk to what is left of your men."

Freddo put an arm around the Redu's shoulders and began to push him toward the rear. Paxon coughed with the smoke and said, "But I betrayed you!"

Freddo shook his head. "No one bears you any ill will." He shoved Paxon toward the smoldering remnants of the barricade. "Now be a good boy and wait for us there."

Once he had made certain that Paxon was indeed heading away from the battle, Freddo returned to the action.

Once the Norakamo joined the battle, the Redu defeat was inevitable. On the one side of them were the men of the Kindred, each man leaning on the man in front so that the whole mass of them formed an immense human roller, pushing and pushing and pushing the Redu back toward the end of the pass. On the other side were the Norakamo and thousands of pounds of horseflesh pushing the other way. Many of the Redu, caught in the middle, died from being crushed to death by their fellows.

Yet still the Redu fought on bravely, though most of their spears were broken and they were reduced to trying to kill the enemy with rocks they had picked up from the floor of the pass. They fought with a reckless fury, but it was not long before only a remnant of the once proud tribe of bowmen was left, desperately trying to hold out against the onslaught that pounded them from front and rear. That was when Nardo got Paxon and laid out his terms.

Once the Redu understood what they were being offered, they did not take long to lay down their arms and agree.

Midday, when the sun was at the top of the sky, was the only time that its rays reached to the bottom of the pass. On this day it shone down on a shambles of the dead and the dying. Blood lay in pools on the trampled ground. The place where the Redu had held their position was choked with bodies.

Nardo's clothes and hands and face were covered in blood. He stood in silence, regarding the carnage before him, and felt a fatigue so great that he wondered if he would be able to keep his feet.

So many dead, he thought. He ran a bloodstained hand through his already blood-splattered hair. *So many dead.*

Through the mist that suddenly obscured his vision, he saw a horse approaching. He drew a deep, steadying breath and blinked his sore eyes several times.

"Rune," he said.

In a moment Alane's brother was beside him. Nardo enveloped him in a huge bear hug, which was returned vigorously. "Thank the Mother that you came!"

"I'm sorry I was late," Rune said. "Your messenger didn't make it to my camp until the day before yesterday."

"What?"

Rune gripped Nardo's arm briefly. "I'll tell you about it later. What we need to do now is clear the dead out of here." He glanced upward at a huge, bearded vulture which was gliding smoothly along the vertical walls of the pass.

"Sa," said Nardo. "We'll dig the graves in the valley, where the ground is softer."

"You will bury the Redu dead also?"

"Sa. We will bury them all," Nardo said, and signaled to his clan leaders to give the orders.

Chapter
Twenty-Nine

Back at camp, the women of the Kindred waited for word from their men. They had made no preparations for flight in the event of a defeat. They did not expect a defeat. Either the Norakamo would arrive, in which case there would be a battle and the Redu would be defeated, or the Norakamo would not come and the Kindred men would themselves evacuate their women and children via the High Col.

The worst scenario, the one no one liked to talk about, was that if the men of the Kindred should be slaughtered, the Redu would enter the valley, claim the Kindred women and children as their own, and the women would submit. With their own men dead, they would have no chance to live on their own. Such a large number of women and children could not feed themselves without meat, and the women could not begin to bring in the amount of meat that would be needed.

Nardo had told Alane, "If things do not go well for me or the tribe, then you must do what is best for you and Nevin."

She had wanted to cry, "*Never. Never will I take another man to my bed, never will I lie in other arms than yours. If you are dead, then I am dead also.*"

But he had not needed to hear that from her. Nor, to be honest, would she have been speaking the truth. The wife in her might have meant it, but the mother knew she would never desert her child. She would do whatever she had to in order to keep Nevin safe.

On the morning of the battle, several of the young girls rode with the men up to the pass in order to watch for the Norakamo smoke signal. When it came, they returned to camp to tell the women that the combined Kindred-Norakamo attack was underway.

"Nardo never doubted that your brother would come," Mara said to Alane as the two of them sat within the matriarch's tent, sewing baby garments for Lora's expected child.

"On the day we were married," Alane said, "two rainbows arched across the River of Gold. They were an omen, my mother said, that Nardo and I would be a bridge between our two tribes."

"I am thinking that your mother was right," Mara replied.

Both women's voices were calm and ordinary. Both of their hands were steady as they pushed bone needles in and out of the softened fawn skin they were working on. There was comfort in the ordinary work, comfort in each other's calmness. Outside the tent the rest of the household women had gathered to talk about what might be happening in the pass. Only Alane and Mara sat within and sewed.

The tent flap was pushed aside and Nevin crawled in. He grinned at his grandmother and said, "I hungry."

Mara smiled back. "Would you like one of my honey treats?"

The child's large brown eyes sparkled. "Sa." Then, as Mara moved to rise, "I will get them, my mother. I know where they are."

"I am sure that you do," Alane said in a faintly ironic voice.

Mara reached out her hand for the leather bag Nevin had brought to her, extracted two nuggets made from a mixture of grain and honey, and handed them to her grandson. Nevin popped one into his mouth immediately.

"Be sure you chew it well," Alane cautioned.

He gave her an indignant look. "I know how to chew, Mama. I a big boy now." The sparkle in his eyes grew more pronounced. "Soon I will learn to fight like Dada."

Alane did not reply, just rested her sewing on her knee and stared into the flames of Mara's small fire. Nevin crawled back out of the tent and Mara said softly, "He reminds me so much of Nardo at that age. The same eyes, the same wonderful smile."

Alane's own eyes were beginning to sting. She blinked them until they cleared, then looked once more at her sewing. There was nothing else they could do in order to pass the time. They had made ready all the mosses and herb ointments they used for dressing wounds. They had laid out piles of buckskin to use as bandages. There was nothing else to do but wait.

Alane said, "I keep thinking how, because he is chief, he always insists he must go first."

There was a rustling noise, and Alane turned in surprise to see that Mara had come to sit beside her. The older woman put an arm around her shoulders. "He will be safe, my daughter," she said. "I feel this in my heart. He will come back to you."

Alane had tensed when Mara first touched her, but at these words all the resistance drained out of her, and for a brief moment she pressed her forehead against Nardo's mother's shoulder. Then she straightened up. "He must," she said, "because I do not know how I can live without him."

It was grim work digging the graves. Over three hundred Redu had been killed in the pass, and the men of their tribe who still lived helped to dig a huge ditch to serve as a mass grave for their less fortunate brethren. Paxon, who by now had figured out for himself why his escape had been so easy, worked among his fellow tribesmen with a scalded heart.

All my fault. The familiar refrain ran over and over through his mind, although the object of his remorse had changed. When he came upon the bloody body of his father, he stared down at Kerk's unmarked, proud face, broke down and wept for the first time since his mother had died.

Aven, one of his boyhood friends, saw him and came to put a comforting hand on his arm. "It was not your fault, Paxon," he said, answering the accusation he knew must be ringing in his friend's brain. "You thought you were giving us a victory when you brought us to this pass. You had no way of knowing of this other tribe. No one blames you."

But Paxon blamed himself. How could he have been so stupid not to suspect that too-easy escape? He had thought Nardo was a fool, when all along it was he who was the dupe.

Over three hundred Redu dead. Only twenty-seven men of the Kindred had been killed, and eleven of the Norakamo men and twenty horses. It had been a slaughter.

"They could have killed us all," Aven's voice was going on. "I still cannot believe that they have offered to take those of us who remain into their tribe. If they had not just defeated us so decisively, I would say that their chief must be a fool."

"Nardo is no fool," Paxon said bitterly.

"How does he know that he can trust us?" Aven asked in bewilderment. "How does he know that we will not rise in the dead of night and kill them all?"

"He will offer you good hunting. He will teach you to ride upon a horse's back. You will have a woman. Why should you want to endanger such a life as that?" Paxon's voice was even more bitter than it had been before.

Aven stared down bleakly at the bodies piled in the deep grave. "Revenge," he answered.

"I think you will find that life among the Kindred is sweeter than any vengeance is likely to be."

Aven turned to look across the beautiful grassy valley that stretched away for longer than he could see. He sighed. "You are probably right."

Nardo had the dead bodies of the Kindred men loaded onto horses and taken back to camp for their women to see to. All of the wounded—Kindred, Norakamo and Redu—were also quickly evacuated back to where they would receive proper attention. The rest of the men stayed behind to help bury the masses of Redu dead. The Norakamo, who found the dead bodies of the Redu more frightening than the living men had been, worked harder than anyone else.

The shadows were growing long by the time the great bulk of the men returned to camp. Nardo had first made everyone wash in a stream, so as not to frighten the children with their bloodstained appearance, and the men looked mainly cold and exhausted as they poured into camp and sought out their families.

Paxon was so weary by the time he reached the camp that he could scarcely stand up. He had shunned the horse Freddo had offered him and was walking instead among the defeated Redu.

"This camp looks nice," Aven said beside him. He sniffed the air hungrily. "I hope there is food for us too."

"*Paxon!*" It was a girl's voice, high-pitched with urgency. He halted and watched the figure that was flying toward him over the beaten-down grass of the campsite.

"Who is that?" Aven asked.

"That is—" The breath was knocked out of Paxon as the girl flung herself against him and gripped him fiercely around the waist. ". . . Pettra," he managed to say to his friend over the brown head that was pressed into his shoulder.

"I told my brothers that if they did not bring you back safely to me, I would kill them all," Pettra said in a faintly hysterical voice.

The full length of her body was pressed against him and, exhausted as he was, Paxon felt his body begin to respond. But he did not raise his arms to embrace her. He said instead, "You should have known that I have no chance against your brothers, Pettra."

She heard the bitter note in his voice and lifted her head from his shoulder, leaning back so she could look up into his face. "I knew nothing about that plan of theirs, Paxon," she breathed. Her green eyes shimmered with unshed tears. "When they told me you had left, I thought my heart would break. Then, when they told me why they had let you go—na, *forced* you to go—my heart was broken for you. It was not right for them to use you that way! It was not fair!"

Paxon said hoarsely, "It was not."

A short silence fell as she scanned his face with her shimmering eyes. She bit her lip at what she saw there. "Do you know that it was because of you that Alane was able to persuade Nardo to spare the lives of these men? Even to offer to take them into the tribe?" She gestured to the hundred or so Redu who were staring with great interest at Paxon and the Kindred girl. "Nardo said that if the rest of the Redu were like you, then we would be getting good men. So you see," she finished anxiously, "you were the means of bringing good to your people as well as evil."

After a moment he answered, "It not feel good." But she had

managed to say the one thing that he most needed to hear. His arms, which had been hanging by his sides, lifted slowly to encircle her. She hid her face in his shoulder and whispered, "I have missed you so much."

Aven, who had not understood a word of what was being said, regarded Pettra with a grin. "I see you did not waste the time you spent among these people, Paxon."

Paxon said stiffly, "This is the girl I am going to marry."

A man behind Paxon said urgently, "Paxon. Their chief is coming."

Very carefully Paxon put Pettra away and drew himself up to face Nardo.

Never will I forgive him for using me to destroy my own people, Paxon thought as he watched the big Kindred chief approaching the group of Redu. *He thinks he is so clever. Well, perhaps he is. But I shall never forgive him for what he made me do.*

When Nardo was an arm's length away from Paxon, he halted. Paxon's nostrils flared with some of his old haughtiness, and, refusing to be intimidated by the other man's superior height, he set his jaw and stared stonily up into Nardo's face.

The first thing he noticed was that Nardo looked almost as tired as Paxon felt. There was absolutely no trace of triumph in the large brown eyes that were regarding him so gravely. Paxon's fists clenched. *If he patronizes me, tells me that the Redu fought well, I will hit him,* Paxon thought viciously.

"I am sorry, Paxon," Nardo said, and there was a note in his quiet voice that turned Paxon's breathing into sudden pain. The Redu couldn't answer, couldn't speak at all. "It was an unforgivable thing to do. I know that," Nardo went on in that same gut-wrenching voice. "But I had no choice."

I will not cry. Desperately Paxon struggled within himself for control. *I will not cry.* His face was stiff, his lips would not move. He nodded. Once. Then he felt Pettra take his hand.

"The men of your tribe are welcome among us," Nardo said.

Paxon finally managed to speak. "If that is the case, why did you force this battle?" His voice sounded like a croak, and it was with great difficulty that he refrained from clinging to Pettra's hand.

"We can take in ten handfuls of men," Nardo replied, "but

it was not within our power to feed the full number of your people. You have lived among us, Paxon. You know the number that our hunting grounds will sustain."

There was a faint line between Nardo's black brows, and he looked exhausted. When Paxon did not answer, the Kindred chief continued with some reserve, "Alane and my mother and Lina have prepared food for you and your men, and they have collected enough extra clothing for you all to be able to change into something dry."

At last Paxon's breathing was beginning to return to something that approached normality. "Lina?" he managed to say. "Perhaps it is a good thing, then, that my men do not speak your tongue."

Nardo's face broke into a radiant smile and, unaccountably, Paxon felt his heart lift. "She didn't frighten you," Nardo retorted. "Dhu, for a while there I thought I was never going to get you to leave!"

Aven and the men of the Redu had relaxed when they saw Nardo smile. "What is he saying?" Aven asked Paxon.

"He says his wife has food prepared for us."

The men of the Redu grinned.

"They're hungry," Paxon said to Nardo.

Nardo said to Pettra, "Show them where they are to go."

It was very late when Nardo finally came into the tent he shared with Alane and Nevin. All evening long the soft and steady sound of women mourning had echoed around the encampment. The following day, shortly after sunrise, the Kindred would lay their dead in the earth of the valley. In accordance with ancient custom, the corpses would be buried so that they faced west, toward Moonland and the western gate of the Mother.

All during the long and painful evening, Nardo had gone from tent to tent to show his respect for those who had died in the fight in the pass. Over and over again Alane had heard his deep voice raised in the strong, pure refrain of the mourning chant.

There was not a clan who had escaped the blow of death. The Wolf Clan had lost Mano, their leader, in Vili's ambush, and of the men who composed Mara's household, Adun, Nessa's husband, had been killed and Pier had been injured. Alane had spent a good part of the evening nursing her brother Stifun, who had taken a jagged gash in his thigh.

But it was over. For the first time in two long years, the tribe could face the future without the threat of the Redu hanging over their heads. Anguishing as the individual losses were, an undeniable sense of relief pervaded the camp.

"You look exhausted," Alane said softly as Nardo came to sit beside her near the small fire she was feeding.

In answer, he rubbed his bloodshot eyes as if they hurt. "I must be getting old," he said.

She shook her head in denial. "You have been striving and striving toward this day for so long, and now that it is over and you have accomplished what you desired, you are feeling what a strain it has been."

"How is Stifun?"

"He will be all right, I think. I packed the wound with the moss your mother recommended. He was sleeping when I left him in the sick tent."

"Rune did the impossible to get to me in time, Alane. If he had not made that magnificent march . . ."

"I know," she said quietly.

Nevin turned over in his sleep. Samu got up and padded to the doorflap of the tent, pushing it aside with his nose. He went out.

"I think the Redu will be all right," Nardo said. "I have set some men to keep watch on them, but I do not think that they will seek revenge. Just in case, however, I am going to divide them up among the various households tomorrow. Best not to give them too much chance to plot together."

She rested her head on his shoulder, and his arm went around her and gathered her close. "I think they will be all right too," she murmured. "They seemed grateful for the food and clothing we had for them. Once they learn Kindred Speak, they will be more comfortable among us."

Nardo grunted, then he yawned widely.

Alane said, "Get into the sleeping skins. I will bank the fire."

Nardo gave her a sleepy smile and did as she suggested. Alane banked the fire so it would smolder through the night, then laid out the utensils she would need for breakfast the next day. Samu returned from his visit outside. Finally, after she had put Nardo's moccasins under the drying rack, Alane crawled inside the sleeping skins, immensely grateful that Nardo had already warmed them up. She thought of the night before, of how terrified she had been that he would be killed in the coming battle. She had lain awake all night, her cheek pressed against his strong back, her heart filled with fear and agony. And the Mother had heard her prayers and returned him to her safely.

She jumped a little in surprise when she felt his arms go around her. "I thought you were asleep," she whispered.

"I was waiting for you," he whispered back, and bent his head to kiss her. After a while his hands went to the drawstring of her trousers.

"I thought you were exhausted!" she said.

He was sliding the trousers off her hips. "Alane, the day I am too exhausted to want you, I will be dead," he replied.

But he was not dead. She put her arms around his neck and felt him against her, strong and alive and full of potency. *Safe.* She pulled his head down to meet her mouth and lifted her hips to welcome him in.

DATE DUE